SEARCH FOR THE INTERFACE
The Aneksaria Book 2

Chris Maries

Gotham Books

30 N Gould St.
Ste. 20820, Sheridan, WY 82801
https://gothambooksinc.com/

Phone: 1 (307) 464-7800

© 2023 Chris Maries. All rights reserved.

No part of this book may be reproduced, stored in a retrieval system, or transmitted by any means without the written permission of the author.

Published by Gotham Books (September 26, 2023)

ISBN: 979-8-88775-535-9 (P)
ISBN: 979-8-88775-537-3 (H)
ISBN: 979-8-88775-536-6 (E)

Because of the dynamic nature of the Internet, any web addresses or links contained in this book may have changed since publication and may no longer be valid.

The views expressed in this work are solely those of the author and do not necessarily reflect the views of the publisher, and the publisher hereby disclaims any responsibility for them.

Table of Contents

Prologue 1

Chapter One 3

Chapter Two 17

Chapter Three... 31

Chapter Four 43

Chapter Five 51

Chapter Six 63

Chapter Seven 73

Chapter Eight 79

Chapter Nine.. 91

Chapter Ten 101

Chapter Eleven 113

Chapter Twelve... 121

Chapter Thirteen 135

Chapter Fourteen.. 149

Chapter Fifteen... 157

Chapter Sixteen... 169

Chapter Seventeen 177

Chapter Eighteen	191
Chapter Nineteen	199
Chapter Twenty	211
Chapter Twenty One	219
Chapter Twenty Two	231
Chapter Twenty Three	245
Chapter Twenty Four	257
Chapter Twenty Five	267
Chapter Twenty Six	275
Chapter Twenty Seven	285
Chapter Twenty Eight	295
Chapter Twenty Nine	305
Chapter Thirty	311
Chapter Thirty One	317
Chapter Thirty Two	327
Chapter Thirty Three	331
Chapter Thirty Four	345
Glossary of terms	347

This book is dedicated
to the memory of my Father

The World of INALSO

SHOOINAR

Yerban Ban Han

Tyrennia
Yerk
Manuka
Malkronin
Yalli
Must
Stepan Kor
Tyber

SHENF...

Jefral
Es...
Agad
Manyl

Pegua

SHENFEWER
Timmer
Shturtan
Victonna
Adyl
Maki
Dorem
Bris
Musgriv
Asman
Kalladon

Wadi
Musuk
Ah...

NUAFRAGA

SHEWICKVAR

Prologue

Cullin was at his desk deep in thought. The Battle of Dundoon had been a mere prelude; an opening salvo from the Frame. What followed was worse, more violent and aggressive. Cullin didn't like thinking about those times or the senseless waste of life that accompanied them. He thought about those people, long dead now, who had played such an important and influential part in his life and the lives of the ordinary folk of the world of Inalsol.

In the course of a millennium, much had been written about those times, but oddly, no one had ever thought to ask Cullin about them. Now, of course, few even realised that he was the same Cullin that had been involved in those legendary events. Even members of his own family didn't know who he was these days.

After so many generations, Cullin himself had lost track of most of them. There were those of the 'New Path' who believed these things to be of great importance, but after so many years recording data they had only demonstrated that all people were related, however distantly, to each other. We are all distant cousins mused Cullin.

It was inevitable that the Frame wouldn't give up on its control of the human race easily. In fact, even before the dust had settled on Dundoon, the Frame had been formulating plans against the muckers and free people who now called themselves aneksa. In essence a war had started that the people and their leaders were still unprepared for.

Chapter One

"Do you think we can talk him out of it?" Cullin asked Dookerock.

"I have tried that. The prophets know that I have tried, but he is adamant." Dook idly stroked the kitten's head as it curled in his lap.

The kitten's mother, a mottled tabby, had been rubbing herself against Dook's leg, now jumped up onto his lap and settled down with her kitten after some judicious licking and preening.

"So what do we do?" Cullin asked exasperated at Yayler's behaviour.

Yayler's plans to leave Rustick More and meet with a group of divines had annoyed and upset Dookerock who felt that they couldn't be trusted.

"We do what we must. You put a team together and search for this Interface. Destroy it if you can. I will continue to build defences here and hope Yayler knows what he is doing."

"I hope so too. I guess I'd better think about whom I'll need with me. Tyber is supposed to be in a desert. I don't know what deserts are like." Cullin idly rubbed his chin, feeling the roughness of unshaved growth.

"Hot and dry, you won't need a morcote."

"I'll need a list, skills and equipment and so on."

"Good idea." Dook stared into the distance blankly.

"Better get on with it then."

"Aye" Dook appeared deflated and hopeless to Cullin. The truth was that he felt badly let down by Yayler and was at a loss to know what to do. Dook was depressed and out of sorts, deflated and directionless. He needed a plan of action that didn't involve help from his oldest friend.

Later that night Cullin was working on his compad, his eyes flicking backward and forward through the three-dimensional display projected from the small hand held device. The compads input came direct to Cullin via miniature hardware in his fingertips that caused an unfocused demeanour whilst he used the compad. Sara lay curled up asleep on their bed. She was used to her spouse working late into the night and it no longer bothered her.

Earlier Cullin had found data that confirmed the position of the Interface as the town of Tyber. Tyber sat inland on a broad river situated thousands of strides away on the other side of another continent. The logistics of such a journey worried Cullin. The distance worried him, his lack of experience in such terrain worried him, and sourcing food worried him.

His mind was buzzing as he closed down the various files he had been viewing and hid his traces from the Frames' internal checks. It was late and he should try to sleep, but knew he wouldn't. He started a new search.

Dundoon, the site of the recent battle between aneksa and divines, was the obvious choice. Most of the historical documentation on the town was benign and uninteresting, yet the Frame had built a surrounding wall, presumably for defence. Cullin believed that the Frame had built the wall for a reason it did not wish to disclose. Cullin presumed it was for defence.

Another wair of searching found him digging deep into the Frames' archives. He repeatedly tried to open an intriguing folder, but found access denied. He needed the identity of someone with authority to open the folder. His mind leaped as he made a mental connection.

He still had Beck25's locater disc from Mark Ossin in a little alcove where he stored his few personal items. The device connected remotely to the compad as soon as he activated it, allowing Cullin to clone Beck25's identity. With that done he could fool the database into believing he was Beck25.

Cullin attempted to access the folder again and the display blinked out. The compad was silent and dead in the palm of his hand. His mind froze with panic. What had he done? By accessing the folder with the identity of a dead person, he had destroyed his compad. He tried to re-boot, but the compad remained lifeless.

Shocked and worried he put the dead compad on the desk and worried now that the Frame would know about his 'snooping' through its data files. Several sents passed by as he anxiously pondered the dilemma. How was he going to explain this security breach to Dook? How much of their activities would the Frame be able to identify?

Chapter One

The compad beeped. Cullin looked at it in stupefaction until he registered the words 'access granted' on the display as it flickered back into life. Another sub-screen opened requesting 're-boot now?'

Cullin closed that and opened the folder. What he found shocked him. Forty-nine years earlier Dundoon had been the site of a revolt by the local muckers. They had marched en masse on the town, angry about recent decisions by the local Divine General.

The Divine General had disallowed muckers from using the towns harbour for their fishing vessels. The divines forcibly removed locals' boats from the harbour or destroyed them. The divines then shot several of the muckers with their staffs after the angry mob damaged property. Though no one had died, the local populace was extremely angry and eager to fight for their 'rights'. The result was a standoff.

The Lord of the Mark had entered discussion with the Divine General and laid down a number of grievances. Eventually it was agreed that the muckers could build a jetty south of the town for fishing vessels, but the harbour was preserved the need for divine business and would remain off limits to the muckers. To pacify the muckers they made an agreement for a new Great Hall to administer the Mark.

The town wall had been built shortly afterward along with an abutting administration block on the south wall. After this, they no longer allowed muckers within the town, as they had 'no need' to be there.

Cullin noted with interest that the Lord of the Mark who had successfully negotiated a solution to the standoff was the same person who had been involved in the current affair. Cullin copied the folder and closed the various files before and turning off the compad.

"You're up early Cullin" Dook remarked as he watched the sunrise over distant mountains to the east of Rustick More. He was wearing the same clothes, as he was when Cullin spoke to him the day before. It was almost as if Dook's black mood had seen him sitting on the mountain's flat summit for a day and night. The cat and the kitten were absent, but otherwise there appeared to be no change at all.

"Aye, it gets a bit claustrophobic inside sometimes. Nice morning, I can't understand why more of us don't come up here to greet the day." Cullin was also looking at bit rough, but only because he hadn't washed or shaved yet. That was also true of Dook, but no one could remember when he had last washed.

"Aye, it's a nice morning. I always think this is the best part of the day, before the hustle and bustle of daily activities starts; space to think and put things in perspective."

"Hmm, I just like the view, it's as the whole world spread before your feet." Cullin rubbed idly at his rough chin before continuing. "I found some interesting data last night. Did you know there had been a revolt in Dundoon forty-nine years ago?"

Dook looked up and gazed at Cullin steadily. "Nay, I didn't, but it sounds interesting."

Cullin went on to describe his discoveries including commenting on their location in the Frames' database. Dook was very curious about those suppressed, concealed files and Cullin's method of opening them.

"There must be a lot of information we can learn, hidden in those files." Dook mused, thinking aloud.

"I'm guessing that a divine has to be at a certain level in the hierarchy to be able to open these files."

"If that's the case then there is likely to be other files at a higher level that divines can't access." Dook leant back against the target rock, his lined face creased in thought.

"There must be a lot of stuff that the Frame doesn't want muckers or even most divines to know about." Cullin added thoughtfully.

"Well, we've always known that to be the case, but now, thanks to you, we have a means of accessing that 'stuff', that concealed data."

Dook had a harder look about him, Cullin noted absently, more focused, and positive.

"Know your enemy, Cullin, then you will know how to beat him." Dook made to get up, but Cullin stopped him with an odd thought.

Chapter One

"Him, you said him. Why are there no female divines? I've never seen one or come across any mention of any."

Dook sat back down with a thump, wincing slightly as he sat down on a sharp rock.

"It's not a policy of the Frame, I think, and the Frame wouldn't care. That's not its nature."

"So there are female divines?"

"Of course, but you know very little of divine society. Such a policy would have been made by your Interface and passed on via hius. Human interface units, you've seen a few of those I think."

Cullin nodded an affirmative.

"There is another possibility. Some Doctrine dictates that women are physically and mentally inferior to men. It's a reference from the 'Book of Hameed'. You might consider it to be utter rubbish, of course, but it remains part of the doctrine that some Ardclerics still teach. Not in Garvamore, but in some of the desert districts it's a common and strongly held belief."

Dook remained motionless for some time as he contemplated a better answer to Cullin's question.

"The thing is, we don't really understand the full role of the Interface. It seems to do more than translate the Frame's policies. I wonder if it creates policies of its own that the Frame implements."

"I don't know Dook. I don't really understand these things that well. What I have seen so far suggests it works down from the Interface to hiu and then to divine. I don't know about upward from Interface to the Frame. It seems unlikely though." Cullin watched a white tailed eagle as it soured on the early morning air currents.

"Unlikely indeed, the Frame doesn't share its rule" Dook agreed.

"So, is it a literal translation of doctrine by the Frame?" Cullin asked as the eagle disappeared to the north. "One day, we'll be as free as that eagle."

"Aye, one day." Dook had also been watching the eagle. "A literal interpretation would appear to be the case."

"But wouldn't simple observation dispute such the validity of such an idea?"

"Hmm, and the Frame records such data so it must realise the error."

"So has the Interface affected the Frame's data and decisions in some way?" Cullin asked as he watched the sky, hoping the eagle would return.

"Could be" replied Dook. "Perhaps the Interface makes judgements on human affairs that the Frame uses to formulate decisions and policies."

"Why would the Frame implement policy made from flawed judgements? Would that be consistent with the Frame's normal methods?"

"Nay, it wouldn't, certainly not."

Cullin scratched his head in thought "I don't understand it then."

"It's confusing, truly." Dook remained silent again as he thought through the complexities of the problem. "So, what if the Interface makes a judgement on what it believes people think?"

Cullin mulled the thought over before replying. "Such as this doctrine of Hameed?"

"Aye, something like that."

"It's a bit woolly, Dook"

"Not really. If the Frame took something as a general belief, then it may well formulate policy and decisions based on errant belief."

"Seems a bit crazy to me, Dook"

"Hah, it seems a possibility to me, otherwise, why would the Frame maintain belief in the four prophets, even though much of their different philosophies is clearly wrong."

Cullin look sharply at Dook and frowned "you've lost me there, Dook"

"As a divine Ardcleric I had to teach much that I knew from observation to be wrong. For example, that the child prophet Hesoos could understand the hearts of men and women and the nature of all things, is about the biggest chunk of unbelievable rubbish that is taught as absolute truth."

Cullin laughed "but nobody really believes it, do they?"

Dook raised his eyebrows and gazed meaningfully at Cullin. "Oh, some do, absolutely. I have known people who believe in the literal truth of the four prophets even when their philosophies are in conflict. The point is that the Frame may believe that we believe such doctrine."

"I see, so it would then make policies based on error. I guess that might be possible."

"And it would explain why women are used for lower administration positions among divines and why all Lords of the Mark are male." Dook added.

Cullin nodded "and why their army is exclusively male even though the likes of Isla clearly demonstrates that women make very capable warriors."

Dook nodded with agreement. "You've met her, I believe."

"Aye, she's almost a match for my brother Ulbin and much brighter."

Dook laughed "I wouldn't repeat that in his presence if I were you."

"No, that wouldn't be a good idea."

Dook mused again "the Frame may also have the opinion that men are more domineering and authoritative than women."

"You've lost me again, Dook."

"Oh, that's a commonly held belief among divines."

Cullin chucked "there are many hen-pecked men about who would disagree volubly with that opinion."

"True enough. Anyhow, young man, I have work to do. It's been a stimulating conversation, but I must get on."

"Aye, and Sara will be wondering where I am."

Ealasat lived alone on a coastal small croft in an isolated valley not far from Tymeum. It was a hard life for a young woman to wrest a living from the harsh landscape. A bitter haar blew along the straits during the hard winter months and the summer was too short to make the smallholding truly viable. There was not much suitable ground in her small valley that could be cultivated for crops and what little available was thin and of poor quality.

She grew onions and turnips, cabbage and potatoes, but not much else did well in the denuded soil. The long furrows of heaped soil fertilised with seaweed harvested from the rocky coast made the best of the poor ground.

Her nanny goat, Gowa, could be as much a curse as a boon if Ealasat wasn't careful as it would eat or trample her hard-won crop. Most of her food came from the sea and the small boat she used for fishing. The boat was old and needed replacing, but the young self-important and rather pompous Lord of Mark Tymeum had refused the tokens.

He was a young man who had only recently started his position and was still wet behind the ears. Ealasat was of the opinion that he hadn't started to shave yet, but it seemed he was old enough to make decisions for the Mark.

In short, he didn't think much of him. He didn't understand the difficulties of trying to wrest a living from her reluctant holding.

Though she was diligent with the tokens she could earn selling surplus fish and shellfish, it would take her years to earn enough to replace or even repair her little boat.

She blamed her parents, but not unkindly, for that situation. There simply wasn't anywhere else to point the finger of blame. They had tried to earn more tokens, but misfortune had raised its ugly head while they had been working for a local fisherman who needed a crew. Rough seas had swept both of Ealasat's parents overboard.

The local village community had been very sympathetic for her loss and wished her well. They had said things like "if there's anything I can do for you –" or "don't be afraid to ask for anything" and so on. Her neighbours demonstrated insincerity in their well-meaning, but empty sentiments when she had asked for help. Her neighbours were always too busy, they'd smile and say they "sorry, next time". The promised help or assistance never came. Therefore, she now found herself coming to the end of the crofts viability, unless she could raise the credits for a new boat.

The young Lord of the Mark had refused to help, but had at least suggested she find the Mark's Advocate, the elusive Dookerock. He gave directions, but these were hopelessly inadequate and misleading. She was now lost on the search for this 'Russet Muir' where he was purported to live.

She was ascending a small ravine with steep craggy sides, but he was unable to extricate herself from its confines. Initially she had thought it to be just a small stream, but it soon became unpleasantly difficult to negotiate.

Chapter One

Perversely she could see clearly ahead a high steep-sided tabletop mountain that fitted descriptions she knew of Russet Muir.

Despite the awkwardness of her position, Ealasat was quite happy, she was enjoying the challenge the topography was giving her, finding it exhilarating. The stream formed clear emerald rock-pools and small waterfalls amongst the boulders. She was thirsty, tired sweaty from her exertions, and stopped for a break, quenching her thirst with the cool water. She then stripped and washed, shivering in the chilly air.

Ealasat was resting, having dressed, when a voice from behind startled her. "It's unusual to see anyone round this way."

She gave the young man a hard stare with her piercing green eyes. He was quite good looking, she noted. He was standing at the top of the crags behind her looking down on her resting place.

"Oh, hello" she responded, not quite sure what else to say. After a pause she asked "do you know these parts?"

"Aye, quite well" the taciturn young man replied.

There was an awkward silence, as neither knew where to take the conversation. After a seemingly endless period of silence, Ealasat broke the silence. "I'm Ealasat, and you are?"

"Oh, Ecta."

Again, there was an awkward silence. Somehow, Ealasat expected Ecta to be a bit more forthcoming. She found his abrupt answers difficult and irritating. "Er, hello Ecta" she ventured. "Do you know where a place called 'Russet Muir' is?"

"No."

The answer was unhelpful to Ealasat; in fact, she was beginning to find the young man quite infuriating. "I'm looking for it, you see. It's supposed to be around here somewhere."

Ecta shrugged.

Ealasat stared hard at Ecta, anger building up a head of steam. She was going to lose her temper soon. "That mountain ahead, what is that?"

"Oh that, that is 'Rustick More.'"

"Rustick More, are you sure it's not Russet Muir?" Ealasat was about to scream.

"Aye."

Ealasat shook her head with irritation. The young Mark Lord's directions were clearly inaccurate. She was surprised to have made it this far without help. The young man standing on the crag above her was not much better and possibly a bit retarded.

"Does a man called Dookerock live there?"

"Aye."

"Well, can you take me to him? I need to talk to him."

"Er, nay, I cannot."

"Why not?" Ealasat was infuriated.

Ecta paused for thought. He knew nothing about the young woman and he suspected that he had already revealed more than he should about Dook's home. "I can take you somewhere he could meet you" he said eventually.

"Why can't you take me to see him?" Ealasat repeated.

"I'll let him explain that when he sees you."

"Oh, so I will see him?"

"Aye, but you'll have to climb out of there first."

"Oh, why?"

"It gets narrower and deeper further up."

Ealasat scrambled out of the ravine with poor humour and arrived near Ecta with several bumps and scrapes. Ecta took her to a small shack a few strides from the ravine. It was basic, bare, and only intended as a rough shelter. A small fireplace made up with peat blocks from a neat stack nearby. A table and a couple of rather dilapidated chairs made up the only furniture. Ealasat was unimpressed.

Ecta left her there and returned later in the dark some wairs later with Dook. Ealasat was in very poor humour, sitting in the dark without food or water.

Chapter One

However, Dook, carrying a small lamp knocked politely on the draughty wooden door he found himself greeted by an angry Ealasat. She gave Ecta an unpleasant scowl before addressing Dook.

"You, I presume, are Dookerock. It is the poorest welcome I've had so far. I was expecting more."

Discomfited by her demeanour, Dook stumbled over his words. "Hmm, ah, well, things are as they are. Ecta tells me that you require my assistance."

"Aye, indeed I do" Ealasat gave Dook her piercing green-eyed stare. She always found that stare put people off their balance, discomfiting them. She placed her hands on her hips, giving Dook a 'well, I'm waiting' look. Dook's appearance didn't help matters to encourage a warmer attitude. He was dirty, his hair was matted, and his clothes stained.

Dook ignored her attitude, putting it down to anger. He believed it better to be sensitive in such circumstances. He tried to put himself in her position and understand. First, he had to learn what her position was. "Why don't you tell me what the problem is while Ecta gets some refreshments? You must be hungry."

Dook listened to her patiently while Ealasat told him her story. He was sympathetic, but he didn't want to set a precedent and allow her to borrow the tokens. He quietly explained this to her. He continued by explaining that muckers' allowances were audited by divines annually and an extra allowance for any particular mucker would be questioned. "Now" he finished "though I cannot give you tokens to repair your boat, I can give you the materials to build a new one, but I would expect some work from you in payment."

A surprised look crossed Ealasat's delicate almond shaped face. "What would you want me to do?"

"Oh, just general work, nothing difficult or too arduous. I will give you food and accommodation as well while you build your boat."

Ealasat looked intently at Dook for several sents trying to see the catch in the offer, but could see none. Though she was angry with Dook's rough manners, eventually she conceded "I will accept your offer with thanks. I get my boat in exchange for work."

"Good" Dook stood up abruptly "we had best get you some food and a warm bed sorted for the night then."

"Dook! You old scoundrel!" Varee called out when Dook's party arrived on the workshop floor of Rustick More "and young Ecta too! It's been a long time."

Dook smiled broadly and gave Varee a big hug at which point Varee wrinkled up her nose.

"I think it must be time for your bath again Dook. You smell like something between a wet goat and a cesspit!" She mimicked choking and pushed Dook away with a gentle hand on his chest.

"Good evening, Varee. Have the others arrived?" Dook asked ignoring Varee's comment, pulling his morcote tighter about him as if it would conceal his odour.

"Aye, Briga brought us. Who is your beautiful young friend?" Varee regarded the young woman with open curiosity.

"Oh, this is Ealasat, she'll be staying while a boat is arranged for her."

Ealasat was completely oblivious to Dook and Varee as she tried to take in the vast scope of the cavern that operated as both workshop and hanger for a handful of fliers. She was gazing about her as she attempted to take in what her eyes were telling her.

She had rarely been beyond her home valley and local fishing villages. She knew the straits and sea for many strides about her home. That was about all she knew outside the fanciful stories told by crofters and fishers.

What she saw before her was completely outside of her experience and previous knowledge. Strange smells assailed her, she couldn't even think about what she saw, the equipment, workbenches with strange contraptions sitting upon them or the sheer size of the place, because it was simply too far beyond her experience.

"Ecta, would you find Ealasat a bed and show her around" Dook instructed. "She's already looking a bit lost."

"Aye, this way Ealasat." Ecta nudged her to attract her attention.

Ealasat drew a quick breath and returned her attention back to the small group with a start. "Oh, Aye, sorry!"

Chapter One

Ecta continued "most of the rooms are on the next level up."

Ealasat gave Ecta a wide-eyed gaze "this place is huge."

"Aye, it's mostly on three levels. Storage and such are on the level below us. We call this part Toiler's Woe."

Dook and Varee had wandered off, talking earnestly in hushed tones leaving Ecta with the awed Ealasat.

"Do you want a tour now, or shall I show you about tomorrow?" Ecta asked politely.

"Aye, tomorrow, I am ready for bed." Ealasat followed Ecta as curiosity began to replace her initial shock and awe.

Chapter Two

The Frame was reviewing the latest reports from one of its spies in the resistance movement of the muckers. They were now calling themselves aneksa, free people. It was a choice of names the Frame did not understand, as its purpose was to administer their lives. This was only part of its purpose, but did take a lot of processing and effort.

There were many reports about resistance cells, but the one recently received was the one that really counted. This recent report that located the very heart of these aneksa had come in two parts. First was the written part from one of its most trusted spies. The second came from an old locater disc owned by that trusted and valuable spy. Years of patient searching had finally paid off. It was something of a surprise to see the location of the cell as it was so far from the recent revolt on Ardbanacker Island. It was not where the Frame expected the cell to be. Its location posed a few interesting problems, but now the Frame could launch a full counter attack and destroy the cell.

That battle at Dundoon had been a very finely balanced affair. The Frame was still trying to piece together what had happened. The fact that these aneksa had built fliers capable of destroying the Frames more sophisticated drones was astounding. More and better-trained troops would be required. A thousand troops should easily have retaken the town, but an enemy wielding wooden shields and firing bows and arrows had defeated them. Though they had developed their own variant of the divine staff, the weapon was a poor substitute.

Now, however, with this new data, the Frame would crush the very heart of the resistance. The base, it seemed, was located within an isolated mountain surrounded by rough country. There was a single track from the divine port town of Innish. The Frame would have difficulty in moving large numbers of troops, aimu, and equipment to the location. The Frame didn't want a long supply line and so had to consider a seaborne assault. A search for suitable landing sites was the obvious next step.

Cullin was thinking about transport. Transport was the key to the problem. On foot, the journey to Tyber would take more than a month and would be a long and arduous trek. They would also have to find food along the way. A flier would be more practical, but too visible. There was a high probability that it would be seen or intercepted, and it was important to remain covert. That left using a boat as the best option.

The only boat Cullin knew of was Pul's badly damaged Banree Na Mur, which as far as he was aware, still needed repairs at Creelan. Cullin wanted people with him he could trust and rely on, so he felt he needed Pul and his crew.

Others would be needed, someone useful in a fight, someone with knowledge of the divines and aimu. Then there would be the problem of deactivating or simply destroying the Interface.

"So we continue to build, strengthen our defences and train more troops. I am convinced that the Frame will strike back, but where is hard to say." Dook was trying to wind up the meeting. Robert the Red had tried to take control and had made many overt demands.

There was, of course, the usual enmity from Red who always had a belligerent attitude where Dook was concerned. Dook had agreed to start supplying short staffs to Red, though he had cautioned him about their availability.

He was happy with the progress at Ecta's Ledge. The new base was now well developed and would be an excellent station for fliers. Dook didn't want all his eggs in one basket, so to speak. Rustick More was best suited to developing technology and research as that was how he had originally set up the facility.

Red's demands for large numbers of the newly developed weapons were simply unfeasible and were unrealistic. Defence of the territory the aneksa controlled was a priority over Red's needs. Varee and Fraze were already aboard the flier when Red and Dook arrived.

"I have a few of the short staffs loaded for you Red, not many, but more will come. It will take time, as they are difficult to manufacture."

Chapter Two

"You take far too long Dookerock. I hate to remind you, but we are now at war and you have 'few' weapons that you can supply me." Robert the Red gave Dook a challenging look full of scorn and dislike.

Dook returned the look with a steady, unperturbed gaze. "Red, I hate to remind you, but your people are not the ones being attacked. Now, do you want those short staffs?"

"I'll take them. Many more are needed. Can you imagine what would happen if we fought aimu or divines with little more than bows and arrows?" Red grabbed Dook by his shirt, pulled him forward so that they were directly face-to-face, and gave him a long hard look. "Get a move on Dook."

"Briga has the weapons loaded in her flier. Look for yourself. There will be more." Dook seemed completely un-fazed by Red's aggressive behaviour and spoke calmly without heat or anger.

Red thrust Dook away from him and strode over to the flier to look. There, neatly stacked, were cases of the weapons. A look of glee crossed Red's face as he picked up one of the short staffs and pointed it at Dook. He laughed and returned the weapon back to its case.

"Caution Red, they have limited power. There are replacement energy packs in the other containers. Use them wisely, they too are hard to manufacture."

"Always with you it's difficult or hard to do. Always excuses. Just get on with it Dookerock. I'll be going now. Give my regards to Yayler, if you ever see him again!" Red laughed. "You're a joke Dookerock, but keep your little people working and you might survive for a while."

"Goodbye Red, I'd love to see you again soon and continue this discussion." Dook watched as the flier lifted off and manoeuvre through the hanger doors into the night sky beyond. He started his way back to his quarters, trying hard to ignore his feeling of loathing for Robert the Red.

He stopped when he saw Cullin standing patiently, waiting for him by Sara's workstation. There was something admirable about the young man, Dook thought to himself. He had never known Cullin to lose his temper or be rude. Unlike Robert the Red who was always full of his own self-importance and had an attitude to others to match.

"Why do you let him be so rude? It makes you look weak, you know."

"I know, Cullin, but we need him and it's not as if I need to see him that often. I can put up with his ignorance for short periods." Dook appeared very calm and composed. If Red upset him in any way, then he hid it very well. "Now, Cullin, I need to talk to you about some Frame technology that I want to give you. It's rare, even among divines and can't be replicated by ourselves."

Cullin remembered the last 'treatment' he had been given had made him ill for several days and wondered what else he could be given that would enhance his, otherwise normal human capabilities. "It sounds interesting, but what do you wish to do?"

"A few more inserts under the skin and one in your left eye. They will allow you to interact with the Frames technology directly without the use of a compad. It's a painless procedure."

"So I won't need one of these anymore?" Cullin rummaged in a large pocket inside his morcote and held up the small compad device that fitted snugly in the palm of his hand.

"Aye, I thought it would be more convenient."

Cullin frowned in thought. "Aren't there dangers? Wouldn't the Frame or aimu be able to enter my mind through these comchips?'

"No, the inserts work as a scape that only you would be able to initiate. Your mind remains the same, so the Frame or an aimu would not be able to read or affect your thoughts."

"Oh, I see. When did you want to do this?"

"Tomorrow, it's late now and I want a drink before bed."

Cullin cast his eyes upward and shook his head slightly in disappointment.

The following morning Cullin met Dook outside the room deep within Rustick More. The corridor, hewn from the rock of the mountain, leading to a large storeroom had a single bend in it and Dook waited there. No door was visible. Cullin knew it was there even though the rough stone wall was blank, bearing no indication there was anything beyond.

It had been Yayler's idea to make the room invisible, but accessible only with a hand with divine subcutaneous microfilament inserts. Thus, only Dook or Yayler would be able to enter the room. This level of Rustick More had originally been Dook's home, but he had found it depressing and so built his upper level apartment. The cavern they called 'toilers woe' came later. The development of Rustick More had taken many decades.

As Cullin approached he hailed Dook "Good morning! How's the hangover?"

"Tolerable Cullin and none of your business" Dook replied tersely.

As normal, Dook had made no effort with his appearance. Cullin decided he'd probably slept in his clothes. After the years, that Cullin had been living at Rustick More he had got used to the odd characteristics and behaviour of Dook.

"This is the hard bit" Dook commented. "I can never find the pad."

Dook ran his hand over the wall in a vertical stroke and waited. Nothing happened. Dook repeated the action and waited again. Still nothing.

"Do you want me to try?" Cullin offered, absent-mindedly rubbing the palm of his right hand over his rough woollen trousers.

Dook gave Cullin a quizzical look, and then his face brightened revealing fine wrinkles around his eyes that Cullin had not noticed before.

"Be my guest, young man." Dook made a theatrical gesture towards the blank wall and stood aside giving room for Cullin.

Cullin could remember his last visit to this place with bright clarity. He remembered his apprehension and nervousness. He made a mental note that he was much calmer this time. He recalled that Yayler had opened this door and he had been standing a little further over to the left. Yayler had passed his hand over there, near that wrinkle in the rock wall. Cullin passed his hand over the wall and heard an almost inaudible click as a rewarded. Slowly the door revealed itself and swung ponderously inward.

"Hmff, beginners luck!" muttered Dook.

As they entered, the room lights automatically illuminated on a room unchanged since Cullin had last seen it. Dook ushered Cullin to the silver table on its crystalline plinth.

"Are you sure you're sober enough to do this Dook?" Cullin was fretting a bit because he knew Dook had drunk more than a few ales after retiring to his apartment and his eyes were still bloodshot from the after effects.

"Aye. It's an automatic procedure. You need to lie on the table." Dook went to one of the cabinets set against the wall and took out a helmet with a number of odd attachments including a long cord with a switch. Dook fitted the helmet over Cullin's head as he lay on the table and launched the operation by passing his hand in front of Cullin's face. The hood emitted a high-pitched note and then went silent. Then a three dimensional hologram appeared before Cullin's eyes.

"There should be a light visible at the centre of the display. Do you see it?" Dook asked as he searched in the cabinet for more items.

"Aye."

"Good. Keep your eyes focused on it. It is important that you don't move your eyes or blink."

"Why?"

"Because the placement of the device needs to be precise."

"Ah" Cullin replied with understanding.

"And it will hurt like Irin if you do move your eye during the procedure. Are you ready Cullin?"

"Aye, let's get it over and done with." Cullin's eyes were beginning to sting, he wanted to blink, but was scared to in case Dook initiated the procedure.

"Ah. Here you are." Dook muttered with quiet satisfaction selecting a small vial from amongst a variety of odd paraphernalia in a drawer of a cabinet. The vial made a slight click as he inserted it into a slot on the side of the helmet.

"There will be a sharp sting, but it will be over quickly." Dook began fussing over the hologram displays from the holoscreens.

"Just get on with it Dook." Sometimes Cullin found Dook to be quite irritating, but he was one of the kindest people he knew. Sometimes, frequently in fact, Dook was completely oblivious to the discomfort of others. This was just such an occasion.

"Oh, sorry Cullin."

Dook pressed a button on the end of the cord attached to the hood. Cullin experienced a sharp pain that vanished quickly and then the procedure finished.

"I still need to add the scape chips. They are inserted under the scalp. You've had those before." Dook was hunting through the drawers in one of the cabinets that lined the wall. "Ah, here it is."

Dook selected a silver coloured needle that he loaded into a gun-like device. "You can remove the helmet now. This next insert goes under the scalp at the back of your head. For some reason, I don't know why, it works best there."

As Cullin raised the helmet visor and slipped the helmet off he asked "how does this stuff work?"

"Ah, I forgot to tell you that bit. When the inserts are initiated, you will see a computer display appear to float before your eyes. The curser blinks. You just have to imagine it moving about the display. It interacts with the other technology you've had added, like the finger microfilaments. Effectively, you will have a virtual computer and display that only you will be aware of. You will also be able to interact directly with hiu and other Frame technology."

"Sure I won't need a compad anymore? I can do all those computations in my head?" Cullin sat up swinging his legs over the edge of the table so he could watch what Dook was doing.

"Oh, Aye, though I can add a few more neuro-chips to boost memory capacity. So you really won't need to." Dook went to another cabinet and started to rummage in a drawer. "It's probably best to keep a compad handy as back up. Both Yayler and I do that though we both have a lot of computing power added up here." Dook tapped his head and smiled at Cullin revealing yellow teeth.

Cullin smiled back. "But it will be useful where I'm going."

"Aye"

"I'm thinking of going by boat."

Dook paused for thought before nodding as he pulled out another drawer. "Good plan. Do you know of a boat?"

"The only one I know about is Pul's boat, the Banree Na Mur, but that was holed awhile back."

"Ah, here it is." Dook withdrew a cylindrical device with a flattened flange at one end. "I heard about Pul's boat. I believe it has been repaired. I'll make some enquiries for you."

Dook snapped open the device and loaded it with a gel coated silver sliver. "You really ought to have had your head shaved for this bit, but I think we'll manage."

Dook brushed hair out of the way with his hand, placed the flange of the device on the back of Cullin's head, and depressed a small button. The device clicked and Cullin experienced a sharp sting. Dook repeated the process a few times then announced that the process was finished.

"Pul isn't well at the moment, but I think I can get Guvin, his son, to captain the boat for you."

"That'll be good. I was thinking of taking the northern route, it makes better use of sea currents."

Dook was busy tidying up. "Really? You seem to have put a bit of thought into this. The wild sea up that way is going to be treacherous. It's probably best if we let either Guvin or Pul choose the best route. Well we're all done here. We should get back to the Toiler's Woe. We'll have a session on the eye technology tomorrow I think."

Back on the workshop floor, they found a large heap of wood and a frowning Ealasat, hands on hips and muttering to herself. Otherwise, the cavern was quiet. A couple of mechanics were busy working on a flier. Sara and Neev sat at benches concentrating the work before them.

When Ealasat saw Dook and Cullin, she gave Dook a hard stare, but said nothing except to carry on muttering to herself. She was wearing the same clothes as the day before, but had gone to some effort to make herself presentable. Her hands and face were to longer travel stained and she had tied back her long black tresses. She wore a simple woollen vest and leather trousers. Her morcote neatly folded on the floor.

Chapter Two

Later that day Dook and Cullin were chatting in Dook's apartment about the journey to Tyber and finding the Interface.

"I've sent a message to Pul and Guvin, but it will take a few days before we get a reply" Dook was saying as he relaxed in a soft chair with his ever-present ale.

"Aye, but we really need better communications, something that will work over long distances and yet not be detected by the Frame."

"I know. We can't use the comsats, as the Frame will detect their use, even if the message is coded or disguised as something else" Dook mused. "Energy waveforms are out as well because the Frame monitors those as well."

"So we can't send a message through space, or the air. What about the ground? We could put cables down and hide them underground, somehow."

Dook considered that and tipped his mug for a thoughtful mouthful of ale, only to be disappointed to find the mug already empty. "No we can't do that either. Point one; we don't have enough materials for the cables. Point two, the magnetic field caused by the cables would be detected."

Cullin was disappointed by Dook's answer, but ploughed on with the thought "what about those light cables we found on the aimu ship at Dundoon."

Dook was looking around him for the jug of ale to replenish his mug, but found it irritatingly missing. "Hmm, that is a good thought. There is a limited supply, but we might find a way to manufacture those light cables." Irritated, Dook placed his empty mug on the edge of the table beside him.

Piles of paperwork for half-complete projects threatened to topple, waiting for the mathematics of cause and effect to determine their fate. Fate decided that they should remain precariously balanced.

"Have you decided on who you should take with you?" Dook changed his direction of questioning, still casting his eyes about for that elusive jug of ale.

"More or less. I'd like Isla to come along, Yasga, Yaren, and Ecta if possible. A mech like Neev might be useful. I don't think I want a big party and we all have to fit on the Banree anyway, so no more than four or five."

"I'm surprised you're not asking for Sara."

"I've already asked her, but she declined. She said it wasn't a good idea."

"Hmm, she might have a point. I'll ask the others though."

"Good, My thanks for that. I'd best be going. I've got duties to do. I've improved the fliers shielding and armament systems. You never know when we may need those again." Cullin stood up and picked up a file Dook had given to him earlier, that contained exercises for him to practice with his new implants.

The file had been casually, but carefully placed, on a pile of Dook's notes and a certain jug of ale. As Cullin left Dook saw the jug and gasped with joy, then realised that it had been deliberately concealed from his view. Dook laughed "too clever by half, young Cullin".

He picks up the jug and without its support, the pile of notes collapsed. Dook laughed again ironically and ignored the disarranged heap as he went to retrieve his ale mug. A broad grin spread over his face as he picked up the mug, a trifle too eagerly as he disturbed the stacks of paperwork on the table. The laws of chaos quickly determined that they would fall, re-arranging themselves into random heaps on both table and floor.

Ale mug and jug in either hand Dook sighed "well, such are the laws of cause and effect".

Air currents disturbed sheets of notes about the room, shifting them slightly affecting the balance of one pile slightly higher than others. The stack of notes and files wavered imperceptibly as its centre of balance subtly shifted and then it too collapsed, knocking into neighbouring stacks, which also fell, scattering sheets of paper and parchment across the floor.

The calamity and an old sideboard that Dook hadn't seen in years revealed old abandoned projects. Dook looked stupidly about the room as organised disorder followed the laws of entropy as several other stacks and half-completed work fell to find new arrangements of their own devising. A shelf above his bed he had believed securely attached to the wall came free at one end tipping Dook's personal effects onto the bed.

The bed that normally was quite happy to support Dook's weight decided the general disruption about the room. A leg at one end broke free and thudded onto the floor, rolling to land at Dook's feet and knocking against a standing lamp in the process, which wobbled, colliding with Dook's ale jug, breaking it along a previously un-noticed crack. The jug and contents crashed to the floor leaving Dook holding an empty mug in one hand and the jug handle in the other.

Chapter Two

"Well, everything moves towards disorder I suppose." Dook muttered to himself, shocked by his room's sudden descent to chaos.

Cullin chose that moment to re-enter the room having forgotten to tell Dook something. He stared in utter confused disbelief at Dook's apartment. "Er, right. I was going to say earlier that I think there is a way to increase the power and life of the short staffs, but I think I'd best leave you to do a bit of tidying."

Dook shrugged "I think it must have been a tremor".

"Ah, that would explain it." Cullin replied ironically whilst making a quick exit.

"Aye, tremors" Dook said to Cullin's retreating. "Aye, earth tremors, indeed!" He suddenly exclaimed with excitement as a thought struck him. He had a method.

He sat down amongst the rooms detritus and began to think. He understood P and S waves; shock waves that travelled for thousands of strides through the crust of Inalsol. He remembered also that shock waves from tremors and quakes passed through the planet's mantle and even its core.

What he needed to do was create a device that could send S waves, detectable up two thousand or more strides distant. As he thought devices formed in his imagination, some feasible, some not. A locater disc could be altered and used as a receiver, or at least translate the signal, he corrected himself.

Subtlety was the key, he thought, now entirely immersed in the project. He couldn't create large quakes, but small ones, something normally detectable over large distances.

How much power would he need? He drew his knife from its sheath and gazed at it, wondering at its limitations. It wasn't as originally designed, those had been developed to create the knife. Why not develop it in other ways?

A code within the shock wave would be needed; well, thought Dook, that was the easy bit. Slowly, by degrees, Dook began to create a mental image of the devices he needed. He sat completely oblivious to the mess about him as he worked on the designs.

It was early evening by the time he stirred with a dry mouth and feeling ravenous. He looked down at the empty mug in his hand as his belly grumbled. "This won't do" he complained to himself.

Two hundred and fifty men women and children needed food every day at Rustick More. It was more usual for Dook to have his food brought to him, but on this occasion, he made an exception. The canteen adjoined Toiler's Woe down a short corridor that some of Dook's 'guests' had decorated with murals and decorations to brighten it up. Several flights of stairs led off from the canteen to the accommodation level above and storage level below. These latter levels were later additions to Rustick More. Dook's private rooms connected directly with Toiler's Woe via a winding corridor carved from the rock of the mountain and remained un-decorated. If Dook's rooms hadn't been so cluttered, he would have been able to enjoy views out over the moors to the east via the natural fissure in the face of the mountain that had been cleverly incorporated into the design of the rooms.

As Dook crossed the workshop floor of Toiler's Woe on the way to the canteen he saw Ealasat still standing over her woodpile. She was clearly at a loss as to how to proceed with the construction of her boat, though she had made an attempt to sort the wood into different piles.

"I don't know what to do with this" Ealasat complained when Dook came over.

"I can see that" Dook replied with rancour or judgement. "I have someone who can do this for you, but in return you must do something for me."

"Must I?" Ealasat looked suspiciously at Dook expecting a catch. "What would you have me do?"

Noting the irritation and bitterness in her eyes Dook considered a gentle approach to be the most appropriate. "Have you eaten?" he asked "because if not we can discuss this matter over a meal."

Ealasat was still looking for a catch, but failing to find one agreed to Dook's suggestion. "That sounds reasonable so far. You are the only person who has offered any help."

"Hmm, the staff are busy and they don't know you. The canteen is this way." Dook indicated a doorway that Ealasat had seen people using frequently throughout the day.

"Aye, I came through here this morning." Ealasat's eyes were drawn to the riot of differing styles of mural along the corridor. A vast landscape dominated one side with mountains and lakes delicately painted with fine detail. There were family settings, crofts, pictures of animals, deer, wicks, dogs, wildcats and so forth. Ealasat's eyes were particularly drawn to a scene of a fishing village with fishermen bent over nets.

The canteen was bustling with activity and noise. Children were running about playing games between the tables, their parents relaxing and chatting with friends. A few families were still eating. One little boy being chased by a couple of older lads ran headlong into Dook, then charged off in a different direction as the less agile chasers struggled to follow. Dook remembered why he didn't eat in the canteen. It wasn't that he didn't like these people or their company. He simply preferred to eat in peace and quiet. Most days he found that it was the only time he had to relax.

The next day Dook met Ealasat at her woodpile, which he noted was now organised into different types and shapes. Planking in one pile, boards in another and so on. "Ah, don't worry about that now. We'll build you a good boat."

He took Ealasat to his rooms, which she had finally agreed to sort out and tidy after much persuasive effort from Dook. When she saw the mess Ealasat was aghast and astonished.

"What by 'Atha and Matha' happened, I think you might owe me another boat by the time I have sorted this lot out" she complained.

Chapter Three

A few days later Cullin was walking along a rocky undulating path that clung to the edge of the sea inlet Lok Kruay. The fearsome teeth of Feeaklan Deyaval loomed high above his left shoulder. He'd been following the path since the early morning and reckoned he still had to walk several strides still before he reached the iron works discovered by his friend Ecta.

Above, delicate blue cloud hung motionless in a blue sky. There was barely a breath of wind to dry the sweat from Cullin's brow. The mountains above were bare, devoid of life, grand and hard and caring not one whit for human needs or worries. Cullin mused that there was a kind of aloof purity about them. Should a mountain have consciousness and be able to think, what heed would it have for human deeds or needs? Very little, he decided. The short lifespan of man would be a fragment of the time allotted to a mountain. A person would be of less regard than an insect or a grub is regarded or thought of by most people.

He had been practising his new eye technology as he walked, finding that he needed to be wary when he zoomed his focus in on an object, a rock or clump of vegetation, caused him to trip and stumble over the small stones that made up the path. He stopped now so that he could view the mountains better. He zoomed in on a on a gully descending from a cleft in the summit ridge. His viewpoint swung crazily about as he struggled to focus on a single point.

He needed to stand still and concentrate harder. He tried again, and controlled the speed of zoom with more care and managed to a single point, a small cleft with an unusual pink colouration. Concentrating hard he moved his point of view about the cleft, beads of sweat dampening his brow despite the cool weather.

What was it that his eye caught? A long pinkish stem surmounted by the bright green of leafy new growth. Small budding leaves spread to catch the spring sunlight. The imperious mountain bore life after all, beautiful and delicate.

He remembered Dook saying to him once that life was insidious, it clung on, it was indomitable and there on a bare stony mountainside there was life. That small piece of vegetation gave Cullin hope, a realisation. That small piece of vegetation could prevail, could survive despite the conscious hubris he imagined of the mountain.

Thus, it could also be for the Frame. The Frame was proud, callous and disdainful of its human servants and ripe with hubris, that is, of course, if a machine could have feelings; no more real feelings or emotions than the mountain he had just been viewing. He understood mountains. He had lived his entire life amongst them, but the Frame was something else. The Frame was the nexus of a vast intelligent network to which humans were an increasingly insignificant part. More machines and fewer humans, that appeared to be the trend of events over recent generations. The Frame could be defeated, but not easily. The mountain had no intelligence, but the Frame did. Concluding his thoughts, Cullin guessed that the Frame used predictive software; it was essentially a difference engine and thus it could be countered.

Ahead the path wound a rough course over boulders and rocks round a headland formed by a steeply descending ridge. His destination, the iron works, lay beyond that ridge. Cullin estimated that another wair would see him arriving there. He pushed on briskly.

As he rounded the headland, his feet skipping with well-practised ease from boulder to boulder the iron works came into view. It had changed a lot from Ecta's description of dilapidated ruins. Wooden out buildings had been repaired and even the stone foundry and chimneys appeared functional and in good order. Smoke emanated from a few of the buildings.

Cullin could see that the jetty across the water from the path had also been repaired and there were two fishing boats moored, tied to the stone structure with long lengths of rope. The ridges of the mountains reflected in the still waters of Lok Kruay. A lone, large white soolara plunged like an arrow into those still waters only to be mobbed by gulls as it emerged with its meal.

As he approached the largest of the outbuildings a large bulky figure with a large mane of red hair emerged. A heavy morcote prevented Cullin from seeing more details, but there was something about the way the figure moved that was familiar to Cullin. Several heartbeats of time passed before he realised with a start that the figure was his brother Hamadern. He zoomed the focus of his eyes on his brother's face and noticed that it was more careworn than he remembered. A few streaks of grey highlighted the red mane. His brother had aged.

He was greeted with a large bear hug. "Cullin, it has been too long! I see you've filled out a bit."

Chapter Three

"Aye, hello brother, it has been too long." Cullin had to remind himself that he and his brothers had never been particularly friendly. They had bullied and demeaned him frequently as he grew up, a situation that had caused him to take long walks in the Mark as soon as he was old enough. As a result, he had got to know many of the people of the Mark that his father had administered. Yet for all that, he was glad to meet his brother again.

"You must be tired, it's a long walk here from Rustick More."

"I'm fine Hamadern. A bit thirsty and hungry, but otherwise fine" Cullin assured his brother. "I thought you were running the weapons camps on Ardbanacker."

"Aye, I don't need to be there all the time though. We'll soon be producing iron here, which will help to speed things along with weapon production."

"You know, you could do with a pad for fliers. It would help with transport."

"Hmm, good idea Cullin. Let's go inside, Pul is waiting for you."

Inside the hut was comfortable and warm. A central fireplace provided heat. Wooden alcoves for sleeping accommodation ran along the far wall and the far end had a small range for cooking. A pot steamed on the range, sending a fragrant aroma of herbs and meat juices that immediately set Cullin's mouth watering. Tables and chairs ranged in groups about the hut in comfortable arrangements.

Bent over the table nearest the fireplace a group bent over a game played with painted tiles. Cullin knew of the game, but was ignorant of the best strategies to employ to win the game. Each player started the game with the same number of tiles, though the initial number varied depending on the difficulty desired by the players. A small box sat at the centre of the table with straws of varying lengths, which the player would draw at random. The player would then move a piece in any direction by the length of the straw.

A player could capture an enemy tile by placing one of his own tiles on top, but could only do this if they drew a straw of the correct length so that their piece would land on top of the enemy tile if moved by the length of the straw drawn.

They could also stack their own stones by the same method to gain a more powerful piece. Once stacked only an equal or greater stack could capture a tile. Tiles could also be grouped and moved as one tile. Then only an equal or greater group could capture a group. If a stack or group toppled then the tiles would remain where they landed and then revert to their own players.

Cullin noted that the red tiles dominated the game having two sets of grouped tiles. The blue tiles were all but wiped out, green and yellow tiles were barely holding their own, but one or two bold moves by reds would easily put them in a weak position.

One of the players looked up, revealing an old grey visage. With a start Cullin realised it was Pul, except that the fisherman had lost a lot of weight and looked ill. Pul's face brightened when he saw Cullin.

"Come in lad, draw up a seat. I almost have the game won. It shouldn't take long to finish." Pul gestured to a nearby chair.

Guvin, the owner of the blue tiles, looked up. "Well met Cullin. Pul's overconfidence is a weakness; I have a few tricks left. He hasn't won just yet."

"Come Cullin, you must be hungry. It's a long walk from Rustick More." Hamadern gestured towards the range.

Cullin found that his stomach was grumbling, protesting vehemently at lack of sustenance. "Aye" he agreed.

Hamadern served Cullin at a separate table, a hitherto unheard of occurrence. The rich flavour of the venison stew and the fresh baked bread were a delight to Cullin and he set to with gusto. Hamadern grinned with amusement.

"We've had a good cook with us for a few days, you're enjoying one of the delights of his stay." Hamadern enthused.

"Mmmm, it is good. It reminds me of Glen Ossin. I've not seen bread like this since then."

"Nor I. I'll leave you to enjoy the food. Help yourself to more if you wish."

"I will, thank you."

"Relax for the evening Cullin, we'll have a look at the boat tomorrow. Now I have a few chores to attend to so I'll see you later."

The years had changed Hamadern, Cullin realised as he ate the stew. He was a calmer, more relaxed person than Cullin remembered.

Chapter Three

By the time, that Cullin had finished his meal Pul had won the game of tiles. With a final set of aggressive moves he had dominated the game to the point that his victory was all, but inevitable. Cullin overheard one of the other players mutter something about Pul always winning. They were packing the tiles into a box when Cullin drew up a chair and joined them.

"Where are you from?" Keri, a thin leathery stick of a man asked Cullin. Keri's face was a study of narrow features and sharp angles. His nose was long and attenuated. Deep-set eyes beneath prominent brows and over-large ears gave Keri one of the most unusual faces that Cullin could ever remember having seen.

"Glen Ossin, but I haven't been there for years."

"Oh, I've not heard of that one."

"It's quite remote, deep in the mountains of Ardyvinland south of the Ice Moor."

"Cold there, Pirt was much more pleasant" Finnan commented. Finnan had been one of Pul's crew members when Cullin had first met them in Pirt. He was quite a rotund man with a round, ruddy face, but he was tough and strong beneath the excess body weight. Cullin remembered him fondly from his previous trips on the Banree.

"Finnan and Keri will be your crew with Guvin as skipper." Pul addressed Cullin, leaning back in his chair.

Pul had lost weight since Cullin had last seen him, but though he was curious as to why and what the cause of Pul's ill health was, he didn't want to intrude into private matters. He would let Pul tell him, if he wished to do so. His face grey and pallid Cullin noted, Pul had lost vitality.

"I'm no longer fit enough for the seas, Cullin." Pul continued "I'm not well and need rest. I believe you've already been told this."

Cullin nodded in affirmation.

"Your brother, Hamadern, wants me to oversee the development of the jetty into a proper harbour."

"That sounds like a good project."

"Tell us what it's like in the mountains, Cullin. We're sea-faring folk and know nothing of mountains. Tell us of your family and friends." It was Keri, eager for stories of other places.

Cullin pondered for a few moments before replying. "I shall tell you the 'Ballad of the Shepherd and the Faery Witch'."

"Ah, we have a drum, if that helps. One of Hamadern's staff left it for practice. Wait a moment." Pul went to one of the alcoves to fetch the instrument.

Cullin found it sound with a pleasing delicate soft tone. He played a few deft phrases. It was old, but a good instrument.

"*On the last day of Rayanam, many years ago, a shepherd was about his useful work*" began Cullin, playing a soft delicate beat on the drum. "*Far he wandered in the heat of the day in search of his sheep, but none could he find.*

"*At last, tired and thirsty, he stopped by an old withered hazel and soon fell asleep. When he awoke an old woman who was as crooked and withered as the ancient hazel was sitting by his side. 'Not many come this way' the old woman croaked hoarsely. 'Lost, you are, methinks, but' continued the old woman. 'I can set you on the right path home.'*

'It is true' moaned the distraught shepherd, 'I am lost and I know not these lands.'

Cullin paused and took a sip from an ale mug set before him by Guvin. He found the flavour light and refreshing and then continued the story.

"Lost your sheep too, methinks, but" the old woman said to the shepherd. "your sheep are well enough in their fields near your home. If you wish to see your sheep and your home again you must perform a simple task for me."

"What is it you wish me to do?" asked the shepherd, fearful that he may never see his home again.

The old woman took a small wooden box from a pocket. "You must take this box high on the black mountain. There you will find a white cairn. You must bury the box by the cairn and then return here and I will show you the way home. A good deed for a good deed, my young friend."

Cullin was playing a faster beat in what he liked to think of as an 'off beat' in that it had five beats rather than the normal four. His intent was to create tension and unease for the listeners. He added more tension with extra strokes every seventh beat, but keeping the sound soft and quiet, forcing the listener to pay attention and draw them into the story.

There was a crash as the hut door slammed shut and Hamadern entered. The fishermen all jumped with surprise. Guvin cursed silently as he spilt his ale down his front; the door had slammed just as he was about to drink from his mug.

"Winds getting up lads, could be a rough night" Hamadern announced. "Are the boats securely moored, Pul?"

The fishermen merely gaped at him until Pul answered. "My crew know their jobs. The boats will be fine. Come in and sit down, Cullin is in the middle of a story."

Throughout the disturbance, Cullin had kept up his complex rhythm and waited for silence before continuing.

"*The shepherd climbed the mountain, scraping his hands raw on the hard abrasive black rock, until at last, he arrived at the top. There he found, as promised, a white cairn. The cairn glinted and twinkled with something more than reflected cold sunlight.*

"*The shepherd wondered what might be so important that it must be buried by the cairn. What was in the box? Torn with indecision the shepherd debated and concluded that the old woman would never know if he'd looked within the box.*

"*His hands shook as he lifted the lid. Surely, the shepherd thought, the lid would have been secured if the old woman wished the contents to remain unseen. There within the box was a single lock of golden hair, braided into a ring.*

" '*What could be so important about a lock of hair*' *wondered the shepherd, but buried the box as instructed and returned to the ancient hazel. The old woman was not there. He waited and at last hungry and tired he fell asleep beside the tree. He awoke to a bright, sunny morning and the old woman sat watching him.*

" '*I did not say to look in the box, shepherd*' *said the angry witch, for a witch she was, cruel and terrible and glowing with inner force.*

"*Terrified the shepherd begged forgiveness, confessing to opening the box.*

" '*Honesty is a virtue and thus I will forgive you, but you must now perform another deed for me.*'

"Fearful was the shepherd 'I will do as you ask, but please show me the way home.'

"The witch took a lock of hair from the shepherds head 'You must climb again the black mountain and return to the white cairn, dig up the box and place therein your own lock.'

"His head bowed the shepherd did not see the witch add one of her own hairs to the lock. 'Do as instructed, shepherd, or you will never see your home again.'

"Again, the old woman was not there when the shepherd returned to the ancient hazel, so, in fear of never returning home, the shepherd waited and slept. When he awoke the witch sat beside him. 'Give this box to your wife and bid her not look within. If she looks within the box your firstborn will be bound to my will for eternity.' The wizened old witch pointed the way down the valley. 'Follow the path and keep to the left and you will find your way home.'

"The shepherd did so and soon found himself treading familiar paths. When he arrived there, his beautiful young wife was waiting. A small child playing near the door looked up at him with wonder in his eyes.

" 'You have been gone long my husband, two years I have waited.'

" 'Two years? I have been gone, but two days. I do have a strange tale to tell.'

A that moment the wind blew the shutters open with a loud crash. Cullin improvised with a loud heavy rhythm in perfect syncopation. He raised the tempo, used the studs on the edge of the drum, and simultaneously pressed the skin altering the pitch and tone. After a final heavy riff as Guvin closed the shutters, he reduced his playing to a soft thrum, waiting for Guvin to resume his seat before continuing the story.

"It was exactly a year to the day that the shepherd was walking with Aluck, his firstborn son, now a boy of nearly a year and a half, when he found himself by the old wizened hazel.

" 'Greetings shepherd; it is time for agreements to be fulfilled.'

"Confused the shepherd cried 'our agreement is done. I have done as you asked.'

" 'Nay, shepherd, you agreed to do as I ask and thus bound yourself to me until I release you from your vow. Know also that your wife looked within the box and saw what was within, binding your firstborn to me, but tell me, what child is this you have with you?'

Chapter Three

"This is my firstborn Aluck, My second son, Ossin, lies asleep in his cradle."

"At this, the witch was enraged and undone. She had desired an enchanted child bound to her will. For all her trickery and falsehood, fate had intervened and all she had was an ordinary shepherd and child for Ossin, enchanted by the triple bound locks of hair, a faery symbol of bonding, was beyond the reach of the witch.

"Ossin grew to be a wise and humane man that many judged to be good and whose leadership was trusted. Of the shepherd, there are no more tales. Ossin's family and descendants grew strong and influential. The witch grew ever more bitter and hateful and winters became ever more harsh and cold until the great northern lok became forever frozen and became known as Ice More.

Cullin let the rhythm run on after he'd finished the tale, and then produced a final flourish in conclusion. Silence greeted him. The crew were a little unsure about the story, but finally clapped and nodded their approval.

"Well, that was an odd tale, young Cullin. I'm not sure what the moral of the story is, but it was certainly interesting." Pul remarked.

"It was our family's story" Hamadern answered. "Though I hadn't expected to hear it here. I haven't heard it told since I was a young lad."

The group relaxed for the evening, exchanging songs and stories. Pul sang a couple of sea shanties and Guvin told a wild and improbable tale of ancient feuding Lords. It proved to be a pleasant evening and Cullin even enjoyed a couple of ales whereas normally he would be quite abstemious.

The following morning Pul and Guvin took Cullin down to the small jetty where the Banree sat in the choppy waters of Lok Kruay. Hamadern was busy with a small group whose quarters were in a neighbouring hut. They were clearing an area of undergrowth from one of the few areas of relatively flat ground in the rocky valley. Hamadern came over to Cullin when he saw them and asked how big a landing pad needed to be. Hamadern was surprised when Cullin suggested that thirty paces on each side would be required.

Down at the jetty Cullin found himself looking oddly at the Banree. It looked subtly different to him, only superficially the same. He looked closer, zooming in with his augmented vision, scanning over the various structures on the boat. He realised that the wood of the hull didn't looked quite right and the sound of the waves lapping against the hull was subtly different. The Cullin had it, he realised that was because the hull wasn't wood.

Curious, Cullin asked the obvious question. "What have you done to the hull Pul?"

Pul brightened a broad grin of pleasure and pride broke his craggy lined face. "That's very perceptive of you Cullin. The Banree has been given a new skin, a metal one, but it has been made to look like a wooden boat, same as before."

"That's awesome Pul."

"Aye, it's stronger and lighter than before, but sadly I won't be able to enjoy it."

Cullin could see disappointment etched in Pul's face and felt a downcast sadness for Pul. "I'm sure that's not true. I don't think the sea has done with you yet, you are too much a part of it."

"That's kind of you Cullin, but my sailing days are over. My heart won't cope with the stress anymore. Guvin has agreed to be your skipper."

Cullin was aware of the pride Pul had for his son and nodded quietly, accepting that even the most vital and energetic people get old. He changed the subject, not wishing to be insensitive about the man's feelings. "How have you done this?" Admiring the boat, Cullin ran his hand along the steel hull. "I'm amazed, where did you get the tokens?"

"Tokens? My dear lad, the cost is measured in horses. Many, many horses. I won't tell you how many. I've been given a new life here and so have my son and crew, but we owe it to your friend Dookerock. It is he who has made this happen for us and to him we owe a life's fortune."

"He wouldn't do that!"

Pul shrugged "he asked, we agreed".

"But you'll never be free of the debt."

"We knew that, but it was Guvin who made the decision and he will carry the debt."

Cullin was aghast. "Why?"

Pul looked steadily at Cullin. "Guvin believes in you, in Dook and Yayler and what you want to achieve for the people."

Chapter Three

Shaking his head with disbelief, Cullin pressed. "Pul, he's enslaved himself to a cause he was free to join."

Pul gazed with sad eyes for a long moment before continuing. "That's true Cullin, but I understand that this venture will pay off a large chunk of that debt. That may be what Dook had in mind to start with. The debt will be greatly reduced when this is over."

The conversation continued as Pul showed off other changes such as the cabin, which now had a hatchway to one side that descended to the hold. The hold was smaller to create space for more crew quarters. That made sense to Cullin as the extra space would make long trips more comfortable.

As Cullin was leaving to return to Rustick More Hamadern called him over and gave him a leather belt with an iron buckle fashioned into the family rune of three interlocking circles. "The leather" Hamadern explained "comes from Mark Ossin and the buckle was cast here and is from the first test batch we have produced. We will be able to produce better quality in time as the restoration continues."

"This is beautiful Hamadern, I'm sure Dook will be impressed. It's a great thing you're doing here."

"Thank you Cullin. Good luck with your venture. It's important to us all."

A couple of wairs later Cullin had left Lok Kruay behind and had started the long steady uphill stretch to Rustick More. Ahead he saw an oddly shaped aytyen bush, larger than normal. Curious, he used his augmented vision to look closer and laughed to himself.

He called out, for it was a person trying to hide behind the bush. "Big Jon! You can't hide from me! Those bushes don't grow that big!"

The giant of a man stood up sheepishly, but managed a rueful and happy smile. A smaller man stood up beside Big Jon, looking down into his boots as if he wished he could disappear into them.

"So, what are you doing in these parts, Big Jon?" Cullin called out.

"Cullin? Is that you, Cullin? The guy at Rustick More wants a cook" Big Jon, thumbs tucked into a hefty belt "so here I am."

Cullin could see by the girth contained by Big Jon's belt that the cook had put on more weight and thought the man must be struggling on the climb to the mountain base. He was certainly red faced and sweating.

Cullin sat down beside the cook from Dunossin. "Who is your friend?"

"Oh, ah, sorry." Big Jon had forgotten to make the introduction. "This is Goram; He's a crofter from home. I believe he lived not too far from the Dun."

Goram nodded his agreement silently shifting his feet awkwardly on the stony path as if embarrassed about something.

Cullin smiled a broad and friendly, cheerful smile. "So, what brings you to Rustick More Goram?"

If anything, Goram became more awkward and embarrassed and stumbled over his words. "Er, I, er, Uhrmm, Sir" began Goram and took a deep breath. "I was accused by a young girl of doing something I didn't do. It was thought best if I was somewhere else."

"What Goram didn't say is that the girl has made such accusations before and frequently stirs up trouble. No one believes Goram is guilty, but the talk continues." Big Jon supplied.

"Ah, well, I'm sorry to hear that Goram. I'm sure Dook will sort it out at Rustick More. He's a fair man." Cullin sympathised, trying not to judge the man without knowing the details.

Chapter Four

Yayler Poddick was descending the verdant green slopes of fields that surrounded the port town of Stepan. The fields had little purpose anymore, though once they would have raised crops or held livestock for the human inhabitants of the town. Sadly, aimus ran the town, which existed entirely for the benefit of the Frame.

Though a number of divines lived within the town, they were only required for the occasional manned ship that docked in the port and administrative tasks with divines in other towns. It seemed odd then that the fields around the town were beautifully maintained though they no longer had any function.

Even the town itself was maintained in a clinical fashion and scrupulously clean. Various automated units carried out all such work. Seus that detected faults or maintenance problems endlessly patrolled the town. Clus cleared away any rubbish or debris and even moulds, mosses and lichens that would otherwise grow on building and roadway surfaces. Mads performed the maintenance tasks detected by seus. Aimus prioritised tasks as determined by seus.

The port was the central hub of the town with straight terraces radiating out to form a half wheel. Each white building constructed of plaz connected seamlessly with the next so that the terraces appeared spoke-like.

All the buildings were of the same general design, giving the town a monochrome appearance. Its meticulous cleanliness combined with mechanical precision and lack of variation made the town feel cold and inhospitable. It was inhuman, like part of a machine, which in many ways it is. Designed to be functional and perform the Frames purposes. The human inhabitants were just another part of that machine.

There are no places of entertainment or other opportunity for frivolous idleness. The resident divines had little in the way of entertainment. They worked, they ate, and they slept. They had little imagination. Yayler found them joyless people who cared more for rigid rules and regulations than for their colleagues and friends.

Yayler always struggled to empathise with them and had little patience for them. However, they were not the object of his journey. They were a means to an end. What Yayler wanted was transport to the nearby island of Mustan where a group of divines existed who lived outside the rigid social structures usually defined by the Frame.

It was very unusual for divines to walk far for any distance without the use of transport. The Frame demanded efficiency and considered walking inefficient. Arriving by foot would cause difficulties for Yayler.

As he walked through the town, he watched a seu glide along its strip down the centre of the street. A rotating sphere surmounted a rounded cylindrical body as the machine meticulously surveyed the street recording defects, rubbish, and detritus and downloading the accumulated data at the strips terminus near the town hub.

It would record his presence, but this didn't worry Yayler, as the seu couldn't differentiate the difference between him and the resident divines. Other droids busied themselves on appointed tasks.

The terrace spokes blended into a plaz gateway ten paces high. Before the gate stood a com-post that droids used for downloading data. Yayler used it to open the gate by placing his hand on a touch-plate set into the smooth, otherwise featureless surface. Yayler passed into the docks area of Stepan and headed for the quay where he knew he would find an office.

The office was not difficult to find, it was the only building with a window. For what need have machines for windows? As he entered the office, Yayler cringed at the image that greeted him. Firstly, his eyes set on the wizened husk of a man sat behind a clear plaz desk with a single curved leg. The man's right hand rested on a scape pad. Otherwise, the desk was completely clear of objects.

The office was empty except for the old man and his desk. There was no odour, no character, or ornamentation of any kind. The small room minded Yayler of the stark contrast between the tidy, but soulless office and Dook's Rooms at Rustick More that held the accumulated junk of a lifetime, incomplete projects and rubbish. This office was no more than an extension to a machine.

The wrinkled ancient was completely motionless excepting for the occasional twitch of his flaccid features. Yayler waited for his attention, but the man appeared to be oblivious to his presence. He waved his hand in front of the man's face, but still got no response. He coughed, but the official's mind was focused entirely with his work on the scape pad.

"Ridiculous" muttered Yayler under his breath. He looked about the office, but could see no button or bell to call for attention so, calmly; he lifted the man's hand from the scape pad, breaking the contact with the computer.

The man blinked, trying to refocus as he was wrenched from one computer based environment and dumped into reality. "What? Why did you do that? I will have to re-do several wairs of work now."

"I need a boat" Yayler said flatly.

"Come back later" the official commanded trying to re-connect with the computer, but finding his hand held firmly by Yayler.

"I need a boat" Yayler repeated more forcefully.

"Go away! I need to re-do all this work you've just destroyed."

"It isn't destroyed; it will be on your 'topdesk', touch the image-rune and you'll be able to continue from where you left off." Yayler calmly informed the official, though why the old man wasn't aware of how the computer system worked Yayler couldn't understand, nor did he care.

"Oh, it's a new system. I haven't worked it all out yet." The old man stammered.

"I can see that" replied Yayler, unimpressed with the lame excuse. The old man was probably incompetent, but that suited Yayler's purposes.

"What is your destination?"

"Mustan."

"Why have I not been informed? I need the instruction code."

"I can download the instructions and codes for you. It will only take a few sents." Yayler offered his hand to the divine. It was a simple process for divines to exchange data through their finger implants.

The official, however, cringed away from the proffered hand and indicated the scape pad on the desk.

'Better and better' thought Yayler and placed his hand on the pad. Of course, Yayler had no codes of instructions, but once connected with the computer it only took him a few moments to create them.

"How did you get here?" The official asked frowning at Yayler's hand. Only now did he realise that he had no access to the computer himself until Yayler was finished.

"I walked."

The official stared with his mouth agape. "No one walks." It was as much a statement as a comment.

"I finished the download, I've left the documents open for you to check." Yayler gestured to the pad for the official to view the fraudulent documents. "You do walk if your transport breaks down and it's getting late."

"Broken down you say? I've never heard of that happening before." The wrinkled face glanced at Yayler with disbelief.

"Nor I, but it has. I didn't have time to wait for a replacement." Yayler exuded an authoritative calmness, daring the official to deny his statement.

The old man shook with horror at the thought of using walking as a means of transport. The concept was completely alien to him. "What was the transport ID?"

"DT577418\210421."

"Ah, I've found it. It is reported as having a critical software failure ten strides north-west of here. You have walked a long way! How long have you had the transport?"

"Six days, I think."

"Hmm, that checks out, so do your instruction codes. Let me check what is available for you."

"Thank you, you have been very helpful."

"I have a small vessel available with ID DOV1891\210427. It will be programmed with your instructions and destination."

Yayler found the boat moored by the quay. He had left the office and the old man had returned to the alternate reality of his scape pad. The boat was a sleek vessel with a hull shaped like a silver knife and a clear plaz canopy. He found sleeping accommodation for two and a larder well supplied with regeneration packages.

The boat was fully automated. All Yayler had to do was to connect with the ship's aimu to initiate the downloaded instructions. That process only took a few moments and then, humming quietly to himself, Yayler headed for the galley in search of food that was reasonably palatable. He disliked the processed food supplied to divines. He always found it bland and devoid of character. The food provided a balanced and nutritional diet for divines, but failed to satisfy. It lacked the heart and passion good food possessed.

He would break the computer coding later and take full control of the boat. Outside droids released mooring ropes and the boat slid effortlessly out of the port. Yayler had a long journey ahead and settled down in the pilot's seat with a pot of 'spicy beef' except that it was anything, but spicy. He ate without joy as the small boat sped toward Mustan and the town of Korak. He would have like to have continued relations with Dookerock and Cullin, but he had to go his own way and they either wouldn't or couldn't follow.

He was sad about that, but they had to follow their own roads, they had to make their own decisions and he, his. He had to bury his feelings and move on.

Yayler rested for several wairs and then returned to the galley to find water. Sipping the water casually he sat in the pilot's seat and checked his position on the charts. It would still be several wairs before he reached the island. He settled back, letting the aimu and the boat do the work for him, and considered what he needed to achieve.

It was dark outside and the nav-console reported a dry moderate desarward wind. That wind would bring rains from the south later in the year. At this time of year, the island of Mustan had a pleasantly warm and dry climate. Yayler looked forward to that after many years living in the semi-arctic weather of the islands of Garvamore.

When the first glimmering of dawn lightened the eastern horizon, Yayler rubbed his hands together and flexed his fingers. He was still a wair away from Mustan. "Time to get to work" he muttered under his breath.

He placed his hand on the scape pad, which lit up with a blue nimbus. His hand jerked off the pad almost immediately as the boat crashed its way through a wave crest. The nimbus enfolded his hand and maintained contact with the pad via the glowing thread of blue light, which stretched and contracted as his hand moved.

"Nice" Yayler grinned. "A new trick."

The display flickered into existence as a two-dimensional image projected above the pilot's console. At its highest level, the computer provided limited functions to the user. The speed of the craft could be altered, the temperature and the humidity. Yayler could display the boats position in three dimensions in any part of the boat. He could download or upload from data banks, but beyond that, he could do very little.

Yayler found the next level blocked with password and security questions. The password he knew to be generic, alterable by an authorised user. He entered the figures A34211385321 and waited for the next prompt. The question, when it came, blinked on and off and was cryptic, comprising of the single word 'origin'.

'Hmm, origin of what?' thought Yayler. He sat back, frowning with concentration. After a few sents, he concluded that it must be something pertaining to the boat, not something random. He entered Malkronin, a town on the west of the continent that was a large manufacturing base for the Frame, where the majority of shipwrights worked. Malkronin was therefore almost certainly the origin of manufacture for this boat.

The word 'origin' changed to 'error', displayed in red. Yayler knew he would have two more attempts at the security question before the aimu shut down the boat.

Yayler realised his mistake, it wouldn't be the origin of the boat. It would be the origin of the aimu and that would be, Yayler entered 'Estraya'. 'Error' continued being displayed, Yayler had one more attempt, which had to be right or he would be stranded for several wairs. At that point, the aimu would send a message requesting support from one of the Frame's security vessels. If they arrived before he was able to start the boat functioning again, they would take him into custody. He was confident he could start up the boat again, or he wouldn't have started to hack into the aimus programming.

'Egg', the origin of life, was another possibility, which he dismissed almost as quickly as he thought of it because no one really knew what the true origin of life was anyway. Life was not relevant to the boat anyway.

Chapter Four

'Centre' he thought a possibility, but no, too cryptic as 'big bang' would also be. 'Beginning' then or 'Genesis', both possibilities, both would be correct. What about 'zero', 'nought' or 'nothing'; they too had possibilities. Yayler pondered for what seemed an age, steadily eliminating the least probable choices until; finally, only one remained. Even then, he did not enter the final choice until he was sure he had not omitted any options. Tentatively he entered the word 'zero' knowing that he could still be wrong. The display flickered again briefly, and then blinked several times before turning blank with a single winking curser.

"Oooff, that was a bit nervy" Yayler noticed his hands were shaking very slightly. He already had the software he needed to take full control of the boat; he was well prepared. The codes were stored in his head on neuro-chips. He only needed to check the version number of the aimus software before downloading. He had now done the hardest part, gaining access to the aimu's programming. He could now play with it as he would a yayl.

He hummed as he downloaded the software and settled back in the chair, letting the software do its work. Ahead was a dark smudge on the horizon, land. Mustan was a large volcanic island with a warm climate, especially in summer. The northern part of the island was typically dry and arid, bordering on desert. Much of Mustan was mountainous with several volcanoes. Desarick currents brought warm moist air and frequent heavy rains.

Korak, his original, destination lay on the east side of a long peninsula of rain forests and swamps. Yayler knew the town from personal experience of many years previous and disliked the place intensely, chiefly because of the myriad of biting insects that proliferated in the surrounding swamps. Korak was the main administration centre of Mustan and Yayler couldn't think of a more unpleasant location for it.

Yayler's chosen destination was a small sandy beach in the northern part of the island where he had arranged to meet an old friend, Clar15. He had once saved her life and they had remained in contact ever since. He settled down and relaxed, running through his mind his aims for coming here and the various scenarios that he might expect.

Chapter Five

Dona had been at a bit of a loose end since bringing the warning to Rustick More about the Divines' discovery of the resistance in the Dunban Forests. She had no purpose and no useful skills that she could employ at the base. With Yayler leaving without so much as a bye or leave, she felt depressed and purposeless. It was not a happy position for her mentally, as she was usually a strong minded and positive person.

With that in mind, she sought out Dookerock with the intention of finding a useful niche. She found him in his rooms with Ealasat who was busy stacking paperwork in a corner of the room Dook generally used for meetings. If anything, the room was even more untidy than when she last saw it.

Dona set aside her feelings of distaste for the mess; at least he seemed to be doing something about it. "Dook, I wanted to talk to you."

Dook was pacing up and down staring at a parchment sheet. He made a quick notation in the margin before replying to Dona. "I'm busy right now, Dona." He looked irritated and stressed with nervous energy. "Is it important?"

"It is to me." Dona looked a bit surprised at the question, Dook was always busy; she wouldn't disturb him unless she thought it was important. He did appear agitated and that worried Dona, Dook was normally quite a calm and reserved man.

"Well, help Ealasat move and stack these papers and notes. I'm looking for a large roll of charts about so big." Dook gestured with his hands a distance of two feet.

Ealasat commented with sarcasm. "Of course, if he'd kept his rooms tidy, he'd be able to find what he was looking for!"

"True spoken, you're the woodpile woman aren't you?"

"Aye, I need a boat. What of it?"

Dona found the acidity of Ealasat's remark slightly disturbing. "With that pile of scraps, I think Dook has done you short! What are you going to use for a keel?"

Ealasat simply stared at Dona by way of an answer and then frowned questioningly at Dook.

Dona continued "you build a boat from the keel up. The keel gives the boat its strength."

"Ladies please, I need to find those charts." Dook continued pacing and frowning at his sheet of parchment. At no point did he attempt to look for the charts himself.

Ealasat placed her hands on her hips and adopted an indignant pose. "If his Lordship had kept his rooms tidy, he wouldn't be in a mess!"

Dona laughed with approval at the remark. "Well spoken Eala, 'only the ordered mind achieves success'." She quoted from one of the often repeated phrases of the clerics.

"Bah!" Dook spat with disgust. "That's just one of the Frames maunderings. What does the Frame know of the human mind? It's just a machine!" Dook spoke with such vehemence that the two women didn't even think to question his logic.

"Dook, I need to know what role I have. I have no function here." The conversation had digressed, Dona noted. She wasn't here to talk about the Frame. She wanted a purpose, a role, without which she couldn't see her place here at Rustick More.

"You think I haven't considered that problem? The trouble is that you have few skills that I can employ." Dook made another notation on his sheet of parchment, oblivious to the shocked look on Dona's face.

Dona felt hurt by the comment and cast her eyes downward in embarrassment. It was true and she knew it.

"Don't bully her you nasty man!" The angry outburst escaped from Ealasat in defence of Dona's feelings.

Dook looked blankly at Ealasat, not understanding. It was a typically feminine reaction that he was always at a loss to fathom. Emotion without thought or control, without discipline he could never comprehend. He wasn't intending to be hurtful, just stating the obvious. Was he wrong?

"It's fine Eala. Dook is right. I have nothing to offer. I don't belong here." Tears of dejection appeared in her eyes as she turned toward the door. I was true, she was too old to fight, she couldn't operate machinery, she couldn't

Chapter Five

build anything, and here she was cleaning a dirty man's room. In short, she had no employable skills useful to a place like Rustick More required. It wasn't Dook's fault, but she had expected a bit more sympathy.

"Dona!" Dook raised his voice sharply.

She ignored him and headed for the door.

"Dona, find those charts and I will have a job for you."

"What job Dook, cleaning?" Dona stopped, listening.

"Dona, they are the charts, the maps of this place. The defence systems, hidden entrances and exits and so on."

Dona turned to face him. "I'm listening, Dook."

"Dona, you are a good organiser; I was planning to have you review the defences of Rustick More. If the Frame sends another army, which I think it will, then this place will be one of its targets. Except that it won't be an army of a thousand divines, there will be powerful weapons that could reduce this mountain to rubble." Dook hooped that Dona would understand his need to prioritise and coordinate the resources he had available.

"The Frame doesn't know about Rustick More, so we're safe here, surely?"

"Well, not quite true. The Frame knows of Rustick More, maybe not by name, but it of its purpose as a headquarters for the aneksa. It just doesn't know the where, otherwise we would already be facing a huge army of machines and divines."

Dona shrugged "it can't send an army here if it doesn't know where we are can it?"

"I hope not, but I don't want to take that chance. I want you to be my chief of defence. You're a good organiser and have a good idea of what can be done. You don't need the specific skills to be able to do the job."

Not sure how to respond, Dona replied with a simple "Oh".

"So? Will you do it?"

Ealasat nudged Dona in the ribs whispering "say yes".

Startled and unsure, she found herself speaking without considering the impact of her reply. It would only be later that she would fully comprehend the level of commitment she was agreeing to. "Oh, yes, of course I will."

Ealasat gazed intently at Dook reappraising the man and her judgement of him. He didn't seem to understand people and yet put a great deal of time and effort into their welfare. The two standpoints did not correlate with each other. She found it incongruous that a man with so little empathy for others, managed to do the right thing by them on many occasions. Clearly there were depths to the man she had yet to penetrate.

Dook picked up a sheath of papers that rested on the now clear table. "Now I need to leave you ladies here to find those charts."

"He's been scribbling that stuff all morning, while I've been doing all the work." Ealasat commented to Dona disdainfully.

A pained look crossed Dook's face. Ealasat had been nagging him all morning to help with the clearing of paperwork. "These scribbles are important. They are the plans for a device that will allow us to communicate with Cullin on his search for the Interface."

Ealasat was unimpressed, uninterested in Dook's excuses and avoidance of proper work. She smiled mirthlessly, adding a bitter undercurrent of sarcasm "perhaps you should have thought about it sooner".

"Leave him be, Eala." She surveyed the room and sighed, summoning her resolve and fortitude. "What a mess, this won't do." As Dook left the room, she placed a friendly hand on Ealasat's shoulder. "I've got an idea, here's what we do."

"The device comes in three parts" Dook indicated the various sketches to Neev who tried follow the designs.

"I don't see why you need two spikes. I can fit the parts into one without a problem. It would be much simpler and easy to make the whole thing as a single unit." Neev was intimate with most of the designs that had been adapted from divine equipment. She had lost her partner several years ago in the year NE 1018. They had been childless and so Neev had little else to focus her attention. Initially, after Nial's death, she had worked to blot out the pain

Chapter Five

of loss. Later it had become habit, a determination not to see others suffer as she had under the heel of the Frames minions.

"No, I don't think so. That was my original idea, but the seismology parts in the receiver spike are too delicate to survive the shock from the sending unit. I don't want Cullin to wind up with useless or broken equipment. It's safer to have three separate units."

Neev laughed with pleasure at Dook's comment. "That's what I like about you. You're a stinking wretch, but you always plan for the worst case. Three units would also mean that he could replace one or another unit in the case of a failure or damage. He should have backups, of course."

Dook smiled, scratching a beard of several days growth. 'Perhaps' he thought 'I could get Ealasat to deal with the beard.' To Neev he replied "I agree, a good idea, but we need to have a working prototype first."

Neev continued to read through the detailed notes and diagrams making a mental list of parts available. "Does it have to have a power source from a divine staff. They are in short supply. Wouldn't a unit from of our own short staffs do?"

"No." Dook took his knife from its sheath on his belt and held it up for Neev to see. "This has never been short of energy ---"

"I'm sorry Dook," Neev cut in "what has your knife got to do with divine staffs?"

"This knife is one of first attempts to adapt the Frames technology. It's essentially a divine staff, just not so pretentious."

"Oh, but why insist on a power supply we can't replace?'

"Because we have discovered certain shortcomings in the short staffs. They work well, but they have a limited lifespan. In short, their power runs out and they have to be recharged."

Neev shook her head, dislodging a lock of her carefully arranged hair, which fell over her eyes and nose. She brushed it quickly out of the way. "I'm still confused Dook, don't you have to recharge your knife?"

"Dook shook his head in a negative gesture. "No, and as far I'm aware, Yayler has never had to recharge his staff either. I don't know why, it's something I've never had the time to look into. I tinkered with his staff as well, by the way." He grinned at his own cleverness, which Neev either ignored or didn't notice.

"I see" she commented thoughtfully. "We have divine staffs liberated from Dundoon, of course, but Cullin has used many of them to improve the shielding on the fliers. I think we only have a few left."

"Ah, I wish I'd known that. It's possible we could be grateful for those fliers before too long. Make sure you have as many as you need, even if you have to take it from my knife."

Neev laughed light-heartedly, the sound rippling across Toiler's Woe. "He's full of ideas that young man. Did you know he drew up some defence plans for Rustick More? A shield that would surround the entire mountain. It's totally impractical, it would take thousands of staffs that we don't have, but the logic behind the idea is sound."

"Really?" Dook was momentarily stunned, the idea was astounding, and Neev suggested that it could even work given enough power. "He's not mentioned it; I'd like to see those plans, if possible."

"Of course Dook, no problem, I'll make sure you get them."

"Is there anything else you need to make a prototype?"

"Aye where do I get the compads from? You're quite specific about what you want there." Neev was indicating a roughly sketched diagram.

"I have a couple of those stored away. I'll let you have them. Cullin has one of his own so he is familiar with how they work."

"Really? How so?"

"Oh, he earned it. It was Yayler's idea."

"I'd like to have one myself so that I can get the feel for how they work."

Dook was suddenly evasive, not wishing to give too much away. The compads indicated were a specialist piece of equipment that only an operator with divine upgrades that he, Yayler and Cullin had. No one else would be able to operate the compad. "Ahh, that won't be possible. Just follow the instructions. Cullin will have to test it himself."

"So I can't test it, that's not good, Dook." Dook's evasion irritated Neev, but with an inaudibly muttered expletive, she let the matter drop. This is what happened when working with Dook, the man was often infuriating.

Chapter Five

"There are reasons I can't explain, but trust me; it'll work if you follow the instructions. Can you build it?"

"Oh, Aye, I think so."

"How long?"

Neev considered carefully some of the more delicate operations in the construction of the device. There was a lot to do. "A couple of days, maybe longer."

Dook nodded his acceptance. "That's fine Neev. This is a top priority, so get straight onto it."

Neev frowned, then shrugged. Dook was right, the sooner she started, the sooner the job would be done. Dook, she had noted, looked tired and stressed, like he had too much to do and not enough time to do it in. That was Dook all over, always busy.

As he turned to leave he bumped into Sara. The young woman had been looking for him. As he glanced down on her diminutive frame, he recalled carrying her through the rugged abhorrence that was the Gullet. With a start, he apologised. "Sara, how are you?"

"Dook, I was looking for you, I wanted to talk to you."

Dook groaned inwardly, he was beset by the wants and demands of women today. He had much to do and organise and he the urgent feeling that time was pressing. Still, he liked Sara; he considered her a rare and special person. "Sara, what can I do for you?"

"I was asked the other day to help with a birthing. I wasn't much help. I don't know anything about such things." Sara was earnest, feeling that this was a failing on her part.

Dook thought about that for a moment, lines puckering his brow. "You always amaze me Sara. You have crammed a lifetime of learning into a few years and you still want more?"

"Well, I like learning new things. I think I should know more about how the body works. Is that possible?"

A low rumble of amusement escaped from Dook. It had a deep base quality with rich resonance. "It certainly is. You should be able to access training schedules. I can show you how."

As Dook guided Sara to her workstation, he continued talking. "You're one of the best navigators I've got and a good pilot and learned both skills without training or coaching. You're also a good mechanic. How much more do you think you need to learn?"

"I like to learn new things. When I was young, the balclerics said that muckers didn't have the ability to learn. Learning and higher skills were only for divines. They taught that the Frame was there to guide and protect and produced all good things. God created muckers to be inferior to divines, who were charged by the Frame to oversee their welfare. They constantly reminded us of our inferiority." Sara was lost in thought as she recollected that part of her life.

"Do you still believe all that tripe?"

"I didn't trust what I was told to believe, but what other reference did I have? I now know that a lot of it was wrong, deliberate misdirection. Until I met you and Cullin, I did believe that the Frame was there to guide us and protect us; that it is the word of God on Inalsol."

Dook pulled at his beard "did the Frame make the mountains? Did the Frame make the seas or oceans?"

"I don't think so, but we were taught that the Frame is the last and greatest of God's Prophets, and delivers us his wisdom."

"More tripe, the Frame merely controls us and contributes nothing. Nothing good comes from the Frame, only pain, suffering and death."

Sara smiled "I know that now. As a slave, I found that the Frame treats us like children and punishes us if we don't behave, but children grow up. We don't need the Frame to tell us what or who to be. We do not need the Frame to tell us how to think!"

"Astonishing! Well I'm certainly not going to try to stop you. Here, this is how you access those teaching schedules."

It didn't take Dook long to get Sara started on the basics of human anatomy. He became aware of a presence behind him as he guided the young woman through the first lesson on bones and bone structure.

The presence cleared its throat.

Chapter Five

"Missed you, Cullin" Sara greeted over her shoulder whilst scanning though a list of names and attaching them to the appropriate image on her screen. "You're late getting back, aren't you?"

"Aye, I picked up a couple of strays on the way back." Cullin rubbed a rough chin. What he wanted at the moment, was a proper wash and shave.

"Strays? What strays?" Dook asked, puzzled.

"Just a couple of duni I met on the track. They're in the canteen getting refreshments. Apparently, you are expecting them."

Dook headed for the canteen mumbling inaudibly to himself and ignoring those who greeted him on the way. The canteen was quiet as most people were at work. In a corner, the two strays sat by themselves, one eating a large bowl of stew and the other quiet and worried.

"You must be Jon" Dook greeted the larger of the two men. "Cullin has told me many stories about you."

"Aye, that I am." Though not a small man, in fact taller than most, Dook found himself looking up at Jon.

Big Jon was a massive, broad shouldered hulk of a man who was also excessively overweight. If trolls existed then Jon could very well be mistaken for one. Trolls were the mythical giants that people once believed to live in the hinterland of faery, straying into the land of men on Oyki na Spirad at the height of Rayanam.

"That would make you Goram." Dook regarded the smaller of the two. Goram was not a young man, but was by no means old. He was a lean, fit man who appeared younger than his years. The odd grey hair and fine lines about his eyes gave his age away.

Goram had his morcote wrapped tightly about him and looked apprehensive. He merely bobbed his head in agreement, not trusting himself to speak.

"Let's move to another table, Goram, I need to talk to you."

They left Big Jon to his food and settled at a table removed from the hustle and bustle of the canteen. "So, Goram, what am I to do with you?"

"I don't know, my Lord." Goram looked as if he wished to disappear. He was in a state of utter dejection and misery. He had done nothing wrong, but here he was being judged and waiting for his punishment.

"Tell me in your own words, what happened between you and this girl Angarad." Dook wanted to hear both sides of the story before making any decisions, though he was at a loss to understand why the man had been sent to him in the first place. Dook rather suspected that Goram's superiors had been a bit reluctant to deal with a rather delicate situation. Any decision might be perceived to be wrong or unfair by one or the other party.

"Well" Goram started hesitantly. "I've known her for about a year. Her parents moved into a clearing not far from me. I was asked to teach them how to grow crops so that they wouldn't be detected."

"Go on, this much I know, Goram."

"Well, the last few months she's been coming to see me. It was just talk, she loved stories about the mountains where I used to live, about the Great Fire and the murder of Lord Ossin and so on. It seemed innocent to me. Was it wrong of me to talk to her?"

"Hmm, how old are you Goram?"

Goram thought about that for a moment before replying. "I'm not sure, but my mother told me that I was born in the year of the great con-, con-, con-something."

"Ah, I think the word is conjunction. That would make you forty-one. You look older."

"I'm told I'm fit for my age."

"That may be, but go on. Is there anything else you think I should know?"

"That's about it, really. The last time I saw her I gave her a hug and told her how much I enjoyed her company."

Dook sat back, thinking. "Actually Goram, I believe you. Sadly though, Angarad's parents do not. They story they have told is somewhat different and more explicit. The girl talks, the tongue wags, but often in her case, the brain isn't connected. I have it on good authority that the girl is still a virgin. So, Goram, you couldn't have performed the deeds that you are accused of."

Chapter Five

Goram looked startled, relief and surprise made him almost speechless. "Ah, thank Hesoos for that" he managed, stumbling over the words.

"Now, I have a job for you in a few days. In the meantime, I want you to help out in the kitchens. That is all Goram. You are free to go."

Chapter Six

Neev was squelching in the ooze that comprised large areas of moors around Rustick More. Perhaps it was Dook's sense of humour, but there were drier places on the moors. There were even perfectly good rocks nearby, but no; Dook had to choose the boggiest section nearby a pink quartzite outcrop.

Recent rain had made the moors wetter than usual and Neev cursed as her leg sank into the soft black peaty mire. "Dook, are you sure this is the best place to do this?"

"Oh aye. The ground near the rocks is too shallow, but here we're in a cup, a hollow in the underlying ground, so it collects water. It needs to be deep enough for the spike on the sender, but there also needs to be solid ground beneath."

"You sure you didn't just make that up? Anyhow, why is it me that has to stand, or more accurately, sink, into the bog and not you? You're already dirty, so it wouldn't make any difference to you." Neev's other leg sank into the ooze.

"You're the operator, you need to know how to do this."

"I know how to do this, I built the thing!"

"Just get on with it, Neev."

"Ah, deetah Dook, it's freezing; I can't feel my toes."

"Well, it is still only early spring, the ground is still cold."

Neev gave up on the argument. Dook was often intractable and frequently failed to appreciate others' points of view. She knew a word that described this occasional attitude of Dook's. He often had these moments where he didn't relate to or understand another person. She sighed and gazed at the distant mountains. It was a beautiful world out there. The vestiges of winter snow were still visible in gullies on the flanks of Rustick More. Distant mountains, glinting in the bright sunlight, still wore their snowy raiment. The air was still and soft cumulus clouds hung in the air. It was a lovely day, so Neev cursed her luck that she was spending it standing in a freezing cold bog.

"Dook, sometimes I think you're a solipsist, you just don't understand other people."

There was a long pause before Dook spoke again. Neev had upset him with her comment though she hadn't meant to offend. When he spoke, it was with a deep, grating rasp. "Neev, please don't use that word again. It is the name of an elite group of divines; they are the brightest and most evil. Quite simply, they only care about themselves."

It took a moment or two before Dook regained his composure. Then it was back to the job at hand. "Ah, I see Cullin and Ecta are set up now."

The two young men had set up the receiver about a quarter stride away and signalled their readiness. "You know what to do Neev?"

"Aye, I think so. All I have to do is press the send button."

"I'll still have to program the sender for you, that can only be done by myself."

"What about the receiver, how will that be set up?"

"Send the message Neev. Let's get the test done."

When Neev pressed the button, the ground shook and there was an audible dull boom. There was a pause and Cullin raised an arm to indicate that they had received a signal.

Dook grinned, happy with the test. "The receiver can be permanently fixed deep within Rustick More and be checked daily. You only need to plug in the transfer drive and messages will be downloaded automatically. You won't need me for that."

"How far do you intend to send messages this way?" Neev was curious.

Dook shrugged, non-committedly. "Maybe a few thousand strides. The receiver is very sensitive and can detect a great many movements within Inalsol's crust. It ignores tremors unless they are associated with a coded signal. The sending times and locations will have to change according to a cipher that both you and Cullin must have. The tremors we create must appear to be a natural phenomenon or risk discovery."

Chapter Six

"It's all very clever Dook; how did you think of it?"

"Oh, something happened to make me think of it, a comment of Cullin's, after that it was just a matter of putting together the details. Oh, you can pack up now."

"Thanks." Neev replied wryly at the reminder that she was soaked in cold bog up to her knees.

Both parties packed up and returned to Rustick More before retiring to Dook's rooms, which had been cleared of clutter and were clean for the first time in many, many years. They could now access two more rooms. A washroom and a small office with Dook's paperwork neatly bound, labelled, and stacked.

After so many years of living in clutter and mess, Dook felt a bit awkward in his rooms. They had become something alien. Before, he could always find things because he could remember where he had left them. Now, when he wanted something, he would have to search for it. He would eventually get used to the system that Dona had put in place, but presently, he had too many other things to think about, do and organise. The extra demand on his time was unwelcome. He couldn't complain though. The job had needed doing, but he was at a loss to understand how Ealasat had achieved it so quickly.

The next day Ecta and Cullin took a flier to the iron works. Ecta was surprised and impressed by the changes. A group of men worked on a new pad for the fliers, which looked almost finished. Cullin landed nearby and disembarked via the tailgate with bits of the receiver.

They had a while to wait before they expected the signal. Ecta was holding the receiving rod while Cullin tapped it into the ground.

"You know Cullin, I thought Dook said this equipment was delicate and there you are hitting it with a hammer!"

"Sensitive, not so delicate. Besides, the rod only transmits the tremors. It's the other equipment that is more delicate. I think that's why we have to attach them afterward."

"That would make sense."

Once the receiver was set up, they settled down to wait. Wrapped up in a heavy morcote, Pul came over from one of the huts to join them. He settled himself comfortably on a large rock. Cullin noted, though, he knew Pul was used to the cold and damp of a seafaring life.

"How soon do you think you'll be ready to leave, Cullin?" Pul asked as he regarded the receiver curiously.

"A few days I hope. This contraption is some of the equipment we'll be taking. We're just making sure it works before we leave."

Pul nodded his understanding.

"Where's the boat, Pul?"

"Guvin's taken it out with the crew. He wants to keep them sharp and not get lazy."

"You're all ready to go then?" Ecta asked relaxing in the sunshine.

"Aye, supplies loaded, new charts drawn up, we're good to go."

"You know Cullin, it's a shame we can't take a flier to this place, but I guess they'll be needed here." Ecta queried idly.

"That's true, but not the reason we can't use one." Cullin explained. "The fliers are simply too obvious and visible."

" That's a pity, I don't relish the idea of spending a month or more on a little boat, especially if the weather is bad. Another thing that is bothering me is how we avoid detection. We are sure to be seen and certainly won't pass as divines. There's not a chance of that, I think."

"We'll be travelling at night. We won't be able to light a fire, but most of the journey will be on the boat. There is a good chance that we won't be caught and we have an advantage in that the Frame won't be looking for us."

"The Banree is a lot more comfortable than she was before and Guvin knows what he is doing." Pul added.

"I know all that." Ecta replied "but I still think we have a slim chance of success."

"That's one of the reasons I want you with me, Ecta. You're very level headed. It's not an easy task and it is dangerous, but you're not unaccustomed to adversity." Cullin tried to mollify Ecta's worries. "I believe we have a good chance of success."

Chapter Six

They relaxed, waiting for the signal, letting time slip by in its own time. Sporadic conversation broke the peaceful quiet, but mostly the three men were content to do nothing. Pul was quietly snoring and Ecta dozing when Cullin suddenly jumped up with a start and started to fuss with the receiver equipment.

"What's the problem, Cull?" Ecta mumbled his voice thick and sleepy.

"We should have received a signal by now."

"Is it not working?"

"I don't know Ecta. I'm just checking."

Cullin fussed with the equipment, clicking his tongue and checking connections and power. He was half convinced that it wasn't working, but all seemed in order.

"Didn't Dook say that it had to be on solid ground?" Ecta asked watching Cullin check the equipment.

"Aye, he did. About a pace under our feet, the ground is solid rock. That isn't the problem. I don't know what is. It is put together correctly, the connections are good; it should be working." Cullin continued fussing and frowning in thought, but after a few sents gave up the battle. "I think we can only leave it and check again later. Perhaps they haven't sent yet."

It was around a half wair later that the equipment beeped quietly. When Cullin checked the receiver again, he found that it had received a signal, though none of them had felt any disturbance from the ground. "We have it Ecta. Let's get packed up."

Cullin and Ecta sat at the table in Dook's rooms back at Rustick More. They convened a meeting with Dook to discuss the results. Dook read through the results with interest. Scattered on the table, there were documents and a plan for the complex of Rustick More, which Cullin and Ecta viewed avid interest.

"This all looks good to me." Dook announced as he scanned through the reports uploaded onto a compad displaying its three dimensional image on the table. "The signal strength is good, so I think you guys are good to go as soon as Neev gets more units built."

"Good, I'd like to get started as soon as possible." Cullin replied looking up from the plans of Rustick More.

"The route is an issue. I understand you wish to head natua and then use the yernan passage. I'm concerned about the amount of ice you'll encounter. Would it not be better to use the desan route?" Dook queried.

"It'll be cold, that's true, but we'll avoid detection better that way and then follow the ocean currents, which will be in our favour then. The route you propose is busy. Pul and Guvin have selected the route and I trust their judgement."

"What about supplies, you won't be able to purchase any on route?" Dook was working his way through a mental checklist, ticking off items as the discussion covered them.

"Again, Pul and Guvin are arranging the food. I've asked for at least a five-month supply and as much fresh water as we can carry."

Dook looked with surprise at Cullin. "That long? Do you think you'll need to be gone that long?"

"I hope not, but I would like to be prepared."

"Good, Well you seem to be organised and good to go."

"There is an issue with the group I'll be taking to Tyber. Ecta is useful to have around and I understand the need to use one of the crew, but I don't see a place for this Goram. What skills does he add to the group?"

"He appears to have good general knowledge and is quite bright if a bit rigid."

"Rigid? He can't deal with authority. Grega, back at Dunossin, used to call him 'the griper' because of the number of complaints and demands he made of the Mark."

"He's not over-bright and very inflexible in his thinking. I had him moved with the first group of refugees from the Mark Ossin exodus, because he couldn't build a decent shelter for himself." Ecta added.

Irritation showed on Dook's lean features as he addressed Cullin. "Nevertheless, he could be useful, but I do need him out of the way for a while."

Chapter Six

"You need him out of the way? What about the needs of the Tyber group? Some military experience would be useful there. Someone with experience with divines would also be a boon, but we get this Goram. I'm struggling to think of what use he will be."

"That I'm afraid you will have to work out for yourself, but he will be going with you. Military thinking or experience will be of little use to you. You will be better to avoid conflict. As for divine experience, you have as much as anybody else does and greater ability and skills. So you yourself fulfil that role."

"I see, so I guess there isn't much else to do except wait for the com-devices." Frustrated and annoyed Cullin gave up the argument. He didn't believe Goram would be foisted on him if he was a liability, but he still questioned his value to the group? "Come on Ecta, I'm going down to the woodpile, see if I can lend a hand there."

"Aye, I'm with you." Cullin's oldest friend replied.

Pyta was bored. All he did was sit outside the Inn, watch and record, and get drunk. He didn't mind the latter and Linn's ale was very enjoyable, but nothing ever happened. It was a dull existence. He hadn't even had a decent fight since working for the 'Boss'. That would've alleviated some of his boredom.

He'd also noticed that he was putting on weight. He was becoming soft, flaccid and rather chubby, rather than the lean hard man he had been. He decided he needed to get some exercise. Walking would be good.

Decision made he went to his room and selected some heavy woollen trousers that stopped just below the knee. Long woollen socks, a finely knitted shirt and his morcote completed the ensemble. The weather was mild, so he'd decided so didn't require anything more extravagant. He made sure his flask was full of whisky and headed for the front door. He would climb the hills behind the village.

They had got used to his presence in Garvin by now, so no one even bothered to look as he strode purposefully out of the village, his boots resounding on the cobbled street. He huffed his way up the initial gentle, grassy slopes and soon began to sweat profusely.

As the ground became more acclivitous Pyta found that he struggled to make any headway at all. He stopped frequently to catch his breath and ease the pounding of his heart. He took regular 'comfort' nips of whisky from his flask as he pushed on. As the grass gave way to heather and loose sliding stones he decided that he needed a break. The slope seemed incredibly steep to Pyta, but he selected a nearby boulder and sat down facing Garvin below him.

Above, the tops of the hills looked further away than they had before. Below the village of Garvin lay spread out along the shore. He could still make out details and realised that he had not attained much height for all his effort.

His sweat cooled rapidly and he pulled his morcote close about him. As he slowly recovered his breath and his heart pounded less aggressively, he noticed that the light was dimming. It was late afternoon, almost evening and the beginning of the fourth quarter of the day.

Where had the time gone? It had been early afternoon when he had set out and he would be lucky to get back before dark. Then he saw the boat, just an ordinary fishing boat, but not one of the local boats with which he was familiar. Then he realised he had almost certainly seen it before. 'What are you doing here?' he asked himself. It wasn't a local boat, so where had he seen it before?

The boat had a distinctive double mast, the stern-most having an odd twin boom configuration that Pyta could only remember seeing once before. He would have to think hard about that. It was certainly interesting, worthy of note, and the Boss might think so too. He committed details to memory and set off back down the hill.

It was indeed dark by the time that Pyta got back to the Inn. Linn, his Landlady, was already serving the evening meal. She was a good cook and Pyta's mouth watered in anticipation. It was only a mutton stew, but Linn had a way of making the most humble of food taste wonderful. The day before she had served lights, but they'd had a deep luxurious flavour that belied the humble ingredients.

Linn was one of the few people that Pyta liked. She never commented on his 'funny' accent and was always in good spirits. He didn't think he had a

Chapter Six

strong accent, but people struggled to understand him and accused him of mangling the language.

"You're late Pyta." Linn called out cheerfully when she spied him entering the front door. "Best get some stew while it's still hot."

"Aye, Ah'l do tha' " Pyta was only too willing to oblige. He threw his morcote over the back of one of Linn's sturdy dining chairs and sat down. He was suddenly ravenous with the expectation of a hearty meal.

Linn gave him a generous portion and Pyta helped himself to a handful of excellent oatmeal biscuits and tucked in. Linn had a knack with herbs, never too much or too little and always subtly balanced.

"So where have you been this afternoon?" Linn asked, breaking his focus on her food.

"Ah wen' oop the heel. Oop thar." Pyta gestured in roughly the correct direction.

"Oh, it's lovely up there. I used to love those little ridges and crags; so wonderful. I'm quite jealous." Linn laughed with a joyful expression full of cheerful happiness.

Pyta smiled with ironic humour. "Aye. It wer' nice." Pyta was embarrassed to admit that he hadn't reached the ridges that surmounted the hills so he tried to look knowledgeable and hoped Linn wouldn't ask too many awkward questions.

"Ah saw a boat oop thar." Pyta commented, trying to divert the conversation away from embarrassing details.

"Really? What? Up on the hill?" Polite as always Linn simply expressed surprise. She was never scornful to her guests.

"Nah, from oop thar, on the wa'ah."

"Well, there are lots of those Pyta."

"Wer'n't from 'round 'ere." Pyta persisted.

If Linn found the pointless conversation irritating, she managed not to show it. "Oh, what type of boat was it?"

"Fishin', bu' naht like 'round 'ere."

"I think it probably stopped for supplies. That happens quite a lot here."

"Ah see." If Pyta had wanted press Linn for more information, he found it would have to wait. Linn had moved on to her next guest, making cheerful, polite conversation as she served and leaving Pyta with any further questions unanswered.

The following day Pyta took a jar of whisky down to the harbour and started talking to Sef, an old fisherman who spent his time doing odd jobs on the quay such as repairing nets, lobster pots and so on. Sef would talk to anyone who had the time and was full of amusing stories that Pyta believed to be pure fabrication and exaggeration.

Pyta supplied Sef with whisky and listened attentively to the stories noting that Sef had done very little work on the net he was supposed to be repairing. Pyta was patient, laughing on cue, and appearing appreciative. He detested Sef intensely, but wanted information and so put up with the charade. If anyone knew the identity of the fishing boat, it would be Sef. Sef spent more time watching and talking than doing.

After Pyta had 'wasted' half the jar of whisky on the old fisherman, who was now quite merry, he steered the conversation towards the various boats and comings and goings of the daily life of the harbour. Sef became excited at the mention of the boat Pyta was interested in and became very animated. Sef's old friend Pul had owned the boat before retiring to run an Inn. Yes, he knew the name of the boat "the Banree Na Mur" though he could not say where it currently harboured or who now owned it. He did think one of the men looked very much like a young Pul, so could be his son, but Sef couldn't say for sure. Sef rattled on and Pyta became disinterested and soon made his excuses and left Sef to the pretence of repairing nets. He had what he wanted. Pyta added the information to his report and sent it to 'the Boss'.

Chapter Seven

Clar15 was one of the few divines that Yayler trusted. After faking his own death and starting his new life among the muckers, Clar15 was the first divine that he had contacted. She had believed him dead and had received his communiqué with considerable disbelief.

Yayler had always been careful not to disclose his location and had not resided or consorted with divines for a great many years. This would be the first time in those countless years that he and Clar15 had seen each other in person.

The sleek boat slid gently through clear turquoise coastal waters now, barely creating a wake. Just beyond a rugged headland ahead was a small inlet that formed a bay with a beach where they had arranged to meet. As he rounded the headland, he saw the lonely figure of Clar15 sat on the golden sands of the beach. She stood up as the boat approached, revealing an elegant, slim figure, despite her advanced years. She was not as old as he was, Yayler reminded himself, not by a long way, but she was old indeed. Her beauty and health at her age were the result of healthy living and the nanos that all divines possessed, repairing the damage and defects that accumulate within the human body over time.

Clar15 wore a white shift dress that, though loose fitting, hugged her body and showed off her figure well. She wore her dark auburn hair tied back revealing a delicate slim brown face. A gentle breeze ruffled her dress and played with a loose lock of hair as she watched the boat approach the beach.

The boats' draught was too deep for the boat to draw near the shore. Whilst working his way through the boats aimu codes Yayler had found a subroutine that launched the shore vessel. He dropped the anchor and deployed the vessel. Both were automatic processes that only required the command from the pilot.

There were several clicks, whirring and clunking sounds. The upper section of the hull behind the canopy detached itself. An arm that formed part of the hull lifted the upper section away. The arm lowered the vessel gently into the water. Small motors provided enough lateral thrust to keep the boat stable. The vessels bow faced the boats stern. The arm provided a ramp that allowed Yayler to step comfortably into the shore vessel. The heat of the air hit Yayler as soon as he exited the air-conditioned cabin. His sweat evaporated rapidly so that he didn't feel clammy or uncomfortable, but the heat was a shock after the cold of his adopted home of Garvamore. A twist of the tiller released it from the arm and Yayler quickly had the little vessel sliding gracefully and effortlessly through the water to the beach.

"Nice boat." Clar15 announced as Yayler jumped with considerable agility onto the shore.

"It's a good boat" he replied as his boots crunched on the golden sand. "How long has it been?"

It was a moment before Clar15 answered "It must be a hundred years". Clar15 spoke with precise intonation, enunciating each syllable with careful preciosity. It was a mannerism drilled into child divines by the aimu teachers from their fourth birthday until adulthood.

"Hmm" thought Yayler. "It might be more than that, but a long time indeed. How are you Clar?"

Clar15 laughed, it was a humourless laugh, without mirth or joy. "Old, but not as old as you Victor." Clar15 used the contracted form of Yayler's divine name, Victor8. Divines generally only used the full name in formal situations. It was acceptable to drop the numeric at other times. It was always necessary to use the numeric when interacting with hius.

"That is true." Yayler greeted his old 'friend' with the traditional gesture, both hands raised with their palms forward.

"I have juices and food waiting for you, not too far. I have a little hut for private use." Clar15 indicated to Yayler to follow her up the beach.

"Good, I have not eaten yet."

They followed a winding path that led onto a rocky rise, their feet raising small dust-clouds as they went. Small bushes of sage and rosemary used for flavouring in the local cuisine dotted the landscape in abundance.

Clar15's hut sat near the top of the rise where it would catch a cooling breeze. The building had wide verandas on each side. Surrounding the two-storey building was a white perimeter wall. A table on one of the verandas had various dishes and bowls laid out with clear plaz covers. Yayler recognised olives, sundried tomatoes, spiced meatballs, and flatbreads that typified the cuisine. He hadn't seen or tasted such foods in such a long time that he could barely remember their tastes or textures. The juices of exotic fruits completed the meal. He tucked into the food with relish, savouring the flavours.

Clar15 waited in silence until he had finished eating before speaking. "What brings you here Victor? Your timing is very awkward. I have a large army due to embark very soon."

"Where are you headed?" It was a polite, softly spoken question and Yayler didn't expect Clar15 to answer it.

"I should not tell you, but, knowing you, you will find out anyway." Clar15 smiled a thin humourless smile. "It seems that the people on a small island to the north of here have successfully taken over Frame installations. Not surprisingly, the Frame wants them back. That is what we do."

"I came here looking for some advice and possibly even borrow a few of your warriors." Yayler didn't want to give too much away, but he wanted Clar15 to mull over just enough information. "So you're going to take these installations back for the Frame?"

"That is correct. We will occupy the local area and bring the populace back under the benevolence of the Frame."

Yayler looked at Clar15 for a long moment, thinking hard. "I know what it is that you do here on Mustan. That is why I came here. Surely though, you don't consider the Frame to be entirely benevolent?"

Clar15 barked a short ironic laugh, her face betraying irritation. "Indeed not Victor. We have always had a certain amount of self-rule and independence here in return for our services. Lately though, the Frame has become more interfering and domineering."

"Perhaps you would prefer less interference and more independence."

"That is true Victor, but we are a tool of the Frame. We tame the rebellious spirit in these remote areas. We get a bit more freedom in return for our services. You know this Victor." Clar15's tone was condescending.

"I didn't think there was enough unrest to warrant keeping a large population of warriors."

"Victor, there is always a revolt or fighting occurring somewhere on Inalsol. The demand for our services increases every year and every year we put down more rebellions. It is such a problem that the population of Mustan can no longer sustain the increasing demand for our services and a corresponding increase in the interference in our affairs by the Frame."

"That surprises me, I had no idea at all that there was so much unrest." Yayler was genuinely puzzled by Clar15's viewpoint. Of all the peoples living on Inalsol the people of Mustan were the best equipped and trained and capable of taking command of their own destiny.

Clar15 smiled "the Frame suppresses the information to prevent further rebellion. So it's not surprising that you are unaware of the amount of fighting going on around the globe."

Yayler smiled back. "I cannot help thinking Clar, that you are fighting for the wrong side."

Clar15 stared at Yayler in open-mouthed shock. He knew that she would rather be free of the Frame, but the idea would be difficult for her to contemplate. As with all divines, Clar15 and the soldiers of Mustan were too entrenched in duty and loyalty to the Frame to consider that they might do better for themselves without the Frame.

"I think I had better go Victor. You are welcome to stay here for as long as you need, but I have other things to do. I will see you tomorrow and we can continue our discussion then. You will not be disturbed here."

The divine left without as much as a backward glance and after a couple of sents Yayler heard the whine of an aimu transport powering up and suddenly felt very alone. He knew the idea of fighting against the Frame would be anathema to Clar15 and hard for her to agree with, but now he wondered if he had misjudged her. Maybe it would be too difficult for her. He now worried that she might do or say something about his intentions, whatever she perceived them to be. It would be a very nervous wait until she returned.

Perhaps he had revealed too much of his intentions too quickly. Yayler had become unsure of himself. Perhaps he should leave, but no, they would track him down as an enemy, a rogue divine.

Yayler spent much of the rest of the day thinking how he was going to persuade Clar15 to join him. He sat by window on the upper floor watching the peninsula for signs of approaching trouble. He slept poorly, frequently waking with a start, but no trouble came. He fretted throughout the morning and afternoon, endlessly running different scenarios through his mind and worrying about what to do.

Chapter Seven

It was late evening by the time that Clar15 returned. By then Yayler felt drained of energy and, unusually for him, tired, very tired. It wasn't a physical tiredness, but a mental weariness that sapped his vitality. He, who prided himself on his mental discipline, would have to do better.

Clar15 slumped into an armchair on the veranda looking exhausted. Yayler had brought the chairs out (one in anticipation of Clar15's return) so that he could enjoy the cool evening breeze. He had set a table with a spread of food from the kitchen storeroom.

"Do you mind? I have not eaten today." She asked as she reached for a glass.

"Aye, help yourself."

As Clar15 tucked into the food she queried "where have you been for so long? Do you know that you have picked up a very strange accent?"

Yayler realised that he had slipped into the local speech used in Garvamore. They called it the true tongue, but divines considered it backward and degenerate. "I have been working in a very remote area. It is how they talk there."

"I see. Do not speak like that on Mustan. People might think you have a speech impediment."

"I will try not to."

"Now Victor, you have put me in an awkward position. Very soon, I have an army of ten thousand embarking. I cannot leave you here and I cannot ask you to leave until I know more. I need to know why you are here." Clar15 was very business-like with a stern, almost emotionless expression on her face.

This was a delicate moment. Yayler chose to lie, a careful distortion of the truth that was not quite untrue. He wanted a positive negotiation built on the long association he had with Clar15. "I am looking for advice and, hopefully a small group of warriors to take with me to that remote area."

"Why can the Frame not intervene?"

"There has been no violence yet. I am hoping to circumvent the need for the Frame's involvement." Yayler felt under interrogation, but knew he needed to work on the trust between himself and Clar15.

"So you want to prevent violence and keep the peace?"

"Yes."

"That is very laudable, Victor." Clar15 appeared to relax slightly. "It would have been better, though had you gone through the proper channels."

"The Frame does not always interfere directly, especially in these remote areas." It was not exactly a lie. Typically, the Frame would only use an army as a last resort.

"That is very true, Victor." Clar15 was now relaxed and picking idly at the food on the table.

Over the next few days their discussions continued. Yayler never pushed or asserted himself, and always avoided giving precise details. He carefully encouraged Clar15 to express her feelings and to trust in them, rather than follow the rigid dogma of the Frame.

The Boss had been searching for the identity of the Boat Pyta had reported to him. He had the name 'Banree' so it should have been an easy job. All he needed to do was to put the name into a search engine and wait for the results. Of course, it would have been easier if Pyta had supplied the correct name, as many, many, boats registered in the Garvamore district included the word Banree. The database did not include a description of the boats. A fishing boat with two masts might be unusual, but that information wasn't included. He didn't even know to whom the boat was registered.

He had to eliminate each item on his search by hand by known locations and guess work. Eventually he had an identity for the boat, the 'Banree Na Mur' that had been missing, presumed lost at sea, for over a year. It was an easy job to request a search for the boats current location through an aimu. The coastal village of Bandrokit, his present location, had one permanently stationed and made regular patrols. He simply added his search request to his normal report. This, he normally did late at night outside the village or at the nearest com-post to his current location. The wrong person witnessing his activity was always a danger, but that was something he could not avoid. He could use a compad, of course, but their use could raise even more awkward questions than questioning by an aimu. He kept such activity to a minimum to avoid needless risk.

Chapter Eight

"I'm amazed, Neev. How are able you to produce these so quickly?" Cullin held in his hands one of the communication devices he would be taking with him on the journey to Tyber.

"It was easy enough when I had all the parts." Neev was finishing the packing of a container with the different sections of the devices. "When do you think you'll leave?"

Cullin handed back to Neev the two sections of the sender he was holding. "Probably tomorrow now. The sooner we go, the sooner the job gets done. I'll need to find Ecta though; I've not seen him today."

"He's out on the moors doing something for Dook."

"Well, look out for yourself Cull, I'll keep Sara up to date on what you're doing."

Cullin flushed slightly as he thought of the young woman. He would miss her. She was a constant source of strength and support to Cullin and he wondered how he would ever manage without her. "I would appreciate that." He realised that he should spend the day with her, though she would certainly protest that she had too much to do.

In fact, she didn't; she thought it a wonderful idea. They would spend the day on the moors away from Rustick More. She knew just where there was a good spot. They got food from Big Jon, who completely taken over the running of the canteen, and took a flier on the pretext of doing a flight test.

The spot Sara had chosen lay Natua of Rustick More, on a hill with views along Lok Kruay and distant snow-capped mountains. Rustick More dominated the view south. Fresh spring growth was turning the dull browns of winter to vibrant green beauty. Small spring flowers dotted the hill with a riot of colour.

They lay their morcotes on some flat rocks near the summit and determined to spend the day doing nothing. Despite a slight chill breeze, it was a lovely spring day. White cumulus clouds glided in silent majesty across a blue sky. It was over a wair before either of them spoke. Talk was an intrusion on a perfect spring day.

The simple joy of watching the world enthralled Sara. It was something she had never been able to enjoy in her earlier life. In the distance a herd of deer grazed, looking for fresh green shoots and leaves. She could see that they were quite heavily pregnant deer in fawn soon. Sara nudged Cullin that she might point them out to him, but all she got was a slight snore. She left him to sleep, and continued her enraptured vigilance of the countryside.

It was a while later that she saw a figure ascending the hill carrying a deer carcass across its shoulders. As the figure approached, she recognised it as Ecta and nudged Cullin into wakefulness. He groaned, muttering incomprehensibly under his breath.

"Ecta's here" she supplied him helpfully.

Cullin shook himself into wakefulness and rose to greet his friend. Noticing the deer he commented "A bit early in the year for hunting isn't it?"

"Aye, but we need the meat and this one has no fawn. She's old and thin and probably wouldn't survive next winter anyway." Ecta dropped the carcass onto the heathery grass that carpeted the hill. "So, what brings you two out here."

"We have everything we need for the journey. Neev finished those communication devices Dook devised last night. So we're just having a break and waiting for you." Gesturing toward the deer carcass, Cullin commented "It hasn't been gralloched!"

"I thought Big Jon would like that job, I always make an appalling mess. So we're ready to go then?"

"Aye, enjoy the day and we'll go tomorrow. We rendezvous with the Banree at Dunirayn."

"Dunirayn, Cullin? Where's that?" Ecta queried.

"It's your iron foundry, silly" quipped Sara.

"Oh, the one I found. When did they start calling it that?"

"Not sure, recently. It was just the iron works when last I was there." Cullin was rubbing his eyes, still not fully awake.

"Well, I guess it has a proper name now." Ecta commented. "I'll get my wee friend to Big Jon and see you in Toiler's Woe tomorrow."

Chapter Eight

"Take it easy, Ecta. Put the carcass in the back of the flier and take some time off. We don't know when we'll be able to relax again."

The following day there was palpable tension between Sara and Cullin. Sara was piloting the flier. She would return with it to Rustick More after dropping off Cullin, Ecta and Goram at Dunirayn. A couple of mechanics had fitted six seats for passengers since the battle at Dundoon, two of which were occupied by Goram and Ecta, who were busy trying not to listen to an argument brewing between Cullin and Sara.

"I can't think of anywhere I would rather you be. Rustick More is a safe place to be. I can't think of anywhere safer." Cullin was more frustrated than angry, but Sara's timing in raising the issue was causing a problem.

"Have you spoke to Dona recently? Dook has given her responsibilities." Sara's voice was clipped as she barked out the words.

Cullin tried to maintain calmness in his voice. He needed Sara to explain what was on her mind, what was irritating her. "Nay, what responsibilities?"

"She's reviewing the defences of Rustick More."

"Dona doesn't know anything about defence. She has no military experience." Nevertheless, the importance of what Sara was saying was not lost on him.

"She knows enough to ---"

"Cac!" Cullin cut Sara short with the expletive.

"What?" Sara snapped.

"That means he's worried."

"Aye, and how do you think that makes me feel?" The pitch of Sara's voice rose a notch in a strident, challenging tone.

"Worried; I think we're all worried about what the Frame might do next."

"Is that why Yayler left?" Sara's voice quivered slightly as she spoke.

"I'm not sure why Yayler left. He didn't go skulking off in the middle of the night. Both Dook and I were there when he left. I believe he will come back." Cullin had no idea why Yayler had left. If anyone knew it was Dook, but he was keeping such things close to his chest.

"What? How could you possibly know that?" The challenging note in Sara's voice had returned.

"He gave me his yayl the day before he left. He asked me to keep it safe. That instrument is precious to him. Not even Dook appreciates quite how precious, but I think I do."

"I don't understand." Sara shook her head slightly, her forehead furrowed with a slight frown of confusion.

"He gave you his yayl?" Ecta queried with surprise.

"What's a yayl?" Goram piped up querulously. He had been surreptitiously following the argument, trying to understand the conversation. He got the bit about defence, but the yayl bit lost him.

"The music Yayler plays with the yayl is important to him. It's an extension of who he is. I'm not keen on his music myself. It's not like the ballads and dances they used to play in the Great Hall at home. It develops in odd ways that I find uncomfortable. Yayler makes the instrument a part, an expression of who he is." Cullin did his best to explain the importance of the yayl to the others, but felt his explanation to be inadequate, only part of an answer. He shrugged.

"So?" Sara asked confused.

"He wouldn't have left it unless he knew it was safe and he was coming back for it." Cullin continued.

"Oh." Sara had never known musical instruments when she grew up. Music to her was entirely vocal. Nonsense words set to ancient tunes that some of the older slaves said went back to a time before the Frame.

"Unless he was going somewhere he couldn't take it, where it might betray him. Are you sure, it wasn't a gift?" Ecta was rubbing at his beard thoughtfully.

"That's ridiculous Ecta." Cullin retorted with mild irritation. Ecta clearly didn't understand the personal nature of the instrument to Yayler.

"Really?" Both Ecta and Sara spoke in unison.

Chapter Eight

Ecta gave up and an awkward silence filled the flier. It was Sara who broke the silence. "Cullin, I'm leaving Rustick More."

"What?" Cullin couldn't believe his ears, how could she leave Rustick More?

"The boat woman, mistress of the woodpile." Sara said by way of explanation.

Completely confused Cullin could only ask "what about her?"

"I'm going to help her finish her boat. Then we're going to go and live on her croft."

"Why, you're safe at the More and can get out quickly enough if needs be." Still confused, a slightly desperate tone had entered Cullin's voice. He couldn't understand why Sara would want to leave him.

"Aye, in truth it is, but I wouldn't want to raise a baby there." Sara glanced over at Cullin to catch his reaction. He was being unusually dim-witted this morning.

"There're lots of children and even babies at the More, but what has that got to do with ---" Abruptly Cullin stopped, startled and simply stared dumbly and wide-mouthed at Sara. A feeling of dread overcame him as cold beads of sweat broke out on his forehead and a churning sick feeling cramped his stomach. He gawped at Sara who looked immensely pleased with herself. "So you're –" he stammered.

"Pregnant?" Sara finished for him. "Aye Cullin. You're going to be a father."

Ecta, sitting behind Cullin, laughed with delight and clapped his friend on the back. "Congratulations Cull!"

Cullin leant forward as another wave of nausea hit him.

"Ahh, we're here." Sara announced as the flier passed over a sharp arête and she started to descend to Dunirayn.

As Sara settled the flier down a bemused Goram said "can I just ask? What's a yayl?"

Cullin looked up at Goram with a disgusted look on his face. Sara and Ecta just stared at him. Discomfited by the reaction Goram stammered "well I've never heard of a yayl before."

Ecta gave Goram and a quick friendly pat on the back and mimed the instrument before disembarking from the flier after Sara and Cullin. Cullin had his arm around Sara's shoulder as she suddenly seemed very fragile and delicate to him.

"Oh, I thought that was a fiddle."

Ecta turned back to face him to explain. "Nay, similar, but a yayl has more strings."

Goram was upset at the attitude of the Lordling and his wife. It was typical of those of, so called, noble blood. How was he expected to know anything unless someone told him? The unfeeling pretentious behaviour of the two imperious 'highborn' sickened him. He felt as if he was being punished for a crime he hadn't committed. Goram's thoughts were dark and negative, but he determined to keep his mouth shut lest he cause more problems for himself.

They headed for the largest of the huts that Cullin knew they used for accommodation.

"Wow, this place has changed since I first saw it" exclaimed Ecta, admiring the new buildings.

"A lot can change in a year, Ecta." Cullin replied.

"A year? Has it been that long? I doesn't seem like it."

Hamadern greeted them and quickly organised food for his guests. "If I had known you were coming today I'd have arranged something better. There will be a stew later, but there is salt-fish and freshly baked oatcakes. The Banree is still out at sea somewhere. Sea trials, Guvin tells me. Pul is about someplace, he doesn't really do much any more."

Hamadern busied himself with mundane chores as Cullin's small group made themselves comfortable. A basket sat on the floor by the range filled with onions and carrots with black skins, which piqued Goram's interest. "The carrots have to be stored in a mixture of sand and dry peat to stop them from rotting" explained Hamadern, noticing Goram's interest. "They'll go into the evening stew later with a few blaeberries."

"You don't grow your own here I noticed" commented Goram.

"Nay, the ground is too thin. Not much grows here."

"You can improve that over time. Composting your waste helps. I can show you how to do that later if you wish."

"I would be interested, if you have time. Er –" Hamadern realised he was short of a name for his guest.

"Goram, I'm called Goram. My Lord." Belatedly Goram added the honorific.

"Just Hamadern will be fine, Goram. We don't stand on ceremony here."

Cullin had neglected to break his fast due to the tension between himself and Sara. Now that had been resolved he realised how hungry he was, and the smell of fish cooking on the range made his mouth water. Hamadern, he realised was not a skilled cook, but then his brothers had never had any call to learn. "Smells good, Ham."

"Ah, Cullin. Your friend is going to show us how to grow vegetables in this place."

"If anyone can do that it would be Goram. Does anything need doing?"

"Aye, there is a bowl of dried fruits in honey and Donal's hooch on the preparation table. There are bowls underneath."

Cullin laughed merrily. "Donal? That man is uncanny. He always knew if someone was looking for one of his stills and always managed to avoid trouble."

Hamadern smiled broadly. "Aye, Father was never able to catch him. I thought he had simply melted into the hills and would reappear when things settled down. I didn't realised he was part of the exodus."

"Nay, he wound up amongst my group of refugees and, of course, did his own thing. He caused a bit of trouble before being tracked down. His whisky proved to be very popular and we had an epidemic of morning malaise. Of course, he moved on before we could catch him. Though, I still don't know how he managed to arrange that."

Cullin had recovered from the shock of learning he was to be a father and was now in a cheerful and light-hearted mood. He was laughing quietly despite himself. In truth, he had always liked Old Donal and had never considered him a problem. "So how did you get hold of his hooch?"

"Ah, one of his stills was found and I got a tip-off. So, I had a trap set up for him and finally caught the rascal. He works for me now. What Father or any of us never realised is that he hardly drinks any hooch himself. He takes some to test it and may have a glass in the evening before bed. He considers himself 'doing people a service'.

"I'm glad he's with you. Now, if you have any of that hooch, come and join us. I have something to tell you."

The next few days were a period of unaccustomed relaxation for Cullin and the little group. Sara took the excuse that she wouldn't see Cullin again for an unknowable duration. She wanted and needed that comfort of being with Cullin for those few days. The couple spent much of their time down at the harbour talking about plans for the baby or simply enjoying the mild spring weather.

Ecta spent his time wandering about the small glen, and Goram, incongruously due to his dislike of 'Lords' and 'highborn' spent time with Hamadern using the foundry staff to move large rocks about with the apparent aim of creating a vegetable garden from the thin soil.

The weather turned cold and wet after a few days, and grey mist shrouded the surrounding mountains and made the sea grey and inhospitable. The Banree Na Mur slid un-noticed into the harbour. Pul, who now spent much of his time at the small harbour gazing wistfully out to sea, greeted them. Guvin and his two crew, wasted no time in heading for the main hut of the small foundry complex with Pul in tow.

They clattered into the hut to find it busy with a gathering of people. Hamadern had declared a rest day and his small group of foundry staff and Cullin's group were exchanging songs and experiences. After hanging waxed atacotes on wooden pegs by the door, they called out for whisky.

A startled Hamadern greeted them. "Fealty lads, drink you shall have, but is it not a bit early in the day for strong drink?"

"Nay Lord Hamadern. Varuna demands our respect and it is not wise to take him for granted." Pul returned the greeting. "You are from the mountains and this is something you are likely not to understand."

"Whisky you shall have." Replied Hamadern formally, found four small antler cups, and poured generous measures for the seamen.

The others at the gathering watched with some bemusement as the seamen raised their cups heavenward and called out as one. "To Varuna we offer thanks for our safe return."

They all downed the whisky in one and bellowed loud and heartily "Slancha Varuna". Guvin then started to sing with a deep resonant and soulful bass.

They all downed the whisky in one and bellowed loud and heartily "Slancha Varuna". Guvin then started to sing with a deep resonant and soulful bass.

> "When north winds blow
> Who heeds our woe
> Through raging seas
> Through ice and snow
>
> To guide our way
> The stars, does set
> Who gives us strength
> To tend our nets
>
> Lets none perish
> In mighty storm
> Until our feet
> Again are home
>
> With Varuna
> Our souls shall be
> And great shall be
> Harvest from the sea."

The four seamen raised their mugs and bellowed "Slancha Varuna" again. After this, Guvin beckoned to Cullin and drew him aside from the excited chatter that followed the bizarre performance. "I'm sorry for delaying your journey, young man, but it is essential to test the Banree before the expedition starts."

"I understand that Guvin. It's not a problem." Cullin was, as always, the quiet diplomat. "Who, or what, though is Varuna?"

Guvin regarded Cullin for a long moment before replying. "Does it not strike you as odd that there are four Prophets?"

"I never really thought about it. There are four Prophets and then The Frame. My teachers Anroshin and Allameud taught me that and my duty to the Frame and the Prophets."

"So you think the Frame created the Prophets?" Guvin pressed with quiet understanding.

"Nay." Cullin laughed. "The Frame is a machine, how could it make the Prophets?"

"Then what created them?"

Cullin frowned with thought, trying to remember lessons long forgotten. "I think God abandoned Man, or something. I'm not sure."

"It's more like the other way round. Man abandoned God and now we have the Frame."

"So, this Varuna is what?"

"Varuna is God. Varuna created the Universe and all within it and that includes the Prophets."

"I'm a bit confused Guvin. How is it you know this and my teachers did not, or at least did not teach it?"

"They teach what they are told to teach, no more, no less. Out on the ocean, who can hear us? Not the Prophets, they are long dead. Not the Frame, the machine cares not for us. Nay, not to them is our obeisance made, but to Varuna, the Creator."

Cullin tried to fit the concept of Varuna into his understanding of Inalsol philosophy, but failed, unable to connect disparate parts into a single entity. "I don't truly follow, but I think we should at least honour Varuna before we set sail."

"Indeed we should. It is something a sailor will always do before venturing out to sea."

Chapter Eight

"Hey Cull, stop talking about work, the lads want a story." Ecta dragged his friend from Guvin and thrust him toward the main group of gatherers.

"What shall I tell them? I'm no bard or peripatetic wait."

"Go on lad, give us a story." Guvin urged.

"What about the lost souls of Ice Moor? That's always good entertainment."

Chapter Nine

"There is no reason to believe that the Frame knows where Rustick More is, Dona. It has always depended on the Frame not knowing. You can't attack something unless you know where it is." Dook and Dona were walking around as Dona pointed out defensive weaknesses she had found.

They were currently by Ealasat's woodpile that was taking shape and was now recognisable as a boat, small, but suitable for inshore fishing. It had become a community project led mostly by Sara. Ealasat sat contentedly weaving nets made from rope made from beetick fibres.

"You asked me to assume an attack would come. I have done that."

"True Dona. I appreciate your efforts."

"Your best defence is the steep sides of the mountain and the few entrances."

"Aye, that's why it was built here in the first place and the entrances are all concealed."

"But, Dook, you have nothing to fight back with." Dona was talking earnestly, trying to make her point by force of will.

"Not entirely so, Dona, the fliers are useful offensively. Cullin and Sara have demonstrated that effectively."

"But both got shot up quite badly." Dona faced Dook down, hands on hips, her dark eyes flaring, daring Dook to deny the truth of her words.

"Cullin has made improvements ---"

"But they are still outmatched by the Frame's drone fliers."

Dook expelled a deep breath in exasperation and rubbed his lined face with his hands. He knew Dona was right; the defences of Rustick More were hopelessly weak. "So, what have we got?"

"There are several thousand of Cullin's grenades and enough short staffs for everyone here. Good for man to man combat, but hopeless against machines. What you really need is some of those plazgunna the divines used at Dundoon."

"I have designs for them, but not the materials. We don't have and can't make the high grade metals required." Dook shook his head regretfully, silently cursing events that precipitated conflict before the resistance groups were in a position to fight back.

"What about making a bigger and more powerful short staff?"

"Ah, hmm." Dook rumbled thoughtfully. "That's a good idea, I'll get Neev to look into it, she's good with that kind of technology."

"Isn't she busy with that communication device you invented?"

"What? The seismocom? Nay, not now, Cullin is finally on his way. That's his term for them, by the way; I never thought of giving them a name."

Dona grinned "he's a bright lad and no mistake."

Suddenly Dook clapped his head with his hand and exclaimed "what a fool I am!"

"What?"

Dook grinned at her with delight revealing yellowed teeth. "We should be using the seismocoms to communicate with other bases. We're still using runners and we don't have to."

Dook was suddenly all frenetic activity and rushed toward his rooms calling back to Dona over his shoulder. "I have a lot to get done, Dona. My thanks, and we'll talk again soon."

Dona replied, shouting "do you want me to talk to Neev about the short staffs."

"Aye, that would be good." Dook hollered in back. "Oh, can you find the plans for the short staff, I have them about somewhere."

Dona shook her head with amusement and tried to raise her voice further to catch the retreating figure. "Aye, will do."

"Oh, and Dona" Dook bellowed. "Look into improvements in anti-personnel defences."

Chapter Nine

Dona just waved her acknowledgment, but muttered quietly to herself. "Doesn't want much does he."

It wasn't long before Neev had both Dook and Dona at her workstation with long list of urgent jobs that needed attention. "Dook, I can't manage all this. It's too much! I only have one pair of hands!"

Dook had found geological maps of Ardbanacker and Anklayv islands and had marked various places. "I need seismocoms placed at these locations as soon as possible."

"They have to be made first, Dook. I don't have enough parts." Neev was furious with Dook; he always asked for the impossible and expected it done immediately.

"Find me the power packs and I might manage, but it will still take time."

"There must be some at Dundoon, take a flier and get what you need from there." Dook failed to see what the problem was. If the parts were available, she just needed to go and get them.

"And what about these, what do you want me to do with this lot?" Neev thrust a sheaf of papers with scrawled designs and notes written on them. "Cullin's plans for a defence shield for Rustick More. The ones you asked for. Also, you want me to design a bigger short staff. Any more jobs you have in line for me?" Neev gave Dook an evil look, daring him to add to the list.

"Er, well, I was going to ask you to help Dona with anti-personnel defences and I need to get as many light cables as I can so a message system can be set up to Dunirayn." Dook said helplessly. He hadn't realised how much he was expecting one person to accomplish.

Dona began laughing; she had her own pile of papers to which she was trying to draw Neev's attention. "You are asking too much, you know Dook."

Neev open-mouthed with shock at Dook's audacity in extending the job list even further and found herself nodding in agreement with Dona, but she wasn't laughing. Her fists were balled and resting on her hips. She wasn't going to let Dook push her into taking on too much work. Dook would have to find someone else.

"I know it's a lot" Dook said in a placatory tone voice. "It does need to be done. Communication is the top priority. The other things will have to wait."

Still not satisfied, Neev thought carefully, there was someone who might be able to help. It surprised her to think that out of the two hundred and fifty or so personnel currently at Rustick More, only a handful had the skills necessary to do the jobs Dook was asking her to do. "Dook" she said finally. "Why don't you ask Troomey? He knows these systems."

Troomey was a small man in his late fifties, balding and as thin as a rake. He was quiet man who had few friends, and often went un-regarded as a result. More recently, he had been working on the transport ship aimu captured at Dundoon and had been able to learn a great deal about how they operated and extend the databases at Rustick More considerably.

"Where will I find Troomey?"

"I'll ask him, Dook, he's a bit leery of you. He thinks you're a bully and ask for too much. He's sweet on me though, so it's better if I handle him." Neev gave Dook a stern look.

"Can I leave this in your hands then?"

"Absolutely not! You'll go away and think up some other urgent job for me to do. No, I think you had best help organise and co-ordinate this effort."

"Aye, I will help in any way I can."

Neev scribbled a list on a sheet of paper with a charcoal stick and then thoughtfully picked up a parchment covered with Dook's sketches and notes. "And this is another thing. Do you know how long it takes for one of us to make a parchment like this?" She held up the offending article between thumb and forefinger and flourished in front of Dook.

With two strong-minded women glaring at him, pointing out his flaws, and using them like verbal weapons, Dook felt uncomfortable, humbled, and even embarrassed in the face of the onslaught. "I confess that I don't." Pinkness showed through Dook's rough tanned face.

"Then perhaps you should make one and find out. Then perhaps you wouldn't be so casual using them."

"Alright, Neev." Dook put his hands up in surrender. "I'll try to be more careful in future." Dook felt like he needed a drink. The onslaught from Neev had unsettled him. A strong ale would settle his nerves, but recently the supply had mysteriously dried up. Resigned to his personal misery he tried to appease Neev. "Anything else I can do to help?"

Chapter Nine

"Aye, take Fil and get these parts from Dundoon." Neev thrust her hastily scribbled list at Dook, who studied it and managed a thin smile.

Neev and Dona took armloads of papers and parchment documents to Troomey's workstation, where he was busy studying data from the aimu transport ship captured at Dundoon. "Are you busy, Troomey?" Neev asked sweetly.

"Only always." Troomey smiled at her happily until he saw the documents. The smile died on his face, leaving a horrified grimace that slowly dissolved into look of resignation. "What, by the two moons, have you got for me, Neev?"

"Presents from Dook, he's very generous, don't you think?" Neev persisted with her sweetest smile.

"So, Dook gave you that lot and you, very kindly want to give it to me?" Troomey gave her a studied look and made no attempt to accept the documents.

"But you know how much you like a challenge." Neev cajoled.

Troomey glanced briefly at the top sheet, grunted, and shoved it back in Neev's arms. "The point to a challenge is that it is possible. What you have there, looks like a lot of incomplete ideas, that may or, more probably, won't work."

"It's important, Troomey."

"That, I grant you, may be the case, but I am busy with other things as well; things that are just as important as that lot. How soon does our esteemed leader want it all done by?"

"As soon as possible of course. I think yesterday would be acceptable. Highest priority."

Troomey reached for the top sheet again and studied it more thoroughly. Finally, he put it down on his desk. "This project alone could take years to accomplish. I'd need the resources of a wizard or a magic wand to do it any quicker."

"Will you at least look through them and sort out what can or can't be done?"

Dona chipped in. "We are relying on you. Please help. If there's anything you need, just ask, I'll get it for you."

"A magic wand would be nice." Troomey retorted with sarcasm.

"I do mean that, Troomey. We can't do magic wands, but if it can be got, we'll get it for you."

Troomey threw his hands in the air and gave up on the unequal fight. "I'll look at them, but I won't promise anything. Put them there."

Neev and Dona immediately relieved themselves of their burdens and Neev grinned pleasantly. "We'll let you get on then."

Troomey looked at the retreating figures and then at the heap of documents, and buried his face in his hands, silently berating himself and thinking "why do I let her do this to me?" He shook his head and gave the pile an accusing look. "Still there?" he questioned the pile, which flatly refused to answer. "You know," he continued to address the pile "it's not a magic wand I need, but more time". He thought about that for a moment and spoke to the pile again. "Hah! If I had enough time, they'd soon find something to fill it."

Troomey took a deep breath and took the top sheet again, read through it and placed it on the floor. He made a few notes and continued to the next sheet with the same process. Over the course of the next few wairs he sorted the jobs into several piles, which he ordered by their priority. He had a thick ream of notes. He sat back satisfied, that at least, he had a few ideas to work on. He looked up intending to address his lists of requirements to Neev, but found she was nowhere in sight. Nor was anyone else. "Last to leave Toiler's Woe again, Troomey" he muttered as he headed for the canteen.

"Halloo!" he called out. The canteen was closed for the night. This was not an unusual occurrence for Troomey and it didn't worry him.

"Troomey, late again I see." Elid, a woman of middle years with short-cropped greying hair answered.

"Aye."

"You're lucky I'm still here. I'm about to finish, now."

"I'm sorry Elid, I've been given a lot of work to do."

Chapter Nine

Elid wandered off, returning after several sents with a rough bannock and sliced meats and a generous portion of preserved fruits. A jug of ale accompanied the meal with a large earthenware mug.

Troomey smiles with gratitude, but eyed the ale jug with a bit of concern. "I think you'll get me drunk, Elid."

"It'll do you good, Troomey." Elid was about to return to her cleaning when Dook wandered into the canteen. "Ah, the big boss comes to raid the stores."

"A man has to eat. I don't suppose there is any more is there?"

"Aye, there is no shortage. What would you men do without us women eh? Probably starve to death, but at least an important job would be done!"

Dook sat silently, he was tired and stressed with too many things to worry about. Since the events at Dundoon, he had felt an urgency, a desperate need to improve the security, defensive and offensive capabilities of the aneksa. Events had moved on too quickly. They were in a poor, weak position. If the Frame launched an offensive, it would quickly destroy everything that had taken decades to build. He was fearful with pent up anxiety and worry. His anxiety threatened to explode in violence and aggression. He dare not let that happen.

If the people at Rustick More knew how precarious and delicate their freedom was, they might not have the will to keep going. Social inertia could set in, preventing essential work from completion. He had to keep the pressure up and entice, coerce, cajole or even threaten people to complete work faster or risk losing everything.

"Up late too, Boss?" Troomey interrupted Dook's dark thoughts.

"Aye."

"You don't look well, Boss." Troomey observed.

"Just tired." Elid returned from the kitchen at that moment with a tray set with Dook's food. "Ah, excellent, you are an angel; truly sent from Neev."

"Nay, not I, but I would not see a man go hungry." Elid replied.

Troomey shuddered. "Nay, she only brings more work. That's why I'm so late. That's why I'm always late."

Dook blinked, not understanding Troomey's comment for a moment. "Nay, I didn't mean her. I meant the 'Halls of Rest', the place we go after death."

"Oh, I thought you meant her, she's more like a witch, Kaylick, they should have called her, certainly not Neev."

"She gets a lot of work done for me. Neev and Cullin have got through a huge amount of work for me." Dook was a bit confused by Troomey's attitude; Neev had always been able to absorb large workloads and produced results that worked. He was heavily reliant on her continued support and hard work.

"Hah, you give the work to her, she gives it to me." Troomey regarded Dook with sardonic humour. He knew the work had to be done, but it, too often, felt as if he had an unfair proportion of the workload.

At that moment, Fil came in from Toiler's Woe. Seeing him enter, Elid calls out. "You too, I guess you want food as well?"

"Aye, Elid, I would be grateful. I've been to Dundoon with Dook, getting parts and equipment." Fil looked haggard. He was one of a handful of people at Rustick More able to pilot and navigate a flier. Though on this occasion Dook had piloted, he'd still had to concentrate on navigation. He looked over at Dook, who was busy tucking into the food Elid had provided and wondered why the older man looked less tired. True, Dook appeared tired; there was a clear weariness in the way he ate, a mechanical effort that showed no pleasure in the act of eating. Fil knew from previous experience that tomorrow, Dook would be full of energy again. Fil knew he would still be inefficient, run down and would struggle to perform his duties. When his food arrived, Fil thanked Elid and took the laden tray to his bedchamber where he could enjoy some privacy.

Dook savoured the ale brought to him by Elid, which had the desired calming effect he was after. He knew he drank too much, but never thought it a problem. He slept better and had a brief period of relief from stress. He would often drink until his mind reached a nice, calm, and peaceful place that suffused his consciousness. There was, of course, potential physical damage, but he trusted in the nanos implanted into his body to alleviate the negative long-term side effects of too much alcohol. The only ones who knew of this physical advantage of his were Cullin and Yayler; neither of whom were likely to divulge or comment on the existence of nanos and neither were currently at Rustick More in any case. Dook trusted such secrets to remain hidden.

Chapter Nine

"So, what jobs has she given you?" Dook asked Troomey, feeling calmer and more in control of himself.

Troomey gazed over the rim of his ale mug, thinking as he spoke. "Too many. The 'big' short staff is just a matter of scaling up and sorting out the power supply. The light cable idea is a great idea as it utilises technology we already have. The difficulty there is the amount of labour involved. I've already roughed out a route, but someone will have to check it and it will take a lot of physical work to lay the cables.

The job that really gets me interested is this idea of a defence shield. It would require a great deal of energy. The engines from those shot down drones might produce enough power. They can be stripped down and re-engineered. I was going to start on designs for that tomorrow."

"Get the plans for the light cable idea done first. That must be a priority. I will help you with scaling up the short staff, the big staff. I know that technology well. Don't worry about putting this stuff together. If necessary, I'll get people from Ecta's ledge to do that. Just work out how to do it." Dook gave his directions sincerely. He wanted progress as swift as possible. Once these jobs were well on the way he could concentrate on other things.

"Well, I'm happy enough with that, Boss. There is something though that bothers me about the divine technology we're using."

"Oh? What's that Troomey?"

"Well, the engines from the drones don't work. I stripped them down from the wreckage when they got here, but I can't get them to power up. It seems that they draw their energy from somewhere else."

"I'm confused Troomey. What do you mean 'draw energy from somewhere else'? Can you make them work?"

"Oh, Aye, I believe so. I found what appears to be a 'collector' that sends energy to a capacitor that works as a power pack. I think the energy is somehow 'beamed' to the engine, so the engines would have to be on the summit of Rustick More to work. There's too much rock surrounding Toiler's Woe for the 'beam' to get through."

Dook became quiet and thoughtful as he absorbed the new information. "So they never run out of power so long as they receive a 'beam'."

"Aye that's about it." Troomey agreed.

"But if that 'beam' stopped for some reason, that technology would cease to work." Dook continued the logical process drawing further conclusions.

"That also is true." Troomey grinned.

"Interesting."

"Aye." Troomey's grin grew broader and somehow vicious.

"Good ale." Dook grinned back.

"Aye."

Chapter Ten

Guvin had split the six crewmembers of the Banree into three teams, each led by either him, Finnan or Keri. One team would be on deck duty, one on 'stand down' and one on sleep or rest period. The idea was to have one experienced crew and one 'raw' crew on duty at all times.

They had been at sea for two days heading in calm weather for the Wild Sea. The sea was quiescent, almost benign. Guvin knew that would not last and so gave Cullin, Ecta, and Goram as much down time as he could. They would be busy later, but for now, he wanted them to relax and get to know Keri and Finnan. Over the next few days, he planned drills for Cullin's group to ensure their readiness and capabilities in rougher seas.

Five of the crew chatted in the cramped cabin. Only Guvin remained on deck at the tiller. During the re-fit Guvin had wanted a second, rear cabin to protect the steering crew from the elements. The idea had been discarded in favour of keeping the appearance of the vessel as traditional, or normal, as possible. Dook's technical staff had suggested the compromise of a steering system operated from the cabin with forward-looking ports. Guvin discarded this idea, pointing out that the steersman needed to be able to see the sail. In the end, they chose a temporary shelter constructed from tough plaz sheets and rigged to the Banree's rear mast.

Keri was in charge of food for the day. This was another duty that Guvin rotated. The others did not Think much of Keri's cooking. He had produced hard biscuits and thick cut ham rather than use some of the fresh meat, vegetables, or fruit from the stores with a more limited storage time.

Keri had placed a large bowl on the cabin table filled with hard oat biscuits. He'd placed vegetables pickled in brine in another bowl despite the availability of fresh vegetables. Keri carved thick chunks of ham, which he served on platters. He had not attempted to use any of the limited supply of fresh meat stored in the hold. He plated one portion for Finnan who was in his bunk, asleep and took another out to Guvin at the tiller.

Ecta bit into one of the biscuits and groaned inwardly. Even Dook's attempts to cook surpassed this desultory, paltry effort. Guvin had warned them about Keri's idea of cooking and warned them not to say anything. He cautioned that Keri had avoided cooking duties for months on end by doing the duty so poorly that another member of the crew took over the job. "I hope they manage with food at the More."

"Why wouldn't they?" Cullin asked cutting through his ham with a utility knife and chewing thoughtfully. Keri, it seemed, had forgotten to provide cutlery for the meal. "Ham's good." He added pleasantly.

"There's a lot of mouths to feed at the More and stores are always running low." Ecta explained.

"I can't say I've noticed any lack of food." Cullin sounded doubtful.

"That's what I was doing the other day when we met on the hill. Food for the larder."

"We struggled to find enough food for this journey. It took a lot longer than Guvin anticipated." Keri added, munching idly on a biscuit.

Cullin was more than a little perplexed. "Really? I never thought food was such a problem. I know crops are difficult to grow, but there always seems to be plenty of game and I've not heard of anyone going hungry."

"I guess not, Cull. You never see the lack, or experience the difficulty in producing it." Ecta was picking at his food with disinterest. The ham was fine, but it was just a slab of meat and there was too much of it. He had grown up on a small croft near Dunossin with his parents who never allowed him to waste food. You ate what was put on your plate even if you didn't like it.

Cullin didn't like the idea of food shortages and had never considered it an issue before. Still, if Ecta thought there might be a problem, he respected that and that raised his concern. "Big Jon always had well stocked stores. I should know, I raided them often enough. Though he was always grateful for the odd carcass brought in by yourself, Ecta, or by me."

Ecta had laughed at Cullin's comment of raiding Big Jon's stores. Goram, however, found the idea of a Lord's son casually raiding stores for food, which he certainly wouldn't have needed, quite annoying. Goram saw Cullin as a well-meaning, but naive young man who had never had to go without. "Food that he redistributed. Never very much, but it made a difference." He looked significantly at Cullin, hoping, but doubting that the young man would understand his point of view.

"I'm aware of that Goram. It is something he was very much encouraged to do."

Chapter Ten

"Big Jon's problem was never meat at Dunossin. It is not meat at the More either. It's vegetables and grains. At the More, they have to be brought in. Nothing can be grown around the More." Ecta explained.

"It's the ground." Goram explained "the soil is very poor."

"Of course, and the Frame would spot any vegetable plots or grain fields and investigate." Cullin agreed.

"Aye, that's what the aneksa trained me to do." Goram continued. He remembered his clearing in the Dunban Forest and the frequent, stern and, sometimes, angry advice whenever he'd planted food for crops incorrectly.

Guvin stuck his head into the cabin and called them out onto the deck. "You might want to come and see this." As they emerged, blinking in the bright sunshine and wondering what the commotion was.

A pod of porpoise followed the Banree, their sleek bodies leaping from the water with playful exuberance. Keri, who had seen the phenomenon before soon headed back to the cabin. The others turned the collars of their atacotes up against the chilly air and watched spellbound.

"Why are they following the boat?" Goram asked, thinking it was very strange behaviour.

"Most of the boats on the Varamor Sea are fishing vessels, much like this one. The fish need gutting and the guts are thrown overboard. The porpoise are just hoping for an easy meal, but mostly, I think they do it for fun." Guvin explained.

"Ah" Goram didn't really understand, but then, he didn't understand the sea either.

"While you're here, Goram, you can take over the tiller."

Suddenly nervous, Goram licked his lips and found his mouth had gone dry, a reaction to the new responsibility. He took the tiller from Guvin's hands, sat down, and stared at the wooden tiller as if it might bite.

"You don't need to grip it so tightly." Guvin instructed the older man. "Keep an eye on the compass and make sure the red end of the needle is pointing to the 45° mark."

The compass sat on a pedestal below the tiller. The needle shifted slightly to the right as the bow turned, riding the swell. Goram tried to correct the direction of the Banree by moving the tiller to the left and the needle swung further to the right.

"Move the tiller the other way." Guvin instructed

"Like this?"

"Aye, you'll get the hang of it."

Goram quickly got used to the tiller, held a steady course and began to relax. "Guvin, can I ask a question?"

"Aye."

"The heading we're on is more Arward and I understood we were using a Yerward course, toward the setting sun. Why is that?"

"Ah, we are heading into the Varamor Sea Natua of Yarvik. Once far enough north we can change course."

"Isn't that a long way round?"

"No, we could head through the Straits of Wrath, but there would be strong currents and tides against us. It's a very dangerous stretch of water. It is safer and quicker to use the route we are using."

"Oh, I see."

The porpoises followed the Banree for another wair and disappeared for no apparent reason. The Banree continued its course for another day without incident. As the sun began to rise above the horizon on the following day, Cullin sat at the tiller feeling a cold bite in the air. A baleful orange glow suffused the sky and there was only a very slight breeze.

Finnan, who sat hunched up next to Cullin, suddenly shivered violently. "Shift'll be over soon" he commented.

"Aye, it's been a cold night, such as night is this far natua. I'll be glad to get into a warm bunk." Cullin shifted his hands on the tiller, flexing his fingers in the process to get some life back into them. Despite wearing a thick pair of mittens, the cold had penetrated and his fingertips stung with the cold.

"Get some food first, you'll warm up quicker." Finnan advised.

Guvin came on deck with a worried expression. "Pressure's dropping Finnan, are we tightly battened down?"

"Aye." Finnan did not attempt to move, remaining hunched over. "Everything is secure."

"Good, we could get a bit of a blow."

"Aye." Finnan was not the least bit concerned about the idea of bad weather; in fact, he would have been surprised if they didn't experience poor conditions at some point. He considered it part of the work. "You want the sail adjusting Guvin?"

Guvin looked up at the triangles of slack mainsail and foresail that were barely catching enough wind to propel the Banree forward. "Nay, drop the foresail if the wind starts to pick up. Ecta has a brew on, honeyed herbs, though I suspect he's adding a bit of 'Donal's Hooch'. I'll ask him to bring some out." Happy that everything was in order on deck, Guvin disappeared back into the cabin. He would take over on deck in another wair. For now, he was hungry and Ecta was on cook duties, so the food promised to be good.

As the morning wore on the breeze strengthened, coming almost directly from Yerward, and the Banree began to make good speed. The temperature dropped, becoming bitingly cold as wind chill reduced the apparent temperature still further. Ice began to foul the rigging, but Guvin paid little heed, pushing the little boat to its limit.

Towards midday, a dark smudge appeared on the western horizon preceded by heavy clouds that streamed across the sky. Noting the deterioration in the weather Guvin called out to Goram who was knocking ice from blocks and pulleys to keep them free. "Guvin, call Keri and Finnan onto the deck."

"Finnan will be in his bunk." Goram called back, but leaving the ice clearing duties to head for the cabin.

"Then wake him, I need him on deck." Guvin bawled, raising his voice.

A few sents later, both Keri and Finnan were on deck. They brought out a large sheet of plaz, with eyelets at strategic points brought out from the hold with eyelets at strategic points. This, once attached between the mizzenmast and the stern, created a shelter over the tiller. It restricted the view of the steersman, but provided protection from weather.

"Expecting bad weather?" Finnan asked whilst making fast a corner of the shelter to the gunwale.

"Aye, the pressure's been dropping all morning and that mass of black cloud looks bad."

Finnan glanced at the brooding mass of cloud and grinned back at Guvin revealing a row of broken front teeth. "Guess we had to get a blow at some point."

"Aye, Finnan, when the shelter is secure I want you and Keri to clear as much ice as you can. Get the others to help."

"Aye, will do."

The work of clearing the ice took another two wairs, by which time large waves were throwing the Banree about on the sea. Cullin had joined Guvin on the tiller as an extra pair of hands. Plumes of spray enveloped the bow as the boat dove into troughs between wave crests.

"Can the Banree cope with this?" Cullin had to scream over the noise of wind and sea.

"Aye." Guvin, grim faced bellowed back the affirmative as waves crashed and boomed into the hull.

Cullin had no way of knowing what the limits of the Banree were and had to take Guvin's assurance at face value. He knew from conversations with Ecta that things could go wrong, and the seas appeared rougher than those Ecta had described to him of the occasion when the Banree had struck hidden rocks.

Guvin had sent Ecta and Goram back to the cabin, considering them to be of limited use in the rough sea. He let them get what rest they could for now. They were likely to be needed later.

Keri and Finnan had rigged the storm sail; a smaller foresail used in rough weather for steering, and then lowered the mainsail. Keri was now busy tidying the decks whilst Finnan stationed himself forward looking out for growlers and brash or bergs that might be hazardous for the Banree. He would use a system of arm signals in the event of a sighting.

The sea grew heavier and Guvin could no longer maintain course. Ice and rime built up on rigging as spume from wave crests covered the Banree. It was bitterly cold. Storm and current forced them arward, toward the rising sun.

Chapter Ten

It was nearly impossible for the crew to rest or sleep. Their clothing became soaked and quickly froze whilst on deck. Guvin reduced deck duties to two wairs at a time. Off duty, they huddled about the stove in an attempt to absorb what little warmth it could provide. Their bunks were sodden and gave no comfort or reprieve from the constant yaw and pitch of the Banree.

Goram rarely moved from his bunk and was frequently sick. He was foul tempered, grey faced and very poor company in the cramped accommodation of the Banree. When he spoke, it was to snap some complaint or other at Cullin. In Goram's pitifully miserable state, Cullin had become the focus of his ire.

Cooking became an impossible task. The violent motion of the sea caused water to spill onto the stove that then have to be re-lit. The storm raged for two days. They had little to eat and only water to drink. Guvin spent as much time on the tiller as he physically could, but suffered terribly from the cold. He would shove his hands under his armpits whenever he could, in an attempt to keep them warm enough to stop the sting of the frost. He would chant a prayer to himself, a cyclic litany dedicated to Varuna to combat fear.

The constant battle against the cold wore the crew down. Everyone was irritable and waspish. Although they were now into the Wild Sea, Guvin pushed on further into the frozen Natua latitudes, ever fighting against ocean currents. The fierce storm winds and tiredness took their terrible toll.

Keri was forward on iceberg lookout, clinging to the woodwork about the cabin doorway and peering over the top. Guvin was on the tiller, assisted by Cullin. They had all been on deck for nearly two wairs and Cullin and Keri were due for relief by Ecta and Finnan. After a deep trough followed by a wave that towered over the Banree Cullin peered forward, wiping spray from his eyes. The salt stung and he struggled for long moments to see and then noticed that Keri was absent from his position.

"Guvin!" He shouted against the constant noise of the raging sea. "Where's Keri?"

Guvin stared forward and cursed, then screamed back. "Go forward. See if you can see him."

Cullin searched, looking over the gunwales to see if Keri was by some miracle, clinging to the hull, perhaps clinging to tackle or a sheet. He could see no sign of Keri. He could hear no sound of voice above the noise of the sea and mountainous waves reduced the chance of sighting the lost man to almost nil.

Cullin struggled back to Guvin with a knot of sick dread churning in his stomach. The look on Guvin's face reflected Cullin's fear knowing Keri's fate. "He's gone! I can't see him anywhere!" He shouted into Guvin's ear sitting down with his back to the transom, his face buried in his hands.

Guvin shook him roughly. "Go and tell the others. There's no more you can do."

Finnan was left alone to man the tiller so that Guvin could talk to Cullin's group. "He's gone; we can't change that. We have to continue or we'll all be lost."

"How did it happen?" Ecta asked, stunned at the idea of losing a crewmember.

"I don't know. Perhaps he let go of the grabrail at the wrong moment. A momentary loss of concentration. We'll never know. Now, Ecta, you will assist Finnan. Cullin, get some rest. I need to talk to you, Goram." Guvin glanced over at Goram who had been dragged from his bunk at the news of Keri's death.

If it was possible, Goram looked even greyer and more sick than usual. "Why is the sea so rough? I didn't think it could be this bad."

"This far natua, there is nothing to stop the waves, so they get big. You should eat something. It would make you feel better." Guvin bore Goram no ill will for his malaise. It happened even to the most seasoned veteran of the seas, but Guvin needed Goram to be more active, to be of some use to the rest of them.

With paroxysmal, convulsive retching Goram grabbed his sick bucket, but it was dry. His stomach was empty even of fluids. Goram ached and sweat beaded his brow despite the cold. Repeatedly he retched until finally he lay back exhausted. When offered food Goram refused saying that, he'd only be sick again. Guvin gave up on him.

They continued Yerward on large tacks against prevailing wind and currents for the next several days. The storm had finally abated, but the seas remained rough as big waves continued to roll inexorably and irresistibly in their endless passage toward the rising sun.

They held a service for Keri, commending him to Varuna and routines returned to normal. They regularly had to knock and hack ice off equipment in a continual effort to keep the Banree seaworthy. They worked in shifts of two wairs on and two wairs off, but no one could rest properly.

Chapter Ten

Guvin and Cullin were about halfway through their watch. Guvin was taking sightings on the sun as best he could with a quadrant. It was a difficult and wildly inaccurate job as the Banree pitched wildly causing a big variation in readings. Guvin would take an average reading to make a rough calculation of their position. He could always rely on an accurate time though, as for some reason he didn't understand, Cullin always knew.

Guvin gave up on the quadrant and rammed his hands under his clothing to warm them up when Goram appeared on deck for the first time since the storm had begun. He was white and pasty faced, but slithered his way doggedly to Guvin's side.

"Is there work to be done?" Goram asked, knowing the answer would be affirmative, but not able to think of another way to broach the subject.

"Aye, indeed." Guvin gave him an expressionless look. "Are you fit to work?"

"Nay, I couldn't possibly feel worse. Work won't make any difference."

"Then help Cullin on the Tiller. I need to chart our position." Guvin headed back below deck leaving Cullin in charge.

Goram looked at Cullin meekly. "I've not done so well so far have I?"

"You have been ill. You still are unwell, but none of us are in good form. Did you notice Guvin's hands, how red and swollen they are?"

"Nay."

"The cold has got to them. He is in a lot of pain."

Goram winced at the thought. Most people from Mark Ossin and surrounding districts learned at a young age about frostbite and knew how to prevent it. Therefore, it was relatively rare. Goram wondered how difficult and extremely uncomfortable it must have been for Guvin to operate the quadrant. "How does he cope with the cold and the pain?"

"He endures, we all do. In truth, the Banree wasn't designed to go this far Natua, but she's a good, tough little boat." Cullin licked his lips, which were sore and cracking in the desiccating, elemental weather beyond the ability of the nanos in his circulatory system to combat. "Guvin hopes to be heading back into warmer waters in a few days."

"Thank Hesoos for that."

"Hesoos? Nay. Thank the Banree, she's coping better than we are."

A little while later Guvin came back on deck, a grim, but satisfied look on his face. "Ahh, Cullin. We need to change course."

The new course had them heading back north, Natua in the true tongue. The crew cheered when Guvin informed them that they would be far enough Yerward to start heading toward warmer waters. They had spent much longer in hyperborean waters than he had intended. The storm had driven them off course, extending their Yerward tack.

He had ordered a measure of Donal's hooch for each of the crew to accompany the news and raise their spirits. An orange cast from the low but never quite setting sun as it slid along the horizon, suffused the sky with moody ambiance. Cullin was on unofficial forward watch. He had felt caged in the cramped quarters of the Banree and had sought the space of the open deck.

Momentarily, before descending into the trough between two waves, he caught sight of a glint, the briefest flash of light, then it was gone. He wiped icy spray from his eyes and peered forward again on the crest of the next wave and there it was again. A brief glistening of reflected orange light and then it was gone again.

Could it be light reflecting off wave crests? Cullin didn't think so, it looked wrong, somehow, but he couldn't quite grasp why. On the next crest, he tried to zoom his focus with his augmented vision and save a 'still' to his array of neuro-chips. By closing his eyes and recalling that image, he was able to review what he had just seen and even enhance it.

What that enhanced image revealed was trouble. He made his way with dangerous haste to the stern where Finnan and Ecta were taking turns on the tiller. "Finnan" he bawled. "There's a large iceberg ahead. I think we're heading straight for it."

"Where?" Finnan barked back.

Cullin pointed, but Finnan could see nothing.

"Are you sure you saw something? The sea can play tricks on you." Finnan was concerned about Cullin's alarm though he thought the young man was likely to be mistaken, he wanted to be sure. He went forward with Cullin, leaving Ecta on the tiller. He peered in the direction Cullin indicated, but saw nothing except waves. "I can't see anything, Cullin."

Chapter Ten

"It's there, I assure you."

On the crest of the next wave, just as the Banree dipped into another trough, Cullin caught a glimpse of that baleful reflected orange light and it was nearer than it had been. "There did you see it?" Cullin gesticulated in the direction of the iceberg, hoping that Finnan had seen enough to convince him.

Finnan stared ahead, still unsure. Had he seen something or was Cullin's assurance sweeping him along? Then, on the next crest as the Banree dipped again into the next trough, he saw a brief fulguration of orange light. "Cullin, go and wake Guvin."

A disgruntled and tired Guvin appeared on deck with Cullin and a bemused Goram a few sents later. Guvin peered intently in the direction Cullin indicated and caught the tell-tale flash of light and cursed. The curse was lost to the wind and rain as Guvin made his way to relieve Finnan on the tiller.

The light was fading fast as Guvin steered the Banree away from the iceberg, heading at an angle between the waves causing a pronounced yawing and pitching motion. His many years of experience on the seas came to the fore as he masterfully and subtly changed direction of the Banree so that he crested head on to the waves, but steered away from the iceberg between them.

The iceberg loomed closer and closer, no longer a distant, unseen threat, but clearly visible in the orange gloaming light. It was a huge mass of ice and, despite Guvin's best efforts it was still bearing down on them, drawing ever closer. Finnan had readied the others with boathooks and anything else he could find to fend off the banree from the iceberg if they got too close.

As the time passed and light faded utterly from the sky, only Cullin was able to indicate the direction of the iceberg. Still it loomed closer, inexorably bearing down on them with unremitting, un-cognizant inevitability.

The huge mountainous iceberg was close, towering above them with overhanging ice-cliffs. Guvin was attempting to sail before the cliffs, drawn ever closer between wave crests, but had lost the wind. The single, reefed sail flapped uselessly and the masthead clipped the ice-wall.

"Fend off!" Finnan shouted as the Banree almost crashed into the wall of ice. The crew thrust four poles at the icy terror, but the starboard gunwale scraped the ice, tearing rails from the hull. The impact rocked the boat violently, throwing the crew to the deck. Guvin desperately clung onto the tiller, but managed to move away as the Banree rose on the swell.

The Banree crested again and dipped back toward the ice. "Fend off!" Finnan shouted again as scoured across the face of the ice.

Again, the crew thrust out their poles and again they scraped along the ice-wall. The grinding noise was horrendous as the ice tore at the hull. Time and again, they pulled away, only to be thrust back to crash into the wall of ice, but they made progress, by degrees, until finally the ice-wall curved away.

Wind finally filled the sail. Guvin bore away and put distance between the iceberg and the Banree. Only then could they appreciate the true immensity of the iceberg. It was a true mountain of massive brooding ice over a stride width.

"Finnan!" Called Guvin when he was satisfied that they had attained a safe distance from the frozen menace. "Check below for any leaks. Find out what damage we've sustained."

Finnan nodded wearily and headed below, taking Ecta and Goram with him. Guvin remained, dauntless, at the tiller. Cullin remained on deck, searching the dark horizon for further threats or icebergs until the sun lifted from the horizon, auguring a new day.

Chapter Eleven

Yayler found that he was intensely frustrated. It would take him days to make a single point and get to a stage where Clar15 seemed to agree and accept the point only for her to revert to her original position.

"The divine Warriors of Mustan only exist to do the Frames' Bidding." Clar15 was saying "There are frequent revolts on Inalsol and it is our duty, our purpose to restore order. It is true that we have our own culture and identity. The Frame allows us that Privilage, provided we do its bidding."

"I understand that Clar, better than most, but do you not think that the Mustanians are better able than most cultural groups to determine their own future, if they chose to?" Yayler had made this point the previous evening, but found he had to waste half of this evening steering the conversation back to its conclusion the previous day.

"We are more than capable, on Mustan, of doing this. I hope you are not going to insult me by suggesting otherwise." Clar15 had an amused expression on her face, almost as if she was toying with Yayler.

"It occurs to me that if a handful of muckers with primitive weapons can take an entire island from the control of the Frame, then your people are capable of doing a great deal more than that?"

"You mock me Victor. We both know what the Mustanians are capable of."

"Do you not see Clar15, that your people have the power within their hands to defeat the Frame and allow the human race to determine its own future."

"Now you insult us, Victor. Do you not see that without the Frame the Mustanians have no function, no point to their existence?"

Yayler stopped to consider the latest argument that Clar15 had not used before. He covered the pause by topping his glass from a jug set on the table between them. "The point is that they do exist and should make their own choices and decisions."

"Victor, Victor, stop this. Who would produce food for us? Where would the food come from?" Clar15 was smiling now; she knew Yayler would be unaware of this.

"You do not produce your own food?" Yayler was stunned at the implications. He knew the Mustanians themselves believed that they were the pinnacle of human society. Without support and infrastructure, their society would collapse.

"Muckers produce food for divines, Victor. We do not concern ourselves with such menial tasks. Food is packaged and delivered to Korak ready for us to eat."

"You mean no food at all is grown or produced on Mustan?" The idea was profoundly shocking to Yayler. He had never thought that any group of divines would be so disdainful of physical labour that they would separate themselves so entirely from such essential, basic work. Such hubris was deeply disturbing to Yayler.

"We have a few orchards on Mustan, but you have to realise Victor, that we do not have the best climate here for growing crops."

"Indeed, irrigation for fruit crops in this type of hot climate is quite normal. Muckers manage to grow their own food in much harsher environments."

"Victor, I hope that you are not comparing us to such worthless scum. They are barely evolved beyond bonobos."

Yayler laughed, though he realised that Clar15 had made her comment seriously. "Of course, I would not wish to make such a comparison, but muckers do manage to produce what they need for themselves. I do find it strange that you do not."

"You almost sound as if you admire muckers, Victor."

"They are self-sufficient whereas you, yourselves, are not. You allow yourselves to rely on the Frame for your existence."

"The Frame gives us a comfortable lifestyle in return for our services. If Mustanians followed your suggestion, they would lose much that they take for granted. It is unreasonable to expect them to do that."

Yayler paused before replying. Clar15 had a good point. The Mustanians had a comfortable, even luxurious lifestyle that they would never give up willingly. It was a selfish point of view, but entirely human and understandable. Why should Mustanians worry about the welfare of others when they had everything they needed or wanted provided by the Frame. "I can see that and you would lose the technology too."

"Of course, Victor." Clar15 beamed broadly at Yayler. It was a presumed victory that Yayler finally understood the point of view of the Mustanians.

"Did you know that the muckers are developing their own technology?"

The smile on Clar15's face died. "Not so, what they have is stolen from the Frame."

"Indeed some is, but not all. They have their own fliers now. Crude and slow, but they will improve."

"They are no match for the Frames droid fliers."

"I agree that would appear to be the case and if that is so, how did two crude and unsophisticated fliers without battle aimu manage to destroy two of the fastest and superior droid fliers? That should not be possible." It was Yayler's turn to be victorious. He knew Clar15 would be aware of details of the Battle of Dundoon. She would have received detailed reports of the conflict so that Yayler was confident that he was giving away nothing sensitive.

"Victor, they are not a significant threat. The Frame is already designing faster and better-armed droid fliers. They cannot hope to win again, it is impossible."

"I agree with you Clar, but it should have been impossible for them to win in the first place. Do not be surprised if they do it again."

"Victor, the army that was sent to Dundoon, was an inferior army. The Frame drew most of them from slave labour. They got a choice. Fight for the Frame and possibly die or continue a life of slavery. They were not the best-trained warriors available, nor did they have the best weapons available. They were mostly muckers, offered the chance to improve the quality of their lives."

"Can I remind you Clar, that the Mustanians themselves are descended from such slave labour. The Frame has always suffered from revolts and needed a ready-trained professional army. That is what the Warriors of Mustan are and you are still slaves. You live or die at the whim of a machine!"

"That is a disturbing viewpoint Victor and one I have considered at length." Clar15 clasped her hands together and leaned forward towards Yayler, her chin resting gently on her hands.

This was a revelation to Yayler, whose eyebrows shot up in surprise, but he said nothing, waiting for Clar15 to expand on her statement.

"It is not me you need to convince, Victor, but an army. We are a culture comprised of people who spend their entire lives training for battle. For most of us, our entire ethos is to win glory in battle or die trying to achieve it. Freedom means little."

"Are you not in charge of an army, Clar?"

"Indeed not. The Frame commands the army to leave for a district called Garvamore tomorrow. Have you heard of it?"

Yayler realised that he had been defeated. His arguments meant nothing. Clar15 had been playing for time. Whether she accepted his arguments, or not, she would lead an army against the aneksa; the muckers, who had won freedom for themselves against immense odds, were now at great risk. A knot of fear for them grew in his stomach as he realised that his gamble had failed. Dookerock had been right and he should never have attempted this course of action. The Mustanians would do what appeared best for them and that meant fighting for the Frame. He had come here in an attempt to garner support for the aneksa, but had instead put their existence in serious jeopardy.

"I see that you have Victor, so you should be grateful that I am going to do you a favour. You saved my life once and now I will return that favour and save yours. As a traitor to the Frame you should be summarily executed, but you are more valuable alive. You will be accompanying the army and provide what information you have. You will see the utter destruction of your friends and their base, Rustick More." Clar15 continued to gaze sternly at Yayler until she was satisfied that he had accepted defeat.

As usual, Clar15 left Yayler alone in the hut. He had no means of escape. He might get away in his purloined boat, but it would not be long before they caught him. He believed his best course was to play along with Clar15 and appear co-operative. At least then, he could provide false or misleading information and might even be in a position to hinder their progress. If he waited and bided his time, opportunities to improve the situation might arise.

The following morning Clar15 arrived early with another divine who towered over her. Both wore battle dress of knee length boots, drab yellow plaz leggings, and an armoured shirt of the same uninteresting colour worn over a light smock. The arms remained bare. Both divines wore a thick belt from which hung a hard plaz helmet.

Clar15's companion was dark skinned and heavily muscled, and his alert eyes indicated a keen intelligence. He remained with the aimu transport, a massive, brooding presence, as Clar15 walked toward the hut. Hut, thought Yayler sardonically; that would pass for a luxury home in most places, but was insufficient to be anything more than a hut here.

"It is a fine morning, Victor." Clar15 greeted him. "Today the largest army for over fifty years embarks Natua, for Garvamore and you are privileged to be one of its senior officers. Gulukone, by the transport, will be with you at all times to ensure your comfort."

"I am sure he will do an excellent job, Clar." Yayler avoided making any formal greeting, but did not wish to upset Clar unduly.

"Indeed he will. He is one of a new breed of enhanced warrior. You will find Gulukone is very strong with great endurance. He also has a very quick mind. Do not be tempted to underestimate him. He will ensure that you do not do anything stupid." Clar15's meaning was not lost on Yayler; Gulukone was to be his guard, nothing more, nothing less.

"Oh, and Victor, we will be taking your little boat to Korak where it will make a nice little addition to our fleet. We are not sure how you managed to break its programming, but I would be grateful if you do not do it again."

"I will endeavour to avoid such temptation."

"Good, shall we go then?"

Yayler shrugged, Clar15 was not really asking him, she was merely being polite, and he was in no particular mood for pleasantries.

The journey to Korak took most of the day, and the sun was low on the Yernan horizon before they arrived. It was a typical divine town in that function was integral to its planning. Rows of identical accommodation terraces, in a monochrome white, came into view as the launch piloted by Yayler approached the town. Large warehouse structures, also in white, lined the harbour and extended into the town.

Seeing the town set out in a traditional and unimaginative way that was so typical of divine port towns gave Yayler a deep weary sadness. The divines of Mustan, for all their vaunted freedoms and semi-independence showed little imagination or individuality. They were the tools of the Frame as much as any divines, anywhere in Inalsol.

The extensive harbour spread up the broad estuary of the River Korak from which the town got its name. Aimu ships filled the harbour. Some were clearly transport ships and others had a sleek brooding menace about them and clearly had aggressive capabilities, they were vessels designed for war.

"This is just a fraction of the Mustanian Fleet, which is maintained in a state of constant readiness. We can embark at any time to anywhere we are needed." Clar15 informed Yayler. "Take us over to that transport." She indicated a large warship with sleek aggressive lines.

Yayler drew alongside the indicated ship. Officious looking flunkies saluted Clar15 before ushering her aboard by a ramp-way. The salute with clasped hands held against the chest and bowing with a slight inclination of the chest was unique to the Island of Mustan. Yayler remained at the controls of the launched with the quiet immense figure of Gulukone standing behind him. Yayler waited.

Shortly, two more flunkies descended the ramp and entered the launch. They both bowed respectfully to Yayler. The taller of the two had two vertical stripes on his sleeves to denote his rank as sub-lieutenant. The shorter of the two had a single stripe to denote that he was a Master. There was no ranking below Master in the Mustanian military. A person was either a Master or an ordinary citizen.

The sub-lieutenant saluted Yayler "Lord Victor8, thank you for the gift of this vessel. The Mustanian Army is grateful. I am to escort you to your quarters, where you will remain until told otherwise".

'Interesting' thought Yayler as he was marched to a small room deep within the ship. He had not expected use of any honorific. He took this as a hopeful sign. The show of respect did not stop Gulukone stationing himself outside Yayler's cramped quarters. He was still a prisoner and likely to remain isolated until they found some use for him.

The Frame had an unusual request from a divine operator in the troublesome district of Garvamore, who was curious about the location of a particular fishing boat that he believed the resistance used. Calculations demonstrated that the relevance and usefulness of the request was negligible.

Chapter Eleven

How important could one small boat be? In any event, the Frame had an army due to embark for that district that would negate any need or relevance in finding that boat.

The Frame would not waste resources in the search, but it could create a general request for information on its location, and it would cost nothing in resources. With an army of ten thousand elite warrior divines, a hundred enhanced warrior divines and a further two thousand offensive units fully equipped and loaded with offensive strategy software, the Garvamore District would soon be back under control and removal of those human units with violent tendencies from the population would reduce the risk of further rebellion. The species was dying out despite the Frame's best efforts and, perhaps, that process would slow down.

The Frame had already removed many thousands of the human population from inefficiently run beet farms in the area still under its control and put to more useful work. The farms became more productive at the cost of increased mortality among the humans. For some unknown reason the humans bred like rats in these remote districts. Inferior specimens of low intelligence that could barely manage their own affairs efficiently, so a few more deaths from labour in mines, saltpans and places where aimu could not function efficiently were inconsequential, but did enable the Frame to continue extracting the remaining mineral wealth of Inalsol. Ultimately, the Frame could manage without humans and eventually would. For now, the human population under its control, performed useful tasks, but required a lot of time and effort to manage. An ongoing, planned process, progressed to each stage as the Frame developed better and more sophisticated machines.

In the future, such distractions would not divert the Frame's attention from its function of study and the search for other planets. The Frame had sent many probes out into space throughout its existence and received continuous streams of data that needed processing. Other mechanisms for searching the heavens that might reveal potential Inalsol-like planets were available, but progress was slow.

Ultimately, the human species would become extinct on Inalsol. It no longer mattered to the Frame how many humans died. They were no longer important to the Frame.

Chapter Twelve

Troomey was having a rare break. He had been prioritising his work on the defensive shield, scaling up the principle of the repulse shields used at the Battle of Dundoon and in Yayler Poddick's 'divine staff'. He wanted some refreshment whilst he mulled over the problem of the power source.

Dook was very keen on the idea of using power from Dunirayn. Certainly, the big furnaces that were still under construction would produce enough power, but that power produced heat and getting that power from Dunirayn to Rustick More was a difficult problem. Making cables to transfer energy to Rustick More was a long-term project and heat energy would need conversion to something else before transmission. Troomey wanted a simpler and quicker solution.

The canteen was quiet and Big Jon brought Troomey's food out himself. Troomey had ordered a light meal, as he found that if he ate too much during the day, he worked and thought slower and felt sluggish and lethargic, so it was his general practice to eat lightly or not at all during the day and ate well when his daily work was done. Big Jon brought him a large bowl of onion and barley broth and a hunk of freshly baked barley bread. A jug of water accompanied his meal.

As Troomey poured a mugful of water for himself, an odd thought struck him. Odd, that is, that he had never thought of it before. Where, he wondered, did the water come from? As he was mulling over the thought Big Jon came back from the kitchen with a large mug of herbal infusion made of mint, parsley and juniper sweetened with honey. It was Big Jon's own concoction, which he insisted was refreshing. He, too, was taking a break.

Troomey indicated his repast and asked "where does all the water come from?"

The question took Big Jon a little aback. "Its' source you mean? I have no idea. We have to draw it by pump several times a day. Dook might know. After all, he's been here longer than anyone else."

While they were relaxing and engaging in idle chatter Dook wandered into the canteen and, seeing Big Jon and Troomey, came over with a big grin on his face.

"You look cheerful today." Troomey commented, dipping a chunk of bread into his soup.

"Aye, Ealasat's boat is finished. She is going home tomorrow."

"It'll be good to have the space back on Toiler's Woe." Troomey mumbled through a mouthful of bread.

"Aye, but I shall miss her."

"Really? She's a little sharp tongued for most peoples' taste."

Dook grimaced, as he pictured the penetrating gaze she adopted whenever she wanted something. That gaze was a warning and frequently preceded a caustic remark. "That may be true, but I shall miss her all the same. Anyway, they're blessing the boat shortly, you should both come through."

"Aye," Big Jon got up, mug in hand. "I think Troomey wanted to ask you something."

As Big Jon headed towards the passageway to Toiler's Woe Dook glanced questioningly at Troomey. "Oh? What was that?"

Troomey swallowed a last mouthful of soup before replying. "I was wondering if you knew where the water comes from. I'm thinking about using it as a power source."

"That's an interesting idea Troomey. What made you think of it?"

Troomey shrugged. "I don't know. The thought came to me just now."

Dook grinned. "Well, let's go and bless this boat, then I'll show you where the water comes from."

There were several dozen people congregated about the boat including children who were not normally in Toiler's Woe. It was a happy, cheerful affair despite Ealasat's aloofness towards most of the people. Children played in the boat, sinking other illusory enemy boats in monster-infested waters with imaginary guns. They blessed the boat with whisky and named it Kooinag after some wag had likened it to an oversized bucket. It had a broad beam and was quite short and stumpy due to a lack of materials to make a keel, but otherwise it was a solid little boat.

A small group of well-wishers including Sara and Dona clustered about Ealasat, who was in a buoyant, light-hearted mood as she would be able to go

Chapter Twelve

home and resume her previous life. Seeing Dook with Troomey, she hastened over, smiling with happiness.

"Dook" she greeted him "you're a smelly old individual, but I'm very grateful for what you've done for me, even if I've had to do most of the work myself." There was no physical sign of her gratitude however. She offered no peck on the cheek, hug, or handshake. In fact, typical of her general aloofness, she kept a distance between them and held her arms behind her back. She ignored Troomey completely.

As Ealasat returned to the small group she considered her friends Dook turned to Troomey. "Let's go and see this water supply."

"Aye, good idea."

Dook led Troomey down to the storage level of Rustick More and then down a flight of steps roughly hewn from the rock, passing an adjoining passage that led back up to the kitchens. A number of pipes ran along the walls that bore the water to the upper levels.

As they descended, Troomey realised that the narrow passage continued deep into the ground. Deeper and deeper they went, their way lit by one of the many little gadgets designed on Toiler's Woe. The rock changed hue from greys to red with dark black veins thicker than a man's body and others of white and yellow tones. It seemed to Troomey that they were descending into the very bowels of the planet.

Soon, though, they could hear the unmistakeable roar of water ahead as Dook brought them into a large chamber. A waterfall crashed into a dark pool of water causing a damp misting to permeate the air. The water exited the chamber, surging through a narrow hollow. The sound of the falling water reverberated into a continuous hum of white noise within which a discerning ear might detect subtle variation. The unnatural light they carried cast stark shadows on the walls and ceiling of the cavern creating an otherworldly, alien atmosphere.

Dook's voice suddenly intruded into the nether-realms ambience. "We draw the water from a channel down that way." Dook indicated to his left with a casual gesture.

They stood on a platform carved from the rock and ran along the chamber wall in the direction indicated by Dook. The chamber tapered and funnelled the water into its constricted exit so that it gained significant speed and force.

"We are below the level of the surrounding hills here so that at times this entire chamber is filled with water. At other times, it is not so high, but there is always a good flow of water."

Troomey was looking about the chamber, trying to gauge the dimensions. "How deep is the water here? Do you know the dimensions of this chamber?"

Dook made a dismissive gesture and scratched his wrinkled face thoughtfully. "In all honesty, I don't know. It's never been a significant issue before."

Troomey grimaced with mild irritation. "I see. I'll have to make some measurements then, but I think there is sufficient energy here for what I need."

"Sufficient?" Dook looked suddenly with intensity at Troomey. To him the chamber looked large and impressive. The thought that it might not be large enough for the needs of Rustick More he found profoundly disturbing. "Good," he managed finally "I'll leave you to get on with it then."

Dook closed his eyes and calmed his mind. There was so much happening at Rustick More and yet more happening on Ardbanacker, that he frequently struggled to keep everything in perspective. He longed for a simpler, less complicated and peaceful life. He sighed regretfully; such things would have to wait. They were always elusive, a distant future utopia that was always just out of reach. "I need to find out how other projects are progressing, Troomey. I will sleep better when this defence is working and better still if similar systems can be installed at Dundoon, Tuaport, and Ecta's Ledge. That would be a great help. Then we'll have to think about offensive weapons."

Troomey was dismayed. He had hoped there would be less pressure on him once this project was complete, but Dook appeared busy thinking up more work for him. Understanding the task did not, nor ever would, provide sufficient time to complete the work. He shook his with apprehension, but finally managed to say "I'll have to get something to make the measurements".

"Now?" Dook was a little startled at Troomey's apparent keenness, but then reconsidered. Troomey wanted the job out of the way as much as he did.

"Why not? I need to know how much energy can, usefully, be expected from the water flow. The sooner I know that, the sooner you can have your defence system in place."

Troomey spent much of the rest of the day drawing plans and making measurement and calculations, working out where he could make anchorage points for equipment and so on. By the time he was finished, he was satisfied that the project could be completed and in less time than he had originally anticipated.

Dook left Troomey to do his work and climbed back up the stone steps in search of Neev. She shuddered when he found her on Toiler's Woe with parts of a seismocom spread out on her workbench, ready for construction. She had been working hard to produce enough devices. She was very tired and wanted a break from the intense workload. She gave Dook a withering look from tired, baggy eyes. "I suppose you have more work for me, Dook? That is very thoughtful of you."

The sarcasm was lost on Dook, who tended to be very literal-minded. "Nay, not unless you wanted more."

"More, I'm very busy, Dook. In fact, after this unit I'm ready to start installing units. Briga should be here tomorrow, so the system can be set up at Ecta's Ledge."

"Oh? That is excellent news. I'm very impressed; you must have worked very hard to have achieved so much in so time."

That Dook was aware of how hard she was working was keenly annoying to Neev to the extent that she thought he was being sarcastic. With difficulty, she ignored the supposed barbed comment on her ability and smiled. She felt like hitting Dook, but resisted the temptation and maintained her ingenuous smile.

"Ah, good. I might join you. I need to know what is happening there."

The smile died on Neev's face. The last thing she wanted was for Dook to be breathing down her neck as she installed the seismocoms. "I'm certain Briga is doing a fine job."

"Aye, she is very efficient."

"I could compile a report for you and use it to test the seismocom. You can concentrate on your work here then."

"Good idea Neev. You do that then."

Briga arrived later that day, sooner than expected, and settled her flier next to Ealasat's boat, the Kooinag. She spent several sents admiring the workmanship of the little vessel until Neev came over.

"She's finally finished it and made a fair job of it too." Neev said, distracting Briga from her study of the boat.

"Aye, it's a good sturdy boat. How did she intend to move it?"

Neev looked oddly at the boat with its name proudly painted in bold letters on the bow and burst out laughing. After all the effort of designing and building Kooinag it had never struck anyone that a mountain, strides from the nearest navigable water, was an incongruous place for a boat. Apparently, no one had ever considered the problem of how to transport it. Briga attempted to heft the bow of the Kooinag with her arms, raising it a mere fraction and grunting with the effort. She let the boat settle back on its supports. "She's heavy and solidly built. A flier might lift her, but she's too big to fit."

"Aye, it will be a problem for her. I don't know where she is right now, but I'm sure a solution will be found." Neev turned her mind to the problem at hand, that of transporting and installing the seismocoms. She indicated a number of boxes filled with equipment and stacked to the side near her workstation. "Let's get these loaded."

There was the usual comings and goings of staff on Toiler's Woe, constructing new fliers or weapons, carefully re-packing grenades fabricated deep in the forests of Ardbanacker in boxes and storing them deep in the lower level of Rustick More, or labelling boxes ready for distribution, or any of a multitude of other jobs. Short staffs and Repulse Shields found temporary homes at Toiler's Woe prior to distribution.

In one area, several unusually shaped objects were taking shape. Generally known as Dook's Follies, they were inelegant, blockish and a mess of different components bolted together and mounted on a tri-pod platform. A short, thick, barrel protruded from the jumble. Constructed from hastily sketched designs produced by Troomey, they were incomplete; no one believed that they would work.

The loading of the boxes did not take long and Briga and Neev were preparing to leave, when Ealasat and a determined Sara approached them.

Chapter Twelve

Sara broached the subject of the boat. "Neev, Eala has a bit of a problem." Indicating the Kooinag, she continued. "A cavern is not the normal place for a boat. We need to help Eala move it so she can go home."

"Aye, it's a problem, sure enough." Neev answered matter-of-factly. "If you're thinking of using a flier, forget it. The boat doesn't fit!"

Ealasat looked suddenly crestfallen and spoke with unaccustomed contriteness. "What am I to do then? I need the boat to survive on my croft. It was the whole point in coming here."

Briga laughed, then belatedly stifled it, but still managed a pointed, barbed comment. "Perhaps, you should have thought of that sooner."

Startled into anger by Briga's comment, Ealasat was about to make a caustic reply but was stayed by Sara's gentle hand on her arm. "I have thought about it." Sara spoke in Ealasat's stead. "I know what a flier can do, and the weight of the boat isn't a problem. It can be cradled and suspended on ropes."

Stunned by the concept, Neev imagined the boat swaying chaotically beneath an out-of-control flier. She shook her head to clear her mind of the image. "That sounds dangerous, Sara" was all she said.

Undeterred Sara continued "Difficult, perhaps. I've worked out a rope system that will work, but then we'd have to borrow a flier. It would be simpler and quicker, and not to mention safer, if another pilot was in the flier as well."

Briga sighed. "Let me see your rope system. If I'm happy, I'll take the boat for you. After all, I've transported large blocks of rock from Ecta's Ledge to Tuaport before. There isn't anyone better qualified for the job."

Neev looked at Briga in complete shock, thinking that the woman had gone mad. Sara grinned with a glint of mirth in her eye as she gave Ealasat a friendly pat on the back.

"It works like this ---" Sara outlined her plan on a scrap of paper filched from a nearby workstation.

Briga was impressed and listened patiently as Sara explained her idea. "What do these lose ropes do" she asked, pointing at two lines that appeared to trail behind the flier.

Sara quickly sketched in a couple of stickmen. "They are control ropes. Ela and Fil have already agreed to help with those. They help to control the pitch and yaw of the boat as it becomes airborne."

"That's a good idea Sara. Well," Briga paused reflectively as she thought about the plan and then nodded. "All right, let's do it."

Sara had already sourced the ropes they needed and went in search of Ela and Fil who she found at the opposite end of Toiler's Woe working on the propulsion unit of a new flier. It took them more than a wair to set up the ropes, with Sara fussing over their precise positioning. They also had to move the Kooinag over towards the hanger doors of Toiler's Woe, which they achieved with brute force and the willing help of a few burly staff. The ropes must not become fouled. Time and care spent now would prevent a potential catastrophe later. At least, that is what Sara hoped.

Ealasat and Neev became mere bystanders, fascinated by Sara's attention to detail. She had even chosen different knots to do different jobs. Eventually she was satisfied and headed to the room to collect a bag with clothes and items she wanted to keep with her.

In Sara's absence, Briga had manoeuvred her flier next to Ealasat's boat and attached the rope cradle. A small crowd had congregated to witness the spectacle, milling about at a respectful distance and chatting quietly amongst themselves. Sara returned with a large beetick holdall, which she threw casually onto the half-raised tailgate of Briga's flier and vaulted herself up after her bag. The bag was stowed by jamming it between a couple of boxes of grenades and Sara took up the navigator's position next to Briga.

The thrusters whined into life producing an unnatural temperament, a sound that, though not a discord was uncomfortable to listen to. Gingerly, Briga crept forward and across until the flier hovered in front of the boat. As the flier moved forward beyond the hanger doors, Ela and Fil apprehensively took hold of two trailing control ropes.

"I hope she's got this right. I don't like the idea of being pulled over the edge." Ela called over to Fil.

Fil raised his voice over the whine of the thrusters. "We're supposed to let it swing free hauling back on the ropes to control it. There is plenty of rope."

Briga made delicate adjustments to the controls of the flier until she could feel resistance from the weight of the Kooinag, then she paused. She had lifted heavy blocks of rock many times at Ecta's Ledge, but never quite like this.

She angled the flier upward and moved forward by degrees. There was a scraping noise as the Kooinag moved, rasping over the stone flooring. The Kooinag was soon teetering on the edge, balancing midpoint on its keel.

"Feeaklack n'Irin! This is awkward, Sara." Briga protested, feeling the unwieldy weight of the boat through the flier's controls.

"Aye, it was always going to be difficult." Sara replied calmly. "Ah, I think she's tipping."

"Aye, I can feel her going."

Behind them sat Neev and an anxious, but silent, Ealasat in the recently installed passenger seats. Back on the hanger floor, Ela and Fil hauled on their ropes to prevent the Kooinag from swinging and yawing.

Suddenly the bow of the Kooinag pitched forward and the stern rose in the air and the boat slid over the edge. "Haul" Fil bellowed. Ela and Fil braced themselves, hauling back on their ropes with all their strength.

Briga lifted the flier so that the Kooinag swung free pulling Ela and Fil forward until they were several paces from the edge of the hanger. When the Kooinag reached the apex of its forward motion it began to swing back toward the hanger wall.

As instructed, Ela and Fil retreated from the edge and hauled in the slack as the Kooinag swung back towards the hanger, missing the edge by a mere two paces, but at a level above the hanger floor. Ela and Fil now struggled to control the boat for several more ponderous swings until it hung, gently swaying beneath the flier. Ela and Fil released the ropes, allowing them to swing free beneath the flier.

"That was a bit nervy." Briga commented with unflappable calmness to Sara as the motion of the boat subsided.

Sara nodded, white faced from worry and nervous tension. She said nothing, but wondered how Briga remained calm whilst performing such a dangerous manoeuvre.

Behind them Ealasat blurted out with a strained wavering voice "is the boat all right?"

Sara nodded again, still not trusting her voice.

Briga answered for her. "It's fine, Ealasat. We needed to prevent your boat from swinging back into the cliff wall below the hanger entrance. Sara, can you check to make sure the rope crew are alright?"

Sara nodded yet again; then she cleared her throat. "Aye." Her voice cracked as she spoke unsteadily. She checked through the rear of the flier and saw Ela and Fil sprawled on the hanger floor, rubbing at scrapes and bruises. They were fine, but Sara didn't think they would agree to this procedure again. Still, it had worked and they were fine and the boat was undamaged. "We'll see you soon" she called out through the open rear of the flier, not knowing when that would be. She would probably be a mother by then.

After closing the ramp and returning to the navigator's seat, she looked at Briga and spoke more steadily now her composure had recovered. "I'm not sure it's wise to do that again. They're mostly unhurt. We should go, I think."

"Mostly unhurt?" Briga raised her eyebrows questioningly.

"Bumps and scrapes, they're fine. Are we comfortable back there?"

"We're fine, Sara" replied Neev, who had been a silent passenger so far. We should go, Briga; nothing more to be done here."

"Agreed, Sara can you load coordinates for Ealasat's croft?" Briga was unperturbed by the risks involved in extracting the Kooinag from the hanger. She was the epitome of serene professionalism.

"Er, no, we don't have any." Sara looked slightly embarrassed by her admission, but she had again thought of a solution. "If I punch in the approximate position, Ealasat should be able to guide you by sight."

"That's fine. Do it."

"What about those dangling guide ropes? Are they a problem?" Sara asked, suddenly realising they could snag, or cause an accident.

"Aye, we should have set them up so that they could be hauled into the flier. I will compensate and give us plenty of room. Have you got those coordinates?"

"Aye."

Briga waited until Sara had punched in coordinates for the Brayvik Straits and swapped places with Ealasat, before engaging forward thrust. She could easily have flown there without navigation, but she believed that it was the correct policy to maintain good habits. Ealasat looked keenly out of the canopy and her excitement rose as she began to recognise familiar landmarks.

They had been flying for quarter of a wair when Ealasat let out an elated exclamation "Hey, that's The Stack! It's not far from my home. Go that way." She indicated the direction by waving her hand in front of Briga and then pointing. "It's just over that ridge, it's just there."

"Thank you, Ealasat" barely hiding her irritation at having a hand waved in front of her face.

The ridge she indicated was long and high until it terminated with abrupt steep scree covered slopes that descended into the waters of the strait, forming a craggy peninsula. Ealasat inhaled sharply as Briga lifted over the ridge, and her little croft with a seaward row of alben, came into view. Sara manoeuvred herself forward on hands and knees until she could peer through the lower canopy at her new home, a harsh rocky cove.

To Ealasat it was a beautiful sight. It was her home. It was the place where she had grown up and lived almost all her life. To Sara it was a desolate waste and a disappointment. A small stone hut thatched with heather stood alone except for a narrow stony path that wound down to the shore and two small fields that showed clear efforts of cultivation. The poor, thin soil, heaped into long rows, to allow crops to grow.

Briga flew low with the guide ropes trailing in the water. She then brought the flier into a hover and descended slowly. When the Kooinag was resting on the surface of the water, they released the ropes. Briga searched for a spot to land. She made a couple of circuits of the small valley surrounded by mountain crags. Most of the valley floor was a boulder field, which extended to the cleared cultivated fields. Even these contained large boulders, too big to move.

"I'm sorry Ealasat" Briga said at last "I can't land. You might have to jump into the water."

Sara giggled. "Sounds like fun!"

Unimpressed Ealasat pointed to an area of flatter rocks by the shore. "Over there. There are big boulders Atha, Da, used to call them the slabs."

"I see them. They'll do." Briga banked the flier and manoeuvred over to the rocks and with gentle dexterity set the flier down on the slabs.

After brief farewells, Ealasat and Sara disembarked and scrambled over the boulders to the small croft-house. Briga wasted no time in lifting away and heading off over the Brayvik Straits. As they watched the flier recede into the distance, they could hear an odd, slightly a-rhythmic clack, clack.

"That's Gawa, my goat. She's getting old for a goat and doesn't say a lot, but she's the only company I get."

Sara grinned and laughed light-heartedly. "Good name for a goat. What would you call a second goat?"

"There she is, up on the crags." Ealasat started to scramble across rocks and boulders to the goat, which was watching them from the vantage point of a craggy ledge above them. "I know. It's not the cleverest name for a goat. My parents were going to give her a proper name, but I was still young and kept calling her Gawa, so the name stuck." Mentioning her parents caused Ealasat long sents of melancholy. She let the moment pass. Time could not be turned back. Her parents were gone, and she had to endure.

Ealasat nuzzled the goat affectionately and led the beast down from the crags and over to Sara. "Well, say hello Gawa."

Gawa sniffed uncertainly at Sara's outstretched hand and then started to nibble at the cuff of her morcote.

"Leave that Gawa." Ealasat gently pushed Gawa's head away from the sleeve, and then with a sudden, startled exclamation she cried out. "The boat! We need to get the boat before she drifts away!"

The Kooinag was bobbing slightly in the chill waters about thirty paces from the shore. Ealasat had to wade, waist deep, into the water to retrieve the boat and fish about in the bow to find the painter and then tow it back to shore. The two of them soon had it run up onto the small pebble beach where Gawa regarded it with suspicion, sniffing and then nibbling tentatively at the painter.

"Leave it." Ealasat pushed the goat away and led it back up the path to the croft. "Now then, Gawa, let's see if you've left us anything to eat."

Sure enough, the goat had run riot in Ealasat's two small fields. "The light goes quickly here, Sara. We need to find something edible for the pot so we can eat tonight. There's a rope by the croft door, if you tie up Gawa we can look for some food. Don't worry, she won't mind. Gawa looked at Ealasat as if to say she would mind, but followed Sara placidly.

Chapter Twelve

"Come on, beastie" Sara enticed leaving Ealasat to survey the damage to the fields.

The sun only showed an orange half disc that crept down the crags that formed an arm of Ealasat's valley. Sara could see that it would soon dip below those crags only to re-emerge later as it made its passage across the horizon, never quite setting. It wasn't a bad place to have a baby; she mused and wondered what Cullin was doing.

Chapter Thirteen

Whilst Sara was tying up Gawa, she was thinking about Cullin, and Cullin was thinking about her. He was at the tiller of the Banree waiting for his shift to end. They were now on a new course. Guvin had reckoned that they were far enough yerward that they could start to head out to the hyper-boreal waters. The news caused a great cheer amongst the crew who were weary of the endless heavy seas and biting cold.

Ecta would have a brew on soon and Cullin anticipated its wonderful warmth soothing the cold from his fingers. He was used to the freezing temperatures, but the sea had a different kind of cold. At home, a morcote would keep out all, but the worst, winter chill. Here, though, it was damp or frozen. The cold had a biting edge to it that no amount of clothing could dispel.

As Cullin was musing, Ecta came onto the deck with a worried expression. "Guvin wants to talk to us, we have a problem."

"What's the problem Ecta?"

"Guvin will tell us. Rope the tiller, this is serious." Roping the tiller was a simple idea that allowed the tiller to be un-manned for short periods whilst maintaining the same course. Cullin simply hooked a line of measured length over the tiller and made it fast to a leeward cleat.

Finnan and Goram sat glumly in the cabin when Cullin and Ecta entered. Grim faced and concerned, Guvin had charts spread out on the table. "Ah, Cullin, come in." Guvin didn't bother to look up, but frowned at the charts as if they could give him the answers he needed. "Make yourself comfortable. You to, Ecta." He waited for them to sit before looking up.

"We have a problem. Ecta has just broached a cask of water and found it mostly empty. There is a split in the cask. We have two other casks and both are similarly damaged. This means that we have a serious shortage of water. All our water has now been transferred to our one good cask and it has been measured. We will now be rationed to one muga of water per day. Dry food rations only as we cannot afford to use the water for cooking. Any questions?"

How were the casks damaged?" Cullin asked.

"Hard to say. It is possible that they were damaged in the recent storms. I suspect though, as other barrels are not damaged, that the water casks were damaged before loading."

"Who will do the rationing?" Finnan was an old hand whose first thought was to the practicality of the rationing. He saw no benefit in arguing about the loss, just the need to move on with the current situation.

"I will do the rationing, but I want one of you with me when I do it."

"That sounds reasonable." Finnan grumbled.

"How long will the water last?" Cullin wanted to know.

"About two tendays. There is an island archipelago roughly a tenday of fair travelling from here. So the plan is to make for one of those islands and re-supply." Guvin thought the plan the most practical. There wasn't a lot else, they could do.

"Didn't anyone check the casks before they were loaded." As ever, Goram took a negative view, seeking to find blame or fault.

"Of course." Guvin replied, wanting to move the discussion on and not have it bog down on pointless tacks.

"Not well enough, it seems" persisted Goram.

"The damage is hard to see, not visible to the naked eye, Goram" explained Guvin, becoming irritated and hoping that Goram would drop his futile line of questioning.

Goram was perceptibly angry. He viewed this latest problem as an example of incompetence and wasn't afraid to say so. "This whole voyage has been a disaster so far. I hope for everyone's' sake that you know what you're doing Guvin. I don't have much confidence myself."

Guvin was angry now. This man was holding him to blame for situations beyond his control. "We have to deal with the situation we have, Goram, and not dwell on what 'might have been'."

Goram snorted with derision, his anger causing a palpable negative ambiance to pervade the cabin. He was being unhelpful. He was unhappy with the way his life had become difficult and out of his control. He wanted to be back on his croft, doing things he was comfortable with. He did not want to be on this boat with four men he found difficulty in trusting.

Chapter Thirteen

"Goram, you are only here on sufferance. You have no practical skills to offer. I am in charge of this boat, not you. Kindly remember that before you decide to insult me again." Guvin was staring the intractable Goram in the face, daring him to deny his authority.

The stress of the situation and Goram's natural tendency to blame authority when circumstances weren't to his liking, were too much for him and he lost his temper. "And who should bear the blame then. I refuse to believe ---" He could get no further as Guvin's large fist was clamped about his throat.

"Let's see how well you can swim, Goram." Guvin forced Goram toward the hatch.

Goram struggled, but it was an uneven match. Cullin blocked his passage across the cabin. The confines of the small boat were bound to cause tension, but violence was unacceptable and threatened to divide the crew. Certainly, no one expected it from the Captain. "This does not help. Either of you. Stop this now!"

Guvin glared angrily at Cullin, offended by another challenge to his authority on the Banree, but rather than exacerbating the situation, he thrust Goram to the floor and spoke through clenched teeth. "Aye, enough. You others, keep this piece of cac away from me or I will throw it overboard."

"How long did you say, before we get to those islands?" Cullin steered conversation back to a more constructive course.

"About a tenday with fair sailing. Which, of course, we may not get." The tension in the cabin slowly dissipated as the crew now focused on the water supply. "We have a little over a hundred muga of fresh water left. With five of us having one a day we have twenty days at best before we run out."

"So we're not desperate yet?" Cullin wanted the point clear for all to understand, even if the balance between continuing their mission and dying of thirst was precarious. Twenty days seemed enough time to sort things out.

"Nay, but one muga of water is not a lot. We will all be thirsty before we can replace our water." Guvin replied, still glaring at Goram.

Goram was still prone on the floor with a sullen bitterness etched into the lines of his face. He made a suggestion, though his voice dripped with heavy sarcasm. "Can't we collect more? I mean, it falls from the sky doesn't it?"

"Aye, it does. Rainwater can be collected using the sails. Prior to the refit, the Banree didn't have such a system so it wasn't included." Guvin explained.

"Perhaps it should have been." Goram was clearly not going to let Guvin off easily.

After a long pause, struggling to maintain his temper Guvin spoke with long deliberation. "No one thought that the Banree was going to be used for an extended voyage. It wasn't thought necessary."

Goram laughed with derision. " 'Wasn't thought' seems to be a common theme on this journey."

Guvin started to move menacingly toward the recusant Goram, but Cullin's steady hand on his chest stayed the action. "So can we make one now?" Cullin asked calmly.

"Certainly. We can rig something up."

"Good. Well, let's get on with it." Ecta, silent throughout the arguments, was his usual, pro-active, and positive self.

"I agree, let's get on with it." Cullin too wanted to get on. The arguments were pointless, solving nothing.

"Finnan, take this ancac on deck and continue our present course. I'll go with our guest below and see what we can do about water collection." With a plan of action, Guvin felt back in control and had new respect for Cullin.

The idea of collecting water from rainfall using the sail was an ancient one and Guvin understood it well. Not fitting one before was an oversight on his part, but he would never admit that to Goram. Goram would only use it as an example of incompetence. He only hoped that he had the necessary parts.

As they searched for the parts, a few more problems with their supplies came to light. Salt water had contaminated and spoiled dried fruits, grains, and dried vegetables. How that had happened was beyond Guvin. He had a sinking feeling of impending disaster that he felt helpless to avoid.

Furthermore, he realised that all the contaminated foods had come from the same supplier. The containers were at fault. They appeared fine, but when inspected more closely by Cullin, they found the staves were imperfectly joined. Water had seeped between them. It was a devastating blow to Guvin and a dreadful feeling of panic threatened to overwhelm him.

Chapter Thirteen

Activity filled the following two days and Guvin found himself forced to exceed the rationing. They now had sixteen days supply of water and had only traversed a tenth of the distance to the island archipelago where they hoped to find water.

Once they had located suitable tubing and other parts they, fitted them to the foresail rather than the mainsail owing to the lateen rigging of the boat. Cullin had repaired the casks and food barrels as only he could see the damage and they cast the spoiled food into the sea. An open gooseneck formed a pouch at the apex of the foresail to which the tubing fitted and ran back along the bowsprit to where it collected in a cask. Guvin looked over the work and could see no reason why it shouldn't work and pronounced it a good job. They tried fishing to supplement their food stores, running lines from the stern mast booms and landed enough skaden to last for several days.

"I don't quite get" Ecta was saying as he was tucking into a plate of fried skaden "why we now only have sixteen days of water rations and yet we're still nine days from this chain of islands. At this rate we won't make it to the islands before we run out of water."

"Ah, well, we're beating a tack against both current and wind. That slows us down, but in a few days, the current will be in our favour. We'll pick up speed then. We do need to remain careful and conserve our water until it rains." Guvin deftly stripped the fillets off one of his fish and took an appreciative mouthful. "Good fish, Ecta."

It had been another gruelling day and Troomey was tired. As he headed for the canteen, he was thinking that he needed a break. A proper break, just a day or two with nothing to do or think about, time without intense pressure. As soon as one job was completed, another took its place with the same injunction to complete as soon as possible.

Dona and Dook sat quietly together with their heads slightly bowed as they talked in hushed tones. As he collected his evening meal, Dook beckoned him over.

"How's the water generator installation progressing?" Dook asked taking a sip of ale.

"Good." Troomey set his food down and sat down with a thump. He yearned for his bed, but knew he had to eat first. Dona too, he noted, appeared tired and Troomey noted that she was slumped in her seat. Was everybody exhausted? Everybody was dragging their feet lately and looked as though they needed a break. "The generator is in and working. I just need power cabling. There should be sufficient on that ship they had at Dundoon. I'm still waiting on those. I can start putting shields in place tomorrow."

"Dona's going there tomorrow. Tell her what you need."

Troomey shook his head negatively. "I'd sooner go there myself to make sure it's what I need."

"That's fine. You help Dona tomorrow and come back with those cables. It's been a month since the battle of Dundoon and the Frame has not retaliated. We have been lucky. The Frame is up to something and we're not ready. It's hard work, but it has to be done."

"Everyone is doing their best, Dook." Dona muttered. "I'll see you tomorrow Troomey. I'm going to bed."

"Good night Dona." Troomey turned back to Dook "how are the follies going? Are they ready to be tested yet?"

"That's the biggest priority after your shields. I'll look into it tomorrow. How soon can you get the shields finished?"

"A tenday will see the job done, assuming there are no problems." Troomey chewed on bread and sliced ham tasting nothing. It wasn't the food; he was just too tired to have any pleasure in eating. "Where do you think they'll strike first?"

Dook shrugged "I have no way of knowing. Dundoon probably, but it's failed there once. Maybe Tuaport. It will have to land somewhere on Ardbanacker if it wants the territory back. It may land in the badlands to avoid a direct assault. It will come, that is certain and the more systems we have working, the better." Dook a long pull on his ale and regarded Troomey seriously. "Once we have a tested working defence shield and my follies operating we'll be better situated to defend ourselves. Time is short, Troomey. I'm surprised we've had this much.

"What you must understand is that you are very important because you will have to build and install this stuff in other locations. You will have to train others and there is not enough time. You are the only one who knows this technology well enough to make it work. I'm sorry, but I'm going to keep you very busy for as long as it takes."

Chapter Thirteen

Troomey had given up on his food; he had no appetite and finally decided that he needed to sleep. He ached and groaned as he stood up. "I'm going bed, Dook. I'll see you tomorrow."

Dook, left on his own, wondered why everyone was so tired. Everyone he spoke to lately made the same complaint. A month had gone by and they were no better off than before. They had to push harder or all could be lost. He had to make them understand they could not afford to relax.

He downed his ale with one continuous swallow and collected up the crockery from the table and placed them neatly with Troomey's half eaten food. The mention of the aimu ship at Dundoon reminded him that he hadn't looked at the heart of the ship, the aimu that controlled the ship, recently. Everyone else might be tired, but he wasn't ready to sleep yet.

He made his way to a small anteroom that contained the machine. With no means of communicating with the Frame, it could no longer cause any harm, but it still worked. He could even talk to it, though it refused to act on any instruction or command. Ulbin, Cullin's brother had damaged the computer to such an extent that Dook had to improvise a method of re-booting the machine. A single button was all it required to start it. He hit the button and sat down on the single wooden chair that furnished the room.

He waited. It took only a few moments for the machine to come to life and the single word 'ready' appeared on its two dimensional screen. Though it normally operated with a three dimensional holographic display, Dook preferred the basic system because he liked to think that it 'discomfited' the aimu. Of course, the aimu could not be discomfited. It had no emotions, but the idea satisfied Dook's emotional needs. He felt that he had more control.

Dook addressed the machine in a monotone that was empty of feeling or emotion. "Computer, the current date code is NE1021M5D10T4-3.63.95, confirm."

A metallic voice answered. "Data provided conforms to internal memory with ninety-nine point eight percent accuracy. Systems are functioning at less than fifty percent optimal. It is advisable to return this unit to its point of manufacture to address critical performance issues."

"Understood. State current destination."

"Please enter authorisation code." This request came up every time he tried to access any data, but so far, he had been unable to find a backdoor access.

Dook would have liked to have Yayler Poddick to help him. He doubted that Yayler would have much difficulty in getting beyond this point. He tried a different tack to those he'd tried before. "Reset authorisation code."

"Please enter user ID."

Dook's eyebrows shot up with surprise. Why had he not tried that before? It was basic and simple, fundamental. He had an ID he could use somewhere in his rooms, but couldn't think where. He could picture in his mind where it used to be, but the ladies had tidied his rooms recently and he no longer had any idea where anything was. He tried something else. "ID not available. Use DNA match."

An image of a hand appeared on the screen. He placed his hand on the image and waited. "Processing" the aimu said in its mechanical voice that sounded, somehow, rusty. He chuckled to himself at the absurdity of a rusty voice. "Voice sample accepted, please wait." Dook blinked with surprise, this was encouraging; he might actually be getting somewhere.

"Access is granted for Manzen19. Limited functions now available."

"State current destination." After a month of intermittent attempts to break into the computer, Dook now found himself at a loss as to what to do with it.

"Gastron."

Gastron was an insignificant town on a continental island many thousands of strides away. Dook wondered why he remembered the name. Then he recalled the frozen mining town. It was a place of horror and death where he worked as a very young Balcleric. That was a long, long time ago, he mused.

A collated manifest of the ship cargo did not include any mining equipment that Dook could recall. Perhaps it was to pick some up in Dundoon. "State purpose of harbourage in Dundoon."

"Unable to comply."

"List manifest."

A long list scrolled on the screen. Since he already had such a list he didn't pay much attention to what was on it, but one item caught his eye as it flashed past. He scrolled back and gaped at it. It was simply a series of numbers without anything to indicate what it might be. He jotted the numbers down

Chapter Thirteen

and wondered. Perhaps he should go with Troomey to Dundoon and hunt for the item.

The following day was bright and calm in Dundoon. Dook descended the ramp from the flier and looked about the harbour. A scant month before a horrific battle had taken place in the town. Many buildings still bore their battle scars. Many people had lost their lives. Scores of people had been injured and some crippled or maimed for life. Such things upset Dook and he desperately wanted to avoid such waste in the future.

He knew there would be more fighting and he could do nothing to avoid further conflict. The quayside showed few signs of battle and people were wandering about performing one task or another in the cool morning air.

"Do you know where we go, Troomey?"

Standing behind Dook, Troomey shrugged "Nay". He had remained silent for the entire journey from Rustick More.

"Dona?"

Dona shook her head in a negative "Nay, I'm going to that big warehouse at the end of the quay. Why not ask around?" She wandered off leaving the two men to sort out themselves.

"Hmm, must be one of these buildings."

"I guess."

"Well, let's find out, Troomey." Dook headed for the nearest large building where a youth with a narrow pinched face ravaged by acne and a large black eye stood guard by the doorway. "I'm looking for ---."

"Try the Harbour Master." The youth cut Dook short, looking at the scruffy, dishevelled old man with disdain that bordered on disgust.

"And where do I find the Harbour Master?" Dook gave the youth a long steady stare, waiting for some kind of answer. "Where is the Harbour Master?" Dook repeated continuing his stare.

"In his office" the boy finally managed.

"Which is where?" Dook persisted. "This way?" Dook pointed to one end of the quayside.

"Aye" the boy finally answered with complete disinterest and stayed, uncommunicative at his post.

As they walked in the presumed direction of the Harbour Master Dook muttered quietly to Troomey "I don't know what his problem was. Youth of today, I guess."

The office did not impress Dook. It was a complete mess. Not a mess in the way his rooms at Rustick More had been until he had been organised by Dona. They had been untidy because he never got around to putting anything away. This small office looked as if there had been a riot. Broken chairs and a table lay scattered on the floor with sheets of paper and files and an upturned cupboard. A small skinny round-faced man stood amongst the disarray, looking as if he was ready for a fight.

"Er, are you the Harbour Master? Can we come in?" Dook asked tentatively.

The round-faced man turned to look at them directly and regarded Dook as if he was about to commit murder. "Doesn't seem to be a lot of point does there?" The man had a deep gravelly voice that belied his slender frame. "Unless, that is, you've come to help clean up this mess."

"What happened here?" Troomey asked gazing at the disorder in astonished bewilderment.

"This is what happens when you leave a bad tempered gillee in charge of your office while you have a lunch break. Can I help you?"

"I hope so. I need some stuff from that transport ship."

"Not anyone can just take that stuff, you know." The little man picked up a few odd sheets of the scattered paper and looked at them helplessly. "This is going to take forever" he grumbled quietly to himself.

"I'm Dookerock." Dook introduced himself trying to spur the man into action.

The man gawped at him for a long moment and then laughed. "I believe you. The ragged clothes and the smell would be difficult for anyone to duplicate. I'm Krunika. You had best talk to Yaren. I believe he's here today."

Krunika took them back down the quayside to where the youth was standing guard. He glared hard at the youth as he led Dook and Troomey into the warehouse. The youth stood aside, but otherwise completely ignored them. He appeared uneasy in the presence of the skinny man.

"Did you say something?" Krunika asked the youth as he passed.

The youth stared straight ahead, yet his emotions betrayed themselves. As Dook passed, he noticed the youth's eyes follow him and turned his head to look closer. The youth's eyes snapped back to the front and he stared steadfastly ahead again.

Once inside, Dook realised that the building was now multi-functional. About half the building worked as a warehouse. Yaren, the lieutenant who had successfully defeated the divine army in the Battle of Dundoon, sat behind a large desk with piles of reports in front of him. Arrayed about the warehouse floor there were other desks where aneksa officers applied themselves to their duties. Yaren had turned the building into his command centre.

"Ah, Krunika, how's that lad of yours?" Yaren stood and beckoned them over.

"The same rude, bad-tempered pain he always was." Realising something of an explanation was neccessary, Krunika spoke in an undertone to Dook and Troomey. "The lad outside is mine and is the one responsible for the state of my office. I am responsible for his black eye." He turned back to Yaren. "I believe you know this man?"

"Indeed, Dook this is an unexpected pleasure. Is there something I can do for you?" Yaren remained standing.

"Aye there is. This is Troomey. He's working on a defence system we've been developing at the More. I want him looked after. Make sure he gets what he needs." Dook turned to Troomey. "Whilst you're here you may as well figure out how to install the system here. Dundoon is, after all, one of the most likely places for an attack from the Frame."

"Aye, makes sense." Troomey agreed.

Yaren motioned to one of his officers who took Troomey away and turned back to Dook. "Was there anything else? You didn't come all this way just for a few bits of divine equipment."

"Nay, Indeed not. I am very curious about the contents of a certain container taken from that aimu transport. I want to have a look at it."

"Do you have any ID for the container?" Yaren asked, intrigued.

"Aye." Dook fished about in one of the pockets of his morcote and retrieved a scrap of paper with a few hastily scribbled notes and handed it to Yaren.

Yaren looked at the scrap with some surprise. "Is that it? Nothing else? They should have some identification code as well as numbers. Are you sure this is all of it?"

"Aye, it came direct from the data banks of that aimu we took from the ship."

"Really?" Yaren gave the scrap to another officer who scratched his head thoughtfully and then scuttled off. "It shouldn't take long. It is fortunate for you that we don't keep such records in the Harbour Masters office any more. It might take a little while, otherwise."

"I quite understand. I have seen the offices, quite a good demolition job. So, what happened?"

Yaren made a wry face "the lad was due to be disciplined for verbally abusing one of my officers. Krunika, the boy's father, heard about it and delivered his own punishment. The lad is known for his bad temper. I understand that his excuse for wrecking the offices was that he 'doesn't like being told what to do'. He's going get a lot of that in the near future."

It did not take long for the officer to return with Dook's scrap of paper. He also bore a small card. "We've found the location of the item, Sir."

"Ah, let's go and find it then." Yaren gestured for Dook to follow.

"I'm impressed Yaren, that was very quick." Dook approved of efficiency.

"It was. Every item we've catalogued from that ship had an ID that was preceded by a letter. Yours must be unique in that it only included numbers."

"Aye, that's what drew my attention to it in the first place."

The officer led them down a broad central walkway to the far end of the warehouse and then turned down an aisle between racks loaded with containers of all sizes. "Ah, here we are. It is, I believe, that one up there. Wait here, I need a trolley."

The trolley was a mechanical device that was operated by two persons. The officer soon came back with a large man towing the wheeled contraption.

Extendable metal forks protruded from a platform, which lifted on hydraulic jacks. The officer then started to pump a long lever with the man, who was a low ranking aneksa, standing on the platform. When the platform reached the highest level of shelving, some twenty paces above the floor, the aneksa positioned the forks and started to crank them forward under the container. It was about four paces long, three paces wide, and two deep.

Once it was down Dook wasted no time in trying to open the box with his bare hands. "Have we got something to lever this open with?"

The officer stepped in, gently pushing Dook aside. "It's still in its original container, Sir. There'll be a small recess somewhere." The officer cast his eyes about the lid of the container and then exclaimed happily. "Ah, here it is." On one end of the container, there was a subtle, small, and easily overlooked indentation. "I think sometimes, that there is something inherently lazy about divines. Watch this. It is an absolutely absurd, excessive use of technology." The officer pressed it with deft fingers and made a self-satisfied grunt of pleasure.

The lid began to loosen and lift. "The screws that secure the lid have little motors so that they can screw and unscrew automatically. Just to save someone the effort of doing it manually. It's a joke."

As the officer spoke, the lid raised itself on mechanical arms and slid neatly down the side of the container to reveal a single white sarcophagus with a transparent plaz lid. A mist within the sarcophagus partially concealed the contents. Dook peered intently into the mists for long sents, then abruptly stood erect. "Hesoos, there's a body inside this thing!"

Chapter Fourteen

The day was looking quite promising for Krarn. He had checked his lobster pots and now had three fine specimens in the bottom of his creel. The family would eat well today. His arms and back ached from the rowing, as they always did, but he was nearly back home to the little harbour of Garvin. He would have a mug of ale at Linn's, he decided, before heading home to his cottage where his wife and babe would be waiting.

As Krarn ruminated on how he would spend his leisure, an oar snagged on something in the water. It only took a moment to fish it out and put the bloody mess next to the creel. He could feel the broken bones within the corpse and he could see where seabirds had pecked at it. A bonxie nearby, viewed him with displeasure at the theft of its meal.

"Nay for you" he told the bird, which flapped its wings in irritation.

Krarn viewed the white-haired object with a degree of distaste and then realised he knew it. It was Kurra, Linn the Landlady's dog, beaten and kicked to death and then dumped unceremoniously into the sea. His mother had told Krarn that the little dog had disappeared the day before and that Linn was quite upset. The dog was well known about the village as it so frequently made a nuisance of itself. Kurra never caused any real harm and Krarn wondered what or who caused its violent death.

Drunken Pyta sat outside the inn with a large ale-mug and followed Krarn into the building.

"Linn." Krarn hollered as he entered.

She soon appeared from the kitchen and tears sprang to her eyes when she saw what Krarn was carrying. "What? How?" was all she managed to say.

"Oh, it's the dog." Pyta muttered sympathetically. "I'm so sorry Linn."

They took the dog's carcass out the back to bury it. The news of its brutal end was soon about the village and became the main talking point for several days. The tale soon came to the ears of old Sef. At first Sef thought it just a sad story until he remembered something he had seen. That man Pyta had dropped something into the harbour. It had been late in the afternoon the day Kurra had disappeared. The more Sef thought about it, the more he became convinced that he had seen Kurra's carcass thrown into the water.

Sef knew that almost no one would take him seriously if he said anything. He was a teller of tales, an exaggerator of the truth, but the old widow would listen to him. He determined to go and talk to her; maybe someone else had seen something as well.

Sef needn't have worried, as she wholeheartedly believed him. The old widow talked to her daughter, who talked to her friend. Soon people were asking 'what had Pyta dropped into the water?'

Slowly a story emerged. Kurra had nipped at Pyta's ankles once too often and in a drunken rage had kicked the dog. Then, so the story went, he beat it with the poker before discarding the corpse in callous, inebriated disregard for the life he had taken.

Pyta was drinking outside the front of Linn's Inn when they started the rough music. It started with a single pan beaten with a wooden spoon. Others joined in with jeers and more beating of pans, jars, or anything that came to hand. Linn was popular in the village, but Pyta did not enjoy popularity. He was tolerated, but no more. The villagers joined the growing throng making raucous a noise and rounding on Pyta.

They surrounded him. Shoved him, jeered at him, and all the while they maintained the cacophony. Pyta backed away from them, but they continued, mocking him as they forced him from the village. Pyta ran in panic, not knowing what had caused the villagers anger.

He did not run far out of Garvin before slowing to a walking pace. He was angry at the shunning from the worthless people of Garvin. He silently vowed to get vengeance on the people. For now, he needed to work out where to go. Not for the first time in his life, he found himself with nothing. He wandered aimlessly for the rest of the day until he found himself on the road to Balgeel. Balgeel, he knew, was another little fishing village, much like Garvin. Furthermore, he knew the 'Boss' visited the village from time to time.

With the rough workings of a plan in his mind, Pyta set off along the road at a brisk pace. He would have to steal food and he would need shelter. His morcote, he realised, still hung on a peg at Linn's Inn. It was a chilly night, not cold, but cool enough to make Pyta regret not having a morcote to keep him warm. He did not sleep well and woke in the grey pre-dawn light hungry and shivering. It was a relief to get moving.

Chapter Fourteen

Life had become a dull tedium for Yayler. Long wairs with just his own company, he could cope with. How many years had he lived alone at his little bothy? He wasn't sure now, but he measured the time in decades. Then he had always had something to occupy his time. He had always been busy. That wasn't the case now. He had no com-pad or any means of occupying his mind.

He lay down on the bunk, which was the only furniture in the small cabin. Gulukone, the enigmatic giant, stood outside. He was always there, impassive and, seemingly, immovable. At least he could talk to the giant; they probably wouldn't stop him from doing that. He swung himself up from the bunk. Yayler swung the door to his cabin open and Gulukone stood there.

"You are not permitted to leave your cabin." Gulukone had a high-pitched musical voice, that was almost feminine in its tone and quality.

"I am still within my prison." Yayler pointed out.

Gulukone considered that remark. "You are not in a prison, you are here for your protection."

"Protection from who?" Yayler responded immediately and received a blank stare from Gulukone. He tried a different tack. "How old are you, Gulukone?" He got the same blank stare.

"I am not permitted to answer", was the reply Yayler eventually got from the enigmatic giant.

"Not permitted by who?"

Gulukone delivered his blank stare again, as if deciding whether he could answer or not. "My Master does not allow some questions to be answered."

"I see. Who is your master?" Yayler asked, fearing the 'not permitted to answer' response.

"The Frame is my Master."

"So Clar15 is not your Master?" Yayler persisted finding the conversation awkward, almost as if he was talking to a machine.

"No, nor are the aimu. The Frame is my Master. May I ask a question?"

"Of course."

"Why do you not complete your sentences when you speak? You speak in fragments that I find hard to understand."

"Er, I did not realise that I was doing that."

"It is a lazy habit. You should work harder on your sentence structure."

"I will endeavour to do so, Gulukone." It was a bizarre exchange. Yayler could not think of anyone that didn't occasionally use fragmented sentences when talking to someone, but Gulukone seemed to find it difficult to understand an incomplete sentence. It was intriguing, almost as if he was thinking like a hiu. He was a very odd person. Yayler decided that it would be an interesting experiment to pass the time trying to find out more about him. "Gulukone, if the Frame is your Master how do you receive orders from it?"

It was Gulukone's turn to be intrigued. "The instructions appear in my mind. Do they not do so with you?"

"No, they certainly do not. My mind is independent of the Frame. You appear to be different."

"I am superior to divines in all ways. Perhaps this is an example of superiority?"

"Hmm, perhaps, but only from a certain, subjective point of view."

Gulukone furrowed his brow briefly "I do not understand. I can conceive multiple points of view simultaneously. To which are you referring."

"I refer to my own point of view. I do not wish to have a machine in my head all the time. I prefer independence of thought and decision-making."

Gulukone grinned; it was mirthless and mechanical. Yayler found it difficult to interpret as amusement. "I accept that as a point of view, but you are in error. Direct contact is more efficient."

"So the Frame is always aware of what you are doing?"

"Indeed so, this conversation is streamed to the main data banks of the Frame, who is, I must remind you, my Master."

"So you are in a symbiotic relationship?"

"Bio-silicon empathy, there is a sharing of consciousness." A pained expression crossed Gulukone's face as he spoke. "I have erred. I must return to my duties. You must not talk of these things again."

With that, Gulukone gently ushered Yayler away from the door and returned to his silent and implacable guard posture.

It was late at night and the all crew of the Banree were tense with anticipation. The nights were only a few wairs long at this latitude and time of year. They were almost half way through the month of Ooan, the fifth month of the year. Ooan had thirty-six days, so in two tendays it would be mid-year. They were all desperately thirsty and despite their best efforts to maintain Guvin's strict rationing routine, they had very little water left, probably, only enough for a single day. There had been no rain to test their rain collection system.

An island lay dead ahead and the crew nervously poled the Banree ahead towards a stream that flowed into a small bay. Guvin wanted complete silence and had ordered the crew to restrict communication to gestures and hand signs. They knew from charts that the island was remote, had few inhabitants, and didn't expect to be disturbed, but they could not afford any mistakes. The island was marked on the charts as a weather station and location beacon. The soil was a poor quality and mostly given over to pasture for wicks and cattle.

Guvin, Cullin, and Ecta were the shore party leaving Finnan and Goram on board the Banree. The three men dropped over the side of the boat and waded ashore carrying small, empty barrels. Once full and heavy with fresh water, these would have to be carried back to the Banree.

They quickly set themselves up by a rock pool filled by a series of little waterfalls. Guvin hoped that the noise made by the cascading water would mask any accidental sounds made by the crew. Using a pan from the galley Guvin slowly filled the first barrel. It was a painstaking process, as he did not wish to make any sloshing noises.

Ecta slipped quietly upstream, returning some sents later. He managed to report with hand signals that there was a path not far from where they were filling the barrels. Once filled the barrels would contain ten thousand oonsa and weigh in excess of one keakudram, roughly half the weight of a small man. They were not exactly heavy, but difficult to manoeuvre in flowing water. The first barrel was filled and being carried to the Banree when a small dog chanced upon them.

It was a lively, skinny little thing that bounded over the undergrowth, and stopped stock still when it saw the crew of the Banree in the water. It turned and raced back up the slope towards the path where it started to bark. Guvin gesticulated wildly to Cullin and Ecta to hurry with their barrel of precious water and hoicked the one he had started to fill out of the stream.

They could hear the dog barking madly above them on the path, clearly demanding the attention of its owner as they waded back to the Banree. Once they had the water on the deck they scrambled on board and poled the Banree back out to sea, even as a woman appeared looking surprised and dumfounded.

'How very strange' the woman thought to herself. 'Why did they not stop by at the station jetty and ask for what they needed?' The strange behaviour puzzled her. She had finished her duty at the beacon and was heading back the accommodation block located at the weather station. Her excitable four-legged companion had drawn her attention to the unusual, covert activities of the boat's crew. She determined to make a report as soon as she got back to the accommodation block.

The woman, Ani21, made a few mistakes in her report, describing the boat as a double masted tartane rather than a yawl, which would have been more accurate. Ani21 called the crew barbarics because their dress was quite different to anything she had seen before.

She usually enjoyed a glass of mixed juices before retiring. Barely had she started to search the racks for suitable fruits when she heard a chime from her service aimu. The service aimu whirred into the kitchen area and forwarded a request for more information on the boat she had seen earlier. The data request was asking for the boats name, size, the dress of the crew, any identification marks, or anything unusual.

Though she couldn't provide much more detail, she did her best and sent off the secondary report. There was an automated thank you message and she noted an increase in her credit, not that she needed much credit on this island.

She went to bed wondering what all the fuss was about a small fishing boat. Perhaps they were escaped slaves. That might explain their odd clothing. Perhaps they had committed some breach of regulations. That too would explain their odd behaviour. Ani 21 knew was that she would never

Chapter Fourteen

learn why the boat was important, but she went to bed with her might buzzing with possible scenarios.

The Frame had just received a report from an operator at a weather station on a tiny island called Aylanooan. The station was in an important location because it lay between two oceans, the Kuanmorack, the Geran Ocean, and the complex oceanic currents between the two vast bodies of water.

Search engines had identified the boat from a report from Aylanooan as the Banree Na Mur, which was a fishing boat from a small town in the district of Garvamore, called Pirt. The report linked several sightings of an old wooden fishing vessel, of which none came from the coastal waters of Pirt. Both boat and crew, previously assumed 'lost at sea', now appeared to be an erroneous record.

The Frame found it highly unlikely that the boat had made a passage through the frozen waters of the Geran Ocean. The Frame viewed the original specifications for the boat that showed a design for coastal waters and not such rough and dangerous waters. Yet the alternatives either took the boat past Fort Castle and Fort Tower or through the dangerous tidal bore of the Straits of Wrath. A third possibility existed through the narrow waters of Bancaol where the local aimu, posted there for security, was sure to have witnessed it.

Such speculative computations were pointless unless they provided answers to questions. In this case, those answers were not forthcoming. It was less important to the Frame that it understood how the boat made the journey, but why. What was the purpose of the crew and where were they going. The Frame calculated many possible routes and destinations and sent out more requests for information and sightings.

As to the purpose of the crew, the Frame had to presume an aggressive move on the part of the resistance movements. The Frame calculated other possibilities, such as a group of people trying to re-locate to a more temperate climate, but these represented little threat to it. Creation of list of possibilities and correlating probabilities took a while for the vast computer mind of the Frame and required input from the Interface, that group of systems created by the Frame to simplify communication and activities with people. How much easier it would be, not to have to deal with humans in the first place.

Once completed, that list demonstrated a near certainty that the crew of the Banree belonged to the resistance cell located in the district of Garvamore. The Frame calculated a very high chance of a resolution to that particular problem very soon. It seemed highly likely that they were attempting to link up with other resistance groups, if the connection with the resistance proved to be correct. The Frame would prevent that from happening.

Chapter Fifteen

Troomey and a team of technicians from Ecta's Ledge had finished installing cables collected from Dundoon and connected the power. He'd had to install large capacitors and safety devices, as the power from the generator would be constant and exceeded the estimated power requirements of the shield. He hoped there would be enough power left over to test Dook's Folly, another time consuming project.

Briga had been unhappy at Dook changing her duties. She had her own work to attend to, but she had quickly seen the implications of Troomey's work and set to work vigorously. Dook's Folly particularly excited her. Dook had requested her help a few days ago on his return from Dundoon with a flier crammed with equipment and materials.

Those few days had been a fury of activity for the staff of Rustick More. Dook pushed them hard, accepting extraordinary achievements with an unemotional calmness that belied his real feelings, before asking for more hard work and total commitment. The people got on with their thankless tasks, cursing Dook behind his back. 'Why does he not say Thank you' they might say, or 'he's not human, that man', or 'I'm sure he's the Diaval's brother, that man' or other caustic remarks.

During this time, Dook himself had been conspicuously absent, appearing occasionally to check on progress and demanding more work done before heading back to his rooms. Troomey was more used to this behaviour than the majority of people working at Rustick More. However, even he found the intensity and pressure too much.

Troomey completed a last connection with a triumphant flourish and turned to Briga who was testing connections and components on Dook's Folly. "Are we ready?"

"I am, Troomey, if you are. Who put this component in? Its' connections seem to be wrong."

Troomey glanced at a small cubic part and nodded "Aye, it's been put in upside down, probably by one of our young lads. You have all the best technicians, you know." He grinned mirthlessly. "Those connections should be here, here and here." He indicated various metal tabs that were without wire connections. "I'll let you do that little job, I ought to find Dook then." Troomey left Briga cursing about a 'bodge job' under her breath.

Troomey found Dook in his rooms hunched over the sarcophagus, frowning and muttering to himself. "Are you busy Dook?"

Dook looked up with a mixture of surprise and bafflement. "Aye, I can't find a way to break into this thing. The material is incredibly hard and the thing seems to be made of a single piece. There is no lid or opening, so how was the body put in there?"

"I'm sure you'll work it out. Why do you want to open it?"

A look of utter bafflement briefly crossed Dook's face before he replied. "Why? To study it."

"Isn't there enough to do?" Troomey had a momentary feeling of dread as he imagined himself working on a dead man's coffin on top of all his other duties. It passed and he determined to let Dook get on with it, without assistance from him.

", But I want to know more about it. Why go to such effort to seal a dead man in something like this? It doesn't make sense." Dook was clearly frustrated, and would nibble away at the problem until he realise the effort was futile or he found some kind of answer.

"Oh, well, I thought you might like to know we're about to test the shield. I thought you might be interested."

"Oh, aye, indeed I am."

A large crowd had assembled in anticipation on Toiler's Woe to witness the event. A large junction box installed on the wall near the hanger opening had cables leading in several directions. Troomey stood by a large central switch, which he grasped with both hands and heaved into the open position.

Nothing happened and a couple of people wandered off, disappointed with the show. Troomey slid open a panel next to the main junction box switch where there were a number of small rocker switches, each with a neatly written label. Troomey selected one and pressed it, then paused, waiting.

Dook looked profoundly unimpressed and rubbed his face with irritation before sipping from a full mug of ale, which he had somehow spirited from the canteen. "Well, Troomey? Is it on?"

"Oh, aye. It needs to power up though."

More of the crowd began to leave. They had expected a show and this was about as exciting as watching rocks dry after a rain shower. Troomey was unperturbed; he wasn't intending to provide a show. He was watching a little black box next to the rocker switch that buzzed quietly. Suddenly there was a click and a little red button shot out from a recess. He now pressed another rocker switch and stood back, satisfied.

Again, nothing appeared to be happening.

Dook regarded Troomey over the top of his ale mug with raised eyebrows. "Is it on now, Troomey?"

"Oh, Aye, it's on and functioning perfectly well."

"So, why isn't it doing anything?"

More of the crowd departed, scratching their heads or muttering about 'a waste of time', thinking that whatever show there was, was now over.

"It doesn't do anything, unless the field interacts with an object or another field."

"So how do we know if it's on or not?" This wasn't what Dook was expecting either. He wanted something more tangible and positive. He had come over to stand next to Troomey, glancing over the array of switches that had been manufactured in a very short space of time at Rustick More. "Will it do what is needed?

"Er, I see your point." Only a handful of people now remained of the crowd. A few people, Neev, Dona, and a few of Troomey's closest associates remained; those who knew that he seldom failed. Belatedly Troomey realised that they needed a more dramatic demonstration was required, not just the closing of a few contacts and saying 'there you go, it's working'. "May I borrow that for a moment?" Troomey indicated Dook's ale mug and taking it from Dook.

Surprise gave way to horror. Dook's jaw dropped as he watched Troomey stride over to the hanger opening and sling the contents of the mug into the void beyond. They never reached. There was a crackle and buzz as the droplets interacted with the shield creating a mottled green tinge that radiated across the opening before dissipating as equilibrium within the field returned to normal.

Neev slid over a metal rod that someone had left by Dook's Folly. "Here, try something bigger." The rod clattered and clanged across the floor and came to rest close by Troomey's feet.

"Let's see." Troomey picked up the rod and threw it at the shield. He knew that the shield worked against the divines' energy weapons and was not, originally intended as, a shield against solid objects. The ale worked as it contained dissociated ions that interacted with the energy field. A solid metal bar, unless magnetised, might pass straight through.

The bar arced through the air and caused green ripples to flow across the shield. The bar perceptibly slowed in its flight, but passed through to fall, almost gracefully, to the foot of Rustick More. "Neev, do you have a short staff handy?"

"Why didn't it work, Troomey?" called out a disappointed Dook.

As Neev went to fetch the energy weapon, Troomey explained the weakness of the shield. That it could only interact with charged particles.

When Neev handed the short staff to Troomey, he fumbled with it, unsure how to hold or fire it. "Let me." Neev gently urged, knowing that Troomey had never fired one before, or, indeed used any weapon.

Neev aimed the weapon at the centre of the shield and fired a quick short blast. The shield flared a bright green as the energy from the weapon was absorbed. She fired again, a longer, sustained blast and the shield flared again, becoming brighter, almost incandescent as the shields field emitted photons created by the interaction of weapon and shield.

Dook was delighted and clapped Troomey on his back to show his appreciation. "For a moment there, I was wondering if it was going to work. How strong is it?"

"I have no idea. There will be more tests and refining to do." Troomey admitted.

Neev added her congratulations and asked "why does it glow green. I thought the shields were more bluish."

"Aye they do, but I changed the frequency to make it work more efficiently. That will be one of the tests I have to do, erm, see how it works with the personnel shields"

Chapter Fifteen

"Don't spend too long on tests, Troomey. I want that big gunna working too." Dook had his arm about Troomey's shoulder in a friendly gesture.

"We're about ready to start testing that too." Briga called out. She hadn't known Troomey long and still felt a bit awkward in his presence. "There are a few more circuits and components to check."

Dook looked at her with surprise. "Excellent! We may have a few surprises for the narid when they come. I'll want you to go and build a shield for Dundoon next. That is where they are most likely to strike."

Troomey felt deflated at the idea. After the joyful high of completing the shield project (or at least making a successful test), he had hoped there would be a break from the intensity of work, but, as always with Dook, more work followed. He was not a young man anymore and felt the strain of the workload, but he did see a glimmer of hope for a break or rest. At least Dook wouldn't be breathing down his neck at Dundoon, pushing him hard all the time to the extent that he felt he was on the verge of a breakdown.

Dook was in a cheerful mood. He could see the defences of his home looking stronger. "Well," he announced "I'll leave you all to get on. I have my own work to attend to."

Dona made a cheeky rejoinder "probably involving a jar, mug and a lot of ale."

"That would be nice, Dona, but the chances seem unlikely just recently." He mournfully indicated the ale mug that now rested, untidily on its side.

Later, back in his rooms, Dook was indeed enjoying a jar of ale. His staff knew him too well, he thought, but he didn't really mind. He enjoyed ale and that was that. They could think what they will. He sipped contemplatively as he studied the sarcophagus. The thing was a conundrum that had trapped him with his determination to find a solution.

Dook had searched over every miniscule part of the sarcophagus without finding any blemish that might indicate a means of opening it as if someone had sealed the corpse someone within without any intention of ever opening the sarcophagus again. He found that to be a chilling and alarming thought. Could it contain contagion? Perhaps some form of plague? Eventually, he gave up on his pondering and retired to his bed after finishing his mugful with one long swallow, but otherwise leaving the jug almost untouched.

He woke early after a disturbed and troubled night of images of people, places, and projects blended and melded into surreal dreams in his semiconscious. Strange distorted visions formed an artificial and uneasy reality. Dook turned in his sleep, muttering unintelligibly before falling silent again. His dreaming mind filled with visions of wasted landscapes, and people with machine bodies paying obeisance to bizarre flickering lights and machines giving birth to distorted mockeries of life, all blending together into an alarming melange.

Gradually the images faded, becoming lost and irretrievable as consciousness reasserted itself. Dook became aware of another presence in the room. He sat up, stared about him in the half-light, and took several, long moments to realise that the sarcophagus was open.

There, standing at his table was a huge figure with its back to him. Dressed in a single-piece, white body suit, it was steadily leafing through piles of his notes in the dimness. Slowly the figure turned and gazed down at Dook. The next action of the huge figure made Dook think he was still asleep. It lifted the ale jug from the table and croaked a single word "More". Dook's mind raced in frantic panic. He did not know what to do.

"I am thirsty. I need to make micturition." The creature croaked.

Dook decided that 'creature' was the most apt description of the figure, as it didn't appear to be exactly human. It still required the basics of life, fluids, or water. Such simple requests jolted Dook from inaction. "You can use the facilities in that room, there." Dook vaguely indicated the bathing room.

The creature headed into the room uncertainly and returned moments later. "I am unfamiliar with these facilities. I require your assistance."

After explaining how to use the bathing room, and discovering that the creature had no genitals Dook pondered over how to manage this new problem. He couldn't very well have it wandering about Rustick More, but neither would he be able to keep it unobserved and a secret a for long. In the end, he decided not to bother. "I will take you to where refreshments are available, but first you must tell me your name. I am Dookerock and this is my home."

The giant looked blankly at Dook, as if wondering whether to answer, then it croaked "I am Anbooakil. Bring me refreshments now."

Big Jon was the only person in the canteen when Dook and Anbooakil entered and he stared open mouthed, unsure whether to believe his eyes or not. Dook was a tall man and well built. Big Jon was taller and broader, though overweight. Anbooakil was 'head and shoulders' above both of them and powerfully built. The creature's presence was daunting.

"Morning Jon. This is Anbooakil "Dook announced" It is requesting ale. I suspect it will want food as well."

Big Jon would normally have several big pans of milk and oats gently heating before anyone else awoke. This day was no exception and he was able to finish cooking a small batch of porridge that was ready before he was able to broach a fresh ale barrel. Thus, he was able to serve two jugs of ale and two large bowls of steaming porridge in very short order.

Dook poured himself a mugful and drank thoughtfully. It wasn't strong ale, but well flavoured with heather and herbs. Anbooakil downed his jug in one long, continuous swallow.

"More" it croaked, though perhaps less coarsely than before.

"Anbooakil, do you mind if I ask you where you came from?"

"I do not know" came the answer.

"You don't know where you were born?"

There was a long pause before Anbooakil answered and when it came, Dook found the answer astounding. "I am not sure that I was born. I simply was not and then I was."

"I don't really understand that. Let me ask another way. When were you born?"

Again, there was a long pause. "I gained consciousness three wairs and forty-two sents ago. Is that what you mean by 'born'?"

Dook shook his head. There appeared to be some misunderstanding. "That is when you woke up. That isn't what I mean. I was asking when your mother gave birth to you."

"I did not have a mother. I was not and then I was. I have already told you this. Today is my first day."

"That cannot be. You must have grown. You didn't just appear fully-grown with intelligence and knowledge. How did you learn language and how to speak?

Anbooakil looked troubled. "I do not know." The giant went silent and contemplative for a long while before speaking again. "I believe you might be correct. I have no recollection of anything before today. Perhaps I have been ill and have lost these memories."

"Well, Anbooakil, I know of a way to find out."

"I would be grateful for the knowledge."

Dook noticed that Anbooakil's voice was no longer coarse and harsh, but the tone had mellowed, taking on a more musical quality with a higher pitch than would be expected of such a large person. The canteen was now filling with people looking to break their fast and they were looking oddly at Anbooakil as if it shouldn't really be there. Dook decided that he would have to call everyone to a meeting to explain the creature's appearance. First, though, he needed more information.

"Have you eaten and drank enough?" Dook asked thinking that someone as big as Anbooakil would have a vast appetite.

"Thank you" came the reply. "I have had sufficient for now, I will need more food later."

Dook took Anbooakil to the room where Yayler and he had previously implanted divine enhancements into Cullin's body. The giant might find a familiarity about the room. That could trigger some of Anbooakil's lost or suppressed memories. Dook felt certain that the sarcophagus was some kind of medical pod and someone had placed the giant being in it for a reason. Illness was unlikely, so what was the reason?

Dook blinked in the harsh unnatural light of the room. He always preferred the softer, more muted light found elsewhere in Rustick More. Yayler had been responsible for the set up in this room as he understood the technology the best.

The table stood on its crystalline plinth and Dook ushered the giant over to it. "Would you mind lying on the table, then we can start to answer a few questions for you."

"I cannot use this facility" Anbooakil replied looking down with distaste at the delicate appearance of the table.

"Why not?" Dook asked quietly so as not to offend.

"It is too small" Anbooakil replied simply.

Chapter Fifteen

"Ah, that is so." Dook agreed and thought for a moment. "This table is intended for simple procedures, but there is another, larger one for more complex operations."

Anbooakil looked about the room with a slightly confused expression, but waited patiently for Dook to elaborate. A series of cabinets lined one wall, but Dook ignored them and went to the plain featureless wall opposite and, after a little searching, found a small indentation.

"This particular unit is seldom used and I'm not very familiar with it. It mostly works automatically, so I think I'll manage." Dook passed his hand over the indentation and stood back.

Fine lines appeared and hidden partitions in the wall drew back, revealing another, silver coloured, table lengthways within a hidden recess. The table slid outward silently, turning as it did so, until it stood centrally in the room. The table stood as did its smaller partner, on a crystalline plinth. At one end, there were a series of thick, white plaz hoops and a bulbous swelling and a piece of headgear composed of a simple ring of white plaz.

"It is a med-couch." Anbooakil stated simply.

"Aye, that is what my friend Yayler Poddick calls it."

"I can operate this machine. It is a simple piece of equipment."

"How can you know this if today is your first day, Anbooakil?" There it was again, the enigma of how the giant could have language and knowledge on it's first day of existence.

"I do not know. I shall set the med-couch to do an automatic scan. You will only need to initiate the procedure." Anbooakil's fingers flickered briefly over the bulbous end of the med-couch, and then as he placed his hand onto it a three-dimensional display appeared above it.

When he had finished the set-up Anbooakil lay upon the couch and placed the plaz ring on his head. Dook placed his hand on the bulge as soon as Anbooakil lay upon it and his finger implants connected with the med-couch computer. It was simple enough for him to operate as he moved a virtual hand around the display. Dook watched as the plaz hoops traversed along the med-couch, and a detailed three-dimensional image appeared alongside it.

The first thing that Dook noticed was that Anbooakil had a great deal of enhancement technology, but otherwise the giant was as human as any other person. As the scan continued, it revealed no sign of any injury or illness; in fact, Anbooakil was remarkably healthy. A scan always revealed a defect somewhere within a person's body, however insignificant it might be, but with Anbooakil, there was absolutely none. What the scan did reveal, however, was something else.

"This is very peculiar Anbooakil. I don't know how to say this delicately, so I will just say it. You have no gender; you are neither man nor woman. You are not hermaphrodite as that implies both in the same person. You simply have no reproductive capability of any kind."

"Possibly, I have no need for reproduction." Anbooakil remained motionless on the med-couch, but a puzzled expression was present as he spoke.

"Hold still, Anbooakil, the scan is still going."

The brain scan took awhile to complete and revealed a highly developed frontal lobe and a battery of implants, most of which Dook recognised, but not the one that seemed to have a switching mechanism. It was currently in an 'off' status. Dook left it that way.

They returned to Dook's rooms after the scans were complete via the canteen where Dook asked for refreshments.

"How do I refer to you, Anbooakil? I can't call you 'he', or 'she', for you are neither. I can't call you 'it' because that implies that you are not a person. Should I just say 'ey' instead, that implies nothing." Dook was relaxing in his chair with his mind buzzing. The scan asked more questions than it answered. The enigma of Anbooakil was compellingly interesting, proving to be very interesting.

"I am happy to be referred to as ey. It is fitting." Anbooakil sat cross-legged on the floor facing Dook. He was placid and passive.

"Good, now, what do we know now that we didn't before?"

"I do not know. You have seen the scans, I have not."

"Let me try something then." Dook placed his right palm against Anbooakil's and found they were able to connect.

They now had no need of physical conversation as they could converse directly mind-to-mind. Words became superfluous, as one person could understand a concept from another person without the need of clumsy, awkward forms such as words or gestures. This was a deeper form of communication. A person generally translates their thoughts and ideas into words and gestures. Mind-to-mind communication avoided the clumsiness and inherent errors that came with language and gestures.

Dook had created for himself a mindscape that helped him remember details and facts about people he knew. He created a new structure within that mindscape and attached Anbooakil's name label to it. He placed an image of the giant within that structure and addressed it.

'*This is your place within my mind. Here we can communicate privately.*' Dook used no words to communicate ideas, they simply were.

'*I understand.*'

'*This is a copy of the scans we made earlier. You should study them.*' Dook searched his neuro-chips for the scans taken earlier. This took a small fraction of time and the scans appeared as a virtual file, which he handed over to the giant. The file disappeared as Anbooakil held it.

'*It is an interesting file. I have learned much from it.*'

'*Aye, so have I. The scan shows that you are a divine, but not like any divine I have ever seen before.*'

Anbooakil paused as he thought about the new data he had been given. '*I would seem that I greater than divine, I have been enhanced. I have grown from embryo in the diakemaklag and I am now ready for activation.*'

Without being told, Dook knew that Anbooakil referred to the sarcophagus, that was an embryonic growth chamber, which delivered a fully-grown person. The chamber also provided knowledge to the growing person so that they were fully functional from embryo to adult in three years. How very typically efficient of the Frame, mused Dook. '*You are aware that divines are servants of the Frame?*'

'*Affirmative.*'

'*So, what is your allegiance to the Frame?*'

'*It is my Creator!*'

Chapter Sixteen

Yayler felt the quiet and constant thrum of the ships engines change in tone. The pitch became deeper, so he assumed the ship was slowing down. Such a subtle difference made a noticeable change to his dull incarceration that Yayler wondered if anyone else on the ship had noticed it. With nothing better to do, he timed to the next change. He could do this precisely using his cerebral neuro-enhancements and was surprised to note that there was exactly a half wair between changes in engine pitch and tone.

Almost another half a wair later there was a knock on the door and Gulukone entered. "You are to come with me." There was politeness or softness in the giants tone. This was a command, purely and simply a command.

Since their last conversation, Gulukone had barely spoken to Yayler. He gave instructions that were essentially orders. Yayler was now at one of the lowest points in his long life. He was unhappy, even depressed, but he still had determination, a drive that had consumed him for so many decades that the time spent became meaningless. Patience and time would deliver the opportunities to move forward with his plans.

Yayler followed Gulukone along brightly lit corridors and up a number of flights of stairs and finally, along another corridor and into a large room with many divines sitting or standing at their stations. Each station had a three-dimensional display with information about the various functions of the ship.

Three sides of the room had large windows through which Yayler could see a number of other ships. Clar15 was standing before one of the windows with a large aimu, a hiu, standing next to her with its headless form facing the room. Gulukone ushered Yayler over toward them.

"As you can see Victor, we have been joined by an aimu fleet. We shall be travelling now to that insignificant group of islands you call home." Clar15 did not turn to face Yayler as she spoke.

The hiu spoke with a a mechanical grating devoid of feeling or compassion. "You will scape now, or you will be ended."

Yayler had little option, offered up his hand, and placed it on the hiu's breastplate. He took on a slack, defocused appearance as he made the connection with the machine. He would have to be very careful to remain focused. A hiu, once connected with a person, could download data from neuro-chips very rapidly. Yayler had a great deal of data stored artificially in this manner that he wished to keep private. As he concentrated, the muscles in his face twitched involuntarily, as if he was suffering from some form of mental seizure. This was quite normal in these situations and, as a matter of politeness, divine society would not comment on such things.

Without, Yayler appeared slack-jawed, but mentally he entered his mindscape, an imaginary construct that enabled efficient interaction between hius and divines. The hiu appeared in his mindscape as a shadowy figure behind an array of icons. Communication was a complicated mix of imagery, words and data that was almost instantaneous.

The first communication from the hiu was in the form of a command that came with instructions on which icon the hiu wished a response downloaded. '*You will download your intention and purpose.*'

Yayler had to think quickly, but found his mind slow and sluggish after his lengthy incarceration in a single room, He had to hide his real purpose, yet still provide a satisfactory response. He decided to keep his responses simple. '*To preserve life.*'

'*Your response is inconsistent and incomplete. What life do you wish to preserve? Explain your purpose in seeking an army.*'

The hiu's aggressive questioning pushed Yayler into a defensive position. He did not know what information Clar15 had given it. She certainly knew his intentions, but he could not be sure whether she had reported them or not. Yayler thought it would be odd for her not to. Was there trickery in the hiu's questioning? Was it trying to manoeuvre a wrong answer from him? He had to assume that was the case. Again, he made the simplest response he could. 'I wish to defend my home, my life, and those of my neighbours.'

'*Against what do you wish to defend?*'

'*There has recently been fighting on a neighbouring island.*' It was a factual statement, but Yayler knew it did not answer the question.

'*How do you know this?*'

'*News of such things travels fast by word of mouth.*'

'*Your statement is factual, but your knowledge may be incomplete.*' The hiu included a data package that included imagery taken from the recent battle

Chapter Sixteen

at Dundoon and the assertion from the Frame that the rebel army had been defeated. '*As you can see from reports, there is no need for you to make any attempt to acquire an army. The Frame would organise defence of your neighbourhood if that were necessary. There is no such necessity.*'

Yayler continued his prevarication, still hoping he could mislead the hiu. '*I am grateful for this.*'

'*Your disappearance is a troubling matter. Reports state that you died in a mining accident. You are now required to provide more data about that incident. Failure to make a satisfactory response will result in your ending.*'

Why could it not say 'killed' or 'executed'? That is what it meant. Yayler had a sinking feeling, an inescapable feeing that judgement had already been made on him. He had known that it was a possibility, but the reward for the aneksa for his risking his life was immeasurable. Yayler had prepared a file with a carefully constructed explanation of the events of the mining accident based on facts, but not the full details of his part in the incident. He had prepared other, similar files that he might use for his defence. Yayler slid the file into the hiu's pre-action icon.

There was a pause while the hiu analysed the data, comparing it against previously known event data. '*Your report is consistent with known the events and has been added to the Frame's database. Your survival is not understood; you are required to explain your survival.*'

Yayler placed a pre-prepared file into the hiu's pre-action icon. The file contained an explanation that he had been the Security Officer and feared that blame would be attributed to himself for the incident. The punishment for such failure in divine society was execution. They may use the term 'ending', but it amounted to the same thing. Yayler had included in the file an explanation that made the expectation to prevent the disaster unreasonable and, thus unpredictable. If the hiu accepted his arguments and explanations, he might live. If not, then his life expectancy would be very short.

The hiu paused briefly again, analysing the new data. It would be a very literal examination of every word; every item of data studied and compared to the last detail. '*The data supplied is accurate and consistent with previously stored data and will be added to the database. The incident at Resource Mine 279 was a significant one. The resource complex still does not perform at its previous efficiency. The data you have supplied demonstrates a degree of neglect on your part. Your lack of diligence caused significant harm to the Frame which is likely to have resulted in your ending. Your actions are consistent with inefficient human behaviour and are unacceptable'.*

Yayler involuntarily tensed himself for what he knew to be coming. The hiu would deliver the sentence, swiftly followed by its execution. Electronic scrambling of his brain would be instantaneous and he would know nothing about it. There would be no pain. He would have no knowledge that it was occurring. The Frame considered it the 'kindest' way to end a life. It was certainly an efficient method of killing. The Frame though, was a machine and could have no concept of kindness.

The hiu continued *'From the data now available the Frame is able to conclude that you have attempted to instigate rebellion against it and your life is now forfeit. It is possible that you will be of use in the forthcoming rebellion eradication process. For that reason, the Frame will spare your life. The Frame reduces you to the ranking of citizen and Gulukone will continue your protection. Do you have anything to add?'*

'*No.*' What else could Yayler say?

'*The Frame requires data on the place called Rustick More. You will prepare your knowledge and this inquisition will continue tomorrow at this time. Your refusal to co-operate would be unwise. If you are not useful to the Frame, I am authorised to carry out the sentence of ending.*'

Abruptly the images of the hiu in Yayler's mindscape vanished as the connection between them was terminated. Gulukone escorted Yayler back to his spartan room and resumed his post. Though he was feeling quite dejected and hopeless, Yayler couldn't help but ask the giant a few questions. "Gulukone, do you not get tired? You have been stationed outside my door now for, what, seven days? What relief have you been given?"

"Citizen, I do not require relief. I do not tire. I attend to my physical needs while you sleep. You must now attend to the instructions you have been given." As always, Gulukone remained passive and polite.

"I will." Then it struck Yayler, that Gulukone was much like a machine. Many divines strove for machinelike efficiency, but with Gulukone, it seemed to be significant part of his persona. He chanced a question. "What will happen to you, when you no longer serve a purpose?"

"I am unsure what you mean by the question."

"There may come a time when the Frame no longer has any use for you. What happens to you then?"

Chapter Sixteen

Gulukone frowned and then spoke gently. "I would no longer be required; I would be decommissioned, ended."

Yayler settled himself down on his bunk. "How does that make you feel?"

"I do not know." Gulukone had the look of someone greatly troubled by an uncomfortable thought.

"I can foresee a time when the Mustanians will become superfluous. What happens to them, then?"

"If the Mustanians serve no purpose, then they too, would be ended." Gulukone's troubled face took on a new emotion, puzzlement. "It would not be permitted for resource users to continue functioning, if they did not serve a purpose."

Yayler thought about that last statement. He found it very curious and deeply disturbing. "What do you mean by 'resource users'?"

Gulukone's face brightened slightly. "Anything that consumes, uses or alters Inalsol's resources is referred to as a resource user."

"So any resource user that no longer serves the Frame's purposes will be ended?"

"Indeed, that is the case. I hope this conversation has been of use to you."

"It has certainly been interesting and gives me much to think about." Yayler had much indeed to think about. Gulukone had revealed a very dark philosophy. "All life on Inalsol uses the planets' resources in some way, if that life does not serve the Frame, then will it not be ended?"

"I do not know. I do not think this conversation is permissible."

"Why not? Does the Frame control the very conversations you have?"

"The Frame is aware of any conversation that I have and has the capacity to punish me for any errant thoughts or beliefs that I communicate."

"That is interesting. What you seem to be saying is that the Frame controls your thoughts and beliefs, at least to a certain extent."

Gulukone had paused by the door. "That is correct, Citizen."

Yayler continued pressing a point. He doubted it would make a difference to him in the end, but at least he would have said it. He had no idea what his bodyguards reaction would be. "The Frame has a very fixed view of the Universe, but is just another part of Creation, after all.

"Creation is an infinite number of infinite universes, all of which are different. The Frame controls all of Inalsol rigidly, yet different views persist, why? Even if the Frame managed to control all belief and thought on Inalsol and force all to conform to its dictates, then, new ideas would still emerge, and thus different views. Thus, the Frame cannot force its viewpoint on all Creation, nor even all of Inalsol. There has to be variation. The muckers are just such a variation."

"Why do you say this to me? I cannot listen to your imperfect ideas. I do not wish for your punishment." With that, Gulukone closed the door on Yayler and took up his station.

Yayler was plunged back into a long period of solitude and contemplation. He did not know what dark thoughts he had triggered within Gulukone's mind, but the big man had listened.

Pyta was regretting his lack of fitness. After his expulsion from Garvin with rough music, he found himself walking to his new destination, Balgeel. Had he realised it was so far, he would have made different plans. Perhaps he would have stolen a horse. One of the crofters near Garvin had one. It was an old nag, but still able to pull a cart. The journey might not have been much faster, but at least he would not have been so tired. His feet were sore and blistered and his body ached from the effort of continuous walking.

The nights were the worst trial for him. They were cold, not the bitter cold of winter, but a subtle chill that entered the bones and sucked his energy from him. It was a relief for him to start walking again each morning. Of course, after a short while, flaccid muscles would start to complain and add to his misery. Three days of painful footslogging had brought him to the belack above the village of Balgeel.

Balgeel straggled along the road without any obvious centre or focal point, and the best thing about the place was that no one knew who Pyta was. He was confident that he could start rebuilding his life again in such a sleepy, degenerate village and move on again when it suited him.

High on the hillside above the village, prominent and proud, stood the Kirk. Pyta shuddered, 'what a ridiculous place to put a place of worship' he thought. He would have built the Kirk in the middle of the village. Pyta regarded the Kirk with distaste and animosity. What had the people of the Kirk ever done for him? Nothing!

Pyta spat onto the muddy gutter of the track. He regarded the Kirk with sick amusement. Its broad tower with anterooms either side looked comical. Pyta grinned viciously; the Kirks had nothing of value for him, his first stop would be the Inn. There, at least, he could get refreshment. The Kirks gave nothing, but dictates and rules. He was not interested in such things.

Pyta checked his pockets for his pouch of tokens and quickly found its comfortable reassuring weight. He found himself looking forward with anticipation to a comfortable pallet, dry warmth and a few ales.

Chapter Seventeen

Goram was thirsty; in fact, all of the crew of the Banree were thirsty. Although Guvin insisted that the water situation was not critical, as it had been before, he had still reduced the water ration to two muga per day. There had been no rain in the four days since the aborted stop at the island to replenish their supplies. This caused frustration for Guvin, as he could not remember having been at sea for so long without rain.

Because of the neuro-chips, Yayler had given him, Cullin 'knew' where the shipping lanes were and between himself and Guvin, they could plot a route to avoid them. The wind was slack, the sea calm and they made poor headway. They were now in the Kuanmorack Ocean, a vast body of water with few islands and little prospect of collecting more water in the way they had done on their previous, abortive attempt.

Guvin even allowed Goram to take the tiller. There was a lot more time for the crew to relax. They spent time on general repairs to the Banree to keep themselves busy. Toward evening, in the gloaming light, Guvin had tide tiller and summoned the crew to the cabin they used as a common room.

"Well, Gentlemen, there is no way to say this nicely, but if we don't cut water rations, there is little chance of our reaching land before running out of fresh water."

"Don't worry it will rain soon. I can smell it! It will rain before the day is out." Finnan assured Guvin sagely.

"I hope you're right, but there isn't a cloud in the sky." Guvin replied "I suggest we enjoy this evening and get a decent rest, because from tomorrow onwards I'm reducing water rations to one muga per day."

There were groans of dismay around the cabin. Goram was seething with discontent at the news and was about to say something caustic when a gentle squeeze on his shoulder from Cullin warned him to remain silent and keep the peace.

"I know the water rationing is bad news, but we have to be careful. I have a small barrel of whisky we can broach, and suggest a few songs and stories." There were nods of agreement to Guvin's suggestion. Even Goram seemed somewhat mollified. "Why don't you start, Goram? I heard you singing to yourself at the tiller earlier. You have a good voice."

Goram was a little unsettled at being the centre of attention, but thought for a moment, then cleared his throat. He began a slow melody of humorous lyrics about a man who fell into a river after drinking too much with friends, he then moved on without pause to another, faster piece that made no sense at all, but with lyrics that were amusing tongue twisters.

When Goram had finished, Finnan clapped him on the back and laughing, pounded his fist on the cabin table. "Whisky for the bard!"

Guvin obliged and gave Goram a small measure from the now, broached whisky cask. He had fetched the cask from beneath his bunk during Goram's performance.

"The caller must perform" Guvin announced, meaning that Finnan should now provide some entertainment.

This was a game that Guvin had devised to build morale. It did not matter what they did, it could be musical, a story, a joke, or anything that came to mind. Finnan knew the game well and had a long list of stories and anecdotes to call upon. "I shall tell you of Hana of the Croftingway, Finnan began.

> Many a year has gone, they say
> Since Hana of the Croftingway
> Sweet as the morning dew, was she
> Charitable and kind, was she
>
> Her Husband was a beast of a man
> A drunken waste of a man
> He would beat her
> And would demean her
>
> Being kind, she would forgive
> Though unhappily did she live
> Never gaining what she wanted
> Never given love she needed
>
> And one day when feeling low
> Down by the greenwood she did go
> For some time to clear her mind

Chapter Seventeen

And escape from her daily grind

And there the Heraveg Stones stood
High as the silent trees of the greenwood
That could not tell her to beware
Of enchantment that knew not care

For the great stones were a gateway
To a land of faerie and of fey
To the land of the King of Arkell
A faerie King, escaped from hell

Between the Heraveg, Hana made her way
Clouds of her troubled mind did fade away
Her heart, clear and peaceful
And she was happy and joyful

And by the stones there was a stream
Beguiled, enraptured as in a dream
Sweet, and cool and crystal bright
So she followed toward the sunlight

Fairflies danced with twinkling light
Emerald eyes and gossamer sight
Shimmering gold were their wings
Honeyed melodies they would sing

Bewitched she followed into dream
Their song up the golden stream
So long since joy she'd known
Not since from child she'd grown

Hana ascended by the water
To the fall of golden water
There to greet the light of dawn
There she met the resplendent fawn

A magic crystal flute the fawn did play
Entranced, Hana wished she could stay
She danced with the sparkling fairflies
Till the wondrous fawn did rise

Fancy diamond flowers did gleam
Brilliantly lit by magic sunbeam
All these were a heavenly thing
And joy to her heart did bring

Then up above she met a man
And beautiful was that man
Graciously said he would set her free
And offered her all she could see

Said he would give her restful peace
And said all her pain would cease
To her wonderful things would give
If only for him she would live

So enchanted was she
No fault in him could see
Blind to cloven feet he bore
And for him then she knelt before

'Give your heart to me
and I will set you free
no more suffering and pain
There's peace for you to gain'

Hana pledged to him her heart so kind
Yearned for gift of peace to find
Then on that hill, she stood alone
And she was turned to stone

And in his marble hall, did dwell
That wicked man of Arkell
Another kindly soul he bore
As many stole before

As Finnan finished his tale, outside could be heard the light patter of rain.

"Whisky for the Bard" called out Ecta and Guvin duly gave out a generous measure. "I thought you were a seaman, Finnan, but that is very much a mountain-man's story?"

"Aye", Finnan sipped at his whisky before answering "I grew up in mountains nearby the sea. That was a long time ago, now".

Guvin then went out onto the deck, coming back some moments later grinning so broadly that it seemed that his face would split." Your story has caused the heavens to weep, Finnan."

Buoyed by the arrival of the rain, the spirits of the crew rose and the story telling went on. Guvin reduced the measure of whisky judiciously, but they were all a little less than sober when he finally stowed the whisky cask back under his bunk.

Most of the crew retired to their bunks, but Cullin and Guvin stayed up and went out onto the deck. After a couple of wairs, Finnan would be woken and replace Guvin on the tiller.

"I noticed you didn't drink much whisky?" Guvin questioned idly as he settled himself by the tiller.

"Nay, I don't like the stuff particularly. I like to keep my wits."

"Aye, that's a good plan. The game does help the crew to bond, important when you may rely on them for your life."

"Guvin, may I ask how much longer this voyage will last? Only we can't contact Dook until we land, and we do need to know what's happening back home."

"That is a good question, Cullin. Of course, we will reach land when we reach land and no sooner. I expect it to take another tenday, but it may be longer." Guvin was watching the tell-tales on the mainsail and judging the force of the wind from them. "Wind is picking up a bit Cullin. Best make sure everything is battened down."

"Aye, it's dark too, no stars. Good job I can see well in the dark."

Although the Banree was not a big boat as such things go, it still took Cullin almost a half a wair to complete his checks. He noted cheerfully that rainwater was running nicely into the catchment barrel. He could make out the burbling sound as it gushed through the pipes. By the time he finished the rain was falling harder. He returned to a dour looking Guvin at the tiller.

"Checks done, Guvin, everything looks fine" Cullin reported. "Twenty-one days without rain, and then we get it all in one go! Does this happen often at sea?"

"Don't forget the storms in the Varamor and the Wild Sea, they count, even if we couldn't use the water." Guvin was a very stoical man; he couldn't

Chapter Seventeen

change the nature of weather, so he didn't let it worry him. He dealt with whatever fortune gave him by finding solutions and not griping about the problems.

The night wore on and the rain became heavier, the wind stronger and the waves bigger. Cullin assisted Guvin on the tiller until Finnan emerged on deck looking irritable and rubbing his head.

Finnan relieved Guvin at the tiller and shouted at Cullin over the noise of the wind "I fell out of my bunk!"

"What?" shouted Cullin back.

"I banged my head."

"Oh." Cullin was feeling tired; it was a weariness of the mind that drained his will to continue. The voyage had been one trial after another. He felt cooped up on the little boat, trapped, and he yearned for the open space of a hillside and a cool breeze. He knew there was nothing he could do about the weather that had caused most of the problems on the Banree. He knew he had simply to get on with the job, but he felt frustrated and out of control. On land, he was better able to control events rather than let events control him, as on the Banree.

The storm raged on, oblivious to the feelings and exhaustion of the crew. Mountainous seas continually swamped the deck and pitched the boat about alarmingly. The morning saw them off course and dangerously close to the shipping lanes that they had hoped to avoid.

They all needed rest and sleep; but at least, there would be no rest until he could assure himself that the Banree was out of danger. He ordered Cullin below as the others had at least had some rest before the onset of the storm. Guvin set Ecta to checking the Banree for damage whilst Finnan and Goram manned the tiller.

A thick layer of dark, angry clouds obscured the sun, making it almost impossible for Guvin to get an accurate sighting. The only clue Guvin had to plot the position of the sun was a feint orange glow, obscured by the thick cloud layer and close to the horizon. His first attempt put their position inland of Malkronin. It was so clearly wrong that Guvin swore. A second attempt produced a similar result and it was only when double-checking the time on the Banree's chronometer that Guvin found damaged it in the storm. Without an accurate time, he would not be able to plot their position, even if he managed a good sighting on the sun.

"Make a desan course, Finnan. Until I can plot a reliable position we'll have to navigate by dead reckoning."

Finnan nodded grimly "you could ask Cullin, somehow he always knows what the time is."

Cullin was resting in his bunk, drowsy, though not asleep, when Guvin shook him gently by the shoulder. He was finding it difficult to sleep with the rough pitching of the boat and the pounding of the rain.

"Wha'?"

"I'm sorry to wake you Cullin, but the chronometer is damaged. I need the time to be able to plot our position."

Cullin sat up suddenly and banged his head on the bunk above him. He cursed, gathering his sluggish wits. "Time?" Cullin shook his head and thought for a moment. "Did you want 'ship time' or 'true time'?"

"Both would be useful Cullin."

"The 'true time' is NE1021M5D19T2-3.75.81. 'Ship time' is T2-0.42.45 and the sun's angle above the horizon is five point seven five degrees."

"You can't possibly know that, Cullin. The sun isn't even visible." Guvin shook his head in disbelief, but made a careful note of the figures.

"It's a skill I have, Guvin. I always know where we are."

"Well, I trust you, but I'll plot our position anyway. Get some rest, I don't think this storm is over yet."

Guvin was just as baffled when he plotted the position of the Banree, some two-hundred strides off the coast near Malkronin. How Cullin could possibly have known the figures was beyond Guvin. Their position revealed another potential problem. They were now perilously close to the shipping lanes that followed the ocean currents close to the mainland. There was a risk that a passing aimu vessel could witness their passage.

Guvin changed their course, heading away from the shipping lanes. He was considering getting some rest when Ecta approached him. Ecta had checked on the catchment barrel for drinking water only to find it overflowing and the hold awash with water.

"Close off the collection pipe and pump out the water, then transfer the drinking water to a storage barrel. Make sure it's not contaminated with seawater. I need to get a few wairs sleep. Talk to Finnan, he knows what to do." With that, Guvin headed for his bunk, hoping that more problems did not arise whilst he was resting.

Almost four wairs later Cullin, who was back on deck duty, shook Guvin awake. Guvin could tell by the pitch and yaw of the Banree that the storm was becoming violent again. "What time is it?"

"Midday; Ecta's been off duty for the last two wairs."

"You shouldn't have let me sleep so long, Cullin." Guvin complained. He needed the sleep and appreciated the rest, but would have preferred waking sooner, and thus, be back in charge of the Banree sooner.

"Nay, If you can sleep through this weather, then you need the sleep. Goram's managed a brew. It's only roasted acorns, but it'll wake you up a bit."

"What's our position, Cullin?"

"We're still running a desan course, but the storm is pushing us closer to the coast."

Without more ado, Guvin lurched into an upright position and sat on the edge of his bunk. He entered the cabin and found Cullin and Finnan studying the chart with mugs of Goram's steaming acorn beverage. There were biscuits in a container, sliding across the tabletop in unison with the pitching of the Banree.

As Guvin helped himself to a half mugful of the acorn brew and a handful of biscuits, Cullin indicated a position on the chart.

"We've changed the heading while you were resting" Finnan reported, "to two-twenty five degrees, des-yernan, but we're still being pushed toward the coast."

"Change the course to two-seventy degrees. Let the current take us further des. We need to get out of these shipping lanes." Guvin took a swig of the steaming brew and gagged. "Hesoos, that's bitter!"

"It'll be difficult to maintain a course that close to the wind. We'll probably have to tack."

The Banree made little headway against current and wind for the rest of the day. The rain pelted the crew as the boat struggled against mountainous waves and several wairs of effort brought disappointment, as they found they had moved closer to the coast. The wind was beginning to ease off, however, and by dusk, the rain had reduced to a fine drizzle.

It was then that Cullin saw the ship, just a grey dot on the horizon, easily missed. Guvin altered course immediately, bearing away from the ship. Cullin identified it as an aimu transport, fully automated and crewless.

"It won't try to stop us will it?" Goram asked.

"Nay, it's a machine. It will follow its programming unless it's given instruction to do otherwise" Cullin answered, watching the speck intently.

"We've been luck not to have seen another vessel so far. It may not have seen us yet, of course." Guvin was sitting in his accustomed position by the tiller.

"Aye, we should turn back before it sees us." Goram interjected.

"Turn back? Why?" Guvin asked, puzzled.

"This journey has been a disaster from the start. We can't continue like this. Next, we'll all be captured and probably killed." Goram was earnest to the point of raving. Tiredness and the stress of constant battling against the sea and storms had finally beaten Goram. He wanted to quit, ending the unequal struggle.

"We're all tired,

Goram, we know how you feel, but we can't give up now." Guvin tried to calm Goram, but Goram simply stared at him as if he were inhuman.

Cullin spoke gently to Goram, looked him in the face, and saw panic in the eyes that returned his gaze. "I know it's hard, Goram, It's hard for all of us ---"

"What do you know of hard?" Goram snapped, angry now. "Your entire live has been easy, growing up in that big castle and having everything done for you? I've had to work and graft for everything. Don't talk to me about hard"

"I know, Goram, but we have to destroy that thing that makes our lives hard."

Chapter Seventeen

"You've failed!" Goram screamed. "That ship out there, is going to stop us!" Goram sat down heavily on the deck, buried his face in his hands, and began to shake uncontrollably.

"Leave him, Cullin, you can't help him." Guvin placed a gentle hand on Cullin's shoulder. "Do you think it's seen us?"

"Oh, I suspect it saw us first. It has better 'eyes' than any of us. So we can expect it to have sent off a report already." Cullin was still gazing over the stern of the Banree.

Guvin stared toward the position of the aimu ship. "I still don't see it. Am I looking in the right place? "

"Aye. Look on the horizon."

Guvin continued looking, but still failed to see the ship. "You must have good eyes, Cullin, I can't see anything."

"Aye, I can see quite well." Cullin paused. "We could make for land under cover of night. It would mean a longer trek on land."

"Aye, and we're two days off the coast. It would mean we would be in the main shipping lanes during daylight. We have to cross them anyway, but I wanted to be further des, and further from Malkronin before doing that." Guvin scratched his chin thoughtfully. "We'll make a run for it tomorrow night. Now, I need to go and look at the charts. You two stay on deck for the next two wairs, then the others can take over. I'll want everybody well rested before we make the run tomorrow."

At dusk, the crew of the Banree turned the boat about and started their run for the coast. The Banree was a tough vessel, designed for the rough seas around Garvamore. It was not like one of the sleek, swift vessels of the aimu. Cullin knew, of course, that aimu ships were perfectly able to detect them at night and had made sure Guvin was aware of this.

Guvin had merely shrugged saying "we have to go sometime".

Guvin wanted Cullin on lookout duties at night, as he was best able to see in poor light. When challenged how he could see so well in the dark, Cullin simply suggested that he had good night vision. The start of the run for the coast was a relief for Cullin, as it meant the hardships of the journey were almost over. The next two days would be the most dangerous. They would either be seen and captured or they wouldn't be. Cullin felt more relaxed now than at any other time on the voyage.

The Banree cut a broad wake through the waters now that it was following the wind. Two sails caught that fair wind, propelling the boat at a good speed. The sea was much calmer now that the storm had abated. It was still rough, but the crew who had coped with storm, icy deck and frozen equipment and short rations, now found the sea relatively benign.

It proved to be an uneventful night and the following day dawned bright and fair. The day that followed was one of dull routine, though their eyes spent much of the time nervously scanning the horizon for signs of shipping. They saw none, and when Guvin recalculated their position, they found themselves closer to the coast than expected.

However, that meant that they would be in coastal waters at night. Low clouds covered the sky in a continuous layer that obscured stars and the two moons, Atha and Matha.

Cullin, peering into the dark turned to Guvin. "I think we have to be careful, that coastline has many small rocky islands. It's a rugged and desolate area and we don't want the Banree damaged by the rocks."

"How do you know this, Cullin, the charts only show a few islands and rocks, but they are not nearly as detailed as I would like, are you suggesting that they are not good enough?" Guvin shook his head with exasperation; Cullin was doing this sort of thing more and more often. He could accept good eyesight, but Cullin's was beyond good; it was impossible. He also seemed to have an eidetic memory for little details and that ability to 'know' the time was more than uncanny.

"Aye, I studied this coastline back at Rustick More. Your charts have many omissions. I can navigate you through the rocks into a cove where we can hide the Banree."

"I'm astonished, I think there is a lot more to you than meets the eye, Cullin. I have more years on the sea than you have lived, yet I can't do some of the things you do with ease."

"I have prepared for this journey, that's all."

"Nay, I don't think you are telling me all, but I guess that is up to you, as long as you can get us through those islands unseen."

"Oh, I doubt aimu ships will be in these waters, they are too dangerous." Cullin grinned, a friendly, open grin that left Guvin wondering what other secrets were hiding behind it.

Chapter Seventeen

Guvin shook his head to clear his thoughts and concentrated on the matter at hand. A couple of wairs later Guvin asked Cullin to wake the crew. Goram was still in a bad humour, he felt that he had done his bit and had earned his rest.

"Goram, we are all tired" Cullin reminded him "we all need a rest. Besides, we will soon be making landfall and Guvin needs everyone looking out for rocks."

"Landfall? We're there?" Goram sat up suddenly, swinging his legs over the edge of his bunk.

"Aye, we're there."

The news nonplussed Goram and he glanced at Cullin with an expression of mixed confusion and suspicion. "Weren't we supposed to land tomorrow?"

"Aye, we were moving a bit faster than we thought. Come on Goram, once ashore we can all have a good rest."

Noting the exchange between Cullin and Goram, Finnan and Ecta headed for the cabin in wordless silence. They found Guvin studying charts with a frown. Cullin had added details to the chart after explaining to Guvin that the chart had too big a scale to allow for fine details. They had selected a small cove suggested by Cullin, where they now planned to hide the Banree.

Finnan, Ecta, and Goram had scant time for food or drink before they were ushered onto the deck. It was dark, the wind had calmed, and ahead, unseen in the dark, a rocky coastline lay.

As the Banree moved inshore, they could see dark shapes in the water. Making headway as slowly as he could, Guvin steered a course close to steep cliffs to larboard. He was apprehensive about this, but trusted Cullin enough by now. Then, of course, Cullin had knowledge from his study of this coastline. Guvin was far from convinced about that. How he could remember the details so accurately was beyond Guvin. It was a great skill to have, but Guvin distrusted it; it was too un-human, divine.

"The tide is out" Cullin hollered back to Guvin at the tiller. Cullin had positioned himself at the prow of the Banree and was using hand signals to indicate direction. "The channel is deep enough if you stay close to the cliff."

Rocks passed by the starboard bow, small at first, and they even passed some by, unseen under the water. The crew stood ready to fend off with poles. Tension made everyone nervous. The cliff had an overhang that caused further difficulties for Guvin. The last thing that Guvin wanted was damage to the mast.

Cullin indicated a move to larboard was necessary and Guvin cursed. There was precious little room for manoeuvre in this channel. The masthead was very close; barely a handbreadth from the rocks now, and the yard had little more clearance.

"Ready to fend off, larboard." Guvin ordered. Finnan and Goram readied their poles nervously.

The masthead edged ever closer to a ridge in the overhang. Yet, Cullin still indicated to keep to larboard. "We're too close, Cullin. Are you sure we have room?"

"Ready; fend starboard!" Cullin shouted back. Then he added "there's a ridge of rocks just under the surface!"

Guvin cursed as the Banree crept slowly forward. He should have quizzed Cullin more about this cove. The very tip of the masthead clipped the rocks as the Banree slid by even as Ecta thrust his pole into the water. The Banree jerked its bow starboard, throwing Cullin off balance for the briefest of moments. Cullin indicated urgently larboard and Guvin nudged the tiller slightly away from him.

"Hesoos, Cull, those are boulders, not rocks!"

There was a grinding screech as the hull scraped along the underwater ridge of rocks and boulders, and then silence. Cullin ignored his friend and continued indicating larboard, though not so urgently as before. Larger rocks and boulders passed by, but none as closely as the underwater ridge. Slowly the Banree slid into the calm waters of a small bay protected on one side by cliffs and on the other by a long curved peninsula that jutted out into the sea protecting the bay. A small gravel beach nestled within an arc of rocks and crags. Guvin headed for it and ran the Banree aground on the pebbles.

Goram was the first to disembark. With an energetic leap, he launched himself over the side and landed with a heavy crunch on the beach. The others were quick to join him. The voyage of the Banree was over.

Chapter Eighteen

Pyta was not a happy man. The people of Balgeel had not made him welcome, as he had supposed they would. In fact, they had made him very unwelcome. It was his accent of course. They had cursed him because of it. He was without tokens and hungry.

He was a survivor though and a difficult person to keep down. He had waited outside the village, hidden among the hills, and then in the middle of the night he had stolen a small fishing coracle. He had no idea where he would go, but anywhere away from this place, away from these dreadful people would do.

After struggling with the awkward craft, Pyta had to admit to himself that he was not a good boatman. It was a poor boat, made of sticks and hide. It was as primitive boat as it was possible to make with materials available. His choices, though, were limited. If the stupid people of Balgeel had been a bit more hospitable, he would not be in the position where he had to steal a boat. It was, therefore, their fault. Such backward people deserved to have their property taken.

As he paddled a ragged and weaving course over the water, Pyta noticed the sky brightening ahead of him. He must have gone far enough away from the 'odious denizens' of Balgeel, so Pyta headed for shore. He had seen a light on the natua shore; there he hoped he would have a more friendly welcome. It seemed to take an age for the rocky shoreline to near, but Pyta could make out the shape of a building. It was not a large building, having perhaps two small rooms only, but to Pyta it was a welcome sight. It meant the possibility of rest and a meal.

Pyta hid the little boat in a rock-pool and covered it with seaweed, then headed for the little building. Pyta noted with disappointment that it wasn't much of a building. Smoke rose from a stone chimney, but otherwise it had an irregular wooden frame with walls made of withies woven about slender sticks. It was surprising that the structure could withstand winter storms. He hollered out a greeting and a slim woman wearing a simple dress and shawl appeared in the doorway holding a small child.

The woman greeted him with an apprehensive smile "Fayltee gu Taygor" she spoke softly, hesitantly, and for a moment Pyta struggled to pick up her accent. "Where thee be fra?"

"Fra? Ahh, from?" Pyta had to think quickly. He hadn't prepared a story for this eventuality. The woman was making no effort to allow him in. He needed to think of a place distant, but one a woman like this might have heard of. It came to him in a flash of inspiration. "Ah 'ave com from beyon' the 'Pass of Torment'. Ah'm lukin fer a gud place ta live, 'way from the divines."

The woman looked puzzled and frowned. "Your speech is difficult to understand, but you are welcome to take shelter. My husband, Gor, will be back from his work later."

"Ah'm Pyta, thangs fer the welcome." Pyta could see no reason to hide his name. These were poor people, who he guessed, seldom got news from other places. They would probably want news and gossip. He could make up stories for their benefit and they would probably never realise that they were complete lies.

As Pyta entered, he realised that the woman hadn't told him her name or that of the child. Not that it mattered to Pyta either way, but it suggested a degree of distrust, or even fear. Pyta was quite happy with that idea; it gave him power.

There was an appetising smell of stew coming from a pot suspended from a hook in the hearth. Pyta's stomach growled and he realised how hungry he was. The woman indicated a wicker chair and made herself busy adding various ingredients, mostly vegetables, to the stew.

It was customary to offer guests hospitality, refreshment, and food, but this woman offered nothing. He sat in the wicker chair, the only chair in the small dwelling, whilst the woman squatted on a small wooden stool. Pyta felt frustrated, but what could he do? He waited as the child played on the dirt floor, occasionally gazing at him with a stupid, open-mouthed, gawping stare.

He waited, his frustration building into anger. All the woman was doing was stirring the pot and ignoring him. She wasn't doing anything constructive at all. It was no wonder that they had such a poor, mean home. They were lazy people who deserved contempt.

Chapter Eighteen

The wairs dragged by into the afternoon until, at last, they heard noises coming from outside. The woman left her stirring and went outside taking the child with her. As she went, she scowled in his direction as if to say 'stay there'. Pyta soon heard urgent talking, but couldn't make out what they were saying. He was sure about one thing; it wasn't pleasant. He looked quickly about the room for something to defend himself with should things become violent, which he was sure they would.

In a niche by the fireplace, he found a small dirk of poor quality, but testing its edge revealed that it had a keen edge. Pyta tucked it under his morcote and sat down again in the wicker chair, putting on his most sincere, friendly face.

He had sat down, none too soon, as a large heavily built man, presumably the woman's husband, Gor, entered the building. Pyta was not a big man and he was certain that he would not fare well in a fight against this man. He fingered the dirk beneath the folds of his morcote nervously.

"Who are you?" the big man demanded. "There is news of a man called Pyta, he is not to be trusted."

Pyta stood up and smiled. "Ah'm Pyta, a common name where Ah'm from. Ah don' know of this other Pyta yer spik of." He edged closer to the big man as he spoke.

Gor looked down on him with distaste. "The Pyta I speak of had a strange way of speaking, like you." Gor folded his arms across his large muscled chest and glared at Pyta in the dim light. He did not notice Pyta's expression change.

Pyta lunged forward and thrust the little dirk deep into Gor's neck, severing the jugular vein. Shock and rage suffused Gor's face as he put a hand to his neck. I came away bloody. Pyta retreated, throwing obstacles in the way, should Gor decide to attack.

The dirk had gone deep and blood oozed from Gor's neck, he knew the wound be a fatal one, and watched the dark stain of the big man's life-blood seep and spread despite desperate efforts to stem the flow. Gor sank to his knees, a pleading, questioning look on his face 'why?' At last, he sank forward without uttering a word and lay motionless, face down in the dirt before Pyta. Pyta grinned with exhilaration; it had been all too easy. Though he had killed before, Pyta had never experience this 'rush' before. Before, he had always been relieved to be alive. This was different. He felt stronger, superior.

He went outside, blinked in the bright light, and looked down on the woman crouched nearby, cowering, and holding her child close to her. Tears streamed down her face and she looked beseechingly at Pyta. Pyta ignored her silent pleas and leaped forward, slitting her throat before she could react or move. The child screamed once before it, too, had its throat cut. Pyta smiled gleefully and spat on the corpse of the woman. At least now, he would be able to have something to eat, and eat in peace. He left the bodies where they lay and went back inside, helping himself to a bowlful of stew.

For several days now, the Boss had been trying to piece together a jigsaw of events and stories. He was not a happy man. The jigsaw had started with one of his routine visits to Garvin where he had spent a long time apologising to Linn for Pyta's behaviour. They accused Pyta of killing Linn's dog, though the evidence for this was purely circumstantial. They had subsequently run Pyta out of the village. Pyta had since disappeared and where he had gone no one knew or cared.

The Boss had stopped in Balgeel and dropped off a ham to one of his 'lookouts'; those who kept their eyes open for him and often gave him useful bits of information. He had been quite surprised to hear stories of an impecunious vagrant stealing food from crofts at night. Although the thefts had stopped after a few days, it was easy for the Boss to make the connection with Pyta. The stories of the night thief had quickly spread amongst the crofting community.

Pyta's behaviour puzzled the Boss; it was needless and made no sense. He knew Pyta was a thug and, sometimes, prone to aggressive behaviour. It was one of the reasons the Boss used him. Sometimes, unpleasant jobs needed doing, and Pyta was an ideal person for this. However, the Boss had decided that he no longer had a use for Pyta and would make his displeasure apparent to the man when he caught up with him.

There were further surprises for the Boss in Tymeum. He sometimes used a boat from the village for travel along the Brayvik Straits leaving the cart and donkey at the 'Water Hole', the Inn that served as the community social centre. Locals exchanged news and stories over mugs of ale or generous shots of whisky.

Chapter Eighteen

Whilst waiting for the boat he had hired, the Boss heard alarming stories of murder committed over the Straits on the island of Brayvik. A young couple from Tymeum who had started a new croft that summer, throats cut and left to lie where they had been murdered. There was no reason known for the killings. They had been popular in the village and their deaths had caused considerable grief and angry talk.

Divines, who stopped at the village regularly to collect harvested calp, had merely shrugged. It was a matter for the local Mark Lord Tymeum to deal with. The sudden death of his father had elevated the proud, but young and inexperienced son, into the responsible position of Mark Lord. The tumid, bombastic, young man had pronounced that he would look into the matter; that was the day before and nothing had yet happened. Therefore, the landlord of the 'Water Hole' had asked the Boss to look into the matter, 'as he was heading that way'.

Though he was not entirely happy to do so, the Boss did visit the croft and even dirtied his own hands digging graves for the young family. There seemed to be no reason for the murders. Nothing appeared taken. It was senseless. The Boss suspected that Pyta was the guilty party, but there was nothing to connect the man with the crime. What would have provoked a man like Pyta to commit such an act? The Boss had no answer.

It was now late evening and the Boss was finally reaching his intended destination, a sandy cove with views across the broad mouth of the Brayvik Straits. He had two of his lookouts camped here and was delivering food to them. He also wanted reports and to give them further instructions. The Boss knew events would be happening here soon, momentous events.

The fisherman, an old hand called Vreck, had finished mooring the boat that the Boss had hired by some rocks and had joined them in the rude shelter that showed signs of hasty building. His lookouts informed him that they had only arrived at the cove the day before and hadn't had time to build anything 'decent'. The two men, Camrun and Skolta, had done a reasonable job of a temporary shelter, using deadwood and other detritus from the beach. An arch of curved branches formed a broad opening. More branches interwoven with small branches formed the body of the shelter. The whole, covered with grassy turfs and moss, produced a relatively comfortable shelter. The Boss still reckoned on an uncomfortable night. He did note with pleasure that the opening faced toward the mouth of the Brayvik Straits.

"Good shelter Boss?" queried Skolta. Skolta was a small wiry man who had seen too many summers in the Boss's opinion. He was of a cheerful disposition, accepting most hardships with alacrity. The Boss didn't know his real name and didn't ask. The name Skolta referred to the long diagonal scar that crossed his broad face from forehead, across his nose, and cheek, ending in a vicious curl that split his lower lip in two. The man was also completely bald and had deep-set eyes, that combined with his diminutive, wiry frame to produce an alarming visage. In the dim light of the shelter, Skolta's head had the disturbing appearance of a skull.

"Ah'm glad Ah'm only stayin' fer un night. It jus' a bi' basic fer me." In truth, the Boss was quite impressed with the shelter. He had used much worse before, but simply wished these two men to know he expected better.

"You'll be comfortable enough, Boss" remarked Camrun. Camrun was a short, but heavy-set man who, the Boss guessed to be in his thirties. His dark, cropped hair showed the odd hint of grey, an indication of a hard life, even for those who lived in the harsh environment of Garvamore.

The Boss doubted that, he didn't expect the company to be particularly engaging. They served a purpose and that was all that really mattered to him. He had given them a few bottles of whisky, cheap, poor quality stuff, but it demonstrated his good intent toward them. He didn't believe in intoxicating beverages, but they served a purpose. People like this were much easier to manipulate after a few drinks.

They had barely settled down about the fireplace, a ring of stones set before the shelter entrance, before they'd opened the first bottle. It was already half empty. The fisherman had settled himself down and simply sat gazing out to sea, quite disinterested in the Boss's business.

The Boss handed Skolta a com-pad, the one Pyta had previously used to send his reports and returned to him by Linn back in Garvin. "Yer know 'ow ta use this?"

"Nay, Boss."

After over a wair of instructions the Boss was satisfied, that Skolta would be able to use the device. He noticed that the second bottle of whisky had not only been opened, but was mostly consumed. He hoped that his two new employees of his would remain diligent and not simply spend their time getting drunk. "Thar will be mur hooch when ah com' back in a ten-day."

Camrun snorted "bring more next time. A thirsty man doesn't work well."

"Aye, oh don't worry Boss, we'll do our jobs just fine, but we do like a drink to pass the time, like." Skolta tried to be encouraging, but his reassurances failed to convince the Boss.

"Ah'll tek yer request inta consid'ration. Ah wan' ta be oop early tamorah. Gud e'en.' With that, he found a comfortable patch of sand in the shelter and curled up in his morcote. With a grim sense of foreboding, he noticed that Vreck headed for the fishing boat to bed down.

He did not have a comfortable night. Snoring from Camrun and Skolta kept him awake and sand got into his clothing. He rose early, just glad to have the night over. There were three empty bottles by the cold fire. The Boss didn't pity them their hangovers, but if they did their jobs, it was worth it.

He left another bottle for them as he always had a spare bottle or two with his stock as such items frequently came in useful with certain people. As Vreck shoved the small boat off its sandy berth, the Boss decided he had best keep a close eye on those two.

The trip back across the Brayvik Straits took longer than the outward journey due to currents and tides, but Vreck knew the waters well and even produced a breakfast of fresh caught sea trout that he cooked in a small wood burning stove. Once back in Tymeum the Boss headed straight for the Water Hole to collect his cart and donkey. He had other stops on his itinerary and was keen to get moving.

Chapter Nineteen

It had been a long journey for Varee, but after two tendays of footslogging, she had arrived at Rustick More. She was not very happy. After her last visit to Rustick More, Red had decided to transfer all aneksa operations from Bandrokit to Mark Konzie, which was now Red's centre of operations. Those operations were now in the care of Fraze, whom Varee had quickly come to respect. They had not seen or heard from Red in the four tendays since then.

Recent poor communications particularly irritated Fraze. He felt that his unit had been cut off since the Battle of Dundoon. He needed direction, equipment, and supplies. So he had dispatched Varee, who he knew got on well with Dookerock, with a list of supply requests, requests for instructions and so on. It was effectively, a long rant demanding action. Fraze's biggest complaint was that, with fliers now available, why not use them for communication. A visit once every tenday would be useful.

These days, Varee wore her red hair short for practicality. A wore a light shirt and woollen trousers that showed off her slim, but strong body. It was a fine day, so she carried her morcote over her shoulder. On her back, she carried a sack with food and a report from Fraze for Dookerock.

It had been a difficult journey, mostly travelling at night and using known associates of the aneksa. She was tired, but the table-topped peak of Rustick More now loomed ahead of her. Varee knew that there were several entrances to the base, but only knew one, which she knew aneksa guarded. It was not far now.

She rounded a bend in the rough track she had been following for the last two days. Two men sitting by an open fire and a rough shelter of hides strung between two, long dead, trees. "Good morning" she hailed them.

"And who are you?" one of the men queried, looking up, while stirring a pot on the fire.

"I have messages for Dookerock" she advised, noting the slack, casual attitude of their security. She could easily have killed them, had she wanted to. She would have to talk to Dook about that as well.

"Ah, well" the young man looked at Varee steadily "we'll be needing to know who you are then."

"I am Varee of Mark Kyle."

"You wear no marks. How do I know you are being truthful?" The young man persisted.

This was stupid, decided Varee. "There, those are my marks!" She pointed out the U and swirl on the sleeve of her morcote. That coat was old now, but still warm and comfortable, though it now showed signs of its age.

The young man laughed at the sight of the swirl. "That is quite believable and typical. He is always asking for ale."

The other guard smirked "true, but you have no ale with you."

Varee had had enough of these two gillee. "Just send a message for someone who can vouch for me." She sat down on a rock nearby the shelter, folded her arms across her chest, and looked away from the two men with disgust.

They both laughed and the younger added "that has already been done. You clearly, did not see our lookout. Well, you're not supposed to."

This news surprised and had obviously underestimated these two. She looked at them with renewed interest and asked "How long?"

"Oh, the message was sent several sents before you got here."

It took Varee a moment or two to realise the ambiguity in her question. "No, I mean before someone gets back here".

"Ah, that would be telling. Just be patient." He dipped a spoon into the pot and tasted the contents, nodding his appreciation. "I'm Dris and this scoundrel is Mabe."

The other young man made a theatrical bow towards Varee who found that she could not help, but grin in return. Mabe ducked into the shelter and came back out moments later with deep-rimmed wooden plates. Dris took one and dipped it unceremoniously into the pot; thrust the spoon into the food had dumped it in front of Varee.

"You look hungry, eat" he explained. "You forgot the bread." Dris quietly murmured to Mabe.

Moments later Varee had a big chunk of bread dumped into her stew and realised that she was quite hungry. Dris and Mabe, she noticed, did not use cutlery, but scooped up the food with chunks of the coarse bread. She

Chapter Nineteen

followed suit, ignoring the spoon and found with surprise the stew to be quite palatable.

She had barely finished the plateful when a diminutive grey haired woman appeared from around a bend in the track. "You two will be the death of me!" The woman turned to Varee "I am sorry about these two, the day they do something properly, I will be an old woman. I am Dona, and you are?"

"Varee, we haven't met, but I know Dook well." Varee was a little nonplussed as she regarded the woman, thinking that she was already old.

"Aye, I have heard of you. Come with me." Dona shook her head slightly at the two guards then turned and headed back up the track. Another man was waiting by an entrance concealed by bushes, temporarily moved aside. "I have to ask how you know of this entrance. I know you have been to Rustick More previously, but I understand that you came by flier."

"Aye that is true. I had time for a brief conversation with Sara, she told me where I might find this place."

"That is very uncharacteristic of her. She is usually more discreet than that. I will talk to her when I see her again."

"She is not here?"

"No, she is somewhere safe." Dona looked quizzically at Varee. "She is having Cullin's child." She turned to the lookout then "keep an eye on those two and close the door when we have gone in a way."

Varee entered a dark tunnel and followed Dona tentatively along a narrow, roughly hewn passageway. There was no lighting of any kind. What light there was came from the entrance and faded as they progressed. Suddenly, even that light extinguished, leaving the two women in complete darkness.

"Ah, I was waiting for that." Dona remarked; her voice eerily disembodied in the dark.

Varee could see nothing, not even a hand before her eyes, but she heard sounds, movement, and a clinking, artificial noise. "Dona, what's going on?"

"I'm making some light, unless of course, you want to fumble your way along in the dark."

"Nay, I'm not a mole."

"Dook does have plans to put some proper lighting down here, but I prefer traditional ways."

Varee was not quite sure what Dona meant by 'traditional', but light of any sort would suit her at that moment.

Abruptly, Dona laughed, there was a clink and the brief sound of pouring liquid. Then a scraping noise followed and Varee saw sparks.

"Hesoos, missed!" Dona cursed. There was more scraping, more sparks and a blue flame came to life.

Dim shadows danced on the tunnel walls as the flame flickered before the squatting figure of Dona. "It's always useful to be able to do these things in the dark." Dona put a wick to the flame and a steady light shone from a lantern she was holding. She sat the lantern on top of the dish used to make the initial flame, then screwed it into the lantern base. Flint and metal rod then snapped into a holder on the cylindrical lantern's side, which Dona held up proudly. "All in one; brilliant!"

The explanation made Varee wonder if Dona was entirely sane; it seemed like a crazy practice to her. Perhaps Dona was showing off, but that didn't make sense. Varee put the explanations and procedures down to idiosyncrasy.

"There are several of these tunnels under Rustick More, but only a few know all the entrances. So, tell me, how you know Dookerock?"

"He is a friend of my father. Dook appeared at the Tavern once or twice a year."

"A friend, you say? How very unlikely. Dook uses people; I don't think he has any real friends." Dona's voice had a hollow, eldritch quality as it echoed along the tunnel. "We have to be careful down here when it rains; the passageways can fill with water quite quickly. We go down this way. Mind your head."

Though the tunnel appeared to go on, a small narrow entrance revealed a short flight of steps. The tunnel continued, heading steadily downward. After what seemed like wairs to Varee, but was little more than twenty sents, she could hear the sound of rushing water. The sound steadily drew nearer and there was a distinct dampness in the air. Abruptly, as they turned a bend in the passageway, a torrent, a wall of water appeared ahead. In the dim light of Dona's lantern, Varee could see a path skirting around the cauldron and to the right of the falls, another passageway. As they approached, Varee could see that the water plummeted over a shelf and into a deep, dark, black hole with no apparent bottom.

"Dook calls this place 'Eskoramor', he believes it joins up with other caverns beneath Rustick More, but no one has proven that idea."

"Really?" Varee was about to head into the passageway ahead of her, but Dona stopped her.

"Not that way; that's 'Blind Alley'. We go this way." Dona stepped into the misty gloom behind the curtain of water, prudently shielding the lantern. Concealed behind the falls was a flight of steps that climbed steeply upward. "Careful, the steps are wet, we now have quite a climb; we are right underneath Rustick More."

"How long will it take?"

"About half a wair, if you're young and fit, which I'm not."

Varee scratched her head, thinking, trying to work out the timings. "It must take a wair then, from the lookout post to Rustick More."

"Aye, that's about right."

"So, how did you get down so quickly?"

"I didn't. There is a message system. Another lookout on the More saw a signal. I was on the way down long before you came anywhere near the lookout post."

"Oh, how many lookouts do you have?" Varee was trying to work out how many people Dook must employ as lookouts.

"Erm, quite a few."

As they climbed, the sound of the waterfall diminished and then disappeared altogether. They passed through a large, cleft-like, chamber with a high, narrow ceiling lost in the meagre light from Dona's lantern. Varee's mind reeled at the huge scale.

"Dona, this place is so big!"

"Aye, Dook calls this the 'Chapel'. Come on, there is still a fair way to go."

They passed through other chambers, but none quite as large as the Chapel. Varee was feeling tired, fatigued. Her legs ached from the unaccustomed and different exercise. She found steep climbs the hardest. She wondered how the older woman was managing. Varee was forced to admit that there was more to Dona than was, at first, apparent. Grey hair aside, Dona was a strong, fit woman.

They started through another chamber, but this one was different to the others. The walls were less rough and the floor was level and smooth. Varee could just make out a barred doorway ahead.

"Ah, finally." Dona muttered. Then added to Varee, "why Dook can't live in an ordinary village or town is beyond me. This is too much like hard work. Now mind your eyes, as I open this door."

Dona reached into a small cavity to the side of the door and withdrew a large key that she used to lift a heavy plank across the door. Bright, artificial light streamed into the passageway, making their eyes water. Varee blinked and squinted against the unaccustomed light for several long moments. She could make out another passageway with murals and paintings decorating the walls and suddenly, Varee knew where she was.

"Oh, Toiler's Woe is that way."

"Aye, but let's get to the canteen first. I don't know about you, but I'm rather hungry and thirsty."

After refreshments, they headed for Dook's apartments, where they found him talking with Grega, the old Advocate from Cullin's Mark. Dook's face lit up when he saw Varee. Dona left without a word.

"Varee, where have you been hiding yourself?" It was not the answer that Varee wanted to hear.

Dook jumped up from the table enthusiastically, knocking it and spilling the contents of a large jug. Dook ignored the mess, leaving Grega to deal with it as best he could. Grega did not look happy.

Dook gave Varee a big hug, then held her by the shoulders, joyfully. "So, what brings you to my humble home?"

"Dook, you smelly old man, can I sit down?"

"Of course, of course." Dook gestured toward the table where Grega had just finished mopping up the spilt beer with his sleeve. "This is Grega." Dook introduced the irritated man, as Varee sat down.

Varee nodded her head respectfully and gave the old man a sweet smile, then addressed Dook directly. "I have just travelled from Mark Konzie, mostly on foot. Have you heard from Red lately?"

"Nay, but that is not unusual. Why? Is there a problem?"

"He has not been seen for about forty days. You must know that all operations have been moved from Bandrokit to Mark Konzie. Fraze is getting frantic for equipment and instructions."

"Nay, I was not aware of this. Tell me what has been happening." Dook was suddenly very serious.

"I have reports and equipment requests with me."

"Ah, good." Dook scanned through the papers that Varee handed him with an assortment of hmms, ahs and ohs.

Grega and Varee waited in silence until Dook looked up from his reading. "Varee, Grega has some documents that need to be dropped off at Tymeum's Great Hall. He's been nagging me about this for days, but I haven't had time to do it myself. I'll have a reply for Fraze organised tomorrow for you." Then Dook turned to Grega "would you get Fil, or one of the others to take Varee in a flier, then arrange a bed for Varee?"

"Aye." Grega winked at Varee who found the friendly gesture slightly out of place in a serious meeting. "In truth Dook, it's been more than a few days. It's more like tendays. The Mark Lord should have had the population documents completed long before now."

"I have been busy, Grega." An irritated expression crossed Dook face.

"You're Tymeum's Advocate?" The news stunned Varee. It seemed quite incongruous that a man so deeply involved with the resistance movement would be working for the divines in this way. Then she realised that it could have its uses.

"Aye, I don't like it broadcasting though, so keep it to yourself."

Around twenty or so sents later as Varee entered Toiler's Woe with Fil, she saw the huge figure of a man hunched over a half completed flier with one of the tech crew. "Who is that?"

"That is Anbooakil, a guest of Dook's, though he, actually hasn't told anyone much about him. All I know is that one of us has to be with him at all times and we have to be courteous."

"Oh, how very strange."

"Aye, we'll take this flier." Rustick More now had four fliers completed in a neat row near the hanger doors. "I'll drop you off in a little valley a few strides north of the village, so you will appear to have walked in."

The trip to the valley was brief and Varee was soon walking in the bright afternoon sunshine along narrow paths that Fil had assured her, led to the village. The Hall did not greatly impress her when she reached it. Lying on top of a small rise and looking out over the Brayvik Straits, the Great Hall of Tymeum was little more than a large rough yellow brick house, built around a timber frame, black with age and roofed with stone slating.

A large overweight man with a round, flushed face sat on a stool by the large double doors of the hall. Without bothering to rise from his stool, he challenged Varee. "State your business" he grated.

"I have papers for the Mark Lord" Varee stated simply.

With the slightest movement of his head, the doorman indicated that she could enter. Inside, the hall was constructed of bare wood and unadorned. It smelled dusty. Large beams overhead supported the roof. A small white haired woman sat behind a large trestle.

"Can I help you?" the woman asked looking slightly irritated.

"I have something for the Lord. Is he about?"

"He is not here today. Come back tomorrow." The woman briefly glanced at Varee and then continued with scrutinising papers in a pile on the trestle before her.

Varee had the population documents in a leather sack strapped to her back. She started to remove them. "I am afraid I cannot come back tomorrow. I need to deliver these today." She dropped the sack on the floor raising a small dust-cloud in the process.

Chapter Nineteen

The old woman jumped slightly at the sudden thud, but continued studying the papers. Carefully and neatly, she corrected a minor grammatical error, and drew a line through some incorrect punctuation, then placed the paper on top of a separate, neat pile. Varee watched as the woman worked for several sents. Then she uncermoniously dumped her documents on the trestle, making the old woman jump again.

The woman glared at Varee "I cannot take this today. Can you not see that I am busy? Bring them back tomorrow."

"Busy? Busy doing nothing!" Varee snapped at the woman.

The woman glared angrily at Varee, who merely shrugged and smiled insincerely back. The woman then glanced at the top sheet of the documents. "Who are you? These should have been delivered last month."

"Not tomorrow then!" Varee snapped back at the woman, glaring angrily; then turning on her heel, she strode from the hall. Vexed by the irritating, officious woman, Varee charged downhill and soon found herself on a pebble beach looking out over the waters of the Brayvik Straits. She could see the Great Hall facing out over the village and the calm waters and Rustick More in the distance, illuminated by soft hazy, sunlight. She sat on a boulder, watching the waves break over the pebbles with sibilant chatter. Varee beheld distant soolara plummeting from height into the waters and small birds she didn't recognise, picking through the disturbed pebbles for titbits. She found her calmness return.

Varee smiled. 'A drink' she thought, that would complete her feeling of 'the gasda', her inner peace and calm, belonging to 'kroonack', being at one with the world. As she wandered along the waterfront, she saw a familiar figure. 'That's odd', she thought.

A scruffy man with a strange and coarse accent was leaving the Water Hole and talking with the landlord. The way he moved that tweaked her curiosity, but she couldn't put a name to the figure. She thought that she knew the person.

The Water Hole was quite typical of most of the inns that Varee had been to. It was a wooden shack attached to a stone building with rough wooden floorboards and scattered sawdust used to soak up spillages. An odd assortment of mismatching tables and chairs furnished the room and a hatchway that was formerly a window functioned as the bar. A narrow doorway served as the entrance to the stone building from the bar room. A rotund, bald man sat on a child's stool before the doorway. He disappeared, squeezing through the doorway as Varee entered the bar, to reappear moments later at the bar window.

Varee paid for ale with tokens given to her by Dook. It was dark and had a rich honeyed flavour with slightly bitter undertones, yet remained delicately balanced. The excellent ale demonstrated a passion for the art of brewing on the part of the landlord.

"That's an excellent ale, how do you get that depth of flavour?" Varee asked the landlord after taking a few appreciative swallows.

"Ah, that comes from roasting the barley." Leoona, the landlord, was happy to talk to Varee about brewing ale. The handful of customers in the bar simply drank to relax and chatted amongst themselves, idle-talk and sharing news, the horror of the recent killings high on the list of favourite topics.

Their conversation continued, interrupted occasionally by customers purchasing more ale. Leoona was particularly interested in the Tavern and had many questions. Who were their main customers? What did they use to flavour the ale and so on?

Varee discovered that he used ingredients, not available locally, to create subtle highlights in the ale. He had just received a new package of such flavourings, but he had to be careful of their usage due to their expense.

"Oh, is that who the man with the cart was?" Varee went on to describe the man with the cart she had seen earlier.

"Aye, that's him." Leoona smiled shyly. "I have known him for many years. He is very helpful towards the poorer people in the district. He calls himself 'The Boss', but no one knows his real name."

"I wonder where he gets his stock from?"

"Well, that is something he won't talk about. He gets angry if anyone asks. I think he likes to protect his sources, I mean, that's his living isn't it?"

"I guess so. Look, Leoona, I have to go. It's been marvellous talking to you, but I have someone waiting for me." Varee drained the last of her ale.

On her way back to the flier she found the identity of 'The Boss' was bothering her. Though she had only seen him from a distance, she was certain that she knew him. During the short hop back to Rustick More the image of the Boss played on her mind.

Chapter Nineteen

Toiler's Woe was its usual busy, industrious place. Varee ignored the noise, as she still had unfinished business with Dook. She headed straight for his apartment, intending to demand some answers.

"Dook!" she demanded, "where are the weapons and equipment Fraze needs?"

Dook was sitting in his apartment talking with the giant Anbooakil. There were plans spread out before them. "Ah, Varee, come in. A flier has been loaded for you. Fil, or one of the others will take you back tomorrow."

"Oh, Good, Fraze is absolutely desperate for some support and we haven't heard from Red in a very long time."

"So you indicated earlier. Red has suggested that training has gone well in Mark Konzie. Can you tell me in your own words what has been happening?"

"Dook, we continue to train with sticks and rocks. Food supplies are low." Varee went on to describe the day-to-day life of Mark Konzie and the aneksa based there. She explained how Red, last seen over a month ago, and then only briefly, had spoken in private to Fraze and then left. Talking of Red focused her mind on him, and in a moment of synchronicity she knew who the man calling himself 'The Boss' was and why it bothered her. Red and the Boss were one and the same.

"So what is Red up to? Why did I see him in Tymeum earlier?"

This was a total surprise to Dook. "What do you mean 'in Tymeum earlier'? What would he be doing in Tymeum?"

"I don't know, I only just realised now who I saw in the village." Varee went on to recount her experiences earlier that day. There wasn't much to say, just that it didn't seem 'right'.

"Hmm, Red has always done things his way, but usually lets us know what is going on in his own time. I think, though, that I might find the time to go and talk with this Leoona and buy a barrel or two of this excellent ale you talk of."

Varee laughed "I'm surprised you haven't already."

"This other matter of communication bothers me. I have a couple of staff installing seismocoms, devices we have recently developed for the purpose. I will have one installed at Mark Konzie as soon as I can." With that, Varee's discussions with Dook concluded and Dook returned to his scrutinising the flier plans with Anbooakil.

Chapter Twenty

The crew of the Banree spent a day resting and recuperating, using the idle time to make general repairs to the Banree. The boat was in remarkably good repair considering the rough nature of the voyage and Guvin felt justifiably proud that it had done so well. They drew the Banree up the pebble beach, de-masted and disguised with foliage despite Goram complaining that it didn't look right.

Throughout the day, Cullin and Ecta fused over the seismocom, adjusting settings on the receiver to filter out the majority of 'noise'. Cullin found a rocky cleft that he tutted and clicked into, much to the amusement of Guvin and Goram. Cullin waited until early evening before setting the equipment up to 'send'. Guvin and Goram watched the process with interest.

"How does that thing work?" Goram asked, not following what Ecta and Cullin were doing.

"It sends a shock wave that can be received at Rustick More. A message is coded into that shockwave." Cullin answered plainly.

Goram stared at the machine open-mouthed, not quite believing what he had just heard. "It sends a message all that way?"

"Won't the Frame detect it?" Guvin asked curiously.

"Aye, but it will be just one little bit of seismological data amongst millions. The Frame will ignore it. However, at Rustick More they are looking for it and have a code sequence to identify and extract our message." Cullin explained, not sure that his simple explanation was satisfactory. "All we shall do today is to send a message to say that we have arrived and are awaiting a reply. We'll have to do this every day to maintain communication."

"Are we ready?" Ecta asked. He knew how to operate the seismocom, but not the technology that made it work.

"Aye." Cullin simply pressed a single button. There was a booming rumble, longer than the original tests. Cullin checked the 'sender' display, and then he unclipped it from the spike. He re-connected the receiver to the spike and sat back. "All we do now is wait. I doubt we'll get anything this evening, but they'll re-send tomorrow. We should get a message then."

On the night of the second day, having discussed the forthcoming journey on foot, they decided that Finnan would remain with the Banree. Cullin reckoned that they had about one hundred and fifty strides to cover on foot and hoped to average twenty strides per day. They would have to carry sufficient food for that period to avoid having to forage during the trek.

They woke early to a bright cloudless sky that augured warm weather, though Cullin insisted that they take their morcotes wrapped into a bundle with their rations. The four trekkers bid farewell to Finnan, promising to be back in thirty days or less. Cullin soon began to worry about his estimations. The ground was hard and unforgiving. There was little foliage and what they found was woody shrubs with small, needle-like fleshy leaves that Goram collected thinking that they might add a good flavour to their food.

There was no trail or path to follow and feet kicked up dust that swirled in lazy spirals in the light breeze. They steadily climbed throughout the day finding only dry riverbeds, where scrubby plants struggled to draw enough moisture from the arid ground to survive. Distant, sharp peaks shone brightly in the distance.

"Is that snow on those hills?" Guvin asked, not knowing anything about the geography and meteorology of the area.

"Nay, that is just the colour of the rocks. Malkronin lies beyond those mountains. We don't go that way" Cullin replied.

"How does anything grow around here?" Goram asked.

"It is adapted for the dry conditions."

They continued throughout the day finding only brush and dry riverbeds. Cullin pushed the pace hard, ignoring the complaints and protests from his companions.

"We can't go on like this!" Goram protested volubly. "We need water, if we are to go on."

"If you can find water around here, then congratulations. Though I suspect, Goram, that it would be a waste of energy. We need to be the other side of these hills before we can find water. It will probably take another two wairs. We need to press on."

"How do people live around here?" Goram asked with exasperation.

"They don't" Cullin replied. "It's too arid."

Ecta and Guvin ignored Goram's protests and followed Cullin over slabs of friable rock. Grit and sand choked gullies and streambeds. It was a dry and desolate landscape. In the late afternoon, they passed between two broad, low hills and the terrain began to dip toward a wide and green valley. Cullin headed unerringly towards a small knoll that overlooked the valley. Soon a strip of blue-green water came into view.

"That is where we are headed." Cullin pointed out the lake to the others.

"How can you possibly have known about this, Cullin?" Guvin asked.

"Don't forget, I studied this coast before the voyage." Cullin replied.

"Cullin, you can't have known where we were going to land, but you seem to have a route planned out" Guvin pressed.

"There is so little standing water in this area, I simply worked out routes to them from several likely landing places."

It was not long before they reached the lake and Cullin left Guvin and Goram to set up the camp whilst Ecta assisted him with the seismocom. Firstly, they sent a brief report of their progress and then set up the seismocom to receive and waited. They soon heard Goram bickering with Guvin.

"Doesn't that man ever quit moaning" commented Ecta.

"He does seem unhappy about something" agreed Cullin.

"He's always unhappy about something."

"Aye, seems that way. I'd better see what the problem is."

The problem soon became apparent. "When was the last time Guvin cooked anything?" Goram challenged Cullin.

"I'm not sure Goram"

Guvin sat nearby fussing over his kit, looking awkward and uncomfortable, almost as if he was ashamed of something.

"Never, he never cooks. On the Banree, he always had someone to cook for him."

"He wouldn't be expected to on his own boat."

"We're not on a boat, Cullin. You and Ecta are going to be busy with that thing. So who's going to have to do all the food?"

Cullin realised that Goram had a point, but it was a point that should never have become an issue. Both he and Ecta would be cooking, but Guvin's lack of ability was an oversight.

"Goram" Cullin began. "You need to do this together. Tell him what you need, work together and show him what to do. Is that all right with you, Guvin?"

"Aye." Guvin brightened "I can do that."

Not entirely satisfied with the solution, Goram pressed further. "And what about you two? You'll be messing with that thing all the time we're in camp."

"Ah, Nay. We are still familiarising ourselves with it. We still don't know how well it's going to work. We will do our share, I assure you of that. Tell Guvin what you need for now."

"Wood, you can't make a fire with rocks."

"Ah, true. If you go down to the other end of the lake, you will find trees and bushes alongside the stream. Why don't you send Guvin while you build a fireplace?"

As Guvin headed off down the lake Ecta called out "Cull, I think we've got something".

"Indeed we do" agreed Cullin as he checked the readout. "Ah, it's only an acknowledgement. I'm going to give Guvin a hand collecting wood. There may be another message later."

The evening continued with relative peace and Goram's mood mollified when Cullin lent a hand with the evening meal. They slept wrapped in morcotes, much to the dislike and discomfort of Guvin who was used to a more comfortable bed. Goram too, found the sleeping arrangements not to his liking although he would never admit to being less hardy than the 'Lordling' and his friend.

Chapter Twenty

The second day of walking saw the landscape change, becoming greener. Grasses began to dominate and trees were more common. Occasionally small groups of deer, glimpsed grazing on the vegetation were much larger than the dwarf sub-species of red deer of Garvamore that were only slightly larger than a goat.

The journey to Tyber became little more than dull routine in the sparsely populated land. The land became more ordered and managed, though there appeared to be little or no population. Cullin explained this to the others by saying that machines, aimu, managed the land. Fields of oil-beet dominated, set out with rigid square boundaries. Cullin found the formal rows of the bulbous root crop to be soulless and dreary.

Yayler and Gulukone were having an argument. There were no raised voices, but it was an argument nevertheless. The problem was that neither of them could agree on the nature of truth. Gulukone was very self-assured on what was true and what wasn't, and found Yayler's idea very hard to comprehend. As usual, whenever they spoke, Gulukone stood near the door of Yayler's cabin and Yayler sat on his bunk.

"The truth is what the Frame tells us. The Frame cannot lie because deceit is not part of its parameter's." Gulukone folded his arms across his chest, challenging Yayler to deny the validity of this.

"Truth is a place where heart and mind are in synchronicity." Yayler knew this was a rather abstruse concept and he had struggled with the idea himself when Dookerock had first tried to explain it to him.

"I don't understand that!" Gulukone remained unimpressed and gazed back at Yayler waiting for an explanation for the statement.

"The Frame teaches absolute truth. This is so, this isn't. This is not correct." It was another blunt statement.

"How is that so? You speak in riddles; a thing is either true or it isn't, there is no contradiction."

Yayler paused for thought; he needed to explain the idea from a different direction. "I have a friend who was trained as a divine cleric. He had to teach what the Frame dictated, and had specific texts to adhere to."

"I see no problem there. All clerics should teach the same text, otherwise, there would be confusion."

"It is not the truth, though. I've had access to data denied to many other divines, ancient data. The text written by the Frame the clerics teach. The Frames text bears little resemblance to the ancient writings. There is contradiction between the two. In fact, much of the Frames contrived text appears to attempt to control the behaviour of, both muckers and divines. There is another point; the text differs for muckers and divines, sometimes significantly so."

"It is a lie then?"

"Aye, I believe so, but many perceive it as truth."

"I'm confused, why would someone believe a lie?"

"The ancients had many different faiths that the Frame has combined into one single belief system." It was a simple statement, and one that Yayler knew that Gulukone would have difficulty denying.

"This is common knowledge. I do not see where your argument is going."

Yayler paused, organising his thoughts. "A video records exactly what has been done or said, but it cannot replay the experience of the individual."

"I understand, I agree, that is an accurate statement."

"If you ask an individual to recall and record their own experience of an event and then compare that with a video recording they will differ, sometimes significantly."

"The video recording will be accurate. A person's brain is a poor device for memory or recording details."

"Neither is a perfect record. Neither can tell you the whole truth." Yayler wondered if Gulukone would challenge his statement.

"What is the whole truth? Surely, a record of an event is either true or false?"

"Nay, it is never that simple." Yayler leaned back against the cabin wall, waiting for the response from Gulukone.

"Again, I don't understand. Why is truth never simple?"

Chapter Twenty

"A recording of sounds and images is only a record of events from a specific point and then, in only two senses. It does not record emotion and, very significantly, does not record the perception or the personal experience of people. Both perception and emotion are heavily affected by a person's knowledge, life experiences, beliefs, emotions and so on. Each individuals' perception of an event will, therefore, be different, but each will be equally valid."

After a long pause, Gulukone frowned, and then he spoke haltingly. "I understand your point. Simply ask people to recall their experience to complete a true recording."

"Nay, this approach does not work because memory is not perfect. We fill in the gaps, distort our own recollected experience thereby, often to fit preconceived values and ideas. We exaggerate some details whilst ignoring others."

"I see."

Yayler laughed "I doubt it; I never really would have understood myself except for an old lady called Nell. She was the grandmother of a Mark Lord for whom I was Advocate. She always called me her Bonny Jonny; that was her son. She always got us confused.

Nell was always a cheerful woman who loved life. She used to sing nonsense rhymes to herself and was one of the happiest people I have ever known. When she got old, her mind lost the sharpness it once had. Even though I had known her as a child, she still thought of me as her son. That was her perception, her reality, her truth. I loved her dearly and loved her joy of life. That joy was something I lost during my divine upbringing."

"So her idea of reality was different to yours?" The frown had remained on Gulukone's face throughout Yayler's short speech.

"Aye, it was. So which one was the truth, her reality, or mine? They were so radically different that they can't both be right; at least not in the Frames philosophy."

"I think yours was."

"It is to me, but to her, the reality, the truth was that I was her son. To understand truth completely, I believe it is necessary to record all influences of an event, however miniscule. Each event is influenced by other events, so they too need to be recorded and understood. Each of these secondary events is also influenced by other events. In short then, it is only possible to know the whole truth if you record every event, however small, that occurs in the Universe. Even then, the laws of chaos would introduce random variations. Essentially, it is not possible to know the truth, only a part of it."

"It is unfortunate that you believe this. Don't forget that you are to be executed. Debates such as this change nothing of that reality. Stimulating though they are." Gulukone returned to his post outside Yayler's cabin door, leaving the prisoner to his thoughts.

Chapter Twenty One

With back aching and tired arms, Pyta paddled on, striving against a strong current. Ahead lay mountains that were dark against a pre-dawn sky. He headed for a chink of light. That meant people and food.

It wasn't far now and he could see the vague outline of a croft-house. He let the coracle drift with the current and rubbed his arms. Pyta had been paddling all night and had discovered that the little boat highly was unsuitable for the broad channel of the Brayvik Straits. His morcote lay in the bottom of the boat and was soaked. He sighed, a long weary exhalation of breath and started to paddle again.

He landed on rocks not far from the croft and immediately felt extremely tired. He needed rest. Pyta decided that it looked like being a good day. He spread the soaked morcote out on a broad rock, turned the coracle upside down and huddled underneath it. Hungry as he was, he needed some sleep first.

When he woke, it was the middle of the day. He still ached, cramped muscles protested and he was as stiff as the oar from the 'worthless' coracle. He waited, watching the croft for the rest of the day. There appeared to be two women and a goat. This was going to be an easy raid, thought Pyta. He would wait until dark, and kill the goat and then disappear like mist in the hills. The women would never even know he had been there. They would just wake the next day to find their goat gone.

During the afternoon, banks of clouds rolled in, obscuring the moons. Evening turned into dark, moonless night and Pyta made his move. The goat was around the back of the croft and he carefully made his way in that direction. It was difficult crossing the boulders to the cultivated land of the croft. Pyta's feet slipped into the water several times causing splashing, noise he couldn't afford.

He tripped a couple of times once away from the shore, cursing each time, but by placing each foot cautiously and delicately at each step, he managed to get to the rear of the croft without further incident. Where was the goat? In the dark, he could see little as he fumbled for his knife, now his most valued possession.

Pyta could hear the goat eating. It was crunching on vegetation not far away. He moved slowly forward, skirting past a woodpile. He could just make out a wall ahead and started toward it. There was a clattering noise, as something trod on lose rocks. 'That must be the goat' thought Pyta and took a further step toward the wall.

The noise stopped, Pyta held his breath for long moments, then slowly exhaled. The munching started again. Pyta took the last two steps to the wall, which was only waist height. Where was the goat? He should be able to see it.

There was another scrabbling in the rocks, sudden and explosive, and Pyta found himself face to face with the goat that now stood atop the wall. Abruptly the goat reared and head butted Pyta in the face. Pyta fell back onto the woodpile, scattering the wood as he landed.

As Pyta stood up, he could make out the goat, still standing on the wall and glaring at him in the dark. Pyta cursed, wiping blood from his face. The damned animal had probably broken his nose. He still had his knife in his hand, so he crouched and stepped toward the goat intent on making a swift kill.

Pyta was only a step away from the goat when pain exploded at the back of his head. Turning he saw the figure of a slim woman wielding a hefty branch from the scattered woodpile. He barely avoided another strike, ducking to avoid the blow aimed at his head.

Pyta charged at the woman who swung her branch, knocking Pyta's knife from his hand. Pyta pinned the woman down and was about to beat her senseless with his fists, when pain, again, exploded in his head. The other woman had joined in the fray and had struck him with another branch from the woodpile.

It was getting out of hand; Pyta had lost control of the situation. He rolled free and backed away from the two women, frantically looking for his knife, but failing to see it in the dark.

"I don't know what you want, but you're not welcome here." The taller of the two women hollered at Pyta, waving her branch menacingly.

Pyta's nose was bleeding profusely and when he touched his head, he found his hand came away sticky with blood. The women were between him and the scattered woodpile. Grabbing dirt from the ground, he threw it into the face of the nearer, taller of the women and charged the smaller, but

Chapter Twenty One

stumbled over a piece of wood and found himself face down in the dirt. Scrabbling about desperately he found a hard object and grasped it firmly, only realising as he did so that it was his knife. The women had not taken advantage of his stumble, but stood back, allowing him to regain his feet.

"Leave us alone!" It was the smaller woman, screaming shrilly at him. Pyta thought he detected panic in her voice.

Pyta picked a hefty branch from the ground and tucked his knife away. He began to swing the branch in lazy arcs. The women stood next to each other facing him and Pyta grinned at them maliciously. The gesture was mostly lost in the dark. Pyta then feinted with a big swing at the taller woman's head, continuing his swing and changing his attack to the smaller woman who barely managed to block the attack with her branch.

She yelped and scampered back out of his range. Pyta continued the attack on the taller woman with a series of vicious blows toward head and body that the woman was barely able to parry.

"Eala!" screamed the other woman re-joining the fray with a huge swing of her branch toward Pyta's head.

Pyta easily blocked the blow and wrenched the branch from her hands. Then he kicked her to the ground and returned to the assault on the taller woman, forcing her back. She tripped over something, losing grip on her branch as she fell. As she lay panting on her back, prone and defenceless, Pyta aimed a massive swing at her head. The blow never landed.

A blow from behind knocked Pyta off his feet and he landed face down in the dirt. The goat had head butted Pyta again. Both women, having recovered their feet and now with fresh branches, started to pummel Pyta.

It was too much for Pyta. He gave up the battle and scrambled away from the women. He lurched back to the boulders and his coracle and made his escape. He ignored the pain from the beating and made his way back along the coast, allowing the current to propel him. After about ten sents, he came ashore again on a pavement of smooth, flattened boulders, many of which had sides covered with limpets. These he prised off with his knife and ate raw.

His nose had swollen and made breathing difficult. Otherwise, nothing appeared to be broken, but the bruising would take a while to heal. The could tolerate the pain, but the ignominy of taking a beating from a couple of women rankled.

Pyta rested, trying to digest the shellfish, but he knew he had to move on. There might be a search for him in daylight and he wanted to be far away if that happened. Once again, Pyta set out into the Brayvik Straits, thanking his fortune for clement weather.

Daybreak saw him on another rocky shore and another meal of shellfish and molluscs. The next tenday saw him working his way along rocky shorelines by night and sleeping under the cover of his coracle by day. There were few signs of habitation, though plenty of seabirds. If it had been spring, he would have been able to steal eggs; anything would make a welcome change to his current seafood diet.

As morning dawned on that tenth day, he saw a peninsula that looked familiar. Striated rocks dipped into the sea, surmounted with a bold knoll. Pyta was sure he had been to this place before. That meant people lived there, people he knew. It might be possible for him to rebuild his life again. He would find out later. For now, he would sleep, then, later, he would make his way onto the peninsula to find out why it was familiar to him. He camped below a sloping cliff with a waterfall that provided him with fresh water and pondered over his previous acquaintance with the peninsula.

Optimism was a strong characteristic in Pyta. No matter how bad his life got, and it had at times been very bad, he always believed there was a turning point ahead. A time when all would come good and he would be able to live in the comfort he desired.

After a few wairs of sleep, Pyta tried to tidy himself up a bit. It was a difficult job as his hair was matted and he had grown a scruffy beard, his clothing stunk, was in poor repair, and hung off him. He had lost a lot of weight during his travelling. In short, he looked dreadful.

After a good wair making himself look as presentable as possible, Pyta was still the epitome of a vagabond. He secured the coracle above the tidemarks and made his way uphill by the waterfall. His ascent was quick and Pyta soon emerged onto rolling hills of mossy grasses that had a springy bounce as he walked across them. It was not long before the terrain became recognisable and he knew where he was.

He changed direction, heading now to where he knew there was a track. Though muddy and rutted it led to a place he knew. A place he might be welcome. Cheered by the thought of a decent meal and a comfortable bed, Pyta increased his pace and was soon standing on the track, looking out across the broad straits of Marlok. How much time had he spent watching those waters, recording the movements of boats? It had been dull work, but at least he'd had whisky and a comfortable bed at night.

Pyta had no wish to re-visit that part of his life, so he headed the other direction, away from his lookout spot and toward his former abode. Before long, the old croft came into view, though there was no sign of his former landlady, Pibeg. He soon found her in the vegetable patch, working the soil around turnips and onions. He watched her, leaning on the stone wall that surrounded her vegetable garden.

"Hey, Pibeg, yer're lukin e'en fatter than 'fore!" Pyta had never been polite, or even particularly nice to Pibeg. That wasn't about to change.

"Pyta!" Pibeg stood and glowered at Pyta. She stood up slowly and placed her hands to the small of her back. "You worthless cac. What brings you back here?"

"Ah wer' jus' passin' by."

"You're an idiot Pyta. Nobody just passes by here. Why have you come back. We all thought we were well rid of you."

"Ya, ah wer' a fool. Me Boss, he lied ta me. Ah should 'ave stayed 'ere."

Pibeg regarded Pyta with a long, hard and searching look, as if trying to discern an untruth, but this was Pyta, of course there would be an untruth. As far as Pibeg was concerned, Pyta didn't have a single, honest bone in his body. "You're a lying, cheating fool, Pyta, but you can stay, but on my terms. I need a man to do the heavy work around here. So you may stay, as long as you earn your keep."

This was more than Pyta had expected. He had expected to resort to cajoling and lies to gain a bed, but Pibeg had made an offer without his having to resort to unscrupulous or dishonest measures. The only thing about the deal that bothered Pyta was the idea of work. As far as he could remember, he had never completed an honest day of labour in his entire life. It seemed that was about to change.

Later, after Pyta had eaten his first proper meal since leaving Garvin, Pibeg turned to him. "Pyta, I need to talk to you."

Pyta shrugged "wot abaht?"

"You, Pyta."

"Wot abaht me?"

"You are going to be a father."

Pyta suddenly went very quiet. This couldn't happen to him. For a moment, he thought Pibeg was joking with him, but one look at her serious expression Pyta knew this was not the case. He felt trapped, perhaps not physically, but by the unwanted development. Of course, he could leave. The child would be cared for, and he would still be at liberty to do as he pleased.

No one would care if he stayed or went; no one had ever cared about Pyta. He had always been alone; it had always been Pyta against the rest. They didn't matter to him. A child though, would be a part of himself, something that mattered. He nodded his acceptance of the situation, quietly and to himself.

Pyta didn't think he would ever care about Pibeg; the child was the result of a drunken union between them. There was no love or compassion between them; that would not change. At least if he stayed, the child would have a better start to life than if he went. For the first time in his life, Pyta found that he had something that mattered as much, or possibly more than he did.

That night he slept on the bare floor, wrapped in his damp morcote. He still had the best night sleep that he could remember since leaving Garvin. Snores coming from Pibeg woke Pyta early so he went outside where a bright morning greeted him.

The view from Pibeg's croft was aesthetically beautiful, but such things had little meaning or worth to Pyta. In fact, the view disturbed him, not for any meaningless or abstruse esoteric charm, to him, but because of the large aimu troop transport moored about half a stride off shore. A chilling sensation ran down his spine, fear. Pyta could not understand what aimu and, presumably, divines would be doing in a remote area like this. He did not like it; he did not want it, but somehow knew that it was not going to go away.

A tenday after their unwanted evening visitor, Sara and Ealasat woke to find a fleet of ships moored in the waters opposite the croft. They had intended a short trip to check lobster pots, but couldn't agree on what they should do.

Chapter Twenty One

"Ealasat, I don't think it's wise to stay."

"This is my home Sara, this is where I belong."

"The machines on those ships will destroy us. There must be hundreds of divines on each one of those ships." Sara was urgently trying to move Ealasat away, but the taller woman was unyielding to her urgings.

"Sara, this is where I belong. Everything that is 'me' is here."

"And it will stay here, but we need to warn others."

"Who needs a warning?" Ealasat gestured with her hand towards the ships. "Who's going to miss that?"

"What about Dook? You wouldn't have the Kooinag without him?"

Ealasat bowed her head, troubled. She desperately wanted to stay and protect her home, but another part of her knew that was not the best course. Sara was right, she couldn't stay.

The women spent the next wair sorting out what they needed, which wasn't much. A few personal items, a comb, a belt knife and so on. They then drew the Kooinag from the water and disguised the boat as best they could. Having done what they could to make the croft house secure, they left for Rustick More, Ealasat for the second time in her life, not knowing this time, when or even if she would return.

By late afternoon, they were at Rustick More talking with an unhappy Dook. Ealasat's goat, Gawa, almost unnoticed, was nibbling gently at a corner of Dook's morcote. They were standing in Toiler's Woe and had attracted a small, concerned crowd.

"Why would they want to stop there? I don't understand this." Dook complained pulling at his beard.

"We didn't stop to ask them, Dook" Sara advised him with a hint of sarcasm.

"They haven't stopped to make a social call, you can be sure of that." Ealasat pulled gently on Gawa's tether in a vain attempt to dissuade his nibbling.

"Aye, it's certainly not that" Dook agreed. "I just don't understand why they would come here. They've made no attempt to land, no aggressive move."

"Perhaps they don't feel the need to. What's to stop them doing exactly what they want? They can walk into any village, any time they want, we would be unable to stop them." Dona had joined the crowd and raised her voice above the general hubbub.

"Hmm, where's Neev?"

"I believe she's checking for messages on that contraption of yours" Dona answered.

Gawa tugged hard on Dook's morcote, pulling it slightly from his shoulder and Dook tried to push the animal away. "Would someone fetch her? Dona, how are we doing on our defences?"

"There is still a lot to do. There are no field defences yet, and Dook's Folly, the big gunna, has not been tested yet" Dona answered with a worried expression.

"What have we got?" Gawa tugged even harder on Dook's morcote. "And you need to get your dinner from somewhere else!" Dook squatted down and scratched Gawa underneath its chin.

Belatedly, Ealasat pulled the goat away and shortened the leash.

"We are short on hand weapons, grenades, short staffs and so on; most have been sent to Dundoon or Tuaport. We also recently sent a lot to Fraze. Heavy weapons that we can use to fight machines are a problem. We have four serviceable fliers, but only three have weapons. In short, we are not in good shape." Dona reeled the list off, counting on her fingers, then shrugged, not sure what else to say.

"Right people, we have a problem." Dook called out to the growing crowd. "The machines and the divines are in the Brayvik Straits, we don't know their intentions yet, but the chances are that they will come here. We don't know how much time we have. First of all, let's get as many short staffs and grenades made as we can."

Dook gestured Dona to follow him and headed off to his rooms. Anbooakil was there poring over technical plans for the repulse shields. He looked up as Dook entered and ruffled the plans in the air. "These are quite a quite remarkable demonstration of lateral thinking. It is quite impressive."

"Ah, thank you. I need to talk to some people privately. Would you mind helping on Toiler's Woe. There is a lot to be done there." Seeing a blank look on Anbooakil's face, Dook continued. "There are aimu ships moored in the straits, not too far from here, would you know anything about them?"

"My knowledge of such ships is limited as I am not connected with the Frame. I will gladly help."

As Anbooakil left, Dook added "can you send Fil and Neev up here"

"I will do so" replied Anbooakil, making a slight inclination of his head as he did so.

Dook and Dona were compiling a list of priorities and essential needs for defence when Neev and Fil arrived. Dook beckoned them in. "Fil, I need you to take a flier and see what is happening with this fleet in the Brayvik Straits. Keep your distance, mind, we need that information."

"Aye, I spoke briefly to Sara on the way up here. My guess is that they are making preparations for a landing, though, for all we know, they may move on tomorrow."

"I suspect that they won't. I'm going to work on the assumption that their intent is aggressive. I want to know what they are doing." Dook turned to Neev "I want you to message with the seismocom both Dundoon and Cullin. Let them know what is happening."

"Aye, what about Ecta's Ledge? I think they're about ready for messaging now. I'm just waiting for the first contact." Neev answered.

"Good, I want you by that machine all the time; sleep by it. I'll relieve you when I can, but I must have messages sent to me as soon as they arrive."

"The Frame may decide to attack there as well." Dona chipped in.

"Aye, it may; it certainly has the resources to fight on two fronts. Let's find out what is happening before jumping to conclusions. Get those messages sent as soon as you can Neev."

As Neev left, Dook turned to Dona. "What were you saying earlier about field defences?"

Imperceptibly the staff at Rustick More stepped up a gear, if Dook had pushed them hard before, now they pushed themselves even harder. Fil returned from his scouting to report that he could count eight ships, most of which appeared to be carrying troops. He had managed to take a few stills with a compad that allowed Dook to confirm his report.

Dona had outlined a few plans for defending the area surrounding Rustick More, but Dook abandoned these as impractical in the timescale available. Instead, Dook wanted manned outposts near the entrance tunnels. He wanted the tunnels set with explosive charges so that they could destroy the entrances to Rustick More if the aimu army got too close. Dook was going to have to depend on the natural defences of Rustick More.

By the time, it got dark and Dook allowed the people to get a few wairs of rest, Dook had made his plans. An inventory of anti-personnel weaponry only highlighted the desperate situation. They had less than fifty working short staffs, almost a thousand grenades, and about fifty boxes of explosive slingshots. It wasn't much.

Dook was in the canteen eating a bowl of stew and a chunk of bread wondering how long the food supplies would last. The answer he got from Big Jon was disappointing; essentially Rustick More supplies were insufficient to withstand a siege or well enough armed to fight a battle. It was hopeless.

Neev came to him with a couple of messages from Dundoon and Cullin that she had scrawled onto a scrap of paper. The report from Dundoon denied any aimu presence in the area around the town. In addition, they requested extra personnel to assist Troomey with completing a repulse shield for the town. Cullin reported that they were making good progress, but had suffered one fatality on the ocean voyage. There were no messages from Ecta's Ledge or Tuaport and the installation of the seismocom devices by technical staff in other places was still underway.

Dook scribbled a couple of replies for Neev to send and told her to get some rest and that he would relieve her later. He wanted time to think. He wanted to talk to the staff and had arranged for a meeting in Toiler's Woe in the morning and wanted time to think about what he was going to say.

Suddenly a loud boom reverberated through Rustick More from Toiler's Woe. Panicked thoughts thrust their way into Dook's mind. Were the machines and divines attacking already? They couldn't be. They hadn't disembarked from their ships yet. Dook followed a group of tech staff through to Toiler's Woe, wondering what had gone wrong.

An excited crowd clustered about Dook's Folly. Anbooakil stood behind the controls looking calm and placid as if nothing was wrong or out of place.

"What in Irin happened?" Dook called out. A crowd of grinning faces greeted him.

Chapter Twenty One

"Your device works" Anbooakil spoke. "It is poorly constructed, but works efficiently. The design is contrary to the intended use of some of the components. The power output is sufficient to damage most aimu and a more efficient design would improve this."

The news cheered Dook for a brief moment, but then he realised the loudness of the blast would have reverberated across the countryside and, he was certain, be heard by the aimu fleet. "Kindly inform me next time you wish to perform a test. That noise was sufficient to raise the dead."

"I could build a more efficient device, but that would require more tests and time."

Anbooakil showed no emotion as ey spoke. Dook had yet to see the giant so much as smile. Anbooakil was very 'machinelike' in eyers behaviour, anhedonic in nature to the extent that Dook thought that a vital part of humanity had been bred out of eym. It did not matter, though, if the 'creature' could produce more weapons. "How much time?"

Anbooakil made an apologetic gesture with eyers hands "I do not know until I see the materials I have to work with. Do you wish me to do this?"

"Aye, even one more big gunna would be helpful, but no more tests without telling me first."

Anbooakil was quite impassive as ey replied. "Then I will train your men in the use of this device, then start on building more."

Chapter Twenty Two

Gilmur49 was a young and successful Divine General. He was tall, slim and had strong features that few would call handsome, and was utterly ruthless. He was in charge of a ten-thousand strong divine army given the job of crushing the rebellion. The defiant spirit of the region of Garvamore caused many problems for the Frame. Though he was not normally interested in the Frame's problems, this particular one was his to sort out. He had studied reports on the Battle of Dundoon and had no illusions about the job. He expected it to be difficult.

The first job was to establish a bridgehead and then to take control of as much ground as he could before advancing on the mountain stronghold that was believed to be the centre of the resistance movement. His aimu masters had been very specific in their instructions. The local population had to be subdued, pacified, and totally dominated by a show of force before the main offensive could begin. Gilmur49 did not agree with the tactic. He had wanted to move directly to the main target, this 'Rustick More' to prevent them from preparing defences.

Initial scheduled landings were to start the next day. First, there would be meetings, planning, and analysis. Everything had to be organised down to the last detail. Gilmur49's aimu masters wanted no mistakes, no errors.

Gilmur49 stood before a three-dimensional chart of the area, studying a long, slender, and very rugged peninsula. The small village of Tymeum stood at one end surrounded by hills. The terrain was not as rough as further inland or as difficult as the sharp ridges of the peninsula. A rough track linked the village with other communities, but was not wide enough to be of great use for logistics. Gilmur49 had to consider how he was going to move equipment and supplies on a single rough track, which was simply, inadequate.

Tymeum would have to serve as a headquarters for the divine army. A constant reconnaissance of the area by droid fliers would maintain an aerial watch. Gilmur49 was aware that the enemy had their own fliers, but they were no match for the craft of the Frame. Aimu battle units were to be reserved for the assault on the mountain fastness. The strength of the two armies was an overwhelming force. It would not be swift, but it would be inexorable.

Fil landed the flier and powered down before allowing his ten passengers to disembark onto the floor of Toiler's Woe. He had already made the trip to Dundoon several times during the night and now felt ready for a few wairs of sleep. What he hadn't anticipated was Dook climbing into the flier.

"It is a fine morning Fil. How do you feel about a quick flight to have a look at our new friends?" Dook seemed to be in a very untypically jovial mood.

"Not happy. I've been ferrying passengers all night. I need to sleep." Fil stared Dook in the face.

"I can pilot, but I need someone to operate the cammic equipment. I won't take long. You can get some rest when we get back."

Fil didn't believe Dook. Somehow, it would take longer than anticipated. There would always be another image to take, or something else to investigate. "It's still too dark to get good detail. Wouldn't it be better to wait until it's a bit lighter? One of the other pilots can do it then."

"I think the cammic will work fine. You won't need to do much, just point the cammic at the aimu fleet."

Fil realised that Dook was not going to back down. This was typical behaviour from Dook, he simply expected people to keep working through exhaustion, and recently he had become worse. "Well, let's get the job done then, but if I fall asleep on you, don't say I didn't warn you."

"That's fine Fil. Let's go then."

Within fifteen sents, the flier was high above the fleet moored in the Brayvik Straits. The ships looked very small to Fil. "Will you get enough detail from this height? It is very difficult to see what is happening down there." Fil was lying face down in the front of the flier, pointing the cammic through the lower clear plaz nose canopy.

"Aye, I'll get what I need." Dook made a large circle about the fleet in the dull grey early morning light. A bolt of energy shot from one of the smaller, barely visible aimu ships, missing the flier by a good distance. "I think that is the signal for us to leave."

"I'm happy with that plan, Dook." Fil began to pack up the cammic in a small case and returned to the navigator's seat. "You'd think they don't want us around."

"In more ways than one, I fear, Fil. Get yourself off to bed when we get back. Don't worry about the meeting."

Fil smiled. It was a weary, forced smile. For once Dook had been true to his word and Fil felt his eyes drooping with the desperate need for sleep. Back at Rustick More, people were beginning to assemble for the meeting called by Dook. Dook ignored them, taking the cammic to his rooms instead. What he found didn't surprise him, but filled him with a feeling of dread. The enemy were making their first move.

He found Anbooakil pouring over flier plans. "Busy as always I see" he greeted. "Can you do something for me?"

Anbooakil looked up and bowed his head imperceptibly. "If I can be of service, I will."

"Good, thank you. Can you take the captured ship aimu to Toiler's Woe and power it up. I will need some of its functions."

"It is in a poor state of repair, but I will do as you ask." Anbooakil left without ceremony or any display of emotion. Dook sometimes wondered if the Frame had removed emotions during its creation. Such formal anhedonic politeness gave the giant an inhuman countenance that many of the aneksa at Rustick More found uncomfortable. Many distrusted the creature intensely. Dook himself wondered how far he should trust the creature.

"Thank you. I will be down there shortly." Dook turned to the cammic and quickly viewed the images, making mental notes as he inspected each still image. They would need to be analysed in detail later. He wasted no more time. People were waiting and he knew what he needed to know, details would have to wait.

Twenty sents later, he stood in front of an impatient and nervous crowd. Dona, Neev, and Anbooakil were by his side next to the aimu they had taken from the transport ship captured in Dundoon, powered with cables linked to Dook's Folly. Isla and a contingent of twenty troops from Dundoon stood impassively and slightly to one side of the main group. Dook had restored its three-dimensional display, which now projected a blank image in the air between Dook and the crowd. "Good morning all, I am sorry to have kept you waiting."

There were muttered greetings and shuffling of restless feet.

"Many of you will recognise the machine here, and know that I have spent many wairs trying to extract useful data from it. Well, as many of you know, it is a navigational computer taken from a transport ship. It is intelligent in its own way, but as a part of a 'hive mind', subservient to the Frame." Dook paused. His mouth was dry making it difficult to deliver his unaccustomed speech.

"There are twelve more ships moored in the Brayvik Straits." Dook paused again to let the information sink in. "A little while ago I took a flier and managed to record a few images." He fussed with the aimu for a few moments. Then an aerial image of sea and a few small dots materialised in the display.

"The larger ships are transports and the smaller are support vessels. Now, if I enlarge the image near one of the transports". The image zoomed in on a selected ship, producing an uncomfortable feeling of falling at great speed "you will see smaller landing craft heading in the direction of Tymeum.

"By now, it is probable that the area around Tymeum is under direct control by the machines. I am also certain that the position of Rustick More is now known to the Frame. I have made an estimate based on these stills, of the number of troops. There are probably two and a half thousand or more troops on those ships."

There were gasps and whispered mutterings from the gathered people. A voice from the back of the crowd spoke out loudly "we beat them at Dundoon, we can beat them again." The crowd responded to the comment with a general babble of "ayes" and cheers of approval.

Dook waited for the noise to quieten before continuing "we have scouts out now, watching their every move, but we don't have much time. They will be coming here, and soon."

Dook raised his voice slightly to make his next point more forceful. "The army we face is better equipped and supported and we are not in a very good position to fight back."

There was a general murmur of disapproval among the crowd, which Dook wanted to dispel quickly. "How many of you have been trained to fight?" A very few hands went up. Dook continued "we don't have enough people at Rustick More who can fight. That is because we have concentrated on weapon production and development at Rustick More, and not on our fighting abilities."

The voice from the back of the crowd called out again "we can't just give up without a fight."

Dook had to raise his voice again above the hubbub and noise of the crowd. "We are low on ammunition, we have very little to fight with. Our food supplies are low. We are in a very poor position to fight back."

"So what are we going to do?" It was the voice from the back of the crowd again.

"We do have a plan, and we are not giving up." Dook noted a buzz of expectancy from the people before him. "Rustick More will not fall easily. A relatively small force can defend it. Overnight we have brought in a few Bloody Duncans, the defenders of Dundoon. They and a few essential staff will remain here. Everyone else will be evacuated to Ecta's Ledge where Briga will continue to manufacture weapons. The few who remain will sit tight. Even now, we are mustering an army of trained warriors that will head this way in the next few days."

Dook used the aimu to produce a topographical map of the area around Tymeum and Rustick More. "As you can see from this image, Rustick More lies between Tymeum and the rest of Anklayv Island. The Frame needs to take Rustick More or start another front somewhere else. From here we can disrupt, harry, and make any progress difficult for the Frame. We will use hit and run tactics at night to make life as difficult as possible for the enemy. I hope that this will buy us more time while our own forces assemble."

The meeting went on for a little while longer, but as far as Dook was concerned, he had covered the essential points. He broke up the meeting leaving Dona to organise the evacuation. He would be staying, of course. He beckoned Isla over as the uncertain crowd began to break up.

"Isla, I need to discuss defence plans with you in more detail. How many troops have you got?" Dook noted that Isla was almost at eye level with him, with a lean muscular frame.

"Just twenty, it won't be enough to defend this place."

"Aye, but twenty of you guys are worth two hundred of this lot in a fight. How many more will you need?"

"You said it yourself. Two hundred trained troops would give you a fighting chance. With what you have now, this place would be over-run very quickly. I can't believe you want to defend this place."

"They would learn far too much about the aneksa from this place. We can get more troops in, but I would rather keep them at a distance than fight. They don't know what we have here, so they will be cautious. Come with me, I have plans of this place in my rooms. Let's work out what you need."

Whilst thrashing out details of the defence of Rustick More, Ela, who had been Cullin's navigator earlier in the year, came up to Dook's rooms. "I know you're busy, but there is a craft flying nearby. It looks like one of the drone fliers we saw at Dundoon." The young woman was flustered and rushed through her report, her breath coming in gasps.

"Ah, I was wondering how long it would take for that. I saw the delta wings of a drone on one of the ships earlier today. The Frame doesn't appear to be in any rush to crush us. Keep an eye on those drones and log when and where they fly."

"Aye, do you not want them shot down?"

Dook shook his head vigorously. "Nay. Your fliers are no match for them."

Isla nodded agreement. "It might be worth moving the fliers away from Rustick More, altogether."

"Aye, that is a good idea. Ela, you and the other pilots should get away from here while you can. Take the fliers to Ecta's Ledge. Take the technical staff there too. They will be of more use over there, than they can be here."

It took Dook and Isla another wair to go through all the details of the defence plans. Isla was just leaving when Anbooakil joined them with a worried, almost haunted expression.

"Dookerock, I believe I have a problem. I wanted to ask your advice on the matter."

Anbooakil remained standing as Isla left. Dook had noticed before that he rarely sat. "When I connected with the ship aimu, I learned how to complete my initialisation programming. I am uncertain whether to do this or not. I wanted to ask your advice on the matter."

Dook was startled "what were you doing communicating with it?"

Chapter Twenty Two

"I apologise. You left the aimu on earlier. I was closing down its functions, before returning it."

Dook realised that he had left no instructions with Anbooakil about the aimu. The giant had set it up for him, so of course when his job was complete, returned it to its little room deep in the bowels of Rustick More. "What do you believe will happen if you complete the initialisation?"

"I will become a fully compatible part of the Frames systems. That is what I was meant to be."

"Is that what you want?" Dook realised that this was a very profound choice for Anbooakil to make. The giant had been given a period of independence that it might not wish to give up. How deep the initialising process went was an unknown.

Anbooakil took a long time to answer. Eyers normally placid features creased with unaccustomed expression as he considered Dook's question. "I am uncertain. I am not supposed to have experienced the lives of Muckers, or the way you strive to free yourselves from the Frames guidance."

"I think I understand your dilemma. You need to decide if you are human, machine and part of the Frame, or a bit of both. I can't help you with that. It is up to you to decide."

Anbooakil paused again. This time several long sents went passed before he answered. "You are essentially correct, but it is a difficult choice. Without the initialisation, I am incomplete. With initialisation, I would become a different person."

"I think that I can help you to a certain degree. A normal human learns through experience. Initialisation would deny you that process. How deep the process goes into your conscious and subconscious mind, I cannot know. I can only guess. The Frame is a very controlling entity, so the process is likely to go very deep. I suspect you would become a puppet of the Frame, because that is how the Frame tends to operate."

"I follow your logic. I need to think about this. I will be on the roof." By 'roof', Anbooakil meant the summit plateau of Rustick More.

"Keep out of sight of those drones. The Frame does not need to know that you are here. It must not know."

Anbooakil nodded his understanding, but said nothing.

Yayler stood next to Clar15 on the bridge of the aimu warship, the huge and impassive Gulukone behind him. Gilmur49, the Divine General, stood by the three-dimensional display of the area, which dominated the central part of the bridge. Through the large plaz windows, Yayler could see the mountains of Garvamore and the village of Tymeum, nestled amongst surrounding low hills.

As he watched, opaque blisters appeared in the rigid deck of the ship in two long rows and grew rapidly in size. It was as if the hard metal skin of the deck had become pliable, protecting something underneath. The blisters rippled in unison, then split as the skin pulled back to reveal sleek craft beneath. Yayler heard a howling buzz as the craft lifted and sped off towards Tymeum.

Yayler knew what the craft were, troop transports. The landings had begun. A knot of fear for the people grew in Yayler's stomach. He hoped that they had thought to flee into the hills and escape the destruction that now sped their way. He counted twenty-five of the craft as they flew arrow-straight toward the village.

He turned to Clar15 "why are you showing me this?"

"I want you to see how futile your efforts against the Frame are. This is just a small force. We have other landings in other areas. This area will soon be back under the full control of the Frame."

"There will be a time that the iron grip of the Frame will fail. It is inevitable."

"You are wrong, Victor8, and the cost of your failure is your life and greater suffering of the people." Clar15 looked Yayler in the eye, her voice certain and steady. Her conviction in the strength of the Frame was absolute.

"The people you refer to are part of a chaotic system and cannot be controlled any more than the weather. People resist control." Yayler gestured towards the receding flier troop transports. "What you are doing here is wrong. I had hoped that you would see and understand this."

"Their lives will be better and more productive. The Frame is benign, not evil."

"Really?" The tone of Yayler's voice made it quite clear that he thought that Clar15 was talking rubbish.

"Really, you should have more faith in the machines."

"The Frame may have been benign once, but ask yourself; is this the act of a benign entity? Did you read the statistics I sent you? What harm have these people done, to be treated like this."

Clar15 frowned. Her deeply embedded belief in the Frame was a part of her psyche. That was the case for all divines. From early childhood, all divines had training to believe and follow the Frame's direction. Their conviction in that belief was tested and those who failed the tests never reached adulthood. Clar15 wondered what had happened to Yayler. What had caused him to turn aside from such deep training?

She did not dislike Yayler; in fact, she found his concern for lesser people endearing; another characteristic of the man that Clar15 found to be very un-divine. In the distance, she watched the fliers land and saw the tell-tale flicker of stol-fire. There was little or no resistance.

The old woman sat behind her trestle correcting mistakes in a report so that it would be fit for the young Lord to read. She saw this as being one of her major functions. If everyone who wrote these reports and documents took the time to use proper grammar and punctuation, then surely the Mark would run a lot more smoothly. There had been occasions when she had completely rewritten documents because of bad phrasing or writing.

She disliked disturbances. She would quite happily perform her exacting tasks in a quiet anti-room out of the way, thereby avoiding the disturbances that occurred continuously in the Great Hall. Another person could quite easily do the meeting and greeting.

There had been a lot of hustle and bustle since those ships had moored in the straits. The Lord was convinced that something important was about to happen and wanted all documentation in order. Sovrack was a proud woman who did not want to appear to fail in her duties. She had spent the last day checking that all documents were in place and filed correctly, and was now happy that everything was in order.

Outside she could hear many disturbances and unwarranted noise. Then she heard raised voices and the door-guard came storming into the Great Hall and rushed over to her trestle.

"Sovrack, go and get the Lord. There are divines coming this way, and they are killing people."

Sovrack stared at the large balding man uncomprehendingly as his lower jaw thrust out at her. Most of the villagers called him Lun after his love of ale. His large belly and florid complexion stood testament to his pursuance of that pleasure. Sovrack had little time for such dalliance, but the man wouldn't be told. "Go and tell him yourself!" she yelled back at him. "Can't you see that I am busy?"

Lun swept the papers from the table and bawled back at her. "Go and get the Lord, now!"

Sovrack looked down in bewilderment at the papers scattered on the floor, then stared for a moment at Lun. She then attempted to pick the scattered documents from the floor, ignoring the large enraged man standing by her trestle.

Lun grabbed her by the hair and hauled her to her feet. "Go and get the Lord."

By this time, the disturbances had come to the attention of the young Lord Fin. He had been enjoying a breakfast of cured meats, fruits and a heavy oat bread made in the area. "What in Irin is going on?" Fin demanded.

"My Lord, divines are attacking the village. They are killing anybody they come across."

"Don't be stupid, Lun, they wouldn't do that. You must be mistaken."

"See for yourself, Lord." Lun gestured toward the entrance with an outstretched arm.

Lord Fin rushed to the doors and pushed his way through a cluster of men bearing spades, forks, or any implement that they could conceivably use as a weapon. Down the lane stols flashed. The crumpled figure of an old woman lay lifeless in the dirt.

One of the men shouted in his ear "My Lord, divines have landed in machines."

Chapter Twenty Two

Another man added "they are killing anyone they meet in the streets."

"Inside, everyone." Fin had seen enough. He could see what was happening, but was at a loss to know what to do. The men crowded around him inside the doorway, chattering angrily, but their words did not register as his mind raced. They could not fight with spades or forks. Then he remembered the old hunting bows, hidden long ago. He had seen them as a child. The weapons were banned by the Frame.

"Bar those doors. Lun, make sure all other doors are secure. Sovrack, get the keys to the basement, I'll meet you down there." Fin would defend the Great Hall no matter what. As he headed to the back of the hall and down narrow passages that led to the basement. There, behind a thick wooden door were storerooms, archives and all manner of things too precious to discard including the old hunting weapons that Fin now sought.

He didn't have to wait long for Sovrack. She was one of few people who knew where the keys were kept. His face was hard, set with a burning determination as he selected the key from the ring. He twisted the key with far more force than was necessary, but levers creaked and the bolt slid from its recess. Fin heaved the door open and entered a passageway and the musty rooms beyond. At the far end of the passageway another door stood. Adrenaline pumped, Fin stormed down the corridor, whilst fumbling with the keys in the dim light.

Fin opened the door in similar fashion to the first and stared into the dingy gloom. The room was stacked with old clothing and leather hides, but Fin knew there was more to this storeroom than met the casual eye. He threw aside much of the old clothing until he revealed a large chest. He selected another key to open the chest. There lay arrows and five old hunting bows, short, but powerful. Without ceremony, he slammed the lid back down and dragged the chest from the room. It was heavy, so he simply dragged the chest to the Great Hall where the men were still arguing and shouting belligerently.

"Which of you has handled a bow before?" he bellowed.

Lun raised a hand and two of the other men. "You three get up on the roof. You others stay with me." As the three men selected their bows, he spoke quietly to them. "Keep them off for as long as you can, then come to me here."

Fin upturned the remaining contents of the chest and set it in the middle of the hall. "You others find as much heavy furniture as you can and pile it up here. I'll join you shortly."

"What do you want me to do?" Sovrack asked in a quiet voice.

"Can you fight?" Fin asked.

"No"

"Then all you can do is keep out of the way."

Once on the roof, Fin could see that the divines were almost upon them. Two ranks of five men advanced up the street with stols ready. The men looked at him, waiting for instruction. He ignored them, let lose an arrow at the closest divine and missed his mark widely. The arrow bounced harmlessly down the street.

The divines paused in their advance. This was the first sign of any resistance they had encountered. Without visible sign or instruction, they scattered to find shelter behind the corners of buildings.

Fin let off another arrow, which struck the wall of a stone cottage not two hand spans from a sheltering divine. His aim was closer this time. "Save your arrows, men. Wait until they step out from behind those walls before firing."

Lun and the others nodded. Fin felt exposed on the roof of the Great Hall. It was a civic building, not designed with assaults in mind. There were no crenellations or protection for the defenders on the roof. He squatted down as best he could, and watch for movement below.

The man to his right, Fin had forgotten his name, indicated excitedly towards one of the buildings below. One of the divines was exposed in preparation to fire his stol. Fin drew and fired rapidly and missed again, but the divine had been given time to fire. The man to Fin's left fell forward with part of his head and upper arm missing. The body landed with a dull thump in the street below.

Another stolfire blast hit the wall just below Fin, sending shards of stone and dust billowing about him. Fin felt the shock of the blast and the sting of his face lacerated by the stone fragments. After wiping his face with his hand, he saw his hand bloody from multiple lacerations.

Lun managed to let off a couple of shots, but his aim was poor and the arrows failed to hit their mark. With the defenders pinned down, the divine squad set up a barrage of stolfire and recommenced their advance. The other man, whom Fin recalled was a fisherman, stood to get a better shot and paid for his bravery with his life, as several blasts of stolfire struck him, throwing him back onto the sloping roof of the Great Hall.

Chapter Twenty Two

"My Lord" shouted Lun "we can't stay here. They are nearly at the door."

"Keep at it, Lun" Fin shouted back. He let off another arrow without taking time to aim properly and missed his target by a wide margin.

Lun managed another two shots, the second narrowly missing the head of a divine. "My Lord, this is hopeless."

By this time the divines had set up a barrage of stolfire on the door itself; forcing the defenders to stand and shoot almost directly downward.

"Let's go then" Fin bellowed to Lun. "We'll stand in the Great Hall. We can't do any more here.'

As Lun turned to go, stolfire struck him, leaving a gaping hole in his chest. He gave Fin a shocked, quizzical look as he collapsed to his knees and then forward into the guttering. Lun slid over the edge and landed with a loud audible thump in the road below.

For a long moment, Fin gawped at where Lun had been, and then retreated from the rooftop. He raced to the hall where a scene of devastation greeted him. Where the main doors to the hall had stood there was now a gaping hole. Stolfire lanced about the hall causing wooden panelling to splinter and fly about the hall. Sovrack and two of the Lord's staff cowered behind a hastily built barricade in the centre of the hall.

Suddenly the stolfire stopped. Choking dust filled the air. Fin took careful aim on the doorway and waited. He didn't have to wait long. A hazy, indistinct shadow appeared in the doorway. Without thinking, Fin let lose an arrow, shooting wide of his target and fumbled for another, only realise with horror that he had shot his last arrow.

More shadows appeared and the Lord found himself facing a squad of divine troops with their stols aimed at him. Fin threw down his bow, but summoned his pride and held his chin up as the leader of the squad stepped forward.

"Where is the Lord of this Mark?" the divine trooper barked out.

Fin stepped forward with as much authority as he could muster. "I am Lord Tymeum, Fin of Mark Tymeum. What is the meaning of this assault."

The divine trooper looked at the young Lord with disdain. "You are arrested for harbouring resistance against the authority of the Frame."

Fin gawped at the trooper. "What are you talking about? There is no resistance here. I have always been diligent in maintaining a law-abiding Mark."

"Not diligent enough. You are wrong. The people of the Mark will be interrogated and those found guilty will be put to death. The others will be reassigned."

Cold fear and shock overcame the young Lord as he stared back at the trooper. He began shaking uncontrollably as he sank to his knees. No thoughts or words came as he struggled to come to terms with what was happening.

Chapter Twenty Three

Pyta had slept poorly on the dirt floor of the second room of Pibeg's croft. The bare room was uncomfortable and he had risen early. Pibeg had a comfortable inglenook by the fireplace in 'her side' of the croft. Rather scornfully, Pyta noted that she liked her comforts and even had a cushion to soften the hard stone of the inglenook.

Later that morning Pyta had found a good location for a still. It was sheltered, discreet and overlooked the broad waters of Marlok. Pibeg was still asleep though the morning was wearing on. Pyta had mellowed his attitude towards her; after all, she was carrying his child. He had no illusions about the relationship, however. They would never love each other. In fact, Pyta believed that he would be doing most of the hard work.

He took a long swig of water as he looked out over the water, towards the aimu ship moored not far off shore. As he watched, he saw movement on the deck of the ship as two craft emerged and sped off toward land. He wondered what was going on and was sure that it wasn't good. Only divines had that kind of technology, but why they would bother to come here was beyond him.

Pyta headed back to the croft, deep in thought. One thing he was certain about was that he did not want to be around when the divines began their work. He found Pibeg making porridge. She never used milk and Pyta found it thin and unsatisfying.

"Did you fix that hole in the yard wall?" Pibeg greeted.

"Ah did tha' yester'." Pyta lied, though he had done the work that morning, before looking for a good site for a still. One thing Pibeg was adamant about was that there would be no whisky on her croft. Pyta was equally determined that she would not prevent him from having a drink, she just didn't need to know. "Ah've plotted the foundations fer yer pigpen, a' well."

"Good. You'll need to be tending to the vegetable patch this afternoon then."

"Pibeg, summut is 'appening down the lane. Divines are landing. Ah think we should head fer the hills 'til fings se'le down."

"You are a coward, Pyta. We should find out what is happening. If there is trouble, we should help."

"Ah'm worried, Pibeg. This ain't gud."

Despite his misgivings, Pyta followed Pibeg down the lane towards the small cluster of crofts that served as the village centre. Pyta halted when he saw flickers of stolfire. Although he had never witnessed divine troopers or stolfire before, he knew instinctively that it was best to be as far away from this trouble as possible.

Pibeg however ignored him and headed for the nearest croft. She enjoined her neighbours to head to the village and 'help'. By the time they reached, the small centre of the village there was a small group of men and a few women cursing and angry about the intrusion of the divines.

They found the horror that greeted them to be deeply upsetting. A divine flier had landed in a central green where several lanes converged and the troopers herded tearful women and hysterical children into the flier like so much cattle. They had piled the corpses of several men on the ground nearby, the blood mingling and flowing into the ditch.

The scene enraged Pibeg's hapless cohorts who charged the divines. Pyta held back. He knew the reckless, foolhardy charge would end in disaster and wanted no part in it. He plunged into the ditch and watched in horror as the divines mowed down the muckers with stolfire. He saw Pibeg torn to pieces by a ruthless crossfire and collapse headlong into the lane. The mother of his child was dead and the unborn child within her. Silently, Pyta vowed vengeance against the divines.

Gilmur49 had allowed Yayler to stay on the bridge, with Gulukone as his constant guard, during the assault on Tymeum so that he could witness and be overawed by the strength of the Mustanian army. The General stood, passive and emotionless before the three-dimensional display of Anklayv Island. The display had an overall reddish hue that changed to green as reports came in. It appeared to be projected from the floor of the bridge and only had an illusion of solidity.

Clar15 had been watching sporadic flashes of stolfire around Tymeum through the plaz windows of the bridge with Yayler and

Chapter Twenty Three

Gulukone by her side. There had been a longer period of more intense stolfire recently, but that had now subsided and the area appeared quiet. Clar15 decided it was time to get reports from Gilmur49. Clar15 had overall responsibility for the campaign, but Gilmur49 took charge of the military strategy. To make the point Clar15 took the most direct route to the Generals side, which happened to be directly through the display.

The General frowned, exhibiting his displeasure and irritation at the slight. There were certain rules of formal conduct in Mustanian society. Clar15, the Over-General, should have made her presence known before approaching. In the highly authoritarian militarily society of Mustan, simple rules like this prevented a lot of unnecessary violence.

"How does the fighting progress Gilmur?" By dropping the numeric, Clar15 had made another gaff in protocol. Such informality was fine in private company, but considered impolite in formal situations.

Gilmur49 cleared his throat to hide his irritation. "The area is secure."

"Do we have numbers of casualties yet?"

"There have been no reports of Mustanian casualties. Casualties among the muckers still need collating, though it appears that about two hundred of the population are dead."

"That doesn't make sense. How many injured?"

With a quick flourish of practiced fingers, Gilmur49 brought up a report that displayed on two locations on the three-dimensional map.

"There are no reports of any injuries. So far, it has been an efficient operation. We now have two bridgeheads on these two peninsulas." The General adjusted the display with a casual movement of his hand and the two areas of land turned green. The rest of the display took on a reddish pink hue indicating enemy territory. "Over the next few days our main force will advance on this small village, Balgeel." Gilmur49 pointed out the location on the map before continuing his explanation. "Our two forces will then join in a pincer movement that will effectively isolate the main target, this Rustick More."

Clar15 looked at the projected advance on the display, considered the strategy and could see an obvious flaw. She studied the open stretch of water on the display and read out the caption "this Marvlok?"

"We shall use transport fliers and fortify on the natua shore. We do need that area under strict control, as it is potentially a route of escape from the target.

Gilmur49 continued. "We need to have no route in or out of that area, unless we know about it. I also want the population cleared from the area. The muckers have too much potential for aggression." A light started to flicker in the display over the position of Tymeum as Gilmur49 spoke. "Ah, we have the report on mucker casualties at Tymeum. Hmm, Two hundred and nineteen dead, two slightly injured. There were eighteen survivors in all. The muckers are highly aggressive, this does not surprise me at all."

After a long pause for thought, Clar15 queried. "What weapons did our troopers have?"

"They were only provided with standard light equipment, no heavy assault weapons. They mainly used stols and anti-personnel grenades."

Yayler, who had watched the assault through the plaz weather shield of the bridge with Gulukone in close attendance, spoke for the first time since the assault began. "You didn't use staffs then? What weapons did the muckers have to fight back with?"

Gilmur49 glared at Yayler's back, clearly irritated that Yayler had spoken. "Who is this traitor, who asks questions?"

"We both know who he is, Gilmur. You may answer the question." Again, Clar15 had deliberately dropped the formal numeric suffix of the name. She raised her eyebrows and stared, directly at Gilmur49 This was a gross insult in formal situations.

The message was not lost on Gilmur49. Clar15 was in charge, not him. He cleared his throat uncomfortably, as he brought up another report on the display. "There was significant resistance at the Great Hall. They used banned ancient projectile weapons against our troops."

Clar15 quickly scanned the report. "So, the only significant resistance during the assault was the use of a handful of arrows?"

Yayler interrupted again with a simple, plain comment. "They only want to live their lives as best they can; they do not deserve this."

Both Clar15 and Gilmur49 looked in surprised at the turned back of Yayler, but made no comment.

Clar15 turned on Gilmur49 and with considerable restraint, contained her anger. "I have to report to the commanding hiu, Gilmur. They will want to know why so few of the population survived. They will see the loss of life as a waste of resource. So far, the assault has been clumsy and heavy-handed. This is very disappointing."

A couple of wairs later, Clar15 stood before the commanding hiu after using Yayler's audaciously stolen launch. Not for the first time she felt an absolute loathing for the machine. She was totally convinced that the Frame was beneficial to Mankind, but the towering hiu before was not the Frame. To her it looked and felt like a three pace high monster, utterly devoid of emotion. It was an extreme irony to think that the Frame designed the machine to interact with humans. Clar15 thought the machine very poor at its primary function.

It was generally humaniform in that it had legs, a torso and arms, but there the resemblance ended. The limbs did not look anything like human limbs. They were constructed from plazmetal rods and bars that connected to the torso frame. Various parts and mechanics filled the torso and included the sophisticated aimu computer brain, the zenumerator. There was no head to speak of, just a collar comprising a sensory array. Its chest plate was a pad that enabled a human with the proper implants to interface directly with the aimu 'brain'.

After making the trip to the aimu command ship Clar15 had waited for over a wair. She now stood before the massive intelligent machine and transferred her report to its database. The hiu was supposed to perform at the highest level of human interaction, but was still just a machine. Its designation code was HIUcom01, though Clar15 had never been able to work out what the codes of the hius meant, she did know that the higher the number, the less sophisticated the machine.

"Your report is satisfactory. There will be no requirement for you to scape." The hiu ground out the words with a coarse metallic sound.

Clar15 was grateful for not having to scape. Having one of those machines inside your head was a very uncomfortable experience and one she would much sooner avoid. "Is the high rate of mortality of muckers not of concern?"

"The mucker deaths are inconsequential to the aims of the Frame" came the cold, mechanical reply.

"But so many? Is it really necessary?"

"Your concern for these unintelligent beings has been noted. It is a distraction from your duties. Therefore, your performance will be monitored. The Frame does not need a population of low standard humans in this area."

"The survivors from the conflict are being reassigned. Is it then the intention of the Frame to have a zero population in this area?"

The hiu made a series of clicking noises, almost as if Clar15's questions caused irritation. "The Frame does not wish for any rebellious humans to remain in the environs of the centre of this Mucker Revolt. The Frame wants no distraction from the core aim of this campaign. There must be no population of indigenous muckers in the area around the priority target Rustick More. You are to ensure that this happens and complete your assigned task. Return to your command and carry out your instructions fully."

After that, Clar15 had been ushered away from the hiu with her mind racing. No population to remain at all? Zero population? With a sickening disquiet bordering on disillusion, Clar15 wondered how she was to manage her duty and imagined the huge death toll. Mustanian troops spent much of their time, busily engaged with digging pits for the dead. She had little doubt that Gilmur49 would have little difficulty with his conscience whilst performing his duties. He was young, ambitious and utterly ruthless and would be quite happy to undermine her in an attempt to supplant her.

Dook stood on the summit of Rustick More, gazing towards Tymeum. He was waiting now, for the inevitable. It was most likely that the divines would besiege the base. It would be a difficult job for them to accomplish and would require many troops. Effectively, they would have to besiege the entire mountain. There would be gaps and the divines didn't yet know about the tunnels under the mountain. As long as they remained ignorant of the tunnels, Dook would be able to keep the base supplied with food. Potentially, a siege might last for months, or even years. Dook laughed to himself quietly at that thought.

A bleat from behind him brought him from his dark reverie. He turned and smiled as he saw Sara and Ealasat approaching. "You ladies should have gone by now."

"We are, we just wanted to say goodbye first." As Sara spoke, Gawa started to nibble at Dook's morcote.

"Where will you be going? A lot have gone to the Forests of Ardbanacker."

"Nay, because I can pilot a flier, I'm to go to Ecta's Ledge. I can train others there. Eala wants to learn too."

"Good, you should be safe enough there, at least for the time being. Nowhere is completely safe, and you need to think of the coming baby."

"Aye, it's beginning to get quite big." Sara proudly displayed her belly. "Have you heard from Cullin?"

"They are not too far from Tyber now, travelling at night."

"Well, we had best be going. Fil is waiting for us in the last flier to leave. You should come with us. It's not too late."

"Nay." Dook smiled sadly. "My place is here, it is my home."

"That's a stupid reason to stay."

"I know, but stay I will. The army out there can't leave a base like this to continue to operate. By defending, we tie up forces that would, otherwise, occupy the whole island. I don't believe they are here only to enforce the Frame's authority and set up a more stringent and severe administration. They will wish to make an example. They will punish and destroy before letting the people get on with their lives."

Sara went silent, not knowing what to say. She knew from her past how brutal the divines could be. There was a storm coming to the islands of Garvamore. A storm formed by thousands of divine troops and their machine masters, neither of which cared for the lives of people like herself.

"You take care of yourself then." Sara turned to go, but made a cheeky comment before going. "Do have a wash now and then, you still stink."

Dook laughed affectionately. Sara always nagged him on that subject. A mew from behind him seemed to be in agreement with Sara. Dook scooped up the kitten, now more cat than kitten, and rubbed its nose affectionately. "Don't you start."

Dook was about to return to Toiler's Woe when he saw Isla approaching. "You seem to like it up here, Dookerock."

"Aye. It gives me the space to think." Dook replied. "Call me Dook, you don't have to be formal here."

"Ahh." Isla nodded absently, she wasn't interested in why, and she just liked knowing where to find him. "I want to send out scouts to find out what is happening out there."

"Aye, do that. Otherwise, all we can do now is wait."

Once back in the bowels of Rustick More, Dook looked for Neev and found her with the seismocom. The equipment had been set up in a natural alcove in a roughly hewn corridor. There was an unpleasant dampness in the air and a slight musty odour. Neev was asleep in a hammock slung across the alcove. A single candle cast a feeble light on a table that Dook assumed she had filched from Toiler's Woe. Writing equipment, a hefty pad of paper and a bowl with the remnants of a meal were the only items on the table.

Dook sat down at the soul chair, a rickety wooden affair that had long since seen better days. He glanced through the pad, noting that there were no new messages received. This concerned him, as he had not received a message from Cullin for several days now and that worried him. What could have befallen the group of travellers? Dook didn't want to think about it, but the nagging thought had crept into his mind unbidden, that divines had captured them. He tried not to think about their plight. He couldn't help them and worrying about them would change nothing.

He looked down on Neev. He could do something for her. She needed some relief. One of Isla's aneksa troopers could run this station with only a little training. As she was the only technical staff left at Rustick More, Dook needed her available for other duties. Dook collected her dirty crockery and headed back up to the main level of the base.

Chapter Twenty Three

Cullin awoke thirsty, as he had for several mornings now. He flexed his fingers and toes as best he could, but with both hands and feet bound, movement was awkward and restricted. With clumsy motions, he shifted himself into an upright sitting position. It had been the same every morning for the last several days. The smell of faecal waste mixed with urine from a solitary bucket that served as a toilet, assaulted his senses.

It was hot and stuffy in the almost lightless cellar, Cullin could see with his augmented vision, that Ecta, Goram and Guvin were still asleep. Their bindings kept them in awkward, recumbent positions. Their captor would appear in about another wair, if the routine of the last few days held true. They would then be questioned and given just sufficient water to keep thirst at bay. So far, there had been no food.

Cullin started to click with his tongue. He had done this at every opportunity, investigating every corner of their prison and even beyond the single door to the room using his click sense. He had worked out very little so far. What he had learned was of limited use.

"I do wish you'd stop that dreadful noise; Cull. It is very irritating." Cullin's clicking had woken Guvin who grumbled unhappily.

"I'm trying to find something about our prison. The clicking gives me a sense of what is around us."

"That's ridiculous Cull, how can you possibly do that?"

"I learned through lots of practice. I now know this room is underground and that beyond the door there is a corridor and a flight of steps."

Guvin barked a derisive laugh. "I find that hard to believe, but, I guess I have to take your word for it. I still don't understand why Goram didn't wake us; he was supposed to be on watch."

"Aye, it's hard to fathom, but he is adamant that he heard or saw nothing. He just woke up bound in this room, like the rest of us. I tend to believe him. We simply don't know enough about what happened yet."

Around half a wair later, the door to the room opened and light flooded in silhouetting a caped figure. The figure appeared to have a device in his hand, which it pointed at each captive in turn, leaving Cullin until last. The figure squatted in front of Cullin. "They will sleep for a short while. I require skin samples from each of you so that I may determine who you are."

"That information is free for the asking."

"I see, then we may talk later." The divine proceeded to take samples with a small device that Cullin could not see clearly and then left the group alone in the dark again.

Cullin knew by means of the subcutaneous enhancements he had received at Rustick More that it was two wairs and ninety-eight sents later that the figure returned with an ornately carved wooden chair. The divine set the chair in the doorway. Thus, when he sat down, backlight from beyond the doorway, silhouetted his body.

"Good morning. I note from the DNA samples taken earlier that you are all muckers from the Garvamore district. I was wondering how you all got here?" The figure who they had now discerned to be a man had a soft, polite mannerism about him.

Cullin found the divine's manner un-synchronous with his limited experience of divines. He found himself to be distrustful of the apparent easy-going nature of their captor. However, a response was required. Cullin believed a lie too easily detected too easily. "We sailed in a fishing boat."

The divine looked at Cullin in surprise. "Do you expect me to believe that?"

"I can't help what you believe. Guvin here captained the boat. Perhaps you should talk to him."

"I shall do that later. For now, I will take your word. What I am most interested in is why you have trespassed on this estate farm. What is your purpose here?"

Guvin, Ecta and Goram remained silent, but showed great interest in the interchange between Cullin and their captor. "We are passing through. We have no interest in your estate."

"If that is the case, what is your destination?"

"We are headed for Tyber." Again, Cullin's answer was truthful, but the response from their captor was both surprising and profound.

The elderly divine glared at each of them in turn as if he could detect truth simply by looking at a person. "I find it highly unlikely that you would have any dealings with those solipsists. They could have no interest in meeting muckers in person, so I must conclude that your interest in them is negative and underhand. I shall consider this information at length."

Their captor abruptly left, leaving them in the dark again.

Guvin was the first to speak. "I think you have given him far too much information Cullin. What are you thinking of?"

"Our captor will have other means of gaining information. I don't think there is anything I have told him that he couldn't gain by those other means. We are in no worse a position than we were before."

"You are an arse, Cullin. Don't talk to him at all. I can't think why he would talk to you and not us. He will kill us when he has what he wants." Goram was angry and spat his words through clenched teeth into the darkness.

"At least our captor is taking to us. I think that is a good thing, but I agree with Guvin and Goram. Cull, you shouldn't tell him too much." Ecta had said very little since their capture and had become very taciturn and withdrawn.

"Don't say anything at all." Goram snapped heatedly at Cullin.

"If we have a dialogue with this divine, there is a small chance that we can get out of this place."

"No chance" sneered Goram.

An uncomfortable, tense silence descended on the group. They were in a difficult predicament, but no one had any plan for extricating them from the situation.

Chapter Twenty Four

"I wish they would tell us what in Irin is happening. How are we supposed to do our jobs?"

Mabe looked up from his bowl of soup. "Keep your eyes open and report any movement."

"Aye." Dris griped. "What is that supposed to mean? Movement? Movement of what?"

"You're asking me? I don't know any more than you do." Mabe returned his attention to his soup. He tore a chunk off a heavy oat bread loaf and gazed out over the moorlands and hills that surrounded Rustick More.

Dris and Mabe were at their favourite lookout spot near the tunnel exit station. The last few days have seen a lot of people leave and heading in different directions. Would it have been too much effort for any of them to let them know what was happening? It seemed so. The old woman, Dona, had also ordered them to place a number of explosive charges at the tunnel exit. Again, without any explanation, what was going on?

Dris was about to say something when he saw a distant object in the sky. He watched, transfixed as the object drew closer and the single object became two. With his gaze transfixed on them, they resolved into fast moving triangles that were heading in their direction.

In those scant few sents since he had first spotted the flying objects, Mabe had wandered away from the tunnel exit and was now in plain view. Dris collected his wits, grabbed Mabe by the sleeve, and pulled him back into the tunnel.

"I think we are not meant to be seen." Dris muttered into Mabe's ear.

Mabe nodded dumbly. "I don't like this. What in Irin are those things?

As the two men watched, they could see sunlight glinting off the broad delta wing of the craft and as they slowed down, they turned as one. Thereafter, they seemed to circle a spot a stride or so from the tunnel exit.

"Hey Dris, I think I know what those things are."

"Not good, is what I think they are."

Mabe became excited. "Do you remember those stories from the Battle of Dundoon?"

"Aye, there were a lot of stories and I think the majority of them weren't true."

"I think those are the flying machines they talked of. Those drone fliers, machines." Mabe pointed at the sleek craft and grabbed Dris by the collar of his morcote. "We've got to tell the bosses about this."

"Nay Mabe, we have to stay by our posts. Besides, I think they can see them as well as we can."

"So, what do we do?"

"We keep out of sight and wait."

One of the drones peeled away from the other and made a vertical climb until it was a mere speck, high in the sky. It seemed to hang there motionless before moving off and stopping again.

"What do you reckon it's doing, Mabe?"

"Looking, I guess."

"What? From up there?"

Mabe shrugged and let out an exasperated breath. "How should I know what it's doing? Maybe that's how it looks."

Dris looked doubtful and unconvinced at Mabe's idea and started to scan the sky for the other drone. "Hey Mabe, Where's the other one gone?"

"Ah, cac! Look over there Dris." There was a look of wide-eyed fear on Mabe's face as he pointed into the distance.

"Deetah! That's a lot of dust. You don't think that thing crashed do you?"

"Nay, I think that's unlikely."

"I'm going to take a look."

Before Mabe could say anything or even try to stop him, Dris was off, scurrying over the moorland in the direction of the dust. He returned looking very worried.

"Mabe, Mabe" he hissed, trying to get the others attention. "There's a whole army out there. We've got to get out of here."

"What drivel-brained cac are you on about? How can there be an army out there. We would have seen it before now."

"I'm not so sure Mabe. They're sneaking along streams in small groups. We probably wouldn't have seen them at all if it hadn't been for that dust. You know some of those riverbeds are dry at this time of year."

"Aye, true. How many troops did you see?"

Dris thought for long sents before replying. "Fifty, at least fifty."

"Fifty!" Mabe blurted aloud and Dris hurriedly tried to hush him. "Fifty doesn't make an army."

"I know, I know. I didn't have time to look for more."

"You amadan Dris, you complete konafiog. Is that all that's out there?"

"Nay!" Looking slightly abashed, Dris continued. "I couldn't get any closer, but there are more hidden in those little nooks and hollows in the streambeds. I know I'm right, I could hear them talking and laughing."

"All right Dris, I believe you. Let's blow those charges and get back upstairs."

"Aye, good plan."

It took Mabe and Dris a scant twenty sents to climb through the tunnel system to Toiler's Woe. They soon found Isla talking with a detachment of her troops. As they approached her, a powerfully built trooper prevented them approaching with a large hand.

"State your purpose" the big man growled.

Isla looked up, taking interest, but not recognising the two tunnel guards. Mabe and Dris looked quizzically at each other as neither was now sure who they should talk to. There was a confused pause, during which the trooper tried to usher them away from Isla.

"Er" began Mabe. "We need to talk to Isla." Mabe found his voice quavering as he faltered his way through the simple sentence.

"Why?" The trooper grunted, folding his arms across his chest.

"There is a divine army building up in the foothills yerward from here." Mabe blurted out the words in a rush, the words tumbling over each other, but he managed to maintain a semblance of vocal coherence.

"Where? How many?" The trooper was a man of few words.

"Let me talk to them, Cal." Isla had her full attention on Mabe and Dris. "So, where were these divine troops guys?"

Mabe pushed Dris forward. "It was Dris here who saw them."

Dris had become very nervous and, belatedly, started to straighten his hair, which hadn't seen a comb in a long while. "Er, they was." Dris stopped; his mouth had suddenly gone dry. He glanced down at his hands and saw them shaking. After a deep breath, he tried again. "They're about a stride, maybe less."

If Isla had any impatience with Dris's faltering, her frustration at his halting manner didn't show. "Dris is it?" After Dris nodded a nervous affirmative, Isla continued. "A stride from where, Dris?'

"We was, er." Dris stopped again and looked to Mabe for help.

"We were at the yerward tunnel exit, Venuasal." Mabe supplied without a hint of nervousness or stress.

Unexpectedly, Isla laughed. "I am no Lady, just call me Isla, we don't use titles here. I didn't catch your name?"

"Oh, it's Mabe."

"What else can you tell me, Mabe?"

Mabe composed his thoughts before answering. "We noticed those flying machines, those drones, and Dris went out there to have a look."

"I see." Isla smiled. "We saw the drones ourselves. I saw drones at the Battle of Dundoon, so I know what their capabilities are. That was very brave of you Dris. What numbers did you see?"

Isla's debrief of the two tunnel guards went on for a while as she gradually added more details about weaponry and most importantly, if there was any sign of aimu.

Isla was about to dismiss Mabe and Dris when a scout approached them looking very disgruntled from a direction that suggested that he had used the

'Rake'. The Rake was an exposed gully that cut across one of the steep faces of Rustick More and was the route to the cavern that formed Toiler's Woe. Dook now rarely used the 'Rake'. It was a difficult route. It had sections of exposure that scared many who used it. Thus, Dook had, almost, exclusive use of the Rake. Isla looked expectantly towards the woman, recognising the face, but not remembering the name. "Ah, I'm sorry, what do I call you?"

"Roz, my venuasal." Roz had a slim athletic figure and long braided hair. She was at an age where most women would have children of almost adult years, yet was still single despite having a ready humour and pleasant character.

Isla shook her head and regarded Roz with some amusement. "Just call me Isla. What can you tell me, Roz."

"I have been scouting yerward and have grave news. I would have been here a little sooner, but some amadan has started to blow up the tunnel entrances." Roz appeared haggard and tired, but something in her expression went deeper than mere tiredness. Her eyes conveyed horror at what she had seen. A horror that had burned deep into her soul.

"Aye, I had heard about that."

Mabe and Dris, who were still awaiting dismissal, cast their eyes to the ground and shuffled their feet in embarrassment. Isla glanced at the two men, bemused by their discomfort. "Probably not too soon. I understand that divines are quite near."

"Aye, they are at that. I had a difficult time getting back here."

"Can you give me numbers and positions?"

"Aye, I would estimate numbers between five-hundred and a thousand, spread out into pockets around Rustick More. More divine troops are steadily arriving." Roz stopped as a worried expression crossed her face. "There is something else happening out there that you should know about."

"Go on."

"There are no people left out there. I stumbled across a pit filled with dead bodies, mucker bodies. They had all been beheaded. All I have seen out there is divines and their machine masters, and they are slaughtering the people out there."

Isla looked alarmed, shocked. After a brief moment, she turned to one of her troops and whispered something in his ear, then turned back to Roz. "Carry on, tell me as much as you can."

"I sneaked into Tymeum. There were no people, only the divines using the crofts as barracks. Aimu are stationed there now as well, hundreds of them. I have seen one or two aimu before, but these look different. They look bigger and stronger. I think it is a machine army."

Roz's debrief continued for some time. Roughly, midpoint during debriefing, Dook joined the discussion with Anbooakil in tow and asked for a quick update. Mabe and Dris had become almost un-noticed bystanders.

"Isla." Dook said at last. "I want a raid arranged for tonight. A quick hit-and-run. Let's make these divines think twice they come too close to Rustick More."

That evening, a small group assembled in Toiler's Woe including Mabe and Dris. Keem, Anbooakil and Cal completed the group who were waiting for Isla to join them. They each carried a small backpack with small grenades and a short staff. They each wore black trousers and a loose black woollen smock, but lacked the usual embroidered symbols of Mark and occupation. Sheathed at their waist, each had a large knife. Isla joined them with Dook walking beside her.

Dook spoke first. "I think everyone has heard, now, of the death pits. If any of you have thought that following orders by the divines would prevent harm coming your way, now is the time to think again. There is a psychopathy in the way many divines think. I believe it is caused by the way they are nurtured.

The purpose of your raid tonight is to demonstrate that they cannot murder our people with impunity. There is a price to pay. Get in quick and get out. Don't linger. Good luck"

As the raiding party descended the Rake, Mabe and Dris were whispering to each other. The others negotiated the narrow declivity in silence.

"Hey Mabe, what does Dook mean by 'impunity', what's that?"

"You're an idiot Dris, didn't your parents teach you anything. It means we're not allowed to complain or harm them."

"Oh, but we're going to do that aren't we?"

"Aye."

"Good." Dris fell silent for a moment and then whispered again. "What does he mean by syko, syko-something?"

"I don't know Dris, but did you see how angry he was."

"Aye, he was that."

"I'm worried Dris. My Mother was in Tymeum. She is old. They have probably killed her, they didn't need to do that."

"Aye, they shouldn't have done that. Well, we can show the Diaval Urahar what we think of them!

"Will you two amadan keep quiet." Isla hissed at the two tunnel guards. "Your voices can be heard by the divines."

She took them in single file at a slow pace after admonishing them not to disturb any rocks. They continued in silence down the Rake with Isla in the lead and Anbooakil bringing up the rear. Despite her admonition over rocks, their footfall still disturbed the stony ground. The occasional cascade of stones clattered and tumbled down the rake, though they managed not to knock loose any of the larger rocks. The noise they created on their descent, though minimal, still sounded alarmingly loud.

The stone-choked rake eventually opened out into a gully that disgorged rocks into a broad fan of scree. Isla led the group down the edge of the broad spray of boulders and rocks, where they were less loose. Progress was still slow, but rock slowly gave way to heather and grass, where Isla led them into a dry streambed and called a halt.

Isla beckoned to Mabe and Dris and whispered. "Can you take us to where you saw those divine troops, from here?"

They both nodded an affirmative.

"Aye" whispered Dris.

Mabe simply pointed a direction and then led them over moorland where they forded a number of streams. Both Mabe and Dris knew the terrain well, having worked amongst the rolling hills for many years. They were familiar enough with the terrain that they could navigate easily through the confusing topography. After about a half wair Mabe called a halt, beckoned Dris over, and murmured into his ear.

With confidence, Dris pointed a direction into the dark and set off with the others following. It was only a scant few sents later that Dris urgently signalled a halt, barely seen in the dark. The unmistakable sound of someone urinating could be heard not far ahead of them. Anbooakil moved forward next to Dris and motioned everyone to stay low.

With amazing lightness of foot for such a big person, Anbooakil disappeared into the dark, leaving the others behind. Silence enveloped the others like a nervous shroud as they waited for what seemed an age, but was little more than a few sents. Suddenly Anbooakil's huge figure reappeared, looming over them. The giant beckoned then onward. None of the group had heard him return.

They crawled forward over the heather until Anbooakil called a halt. Just ahead of them lay the slumped figure of a divine. A series of urgent hand signals passed between Isla and Anbooakil; then Isla crept over to Mabe and Dris. She pointed at the two and then at Anbooakil, indicating that they should follow the giant. Isla then disappeared into the ebony dark with Cal and Keem close behind.

Anbooakil indicated to Mabe and Dris the direction they were to follow and then moved forward into the gloom, passing close by the dead divine trooper. Mabe chanced a quick look at the body and instantly wished he hadn't. Anbooakil had cut neatly through the man's throat to the spine.

Soon the ground gave way before them, opening out into a steeply banked streambed. The water gurgled over rocks as it babbled and splashed along its course. Anbooakil motioned Mabe and Dris to huddle down and pointed into the dark. There ahead of them they could discern the huddling forms of divine troops, in small groups of twos and threes. Anbooakil motioned that they should draw their knives, but stay behind him.

They followed the giant along the top of the streams bank and then, quite suddenly, Anbooakil slipped over the edge. Unsure whether to follow or not, Mabe and Dris faltered and looked questioningly at each other. After a moment, Anbooakil reappeared, beckoning them urgently to follow him. As Mabe and Dris slipped over the edge the bodies of three corpses confronted them, one with its throat cut, another with a gaping chest wound and the third with his head twisted in a completely un-natural angle. Neither Mabe, nor Dris had heard a single sound.

Anbooakil slinked along the bank of the stream for a short distance before indicating another halt, and drew the attention of Mabe and Dris to a small shelter a little way ahead. In the dim light, it was possible to make out the forms of two sentries. Anbooakil motioned that Mabe and Dris should stay where they were, but keep their eyes open. The silent assassin, Anbooakil, again slipped into the dark.

Mabe and Dris were both feeling uncomfortably nervous by now, almost to the point of terror. Abruptly a shadow appeared before Mabe and he knew instinctively that it was not Anbooakil. He froze, thinking it might be one of the others. As the figure levelled a weapon at him, Mabe realised that his hesitation had just cost him his life. The divine trooper, however, never fired his stol. Dris had lunged forward, burying his knife deep into the man's chest. There was only a brief struggle before shock and rapid blood loss caused the divine to collapse, sliding to the ground.

As Dris released the divine from the deadly embrace, he clutched at his side with pain. The free hand of the divine had not been empty, but had contained a small dirk. Even as he was dying, the divine trooper had slid the blade between Dris's ribs. Dris staggered and looked at his friend in uncomprehending shock and slumped to the ground.

At that moment there was an eruption of noise and bright flashes of light. Mabe heard confused shouting as he crouched protectively over Dris's body. "Dris" he croaked hoarsely. "Dris can you hear me? Are you alright?"

"Didn't see the knife" Dris wheezed. "The cac had a knife!"

"Come on, we've got to get out of here."

"What about the big man?"

"I think he can look after himself." Mabe tried hard to pull Dris to his feet when he heard an oddly high-pitched voice.

"Eyself, I am not a man, nor a woman, but I am a person. Dook taught me this." Anbooakil stood over them with an oddly serene expression on his face. "Your friend is hurt." Anbooakil seemed completely unfazed by the chaos occurring just out of sight in the dark and lifted Dris easily holding the wounded man across a broad and powerful chest. "We go, you lead."

Dumbly, with his mind reeling, Mabe did so.

Later, back in Toiler's Woe, with Dris patched up there was an excited chatter, buzzing about the cavern. Though Dris had lost a lot of blood, the knife hadn't pierced his lung and he was expected to make a full recovery. Anbooakil had detonated a grenade in the small shelter, that had turned out to be an ammunition dump.

Dook was pleased and deemed the raid was a success, but the truth was that they had killed fewer than twenty enemy troops and almost lost one of their own. The divine army would increase in size faster than raiding parties could reduce their numbers. At the same time, the Aneksa forces within Rustick More would remain static, with dwindling supplies. If this was a cause of worry for Dook, he did his best not to show it.

Chapter Twenty Five

It was hot and sticky in the cellar and the four prisoners were in poor humour. Their captor had questioned each of them in turn, but only Cullin was willing to speak to him. Since then, they were left to suffer without food or water in the stifling heat.

"We've got to get out of here!" Goram was in a foul mood. The force of his frustration and anger overrode his discomfort and the dryness of his mouth. He was desperate to do something to get out of the place.

The others were simply trying to rest and conserve their energy. They just looked at him mutely in the dimness of the cellar.

"If we could get these restraints off we could get out of this place." Though it was difficult to see anything, Goram held his hands up to emphasise his meaning.

"How do you suggest we do that?" Cullin muttered in answer.

Ecta and Guvin had done their best to ignore Goram's ranting behaviour. It had set them all on edge and none of them wanted to talk to him. They had become more dispirited as a result and felt utterly helpless.

"Find something to cut these bindings, of course." Sarcasm evinced itself in Goram's croaking voice.

"I have already tried that several times. I tried when I first woke up in this hole. They resist cutting. These restraints mould to the shape and size of wrists and ankles, leaving no 'wriggle' room. I'm sorry Goram, but that isn't the answer."

Goram was somewhat mollified by Cullin's response, but was still far from satisfied. " Unlock them then."

"Can you see a lock?"

"I can hardly see anything, it's too dark in here."

"Can you feel anything that might be a lock?"

There was the sound of awkward movement as Goram investigated the restraints, but they stopped after a couple of sents. "No, but there must be something."

"I already tried the bindings. They seem to be made of some form of plaz. I remember a reference to something called somaplaz in my studies, that fits the description of these things."

An edgy silence fell on the group as none of them could see a way out of their predicament. At last, Cullin spoke again, his voice hushed and harsh from dehydration. "You have given me an idea though, Goram."

"What's that?"

Cullin replied cryptically. "Quiet; I need to see."

"See? See what?"

"Just be quiet Goram." Cullin made a clicking noise with his tongue against the roof of his mouth.

"What are you trying to do?" Ecta asked, intrigued by his friends activity.

"All of you be quiet. I need silence for this. I'll explain later if it works." Again, Cullin made a click followed by several more at regular intervals.

The process was difficult, as he had only ever used his click sense to see things at a distance. What he was now trying to do was to see inside an object, and the image the reflected sound created in his mind was not what he expected. He could see the bones of his hands as a silvery white shade of blue, but the restraints he 'saw' as a greenish opacity that was amorphous and without apparent structure. His flesh he 'saw' with reddish hue. It was hard to 'see within' the restraints.

He tried different pitches and tones of 'click' mixed with different frequency of clicking, but without appreciable success. The somaplaz simply didn't react to sound in a way that enabled him to 'see' through it. At last, he tried making the clicks as loud as he could before giving up on his investigation. At last, he announced "Dook and Yayler taught me a trick of seeing with clicks."

The others made no reply. They had already heard an explanation of this extraordinary skill.

Chapter Twenty Five

"I never thought to use it to look inside an object though. It is very difficult."

"You mean you can see inside things with those clicks?" Guvin sounded tired.

"Aye, it seems so. There does appear to be something inside, but I can't quite make it out. I need to think about this."

"So there is a lock?" Goram demanded in a throaty rasp.

"Aye, Goram, but I don't know how to unlock it."

Goram's attitude descended into a sullen and wordless quiet. If anything, the heat depressed the spirits of the captives still more. Their futures and even their lives were in doubt and none of them could think of, or offer any plan to improve their situation. So, they waited in silence with the sultry heat of the cellar sapping their energy still further.

Only Cullin, by dint of the enhancements received at Rustick More had any idea of the time of day. The blanket of melancholic inertia enfolded the group with subtle paralysis. None of them even stirred when they heard the door to the cellar open and their captor entered.

Their captor said nothing, but released Cullin's leg bindings with a small hand-held device. "Can you walk?" The divine asked with a surprisingly gentle and polite tone that belied the harsh, callous treatment of his captives for days on end.

Cullin flexed his legs gingerly and decided that he could indeed walk. He nodded an affirmative and found himself suddenly hauled, unceremoniously, to his feet and taken up a flight of stone steps that emerged to a large living space.

"This is my veranda, I hope you don't mind if I don't take you indoors." The captor was again polite and respectful, in complete contrast to the manner he had held Cullin's group captive.

The veranda had just two plain, featureless white walls with no obvious openings or doors. The other two sides of the 'room' presented an open view of an arid landscape. There was no ceiling that Cullin could see, yet for all the apparent openness there wasn't the slightest breath of wind or breeze. The atmosphere was cool and pleasant. It was a total contrast to the atmosphere of the cellar.

The groups' captor settled himself into one of two soft furnished chairs and ushered Cullin to sit in the other, facing him. As Cullin sat, the captor sat forward, speaking steadily with his oddly polite, lilting voice.

"I have decided that it is time for me to introduce myself. My name is Frip17. I have not yet decided what to do with you muckers. It is likely that you will require termination. Do you understand me?"

Cullin tried to speak, but his mouth was so dry that all he could do was to make a brief rasping noise.

"Ah, you have had no water today. I shall remedy that lack." Frip17 went over to one of the walls and passed his hand over the featureless whiteness. A section of air wavered and fluctuated with flashes and streaks of bluish light and resolved itself into a three dimensional display with a variety of icons that seemed to float in the space of the display.

Frip17 flicked his hand through one of the icons and another replaced it. The divine flourished his hand across the second icon and then made a flat-handed gesture. Finally, he made a dismissive gesture and the entire display vanished as if it had never been there.

It took only a sent before an opening appeared in the adjacent wall and a squat hiu glided into the room. The service unit, despite obvious diligent care and maintenance, showed the wear of many years of use. It bore a tray before its squat body on two robust limbs with several empty glasses. A second pair of limbs bore two jugs of fresh water. The hiu halted before Frip17, who took a tray of three glasses and a jug from the hiu. "Help yourself to water. I will deliver these personally to your friends." Frip17 was an old man, one clearly long past his prime.

To Cullin, he appeared thin and emaciated. The divine was bald and had long thin, almost skeletal hands with prominent veins. The divines face was the most striking of all. It was wasted, ancient and seemed to sag from bones, as if there was little else other than skin to hold it in place. He wore a long, calf-length coat of the style that Cullin remembered as worn by Yayler. Underneath, the divine wore white trousers and a white smock-like shirt. It took only a few moments for Frip17 to deliver the water, after which he settled back into his comfortable chair. "I need to know your intentions."

After taking a long drink of water, that Cullin noted was ice cold, Cullin spoke. "This seems to be a pointless conversation. If we are to die, then there can be little for us to talk about. You have nothing to negotiate with. Thank you for the water, by the way."

Chapter Twenty Five

Frip17 showed irritation at Cullin's remark, but remained polite. "No decision has yet been made. I have made a few guesses and assumptions as to your intentions. I only need confirmation."

Cullin merely shrugged.

"You are muckers from Garvamore."

Cullin inclined his head slightly in agreement. "I thought that you had already established that."

"Indeed not. That you are muckers is beyond question, but as to where from, that had not been established." A thin smile broke Frip17's lean features. "I wonder if you are aware of the conflict that is occurring in Garvamore?"

"Much may have happened since we left." Cullin made a dismissive gesture with his hands, making light of Frip17's comment.

"So you know nothing of such conflict?" The old divine raised a white eyebrow in surprise.

Cullin, sensing a trap, felt it better to say nothing and stay mute. It was becoming clear to Cullin that this old man knew more than he claimed and seemed to be trying to trip him up.

Frip17, waiting for a response from Cullin before continuing, relaxed back into his chair and started a casual inspection of his fingernails. With no response from Cullin he spoke. "I'll take your silence to mean that you are aware of such conflict."

Again, Cullin tried not to give anything away, repeated his dismissive gesture and waited for Frip17 to get to the point.

"I see that you are no fool." Abruptly the divine stood and went to a section of wall and passed his hand over it. A previously unseen section of wall slid out with an object nestled within a wrapping of protective film nestled. Frip17 lifted it out and brought it over for Cullin to see. Even with the protective film obscuring the object, Cullin could see that it was the seismocom. "I have been trying to work out the function of these devices. It contains data. It appears to be some kind of communication device, though I cannot discern how it works."

"You seem to have me at a disadvantage."

Frip17 smiled humourlessly, revealing brilliant white teeth. "I have been able to download the data, from which I know that you are not only aware of the conflict in Garvamore, but that you are a part of it. Yes or no will suffice."

"Aye."

"What you don't know is that this 'Rustick More', which appears so prominently in your communications, is now surrounded by a divine army."

Cullin made no reply, though he found his stomach churning from, not merely hunger, but from worry about his friends and comrades back in Garvamore. There was nothing he could do about it, so he tried to put his feelings aside and concentrate on his own precarious situation.

Frip17 smiled humourlessly again. "I find myself forced to conclude that your presence here is advantageous to your cause. Do you know what the function of Tyber is?"

"Nay."

"That surprises me to the point that I find it hard to believe." Frip17 gave Cullin a long hard stare as considered. Was the young man trying to be clever? Did the mucker think that he would believe him? He decided that Cullin was simply trying to be evasive and continued. "Tyber serves as the communication centre for all divines on Inalsol. Are you telling me you did not know this?"

"We do not know the specific function of Tyber." Again, Cullin attempted to provide to minimum of information, but he was now almost certain that the divine already knew most of the answers and was only looking for confirmation. He felt boxed in, trapped and he was getting tired of this charade.

"So you did know that Tyber is important." Frip17 carefully phrased his comment as a statement and not a question and receiving no complaint from Cullin, continued. "Your mission then, is simple. You are here to disrupt communication between the Frame and divines. Is this not so?"

"I think that you would choose to disbelieve me if I chose to deny it."

"Let me give you some information you might not be aware of. Do you know who the Solipsists are?"

"Nay."

Chapter Twenty Five

"That is not surprising. They are an elite group of divines who spend their lives connected to the Frames systems. They are in effect, a human extension of the Frame. I do not consider them human anymore. When necessary they can connect with machine bodies that they control remotely. I receive my instructions from Solipsists." Frip17 settled back, watching Cullin intensely studying and evaluating the young man's reaction.

Cullin considered his response carefully and decided to continue his policy of giving as little away as possible. "I have not heard of these Solipsists. They are not my concern."

Frip17's bushy, white eyebrows shot up with surprise. "Now that does surprise me. You have managed to travel all this way, almost undetected and have no interest in Solipsists?"

"I have not heard of these Solipsists, they are not my reason for being here." It was all Cullin could manage to say, without risking revealing his true intentions.

"For some reason, I believe you. Yet you are here to disrupt communications." Frip17 smiled. It was an utterly cold smile, lacking in compassion or genuine feeling. "Would it surprise you then, if I said I might be interested in helping you?"

Cullin could do nothing else, but stare. Was this some kind of trick?

Frip17 delivered that cold, loveless smile again. "You see, I have a problem. I am coming to a time when I will no longer have a useful function for the Frame. My function here is to manage the land. A function I have been performing for over a hundred years, but the Frame now asserts a machine can do it better. My usefulness to the Frame is now, or soon will be, concluded. Either my life will be ended, or I will be installed as a Solipsist and become a living part of the Frames parameters. Neither choice has any appeal to me. Your presence here gives me a third option."

"So, it seems we have something to offer after all."

" I believe so. So, tell me, what, exactly, were your intentions in Tyber?"

"What would my friends and me gain if I told you that?"

"Your lives!"

Cullin might have considered that Frip17 was being overly dramatic, but the he believed the divine was being entirely serious. "What assurance do we have that you will help us? We have no basis for trust. We don't even have any assurance that you have the power to have us terminated."

"Indeed, that is so. You have no assurances and I offer none."

"Then what basis is there for negotiation?"

Frip17 sipped at his water and then gave Cullin his mirthless, ingenuous smile. "There is none. It is my belief that you wish to destroy vital communications equipment. I will help you to do so. You and I will enter Tyber. Your friends will stay here. If you do not do as instructed, they will die. After conclusion of our business in Tyber you will take me to a place of my choice where I can live my life as I choose and you and your friends will be free to go."

" I don't see as we have much of a choice."

"Indeed not, I have no intention of offering you choices." Frip17 paused, sipping more water. "So, tell me, mucker, what is the target in Tyber?"

"It is something called the Interface."

Frip17 stared at Cullin, shocked speechless it was several sents before Frip17 spoke again, and then it was to himself. He stared out at the bleak arid landscape and paced up and down the veranda before eventually speaking to Cullin. "How is it that you know of the Interface?"

"Is it not enough to know of it? How we learned of it is surely irrelevant?"

"I confess that I am profoundly shocked. I understand muckers to be primitive, unsophisticated and without technology. Yet you have been able to achieve far more than you should have been capable. You and I will destroy the Interface. We will do so tonight."

Chapter Twenty Six

The Frame was analysing reports from the Garvamore campaign. As a whole, the district was unproductive and took more effort to maintain than the value of resources it could deliver.

The reports suggested that the campaign was proceeding well and, if anything, progressing more quickly than anticipated. There were higher numbers of mucker casualties reported than predicted, but they were within acceptable limits.

A statistical breakdown of the campaign so far showed a positive deviation from expected and acceptable Coefficients of Correlation. The close correlation between expectation and achieved results gave the Frame a sense of 'harmony', that is, fewer contingency sub-routines to run and this meant a smoother, more efficient running of the Frames programming. Efficiency always 'pleased' the Frame.

Soon, with the entire divine army disembarked from the transport ships, another objective would be achieved. One process nearer to achieving the main objective of neutralising the target area called Rustick More. The reports suggested that the area was now clear of its indigenous population, which would allow the divine army to proceed with greater efficiency.

The only negative report was that of a minor skirmish that had caused little damage. The Frame satisfied itself that the campaign was proceeding well, and ordered the initiation of the next phase, before turning its attention to other priorities.

Dook was observing the movement of divine troops who were now in plain sight, arrayed in the chilly morning air far below. Isla and Dona were also observing, though from different sections of the summit plateau. As he watched the troop movements, two drones circled overhead, thus he, the observer, was watched being in turn. The time for hiding had passed.

It worried Dook that earlier estimates of the size of the divine army were grossly inaccurate; they weren't even close. He now reckoned on six to seven thousand troops arrayed about the mountain. The main bulk, though, was encamped less than two strides away from Dook on one of the broad hills that surrounded Rustick More. Dook now knew that the divine army occupied the entire area arward from Balgeel to Marvlok. Thus, Dook adjusted his estimates to ten-thousand troops with additional aimu units that were, yet, unrevealed. What other surprises they had in store for those defending Rustick More, he could only guess, but he was sure they have more than a few. Isla and Dona rejoined him after completing their surveillance and Dook quickly glanced over their figures, which largely confirmed his estimates.

"How soon do you think they will attack?" Dona asked. Her voice was steady despite seeing the overwhelming force that faced them.

"I doubt they'll attack too quickly. They'll want to assess our strength first. They haven't brought forward any plazgunna that I can see. I expect they'll soften us up with those first. So, for now, we sit and wait."

Isla was shaking her head in disagreement. "There are large gaps in the army surrounding us. We still have a couple of tunnels open so we can slip small raiding parties out and make quick strikes. It might be little more than a nuisance for them, but it will keep them off balance. I think that the more we do that, the better our prospects."

"Hmm I don't want to lose people on silly little raids. We nearly lost a man on the last one. We have to be careful. " Dook frowned. "They outnumber us forty to one and I don't believe they have shown their full hand yet."

Isla cast her eyes downward as if seeking inspiration from the scattered stones and moss. Nothing came to her mind. "Let me try a few raids with a handful of troops. If one or more get hurt, then we can have a rethink."

Dook considered the idea, looking for a reason to object. Every objection he thought of came from negative thinking and they had to remain positive. What swayed his thinking was that he liked the idea of taking the fight to the enemy. "Find targets then and use the short tunnel. We may yet need the other as our last escape route; five on a raid; a handful, with a clear objective. I also want spotters up here watching what is happening out there. I want regular reports. I'm going

Chapter Twenty Six

to relieve Neev, so you know where to find me." With that, Dook stalked off to head into the depths of Rustick More.

Neev was grateful for the relief and said she needed to get some air. Throughout the rest of the day, Dook sat by the seismocom, reading through the small pile of messages Neev had collated. There was nothing of any great importance. He also created a number of messages for sending at the scheduled time. Dona, was without a clear role, brought him a steady stream of reports. Dook was quick to suggest that she aid Neev and coordinate communication.

With escape routes almost cut-off other than the two tunnels, Rustick More was isolated and under siege. There had been no news from Cullin or Dunirayn since the attacks on Tymeum. There was nothing he could do to help either; all he could do was hope. An option would be to relieve the siege using the aneksa army, but that would mean a pitched battle against a superior force, superior both numerically and technologically. It was highly unlikely that they could win such a battle.

Whilst Dook was thinking, Isla joined him. "I thought you like to know, they are moving up plazgunna."

"Are the shields up?"

"Aye. Any news?" Isla indicated the equipment on the desk before Dook.

"Nay, at least only bits and pieces. It's odd that they should come here. I thought they would attack Dundoon first or perhaps Tuaport. How about the Folly, is that ready?"

"Aye, charging and manned, for what good it will do."

"What do you mean?" Dook was a little confused by Isla's comment.

"It only points in one direction, so it will be of limited use."

"Aye, we ran out of time to sort that one out." Dook felt a little disappointed at the thought, but there was little he could do now.

"A big problem we have is that the spotters can't see at night. I wish that they had the ability of the divines to see at night."

Dook chuckled. "Most divines can't see any better at night than you or I."

"But Sara, when we had a bit of time to talk after the battle of Dundoon, told me that when she escaped from the slave camp, that the divines could find her by using their equipment even in the dark. I'm just saying that it would be nice if we could do the same."

"It would at that." Dook smiled and then abruptly clapped his hand to his forehead. "We can! Of course, we can! I'd forgotten. It's been so many years. There are so many things from the divines in storage here. I'm sure we have some oykaverk. Very old, but I'm sure they are serviceable. We'll go and find them now."

"What?" Isla was alarmed. "Are you joking? The divine army is certainly about to launch an attack and you want to hunt through storage rooms for odd bits of equipment that might not even work."

"Aye. Don't worry about the divines. They'll use the plazgunna first to soften us up before committing any troops. We can defend against the plazgunna with the Folly. That will cause them to pause and rethink. We have more than enough time. Come on."

Isla stared at Dook open-mouthed, and had to jog to catch up with him as he walked briskly down the dim corridor. Dook stopped abruptly, almost causing Isla to bump into him. They were near the terminus of the corridor and Isla could make out a number of old wooden doors on either side. Isla could hear Dook chuckling quietly to himself.

"I can't remember which room they would be in" Dook explained lamely. "Ah, this one, I think." Dook indicated a door on their left.

As they entered, Isla noticed a slight smell of mould. Dook fussed with an old oil-lamp that stood on a small table by the door and soon had the room illuminated with flickering yellow light. The room was small, about four paces wide and six deep. On either side, there was wooden shelving with wicker baskets.

"You look on that side, I'll check the other." Dook started pulling out baskets systematically, rummaging through their contents with the odd, delighted gasp of surprise.

"What am I looking for?" Isla asked.

Chapter Twenty Six

"Oh, it looks like a loop that fits about the head."

As they searched through the baskets, they heard a number of dull thumps reverberating through the air.

"What's that noise Dook?"

Dook stopped and paused his search, waiting for more of the noises. A few sents later, they heard another pattern of dull thumps that were barely audible this deep in the mountain.

"The sound is coming from upstairs. Sound carries a long way down these corridors because it has nowhere else to go. I might be wrong, but it sounds as if the divines have started a barrage with the plazgunna." Dook returned to the baskets calmly pulling out the next in line on the shelf.

For the second time Isla felt shocked by Dook's calm demeanour. "Don't you ever worry about anything? You always appear so calm to me."

Dook paused in his search again as he contemplated Isla's comment. "I try not to worry, but believe me, I am very stressed and worried at the moment; I'm just trying very hard not to show it. Worry changes nothing. If a problem resolves, then of what use is worry? If a problem cannot be resolved, then worry does not help.

"So what is the purpose of worry? We must worry for a reason; don't you think? Surely, the most likely reason is to focus thought on a problem or issue and thus increase the probability of a positive resolution. Now, the most pressing problem is that army out there." As he spoke, Dook pulled out the next basket and grinned broadly when he saw the contents. "Ah, and these will help!"

Inside the basket lay several oykaverk. They appeared to Isla to be woven plaz headbands with a plastic moulding connected to a drop-down visor. Touch sensors on the plaz moulding controlled the various different functions of the oykaverk.

"Now, let's get up there!" Dook the basket from the shelf and tucked it under his arm. As they left the storeroom, Dook lifted the lid off the oil-lamp and peered inside. "Hmm, I must remember to top the oil up."

Sents later they were looking out over the divine army to the rear of which, they could make out the distinct forms of three plazgunna. As they looked the muzzles of the plazgunna flared. Moments later the charges detonated above the hanger entrance with deafeningly loud crashes. Rocks, loosened by the explosions, tumbled across the hanger entrance and thundered down the yernan flank of Rustick More.

"Do we have anybody out there?" Dook asked pointing upwards.

"Nay, we brought everybody in as soon as the barrage started." Cal spoke. The big man didn't even bother to look at Dook when he spoke.

Dook shook his head slightly. "We need to have people up there all the time. We can't risk the divines sneaking up the slopes whilst we're not looking."

The giant form of Anbooakil was nearby. "I believe there is a chart of the mountain in your rooms. I can bring it here if you think it might be useful, General Dookerock."

Dook frowned. "I'm not a General, Anbooakil. I'm just Dook or Dookerock. I think the chart would be useful here, thank you."

"He's very formal isn't he?" Isla whispered to Dook as Anbooakil headed off to find the chart.

"Aye, ey is. He is not 'a he' or 'a her'; so, we use 'ey' instead."

"Oh, I see." Isla didn't really see, but didn't say any more, though she was a bit confused. How could someone not be male or female?

As soon as Anbooakil returned with the chart, which they spread out on a table and Dook and Isla discussed plans with Isla's aneksa clustered around. With broad hand-gestures, Dook started pointing out various features on the chart. All the while, the barrage continued as a rumbling thunder that Dook, pointedly, ignored.

"This area here is Rustick More and you can see it is flanked by steep crags with scree slopes below them. The divines will not be able to get their army up those slopes. Low hills surround the mountain. There are five small subsidiary outer summits with steep ridges radiating outwards. I want two lookouts stationed at each of these points with the oykaverk. I'll instruct the lookouts on their use myself."

Chapter Twenty Six

A particularly savage series of blasts and rumbles interrupted Dook's instructions. "Hmm, that is getting quite irritating."

"I wouldn't want to ignore them for too long, Dook, they might conclude that we are defenceless." Isla spoke quite loudly so that there was no mistaking who spoke, or what she had said.

"True, so, let's see what we can do with the Folly."

Gilmur49 was alone in the command tent. He had noted in the past that other commanders preferred to have a throng of staff around to carry out their commands. He preferred to have the time and space to himself so that he could think more clearly with less disruption. He had the job of weakening the defences of these aneksa, these 'free people' and, so far, their resistance had been minimal. He could go further than that and say that, thus far, defence had been pathetic.

He had a team of sub-commanders at his disposal in a tent adjacent to this one. They could talk and analyse to their hearts content, but they did little in the way of constructive thinking. That was his job and was the reason that they were lieutenants and he a divine Mustanian General. The Over-General, Clar15, remained on the aimu Command Ship.

Before him on a large table, he had a two-dimensional chart spread out before him, a jug of iced water and a single glass. The barrage on the resistance base had been continuing for over a wair without any response and he was trying to decide if this was over-confidence or stupidity on their part.

Earlier he had marked an entrance to the base on his chart, high up on the flanks of the mountain around which the barrage was now concentrated. He had sent a request to the Command Ship for drones to inspect it and was waiting for a reply. It might be possible to drop an assault team onto the plateau, but Gilmur49 wanted to know more before committing troops to an assault. He would like to know how many muckers were hiding up there. Such details were important to his planning. One thing he was certain about was that an assault on the flanks of the mountain could be very costly.

As he was cogitating, a young officer thrust aside the tent flap. "Divine General, your request for drones has been accepted. They will reconnoitre the mountain and this entrance in twelve sents."

"Good. Stop the barrage in eleven sents."

Shortly, Gilmur49 heard the drones and decided it might be useful to watch them. The drones made regular reconnaissance missions, but he wanted more detail from the data on this occasion. Not that he got the data unless he made specific requests. How they expected him to plan an assault without proper data was beyond Gilmur49, but often, that was how his superiors worked.

It was cold and damp outside the tent and Gilmur49 turned the collar of his battle tunic up against the chill air. High up on the mountainside he could see the entrance to the Base, which appeared to be a cave entrance. Gilmur49 mused that it was not surprising that the base had not been detected before.

The drones wheeled about the sky in synchronised pattern, circled the mountain at different heights and then they stopped and hovered in front of Base entrance. As Gilmur49 watched, stolfire erupted from within the Base entrance striking around the nose of both drones. Gilmur49 had read transcripts of the Battle of Dundoon. He was aware that the muckers had such energy weapons. It was no surprise that they had them here. He made a mental note to criticise the person who had programmed the drones' flight pattern. The drones wheeled away from the Base entrance with one trailing a thin vapour trail.

A single, high energy, blast erupted from the Base entrance followed by a loud reverberating boom. Another blast followed and another boom. The camp erupted into urgent frenetic activity. Gilmur49 fixed his gaze on the Base entrance, which was now quiet.

A young officer charged up to Gilmur49 with panic written on his face. "Divine General, two plazgunna have been destroyed. What weapon was that?"

"I don't know. Move the plazgunna out of range, resume the barrage, and tell the communications officer that I need to talk to him." Gilmur49 needed to think about what he had just witnessed. A weapon like that could be very damaging to the offensive. These muckers were clearly more resourceful than previously thought possible. How they had come by a weapon like that was beyond Gilmur49. Further than

Chapter Twenty Six

that, he could not think of a single report that suggested that they had such a capability. This was something new and alarming.

The Communications Officer appeared quickly with a small compad and greeted him with a simple "Divine General".

"Ah, Sub-lieutenant Dunford55, I need you to take a dictated report and send it to Over-General Clar15."

"As you wish, Divine General."

"Initial report – please insert time and date." Gilmur49 went on to describe the recent action and commented on the destruction of the two plazgunna. He concluded the report with a series of requests. "I will need analysis on drone reconnaissance as soon as possible. Also, I need analysis on the muckers new force weapon. Previous analysis of mucker capabilities considered it to be beyond the ability of muckers to field this type of weapon. It would be useful to know how they have been able to develop such technology and estimate the likelihood of other such new weapons."

"Anything else, Divine General?"

"No, that will be sufficient for now. Send that off."

A distant rumble announced the resumption of the barrage on Rustick More.

Chapter Twenty Seven

"My comrades could do with some food before we go." Cullin didn't think this was an unreasonable request. Frip17, who had only given his captives scraps since their capture, seemed to think food unnecessary. "They are tired and need something to give them strength."

"Why should I allow them strength? They are well enough and they will survive until we return. If we do not return, then of what purpose would feeding them be? We must go."

Cullin simply stood and stared at Frip17. He was astounded at the old man's lack of empathy and consideration for others. It was almost as if he didn't care a whit about other people and considered only his own welfare.

"We must go, mucker. It will be dark soon." Frip17 indicated for Cullin to follow him with a simple hand gesture.

Cullin followed reluctantly. Frip17 led them to the corner of the veranda opposite the two featureless white walls and waved his hand briefly before it. A section of the arid landscape scene slid aside and a gap appeared through which Frip17 stepped. Cullin belatedly realised that the landscape he could see beyond the veranda was a projected image, a fake.

As Cullin stepped through the gap, a harsh, dry heat hit him and caused beads of sweat to appear on his forehead. He felt a hot breeze on his face that made his eyes sting and water. The true landscape was different and Cullin paused to look. It was a desert; dry featureless sand stretched into the distance. Cullin thought that he saw hills in the far distance. He realised that they were hills of sand, dunes. The air shimmered in the heat. In the far distance Cullin could make out rocky hills, real hills, not the ones made of sand.

As he looked about, he saw that Frip17's residence sat on a broad, low ridge that rose towards a range of hills. To Cullin, this was an alien world, far removed from the mountains of Garvamore.

Frip17 waited impatiently not far away. He was standing beside a teardrop shaped transport of clear plaz that appeared to float in the air. Cullin could see that two simple, transparent glass-like seats within the teardrop, each with a control pod that extended from the plaz of the teardrop. As Cullin approached the vehicle, a section at the front of the teardrop split apart horizontally. One section rose and the other lowered to form a step at the front of the transport.

"Step inside mucker, sit down on that side and don't touch the controls." Frip17 indicated the left-hand seat and followed Cullin with an agility that belied his apparent age.

Frip17 placed his right hand on the control pod by his seat and the two sections of the canopy closed seamlessly. The seats then moulded themselves to the form of their occupants. Cullin found his seat surprisingly comfortable despite the lack of padding or cushioning.

"This is an old transport. It is not as comfortable as newer variants, but you will find it far superior to what you may be used to."

If Cullin thought Frip17's comment was condescending, he did not let it show. He had decided that Frip17 was not likeable, but his personality was an irrelevance. Cullin had a goal, a mission that now stood an outside chance of succeeding. Friendliness between them was an irrelevance. "Won't your superiors be able to track this vehicle?"

Frip17 snorted a brief derisive laugh. "Yes, but why would they? I just appear to be carrying out my duties. You must trust me."

Cullin laughed in reply, not in derision or sarcasm, but in ironic amusement. "I am your captive. How can I trust you?"

"You have no choice."

Thereafter, Frip17 was silent. The transport glided smoothly through the desert. Cullin noticed that the air was cool and fresh in complete contrast to the environs beyond the bubble of the teardrop. After perhaps a wair, the terrain changed, becoming less arid. Small thorny bushes grew sporadically at first and then more frequently. Other succulent plants appeared.

Within the implants he had been given at Rustick More there was a database that included topographical data of Inalsol. Cullin found that when he closed his eyes, he could imagine a topographical map of the area around Tyber and overlay features he could see. Thus, to

Chapter Twenty Seven

Frip17 he appeared to be dozing, but in fact, was spending his time using this data to work out the position of the transport and the location of Frip17's home. The terrain began to steadily descend into a wide valley through which a broad river ran.

Frip17, who had spent the time quietly, with his hand resting on the control pod, suddenly broke the silence. "Ah, the orchards are ahead. They provide beautiful shade on a hot day."

"Is it not hot today? It seemed very hot to me earlier when I was outside. Much hotter than I am used to."

"You have lived your life in a cold climate. It is warm today, but not hot, barely above three hundred and twenty therms, absolute. There is a small complex beyond the orchards where we will enter the service tunnels."

Before reaching the orchards, they passed through several sents of cultivated monoculture fields. All the fields were identical and rigidly geometric. Even the rivulets that irrigated the crops were set out in a systematic square form. Cullin disliked the ordered, sanitised appearance of the plantation. Here and there, Cullin could see automated machines tending the crops.

Back home when he was growing up, the crofters set out their fields as part of the topography. They knew where certain crops would grow best. The crofters were in tune with the land. Here they twisted cultivation the other way round, against the natural flow of nature.

Cullin saw the same rigidity in the extensive orchards. It was a mechanical approach to growing crops. It viewed the plants as if they were parts of a machine. Although he appreciated the difficulty of growing crops in an arid ground, the system they employed here seemed too far removed from nature.

"Many years ago I produced the algorithms that control and run horticultural estates such as this one." There was a hint of pride in the way Frip17 spoke. "Not a single blemished fruit goes for processing from this estate. It produces some of the finest product on the continent. It is my responsibility to ensure that the highest quality is maintained and continued."

"We can't afford to waste food where I live."

"Efficiency is everything here. Nothing goes to waste."

"Impressive." Cullin wasn't impressed. To him it sounded like the systems wasted a lot of food. "What happens to food that is not of high enough quality?"

"It is pulped and dug back into the ground; nothing is wasted." They continued in silence until they drew to the edge of the orchard. "There is a service tunnel not far from here. The estate aimu use it for access. The tunnel connects to an underground complex that services the aimu. We will use this tunnel complex to start your search for the Interface."

They continued in silence for several sents until Cullin could make out a large structure ahead through the trees. As they drew closer, Cullin estimated that it was about twice the size of Dunossin where he grew up. Up to now, Dunossin was the largest structure that Cullin had seen. At one end were large double doors three times the height of a man. Cullin stared at the structure, wondering why it had to be so large and, for a moment or two, didn't realise that Frip17 was speaking again.

"It is not normal for people to use this service-gate. The aimu use it for access. Once inside we will be able to use tunnels that go deep underneath Tyber. We will leave the transport here."

The transport drew up to the side of the huge doors where Cullin could see a large scape panel. They had to disembark the transport, and again the dry heat hit Cullin. He ignored the heat as he watched Frip17 place his hand on the panel and frown.

"This is most unusual. You are to place your hand on the pad."

For a brief moment, Cullin was alarmed and wondered what the machine would reveal about himself. He hesitated.

"It will only read your finger and palm print as a record for identification. It is nothing to worry about. It may also ask for your name; I don't know, I have never brought a mucker into the city before."

For all his polite words, Frip17 seemed nervous to Cullin, more so than himself. There were tiny beads of sweat on Frip17's brow that Cullin did not think were a result of the late afternoon heat. He placed his hand on the pad expecting his finger implants to connect with the machine.

Chapter Twenty Seven

Instead, a mechanical voice requested "state name".

"Cullin of Ossin."

There was a pause and then the mechanical voice spoke. "Welcome Master Ossin." One-half of the large double doors slid smoothly and almost silently aside.

Inside was a large space that was almost entirely a stark, featureless white. A harsh, blue-white light emanated from broad strips along the walls. At the far end, Cullin could see another scape pad.

As Cullin was about to enter, Frip17 held him back. "Why does it recognise you as divine?"

"I do not know. My father was Lord of Mark Ossin. Perhaps that is why." Cullin could see that his remark angered Frip17 and that the divine hastily tried to hide his emotions.

Frip17 snapped at Cullin. "I do not see the relevance, mucker. Your father was a mucker; you are a mucker; not a divine. This is disturbing. Go inside."

As Cullin stepped inside, he offered another explanation. "Perhaps it assumes that I am a divine. Who else would use this place?"

"It is primarily used by estate aimu. Harvest aimu bring crops in here and then, others transport them for processing. Seed planters, technical service aimu and so on also use this facility. It is very rare for a divine to use this facility, so that might be it." Frip17 laughed unexpectedly as if the idea of Cullin mistaken for a divine was a great joke. "This way then. Cullin of Ossin."

"How far is it to Tyber from here?"

"About another fifteen strides, I believe."

"That could take another three wairs on foot. Is there not a quicker way?"

"Having come so far without a transport, using just your feet for transport, I am surprised you suggest it now. Perhaps that is an inherent weakness in muckers."

Cullin choked slightly at the idea of suggested frailty in muckers and, for a brief moment, thought that Frip17 might be joking at his expense. However, brief glance at the old man dispelled that notion. Frip17 clearly believed muckers to be inferior. "I am simply thinking that it might save time."

"Ah, that is a good point. We can use my transport for part of the way, but the latter part will have to be done on foot."

Without any apparent instruction from Frip17, the transport entered the service-gate, and drew up beside the far scape pad, where Frip17 again placed his hand. "There should be no need for you to identify yourself again. I am merely inputting our destination. I suggest you enter the transport."

As Cullin resumed his position in the passenger seat, the floor of the service-gate began to descend and the lights blinked out. Broad light strips passed them at each level of their descent. Cullin counted eleven levels and presumed there to be more, when the descent abruptly stopped. A single featureless, dark circular passageway was before them, wide enough for two vehicles. The transport entered the tunnel and as it did so, the light strips illuminated, flickering on as they approached and off as they passed. The passageway twisted and turned and Cullin found it difficult to gauge speed or distance. Frip17 remained quietly passive and unmoved throughout the journey.

They arrived at a junction about a half wair later. They had been travelling down a main tunnel, but the transport had stopped by a smaller, unlit tunnel. "We will have to continue on foot from this point on. This is a service tunnel for aimu. There will be no lighting from now on, as aimu do not require it. Of course, being divine, I have certain abilities you do not."

"I will have to stay close then." Cullin replied wondering if it would be a good idea to use his 'click' sense, but he decided it might be better to conceal that ability from Frip17.

They made slow progress through the service tunnel and Cullin found that he was making quite a lot of noise. His augmented vision still needed light and here there was none. He wondered what kind of augmentation Frip17 had, as the old divine had no trouble in navigating the passageway.

At one point Cullin stumbled quite badly and let out an expletive "Cac". It was close enough to his clicking for him to be able to 'see', albeit only momentarily. From then on, he stumbled deliberately and 'clicked' and 'cac'ed frequently.

"Will you be more quiet. It is possible for aimu to detect your noise." Frip17 was clearly irritated.

Lamely Cullin replied. "I am trying to, but it is difficult in total darkness. I don't have your advantages."

"It is imperative, mucker, that you keep the noise down."

"Perhaps it would have been better, then, if you'd brought a light."

Frip17 brusquely snapped back at Cullin. "Just keep it down."

As they continued, Cullin noted that the walls and floor were perfectly smooth, as if polished. He found that by running his hand along the wall he could progress without stumbling, but he still maintained the pretence of difficulty and persisted with the clicking. Frip17 remained stubbornly silent.

After, what seemed, an interminable time Cullin noticed that the passageway broadened and in the distance, it was distinctly lighter. "We must be nearly there now. It is lighter ahead."

"Indeed so. How very clever of you to walk in the dark this far."

"I'm not sure about cleverness. Is that something ahead?" Cullin could vaguely discern a blockish shape ahead.

Frip17 grinned in the darkness, but Cullin could now make out his dim hazy form and the expression on his face. Cullin suddenly realised he was walking into a trap. It was no real surprise as he had never trusted or believed Frip17. "Did you really think that I would be helpful to a stinking mucker, a retard? It is the end for you, mucker, and not soon enough!"

Frip17 drew something from beneath his clothing. It was a stol. "You will be taken into custody by the hiu for processing." Cullin reacted instinctively and rushed the divine. Dropping to his knees and pivoting onto his side, Cullin swept the feet from under Frip17 and made a grab for the divine's weapon, which had clattered onto the ground. Cullin was clicking rapidly by now and could see several other passages ahead, beyond the hiu.

Cullin moved toward the machine, which called out in its grating machine voice. "You are not permitted beyond this point. You are to surrender your weapon."

Cullin charged toward the hiu, firing the captured stol as he went. At the last moment, he changed direction and dropping to his knees, slid past the hiu, narrowly avoiding a mechanical hand. Cullin pelted down the passageway without a backward glance and darted down the first side passage. From behind him there was a flash followed by a panicked scream that caused his heart to miss a beat, then silence.

He did not pause to think about investigating, but kept going. Fear fuelled his efforts, fear that the hiu followed him and he might suffer whatever fate had caused Frip17's scream. He ran, ran through the unlit passageways until his reasoning mind regained control over the adrenaline frenzy.

He slowed and drew to a halt. "This is stupid." Cullin cursed himself. A piece of advice came back to him then, something Yayler had said to him back at the Bothy. "Don't let Bresleek rule. Bresleek is the trickster. Bresleek brings madness, torment and ruin." Cullin quoted the advice given him by the old man. Bresleek was no deity or person, but emotion, acting without mind or focus. Bresleek simply was delirium itself.

He had to slow down and think. He had no idea where he was. For, maybe a whole wair, he wandered the subterranean passageways wondering where he was. There were no signs or indications of location. He had seen no people, but he had seen small aimu scuttling about on whatever functions they had to perform. He was worried about Ecta and the others. They were in a desperate situation, but what could he do to help them? At least now, he reasoned, nothing was controlling him. He was at least free of the divine who had captured them.

"How long has he been gone? I've completely lost track of time." Ecta asked, pitching his voice into the blackness of the cellar.

Chapter Twenty Seven

They were all thirsty again. The water the divine had given them earlier in the day had done little to assuage their thirst. That had been a long time ago.

Guvin's voice answered. "About four wairs, maybe more. Maybe he's been taken somewhere."

"He's abandoned us. That's what's happened. We'll probably die down here." That was Goram in the bitter and vociferous manner that had become his norm since their capture.

Ecta replied "Cullin would never abandon us willingly".

"No? But that divine would." That was Goram again.

Ecta sighed. In a way, he sympathised with Goram. They were all uncomfortably hot, trussed up and not knowing what was going to happen to them. Of course, Goram was angry and frustrated, but his outbursts did nothing to help them.

"Aye, who knows what has been done to Cullin, or what he has been forced to do?" Guvin's voice was course and rough. He sounded tired and sick to Ecta.

"I don't trust him." Goram again.

"Why not?" Ecta inquired pointedly.

"He'll put his own skin before ours."

"Goram, Cullin wouldn't do that. That isn't the kind of person he is."

"He might not have a choice, Ecta." Guvin croaked.

Ecta was certain the man was ill. They had to get out of the cellar. He shuffled to where he thought the door was, and eventually found it. He pushed against it, but the door did not yield. A deep sigh escaped from him as morbid thoughts came to mind. 'No', he reprimanded himself, 'that's Goram's thinking'.

With awkward movements, Ecta forced himself into a standing position and searched for the edge of the door with his fingers. He soon found it. The thin crack was barely discernible, but it was there. For several sents, Ecta tried pulling at the door, but could get no purchase. There was nothing to grip.

"What are you doing?"

"I'm trying to get this door open, Goram."

"We tried that before. We couldn't do it then. Why should it open now?"

"I don't know, but we've got to try. I need something thin, something like a knife."

"Don't be daft, Ecta. That divine took our stuff from us. There must be a door handle, or something."

"No, there is no handle. It's perfectly smooth." Ecta sighed again. It was hopeless. He was tired, so very tired. He slumped down with his back to the door, feeling defeated. As he did so, his head bumped against the door and he heard an almost inaudible click.

Ecta struggled back to his feet and tried the door again. Nothing, he still could not get a grip. There had been something though, he was certain. He probed at the door with his fingers and heard the click again. The door moved. Ecta shuffled back as light flooded into the cellar from the, now open, door. "Ah, for the love of Hesoos, it's open."

Chapter Twenty Eight

Dunford55 hunched down amongst the boulders and crags. The opening was not far above him and his force of a hundred Mustanians. He was only a sub-lieutenant and it was very unusual for a warrior of his ranking to be in charge. 'Test the defences' he had been told. In Dunford55's mind, that could only mean one thing. They expected few to return alive.

The sun was low on the horizon and shone directly onto the rock-face the force was now scaling. They had about fifty paces to climb to reach the opening and Dunford55 had now realised the effort was futile. There was no way that a sizeable force could scale the almost vertical crags and assault the entrance to this lair of rebels. Perhaps they could make the assault from the side.

To his right there was a steep, sloping sharp arête broken by clefts and narrow ledges. It would be a difficult traverse and climb, but a great deal easier than the rock-face they were currently attempting. To the left there seemed to be a steep gully choked with rubble. He looked at the men about him. They were keen and looked at him expectantly. They, like he, were only sub-lieutenants, but highly trained warriors. They might be of low rank and expendable, but this is what they were born to do.

With a cautionary finger to his lips, Dunford55 directed the first half of his troops towards the gully. The other half followed him towards the arête. Progress was slow. The ledges were narrow and Dunford55 found himself jamming his fingers into narrow crevices and cracks in his attempt to maintain his grip. He inched his way along with his force strung out across the crags. With the sun angling across the horizon and casting a baleful orange glow onto the ruddy rocks, Dunford55 reached the relative security of the ridge.

The young sub-lieutenant watched his force creep along the rock-face and glanced briefly towards the sun. He wondered if it would be dark by the time they commenced the assault. The rock had a dark reddish hue as if bathed in blood and Dunford55 wondered how many of the one-hundred would survive the coming engagement.

A clatter of falling, tumbling rocks came from the direction of the gully. Everyone froze. Surely, the muckers had heard the noise. They waited for long sents for the inevitable challenge, but none came. Dunford55 urgently waved his force onward. Time was pressing.

At last, they were able to start along the ledges towards the entrance. Dunford55 took point expecting defending muckers to pick him off at any moment. Surely, they must be aware of their presence by now. Slowly, he approached the entrance. He could just see the other half of the assault force nearing the other side of the entrance. Good, they would be able to set up a crossfire that would give some protection from the defenders.

Finally, Dunford55 had his force arrayed about the entrance. He looked toward the horizon where the sun had finally set. Filaments of icy-blue noctoluminous clouds were now visible, reflecting a faint cold light over the entrance. Dunford55 could not believe his luck. They had made it this far and they were still undetected. He raised his arm with the signal to open fire.

Dris was feeling sore. It wasn't too bad if he didn't move or breathe too deeply. If he moved too quickly, then he got a sharp pain from the stab wound. His old friend Mabe kept an eye on him and ensured he didn't over exert himself.

Wrapped up in his morcote on top of Karn Jerrak, the little knot of rocks that overlooked the entrance to Toilers Woe, he felt reasonably comfortable. They'd given him some special vision glass that allowed him to see in the dark, cautioning him to be careful with it because the equipment was irreplaceable. Oykaverk they'd called them.

The orange globe of the sun sat on the horizon and it would be dark soon. Dris had been practising with the glass. They gave everything a chilly grey and lifeless cast until he found a toggle on the right side of its body that adjusted the spectrum. A similar toggle on the left side, adjusted the depth of view.

Then he heard the rock fall over to his right on the Forked Ridge. He swung his glass round and scanned the ridge, but could see nothing. Perhaps it was nothing. Crags, beyond which the rocks turned into a gully, impeded his view. He listened. For long sents he concentrated,

Chapter Twenty Eight

listening for the smallest sound and searching the crags for any movement. He was about to give up when Mabe re-joined him.

Dris motioned Mabe to keep quiet; then he pointed urgently at his ear. Mabe nodded and squatted down beside his friend whilst Dris continued to scan the crags. After a few sents, Mabe crept slowly down the steep ridge a short distance and peered into the gloom.

Dris rubbed his eyes. They were tired from the endless vigil. The rubbing made his eyes water and he dabbed at them with the sleeve of his morcote. Mabe was coming back and, if anything, more cautiously. Each footfall placed carefully as if his life depended on absolute silence.

At last, Mabe reached Dris. "We have to go, they are down there."

Dris made a single nod and eased himself into a crouched stance. It was a short distance from their lookout point to a tunnel entrance near the summit of Rustick More. A sharp up-thrust of rock, a tor about twice the height of a man, marked the entrance to Toilers Woe. About the rock, there was a cluster of figures. Neither Mabe nor Dris said anything until close enough to speak quietly.

"They are here" was all Mabe whispered.

"Get inside. We'll alert the others."

Dris followed Mabe into a deep declivity by the tor at the bottom of which stood the entrance to a tunnel.

The twilight afterglow lit the entrance with a dull ruddy hue as Gilmur49 watched the progress of the one hundred Mustanian Warriors as they arrayed themselves about the entrance to the muckers' base. He did not give them much chance of success. He expected them to fail, but in that failure, he would learn the mettle of the defenders. The Divine General ignored the lesser ranks who stood nearby. They were of no interest to him at this time; he would instruct them shortly.

He noticed with wry amusement, that many of them had to use artificial aids to be able to see what was happening on the mountain. Whilst still very young, his teachers tipped him for high ranking and, thus he had the full range of implants available to enhance his abilities.

He could see when most of the lesser ranks struggled to do so. His Memory Drives were faster and his intelligence greater. He was stronger and fitter too, though that was less relevant to him now as he no longer had to do any of the physical fighting and work. Others did that for him. He felt disdain for the lesser ranks. There were very few Mustanians that he had any respect for, but that was as it should be.

The approach had been somewhat clumsy, slow and awkward. He imagined that they would claim that the terrain hampered them. There were always such excuses. Gilmur49 also noted that they arrayed themselves haphazardly about the target. They would have to answer for that failure, also. Perhaps, he mused, it had once been the mouth of a natural cave, however now it an engineered gate, an entrance to a den of aggressive revolutionaries. They did not serve the common good. They did not have humility. They did not follow the Frames guidance. They were marked for extermination because they were evil.

Finally, the leader of the strike team raised his arm and clenched his fist, then thrust it forward in a clear instruction to attack. Stolfire erupted about the cave entrance. Blueish arcs of energy created a vicious crossfire. Gilmur49 pitied anyone caught in that lethal web of energy and made the merest inclination of his head. It was the only acclamation those warriors would ever receive from him. It was rare indeed for him to make such a gesture.

There was something odd though. The Mustanians did not move forward to press the attack. Then he belatedly noticed that there was a greenish tinge to the glow about the entrance to the muckers' lair. What was that? He adjusted his vision and looked closer. Some kind of energy barrier absorbed and neutralised the stolfire. He recalled reports of personal shields with these properties used by the muckers at the Battle of Dundoon. He had dismissed them as fantasy and an impossibility. He now knew his error and realised he needed to re-evaluate the capabilities of his adversaries. Then he saw movement in the rocks above the entrance.

"So, where are they?" Isla whispered in Mabe's ear.

Chapter Twenty Eight

They were on Karn Jerrak. Remarkably, Isla already had a squad of troops assembled when Mabe and Dris got to Toiler's Woe. Isla peered down the ridge with the Oykaverk.

"That way, down there." Mabe indicated by pointing. "More the other side."

"Ah, I see them." Isla made a few quick gestures toward Inan who squatted by her left shoulder. Inan was a veteran of the Battle of Dundoon and had become one of Isla's most trusted and experienced troops. He took about half of Isla's squad toward a small cluster of rocks not far away on Forked Ridge. "Now we wait" she whispered to Mabe when she saw that Inan's group were in place.

At that moment, the divines opened fire on the entrance to Toiler's Woe. Without hesitation, Isla's troops returned fire with short staff. The air about them cracked with the energy. Blue and green light flickered as the opposing forces engaged.

The situation was desperate for Dunford55 and his Mustanian Warriors. Astonishingly, the muckers had some form of energy barrier that prevented his troops from forcing an entrance into the rebel base. The muckers had caught them in a deadly crossfire that had his troops clinging close to the rock face with grim determination.

One of the troops near him shouted over the din of the fighting. "We've got to get out of ---." The shout cut off abruptly and Dunford55 saw a huge hole in the man's chest. In shock, the man let go of his grip on the rocks and fell, soundlessly, into the void below.

"Return fire!" Dunford55 screamed the order. They were in in a death zone, with little chance of escaping with their lives. "Head for those rocks."

Less than fifty men battled, inching their way along the narrow ledges toward the ridge of Karn Jerrak. Continuously hampered by short staff fire from the defending muckers, their progress was painfully slow. Dunford55 saw another Mustanian slip from the rocks, then another, swept away by the steady rain of stones from short staff fire striking the crags above them.

The first of the Mustanians reached the ridge, but were quickly became pinned down by short staff fire from the defenders above them. Dunford55 could see the position of the defending muckers by the flashes from their short staffs. He could also see that he had an advantage in numbers. More Mustanians reached the ridge and began to return fire on the muckers above them.

As he approached the ridge himself, Dunford55 spotted a change in the angle of short staff fire. He jammed his fingers into a narrow crack and leaned outward to get a better view above. There, on a small cluster of rocks on the plateau edge above, he saw flashes from short staffs. He returned fire.

His men fought their way up the ridge into defensible positions higher up and forcing the muckers to spread their fire over a larger area. At last, he reached the ridge and hunkered down into a cleft in the ridge. The men nearest to him looked at him expectantly, waiting for orders.

"There must be another way in." He shouted at them.

One shouted back in bewilderment. "You can't be thinking of pressing the attack!" Dunford55 recalled his name, Moor52. Moor52 was a little older than he was.

"We need to force them back, or we're all dead men!"

Moor52 worked his way to Dunford55's side before replying. "We need to go down."

Dunford55 shook his head. "They'll pick us off if we do that. We need to clear that ridge of muckers if we are to have any chance. How many of us are left?"

A quick count determined that they had a force of forty-four. "Moor52, we have the advantage of numbers. We attack!"

"Let's do it then. Let's show these muckers what we are made of."

They stood and hollered the order as one. "Attack!"

Chapter Twenty Eight

The Mustanians maintained constant fire ahead of them and started up the ridge. Scrambling and firing they climbed until they were no more than twenty paces from the muckers' position.

"Grenades!" Dunford55 yelled the order. Several grenades sailed through the air. They landed amongst the muckers, who immediately scrambled away to safety. The grenades erupted with a terrific blast, sending rocks into the air. The Mustanians pressed on through the shower of rocks and rushed the peak of Karn Jerrak.

Dunford55 was one of the first to reach the cluster of summit rocks and fired wildly at the retreating figures of the muckers. As the Mustanians grouped themselves about the rocks, Dunford55 saw with horror, several dismembered bodies, their crude clothing shredded by the blast of the grenades. He looked into the dark night to where the muckers had retreated. He could see another, larger force there.

"What now?" Moor52 shouted in his ear.

"Now, we get out of here!"

Swiftly, the Mustanians scrambled down the ridge. Sporadic short staff fire followed them. Several men were caught in the crossfire. Dunford55 saw one man nearby, missing his right arm. The man carried no stol, he'd lost that with his arm. As the night closed around them, the survivors desolately made their way back to the main Mustanian army.

Of the original hundred Mustanians only twenty-nine returned, those who had been with Dunford55. None of the others had survived the desperate retreat down the slopes of Rustick More.

Dookerock knew that it was a hastily organised defence, but he'd rushed over a hundred Aneksa to the summit rocks of Rustick More. Many had the energy shields that had been so effective at the Battle of Dundoon. From the flashes of weapons, Dook could see that the fighting was getting close. They would come over the top soon. Then he saw them. There was an explosion as grenades blasted the rocks of Karn Jerrak.

Isla had put together a small raiding party and was briefing her Aneksa troops when the report of the assault came from the lookouts. She had split her squad as two separate divine forces were attacking. The divines attacking on his right flank had started an orderly retreat as the small number of men led by Anbooakil attacked them.

The other divine force was more tenacious. He could see them now, clustering about the rocks of Karn Jerrak. Isla and her troops raced back to the summit rocks and the relative safety of Dook's bigger force. To Dook's surprise, the divines didn't press their attack, but turned tail and retreated back down the flanks of Rustick More.

"How many in the second group of muckers did you see?" Gilmur49 asked the young Mustanian before him.

"Over a hundred. They would have picked us off quite easily had we pressed the attack." Dunford55 was tired and bloody from a myriad of small cuts caused by flying debris in the recent skirmish. The General had been interrogating him for almost half a wair. Every answer he provided prompted more probing questions, until Dunford55 thought that there would be no end to the interrogation.

"It was dark up there. On what do you base your numbers?"

"The size and density of their formation could be made out."

Gilmur49 looked at the warrior sternly. "What weapons did they have? What were their defensive capabilities?"

"We could not see in th ---."

"So you don't know!" Gilmur49 snapped back, cutting off the reply. He had heard enough, he wasn't going to get more useful information from this man. "If you had pressed the attack, you would have been able to report on their defensive capability. The whole point of the attack was to gather information. Yet you retreated without learning simple facts." Gilmur55 glared at the young man. "Go back to your unit. I am done with you."

Overall, Gilmur49 thought the attack successful. He would have liked more intelligence on the number of muckers hiding in the mountain. He

Chapter Twenty Eight

doubted another attack would gain anything more detailed. He, at least, had a better idea of what these muckers could do. He knew they were well organised and had sufficient weaponry to be a nuisance. He now knew a frontal assault would be costly with no guarantee of success. He needed a way in. He started to compile his report to Clar15 of the attack. He added another file to his report that included a detailed plan of attack, one that he believed would succeed.

Chapter Twenty Nine

It was hopeless. Cullin had wandered the corridors of Tyber for a full wair and was nowhere nearer finding the location of the Interface than when he started. He realised that he was swithering. "Focus on what you're here for. You'll not find it with a random search." Cullin reprimanded himself. "Think. It must be above somewhere."

He stopped and let himself sink to the ground in a sitting position, his back resting against the plaz wall. Horizontal strips lit the corridor with a cold blue light that made Cullin feel uncomfortable. As he sat, a seu with a rotating sphere passed along the corridor in almost perfect mechanical silence. It followed a guide strip that ran down the centre of the corridor. He had seen several of these machines in the last wair, but hadn't worked out their function. He chuckled to himself with ironic amusement as he watched the seu disappear down the corridor. "At least you know where you're going."

Another machine, different to the first, rounded a bend in the corridor. It wasn't sleek like the first, but had a number of appendages that sprayed an acrid smelling liquid onto the floor, walls and ceiling as it progressed. Another appendage blew hot air onto the areas sprayed with liquid. Cullin watched in fascination as it unhurriedly and systematically cleaned the corridor. This aimu was a clus, a cleaning machine.

When the cleaner neared him, Cullin moved away. The cleaner stopped where Cullin had been sitting and paid particular attention to a dirty mark. Cullin looked down at his boots and noted that they were quite worn and dirty. He chuckled again. Perhaps the cleaner was cleaning up after him.

As he watched, he noted that the cleaner did not follow the central strip as the other machine had done. How did it know where it was going? Now that he thought about it, the answer was simple. The cleaner must have a 'map' of Tyber within it's database. All he needed to do was download that map to the neuro-chip under his scalp that Dook had given him as one of a range of enhancements. He should then be able to locate the Interface.

He made a few marks on the floor to keep the machine busy while he looked around the machine. The cleaner mechanically dealt with the dirt. Cullin remembered the hiu that Yayler Poddick had interfaced with on their trek to Balcon. That hiu had a breastplate onto which Yayler had simply placed his hand.

At first, Cullin couldn't see a similar breastplate. Then he saw it on the front of the machine, directly between two of the appendages and awkward to get at. At the same time, Cullin found it fascinating that the machine completely ignored him. It was a machine, he supposed, and lacked curiosity; it just did its job. He knelt down beside it and placed his hand on the breastplate, not knowing what to expect.

Immediately he found the topdesk of the clus superimposed onto his vision. He closed his eyes and an image of his hand appeared. Cullin quickly read a number of image-runes on the topdesk and dismissed most, such as 'maintenance' as not relevant until he had two choices 'command' and 'navigate'. With the hand image, he clicked on 'navigate'. The image-rune expanded and resolved into a further series of image-runes.

He could find no maps or other way to navigate the corridors of Tyber after several sents of fruitless searching. He returned to the topdesk and tapped the 'command' icon with the hand image. The topdesk disappeared. For a moment, he thought that nothing further had happened. Then he realised that he was required to enter a command. 'Interface location', he thought and the words briefly flashed before him.

In his mind, a three-dimensional image appeared with a flashing beacon near its top. This was the map that he had been looking for. He grabbed the image with the hand image and dragged it to his own, subcutaneous, neuro-chip. He returned to the 'command' page and thought 'show current location'. The map reappeared with the beacon flashing in a different place. Cullin dragged this image to his neuro-chip and disconnected from the cleaner.

The machine then started to behave oddly, wheeling round in a circle and then starting to head down the corridor, only to stop and spin again. The clus repeated this several times, as it made an uncertain course down the corridor in the same direction that Cullin needed to go. Cullin realised that he had not closed down the locations he had opened in the clus, thus giving the machine conflicting instructions that were vying for priority.

Cullin followed the clus. In all the time that he had spent in the corridors of Tyber he had not seen, heard or had any hint or slightest inkling of another living soul other than Frip17. The clus turned abruptly in front of him and entered an aperture in the corridor wall that opened for it. Cullin followed.

Chapter Twenty Nine

The opening was a tube that disappeared deep underground. Cullin had a momentary feeling of vertigo and stepped back. There was no sign of the clus. He looked again and, this time, noticed that the tube went upwards towards a vanishing point as well as down. He frowned. What was this? It took him a moment to find it on his 'map' of Tyber, but only saw the symbol 'X'. The symbol was meaningless to him.

The tubes were oval and about three paces in depth and four paces wide. At the back of the tube, he saw two runes, or symbols. To the left was a ∧ and on the right a ∨. After a moment of thought, he understood. They were arrows. He knew the Interface was above, so he tentatively placed a foot into the up-pointing half. A blue energy field appeared beneath his foot. He tested it by putting more weight on it. Then he put all his weight on it and stepped fully into the tube.

Cullin stood, hanging in the air with only the energy field beneath his feet preventing him from plummeting downwards. A voice grated out the word "level". After a couple of sents pause, the voice repeated the word, then again. He needed to tell the tube, which level he wanted. The Interface was marked at level one-hundred. "One-hundred" he spoke uncertainly into the air.

"Level not accepted." There was a paused and the voice started to repeat the word 'level' again.

Cullin found chambers on his map, marked at level eighty-four. "Eighty-four" He said and waited for that ominous grating voice to reject his request again.

The voice grated out the word "accepted" without any inflection or emotion.

A web of force suddenly emanated, radiating from the walls of the tube and Cullin felt himself held motionless. He started to move upward, initially a steady speed, and then faster as the levels raced past. After less than half a sent, Cullin's rapid upward progress reduced and stopped. The web released him and the voice grated out 'level eighty-four'.

Cullin stepped out into a large room full of plaz cases on slender pedestals, set out in neat rows throughout the room. It wasn't what he was expecting. To him 'chambers' suggested a series of small rooms. He assumed that these plaz cases were the chambers. He looked through the clear plaz lid of the nearest case or 'chamber' and saw a body.

It was the body of a woman, possibly in her thirties. Did all of the chambers have bodies in them? He quickly looked at several others and found that they all had bodies in them. There were men and women of different ages and all apparently dead. 'How very odd' he thought.

As he looked at one old man he saw the chest rise and fall, almost imperceptibly. 'No, not dead' he realised, correcting himself. What was this place? Then it came to him. He remembered the conversation with Frip17 and the mention of solipsists. Frip17 had said that he received instructions from solipsists. Is that what this place was? Did these people conduct their lives entirely from within these chambers? How did they deal with their bodily functions? Curious, very curious.

Cullin became lost in thought for awhile, and had to force himself to focus on the reason for his coming here. How did he get to level one-hundred? He looked about the room thinking that there must be another route upward. In the far corner of the room, he saw another tube, so he headed for it. As he stepped into the tube he stated "level one-hundred".

The same voice as before grated out "Level one-hundred accepted". This time he emerged from the tube to a single, circular room.

There was a single chamber at the centre of the room. As he looked about the room, the clus glided passed him and into the tube, presumably having performed its task.

Around the room were various displays, some streaming data, others with three-dimensional video. One of the screens went blank and then blinked back on with the image of a face. It was the stern face of a divine. Text streamed down one side of the image. There seemed to be some interaction occurring, as the face appeared to be talking.

Another screen showed images of a mountain. Cullin had seen the mountain before, but it was a moment before he put a name to it. "That's Rustick More" he whispered to himself in shock. "What is this place?"

Cullin looked closer, watching the video play. He noticed that there was a large army surrounding Rustick More. As he watched, the video flicked through several different scenarios, each time returning to the same start point. Each scenario was a different assault of Rustick More. Was this real? What was happening here? He hoped the images weren't real, because, if they were, there was little chance of Dook defending Rustick More. There wouldn't be another Dundoon.

Chapter Twenty Nine

Sudden feelings of nausea made Cullin look away. It was such a large army that he struggled to think of any way that Dook and the others would survive the overwhelming force arrayed against them.

Cullin turned his attention to the chamber. Within the chamber lay an old man, slack faced and emaciated. The man was hairless and had his eyes closed. The eyes darted about here and there, as if in REM sleep. The man was dreaming.

A feeling of revulsion suddenly hit Cullin. With sudden realisation he knew what this man was. This was the Interface. "That thing is just a man, not even a real man." The Interface was not a machine. It was just a person.

Cullin wrestled with conflicting emotions. He had come all this way to destroy a machine, only to find that the machine was a living person. He had never killed a person. How could he murder a helpless person? He couldn't.

Chapter Thirty

The sea was calm, as the launch Yayler had purloined in Stepan raced across the water. Gulukone was at the controls with Yayler the only passenger. Yayler was feeling quite edgy and anxious. He had spoken to no one since the meeting on the bridge of the divine warship. Since then he had become withdrawn. Yayler could think of no way to extricate himself from his predicament. He barely noticed when Gulukone spoke. "I am sorry, Gulukone, I missed that."

"It is nearly time. Your efforts to help your friends have amounted to nothing."

"I had to try something, though that might be difficult for you to understand."

"Why did you think it was necessary to help them? The rebels cause great harm to the Authority of the Frame."

"Because I disagree with the Frame." Yayler gazed out at the distant mountains of Anklayv Island. The island group known as Garvamore had been his home for a very long time now. Despite their cold climate and bleak habitat, he regarded Garvamore as a beautiful place.

"I do not understand. How is that possible? The logic of the Frame is perfect in its conception."

"That logic can be analysed in many ways. It may seem perfect, but it is flawed, nevertheless."

"That cannot be, Victor8."

"Call me Yayler Poddick. The Frame commands all people on Inalsol to have the same beliefs."

"That is so. Those beliefs are correct and without contradiction. Whatever your friends believe, they err. Thus, forcing the Frame to chastise them and correct such errant belief."

Yayler noted absently that Gulukone didn't use his chosen name.

"I do object, because they are incomplete. Something will always happen that does not fit in with the Frames 'perfect' system. The human population is too big for this not to happen. Random occurrences are inevitable."

Gulukone was shaking his head in disagreement. "Such random occurrences are few and can be corrected."

"So you agree that they will happen. You might correct one occurrence, but there will be another. The unpredictable will happen. You say that you can correct the thoughts and deeds that do not conform to the Frames system. I would say that even the act of correction introduces new variables into that system."

A frown crossed the face of Gulukone. He disliked these conversations with Yayler, as they always challenged what he accepted to be true. He could refuse to talk about such things, of course, but under the current circumstances, Gulukone felt that to be inappropriate. He shrugged. "I do not understand."

"Consider the sea then, where do the waves comes from?"

This was an easier subject for Gulukone to engage in. There was good data that he could access, though it was a curious shift in the conversation. "There are variations in water and sea currents, sometimes they cancel each other out, sometimes they do not. The moons add a gravitational variable. The sun adds heat. The sea is constantly moving."

"It is a chaotic system."

"Yes."

"Have you ever considered that human social interaction might also be chaotic?"

Gulukone frowned again and didn't reply. Instead, he gazed intently at the approaching village of Tymeum. They were perhaps five sents from arrival when he spoke again. "Will you scape with me?"

"Why do you ask this of me?"

"It is so that I can better understand why you believe what you do. In addition, my instructions are to ensure that you remain calm. I can best do this by scaping with you." Gulukone offered his hand to Yayler.

Chapter Thirty

Yayler felt a wrench he had never felt before as their minds connected. As his consciousness opened to the three-dimensional mindscape, he saw the silvery image of Gulukone. When he looked closer, Yayler realised Gulukone's data was an avatar composed of streaming data. They greeted each other with slight inclinations of their imaginary bodies.

Gulukone made a few hand gestures that replaced the need of ordinary speech. '*There is much I would know of you, Victor8.*'

'*I am here. What is it that you wish?*' Yayler looked at his hand, which in reality was held by Gulukone, but here, was surrounded by the same streaming data that enveloped the giant divine's image.

'*I would understand your reasoning better.*' A stream of data weaved its way from Gulukone and formed an icon of Yayler in the mindscape. The data-stream increased its speed until it appeared as a ribbon of luminous neon light. As the data-stream finished the icon had gained an almost lifelike appearance. All it lacked to be convincing was movement. '*Place your understanding in the icon.*'

'*How do I know I can trust you?*'

'*The icon cannot be accessed by the Frame, only by myself. It will be safe. This is a place where I will be able to consider your arguments without interference from the Frame.*'

Yayler could detect no lie or dishonesty on the part of Gulukone. Trust was another matter, and something much harder to win. He knew that he was due for execution in a few short wairs. This way, at least, something of his life would survive. He started to drag historical data from his neuro-chips to the Yayler icon. He added mathematical equations and emotions that formed the basis of his point of view. The entire process only took a few sents.

'*I offer you my thanks to you, Victor8. It will take me time to assess this data fully. Can you explain this mathematical function, I do not understand it.*'

A complicated formula of letters and symbols appeared, suspended, before Yayler's vision. '*Ah, it models specific individual decisions.*'

'*It is a chaotic model.*'

'*Yes. I have included more quantifiable variables than is usual with such systems. I have not found anything that even approximates this model in the Frames databases.*'

'It is not a practical model. It requires too much computation to be useful.'

'Indeed, that is so. Only the Frame has the capacity to use this model.'

'Then of what use is it?' If Gulukone was being scornful, it didn't show.

'It shows that the Frames concept of human behaviour is wrong, or, at the very least, severely limited.'

'You have given me much to think about. It is time to disengage. We are approaching Tymeum.'

Yayler found himself return to his 'real' body. He felt a numb clumsiness and disjointedness. Yet at the same time he felt calm, resigned to what would happen very soon. He could not escape it. Feeling detached and listless he saw himself guided from the launch and onto a waiting divine flier. He knew the sleek, streamlined craft would take him to his death, yet he felt no fear.

"Dook!" Mabe had rushed from his lookout position and found him in the canteen in discussion with Isla. "You had best come and see this. I think they're preparing for another attack!"

"Where?" Isla barked the question before Dook could say anything.

"They're massing on the plain below the screes. There must be thousands of them!"

"Is the Folly charged?" Dook demanded of Isla.

"Aye, always."

"Then let's have a look and see what these diavals are up to." Dook placed a gentle hand on Mabe's shoulder and guided the man from the canteen.

What Dook saw below put a knot of fear into his stomach. The footfall of the Mustanian army kicked up clouds of dust. This was a show of strength. Already, more than a thousand troops were arrayed themselves in formal squares not more than a stride away from them. More were arriving.

Isla turned to Cal and Inan. "Get everyone ready for battle!" She hissed the order at the two men.

"Don't do anything until I say so, Isla. This doesn't make any sense at all." Dook cautioned the aneksa trooper.

"Aye."

"Let's just wait and see what they're up to." Dook was surprised at how calm his voice sounded, he certainly didn't feel calm. "Where's Dona?" he called out.

Toilers Woe was filling with people and Dona called out from the back of the crowd. "Here!" She pushed through the crowd to Dook's side.

Dook whispered something in her ear and then he turned his attention back to the massing Mustanian army.

Over the next wair, the army arrayed themselves until the plain filled with a grid of formal squares of Mustanian troops. Then they stopped and waited.

At last, from the back of the grid, there was movement. Dook knew the time, as he always did. It was NE1021M6D01T1-3.80.07. Dook frowned at the significance of the timing. In less than ten sents, it would be midday on the first day of Savrah and an auspicious time, as it marked Oosgrim, the exact midpoint of the year, after which all things diminished.

A group of twenty Mustanians bearing staffs marched slowly through the central aisle of the grid. At the centre of that group was a single figure dressed in a white robe with his arms behind his back. A very large warrior followed the man in white carrying the ardclaf, a traditional ceremonial sword.

As the procession approached, Dook looked closer and, suddenly, gasped with dread and horror. The man in white was Yayler. So, Yayler had failed to bring the divines to his point of view. He had not been able to bring any help. The procession stopped at the forefront of the army and the staff-bearing Mustanians fanned out into a semi-circle, with their staffs pointing toward Yayler.

The large warrior, whose build was similar to that of Anbooakil, kissed the sword in ceremonial fashion and then dug it into the ground. Then, with remarkable gentleness, turned Yayler to face the Mustanian army and ushered him into a kneeling position with his head bowed. With a swift and smooth motion, the warrior drew the sword from the ground and with a single stroke severed Yayler's head from his body.

Dook screamed with dismay as he saw the body collapse to the ground. There was no blood as the ardclaf cauterised the vessels to the head of Yayler as it passed through the neck. Tears wet his eyes as Dook watched the warrior headsman hold the head of Yayler up for all to see and witness. The sword had fallen at the exact moment of midday.

"Kill them! Kill them all!" Dook screamed and charged toward the Folly. Even before Dook reached the Folly, the defenders of Rustick More heard the whine of incoming plazboma.

"Dook!" Isla called out as she was watching the events occurring on the plain below. "They're using smoke to hide behind."

"What? I need something to fire at!" Dook let off a couple of random shots from the Folly, but the poorly aimed shots completely missed the Divine army. "Ah, Deetah!" Dook cursed as he saw the Divine army disappear under a bank of smoke. In his dismay, he almost missed a dark smudge in the yernan sky.

Dook looked closer and his feeling of dread increased. The sleek shapes of a hundred or more Divine fliers were heading their way. "Isla, get your people on the plateau. Irin is coming!"

"What is coming? Dook, you've got to calm down. This isn't helping." Isla grabbed Dook by the collar of his tatty morcote and pulled him from the Folly.

"Look, that shadow, there." Dook was pointing at the incoming fliers. "That is a thousand horrors coming this way!"

"Cal!" Isla hollered. "Get a hundred aneksa topside, now! Inan, get as many of those little slinger stones Cullin created up there, quick as you can."

"Aye." Both Cal and Inan called out in response.

Dook looked at Isla in wide-eyed panic. "Isla, we can't fight this. There are too many, it's suicide."

"Nay, it's a narrow passageway up there. We don't need many aneksa to stop them."

Dook just looked at her with awed horror.

Chapter Thirty One

Cullin looked down on the old thin body in the chamber with dislike and enmity. It was still a person; he was still a person, Cullin corrected himself. It was still a struggle to think about killing the man. That went against deep-rooted principles that Cullin believed in. The chamber was a life support machine for the person referred to as the Interface. The body simply lay there, supine, as the chamber carried out all the functions of life for it. The person's mind connected directly into the Frame.

What then of the others he found on level eighty-four? What function did they perform? Were they part of the Interface to, or just the man lying in front of him? It didn't really matter, as it seemed clear that they, as a whole, were the source of instructions for the divines. These people were the Solipsists, the highest ranked people on Inalsol, the pinnacle of human success. What kind of life was it, plugged into a machine? Cullin didn't want to think about that, the idea revolted him.

Were they really the pinnacle of human achievement? Had they become too disparate from the rest of humanity, a humanity to which they could no longer relate? Cullin remembered that his father had died at the hands of a divine who considered himself superior to ordinary people.

The memory of his journey with Yayler Poddick came to mind. The town of Balcon, where divine and mucker lived separate lives, the divines in comfort and the muckers in squalor. He remembered the farms, cleared of people and run instead by machines.

Cullin turned his attention to the chamber and tried not to dwell on the hardships he had witnessed when growing up in the mountains of his homeland. It was a difficult life, as Goram endlessly harped on about to remind him. That life was, by no means, as hard as the life Sara had experienced.

The chamber's lid was of transparent plaz from the lumbar region and above and an opaque white below. There was a pad on the side of the opaque region bearing the image of a hand. Without hesitation, Cullin placed his hand on the image and connected with the controls of the chamber. A bewildering array of available options appeared that he had neither the time nor the inclination to investigate.

He had been in Tyber for a long time now and keenly felt the need to leave as soon as possible, before his luck ran out. He picked an available options labelled 'voice control' and spoke the word "open".

Nothing happened.

He tried again. "Release." Again, nothing happened.

It was frustrating. Cullin realised that he didn't know the proper sequence of commands, that he was working blind and trusting to luck. Perhaps he needed a key, or something, but the chamber had no locking mechanism that he could find, at least nothing like the crude locks he had known as a youth.

"Unlock" he spoke uncertainly and waited. There was an almost inaudible ripple of sound as thousands of microscopic filaments released their grip from each other. "Open" he tried again, and the lid began to split apart down its centre and slide into the lower body of the chamber. Cullin could now touch the body within. As he looked upon the figure, he still felt loathed to kill the old man.

Cullin turned his attention back to the three-dimensional images and watched the images scroll through their scenarios, each time repeated slightly differently. So, Cullin mused, each scenario was a different possible set of events. What he was watching hadn't happened, but could. He watched one scenario where thousands of divine troops assaulted Rustick More with huge numbers slaughtered by the defenders. That scenario stopped abruptly and another that was of an aerial assault replaced it. That also failed and another played in its place.

With sudden realisation, Cullin knew what was happening here. The person that was the Interface was trying to work out the best way to breach the defences of Rustick More. As he watched, one of the displays started to blink. That scenario replayed and displayed machines scaling the sides of the mountain, tearing through the rock into Toiler's Woe. Fliers landed on the plateau of Rustick More and thousands of divine troops pressed the attack on foot. The attack completely overwhelmed the defenders.

Cullin stared with sudden intense dislike at the Interface. It had worked out the best way to attack Rustick More. It would pass that battle plan onto the Frame, which would implement it. He stood over the solipsist, the Interface, and placed his hands about the neck.

As he did so, the eyes of the Interface snapped open. A thin and wasted arm moved, but long years of inactivity had atrophied the muscles. The

Chapter Thirty One

Interface could no longer use his body. He had become a thing of mind only, trapped within a useless body that could only maintain itself with the help of the chamber.

Cullin squeezed and saw panic in the eyes of the person who was planning the death and destruction of his friends. He was angry now. He squeezed harder and felt bones crumble and the trachea collapse under his hands. The panicked Interface could do nothing to defend himself. Cullin ignored the panic in the eyes of the Interface, though he felt wretched. Tears coursed down his cheeks as the Interface died.

The scenario displays went blank and Cullin knew that the Interface was dead. He collapsed to the ground feeling utterly dreadful. He had committed the worst crime it was possible to commit. He shook with grief and self-hatred.

Gilmur49 was in a cheerful mood as he watched the strike force fly overhead. He had just sent the signal for phase two of the attack to commence. Phase three, the attack by ground troops, would commence shortly as soon as the success of phase two was irrevocable.

That second phase was the key and it had taken him some time and effort to convince Clar15 that it was necessary. Approval for the plans had come only a wair ago. Everything had been prepared, waiting for that approval.

He knew that an aerial assault alone would be almost certain to fail. A handful of troops could defend the entrance on the summit plateau. The energy shield and difficult terrain made a ground assault virtually impossible. He had needed something to hammer through those defences. He had needed the battle aimu.

Gilmur49 turned to First-lieutenant Rothry37 who stood behind him with a handful of lieutenants awaiting orders. "Any confirmation from the Command Ship yet?"

"Not yet, General." The First-lieutenant was a small wiry man with grey hair. He was a man with a lot of experience in the field, but lacked that spark of imaginative thinking needed for command.

"Send the signal again. I need those battle aimu."

"It will be done, General." Rothry37 spoke to a Lieutenant heatedly and returned to his post. "Still awaiting confirmation, General."

The fliers had started to circle the summit plateau and would start the landings soon. They were under heavy fire, but their plazmetal armouring could take many strikes from the muckers' energy weapons. Why was there no response from the command ship?

It was difficult to make out what was happening on the mountain, there being no direct line of sight. The flashes of energy weapon discharges provided scant detail. For several long sents, the battle for the summit plateau continued with neither side gaining the upper hand.

"Rothry37, is there any news on those battle aimu?"

"We are not getting any communication from the Command Ship, General."

"Well, find out why." Gilmur49 snapped out the order, not caring if his irritation showed.

"General." Rothry37 acknowledged.

It was not a good time for technical problems. He had two-thousand troops poised to assault the flanks of the mountain that he was reluctant to commit without support. As he watched, one of the fliers turned away from the battle, heading for the Brayvik Straits trailing thin whips of vapour. A sent later another flier, damaged by concentrated short staff discharges, weaved an uncertain course for a few moments before crashing into the mountain-top.

"Rothry37, call those fliers back and order the troops to stand down." Gilmur49 started towards his tent. He needed to report on the battle. "And Rothry37, have a flier standby to take me to the Command Ship."

"General."

Short staff and stolfire lanced across the sky in a web of electric discharges as Isla's troops defended the summit tor of Rustick More. She had created a defensive arc about the tor with a hundred aneksa troops. The arms of the arc embraced the tor to prevent the divines attempting flanking manoeuvres.

Several of the divine fliers had already been repulsed by concentrated fire from short staffs.

"Isla!" Cal yelled in her ear. "There's another on the right trying to land."

"I see it. Concentrate fire on that flier." Isla turned and adjusted the position of her shield and fired a series of short bursts in the direction of the flier.

Several bursts struck the craft, but the tough plazmetal armouring absorbed without harm. More bursts followed from the defenders, stabbing into the flier, which turned and lifted away.

"Another, near the Target Rock." That was Mabe shouting.

"Another behind it!" Inan shouted with his voice shrill with nervousness.

Anbooakil spoke in her ear. "Several fliers are coming in towards our left flank. They do not appear to be trying to land."

Isla looked even as the trio opened fire on their left flank. The defending aneksa hunkered down behind their shields, which flared with a bright blue glow. Isla had no idea how the heavy, cumbersome shields worked, but she was profoundly grateful that they did.

"That flier's landed!" Mabe bawled above the din of the fighting.

Isla turned her attention back to the two landing fliers. One of the divine fliers now trailed a thin vapour trail and pulled away from the fight. It had acted as a shield, allowing the other flier to land. Ten divine troops were now busy setting up a defensive position behind the Target Rock.

"Inan! Get some slingers out there."

Inan quickly picked a handful of aneksa who started to crawl their way across the ground towards the rock and the divine troops.

'Not quick enough' Isla thought. "Give those men some cover fire" she shouted.

It only took a sent for them to move into position a short distance from the target rock, but it seemed like an age to Isla. Finally, they sent the first few slinger stones flying. The stones exploded on impact, forcing the divine troops to take shelter.

Inan pushed his little force forward towards the target stone under the defensive fire from Isla's main force at the summit tor. He shouted into Mabe's ear "Mabe, have you got any grenades."

"Aye, a few" came the reply.

"Can you drop one or two behind the Target Rock?"

"Aye, I think so."

Mabe threw two grenades with high trajectories in quick succession. He was not accurate enough, though. The first grenade landed just before the target stone and the other to the right of it. Mabe sent another couple of grenades flying. This time his aim was better. The grenades landed a few paces behind the Target Rock. As the smoke from the explosions cleared, Mabe saw three of the divines trying to crawl away. More slinger stones went flying. One of the divines tried to run for it, but a slinger stone struck him in the back. The divine died instantly with a massive hole where the explosive packed slinger stone had struck him. The remaining two divines crawled to make their escape, pursued by Inan and Mabe.

A trio of divine fliers began to attack the aneksa spread about the summit tor. They came in low with withering stolfire scything the ground ahead of them. So intense was their concentrated fire that Isla's troops could make token return fire until they passed overhead. Then the aneksa could fire on the retreating fliers with short staffs. Another trio of fliers came in.

"Get your people spread out further." Anbooakil shouted into Isla's ear.

Isla nodded, they were too much of a group. Individual, widely dispersed aneksa would be harder targets for the fliers. Another trio of fliers started to attack, skimming low over the rocks and moss.

The two Mustanian troops had reached the edge of the plateau by this time. Inan and Mabe had almost caught up with them when one of the divines made a critical mistake and took too long to duck behind cover. Inan had him. A quick, short discharge of his short staff struck the man's shoulder. Inan and Mabe continued to crawl forward. Inan quickly dispatched the injured divine with his utility knife and a swift slash that severed the man's carotid artery. When they reached the edge of the plateau, they could see the remaining divine climbing down the crags and some distance below.

Inan turned to Mabe. "One of us has to go down there."

"I guess you mean me."

Chapter Thirty One

"Aye, I can cover you, but I'm not good at climbing on this stuff." There was a clatter of stones as the escaping divine slipped. The Mustanian was now about thirty paces below them on steep crags. "Hurry, he's getting away." Inan urged.

"Cac! I doubt I'm any better than you." Mabe reluctantly started down the rocky crags.

Mabe tried to follow the divine's route, but the man's descent was reckless and dangerous. Loose stones made his progress difficult, but Mabe managed the first paces. He continued down with his heart thumping. The steep rocky slope abruptly stopped with a vertical rock face.

"Get on with it!" Inan called from above.

Mabe ignored him. He risked a glance down the cliff and got a brief glimpse of the divine clinging desperately to the rock about twenty paces below him. He could not see where the man had started his descent.

"What's the problem?" Inan called urgently.

"Shut up!" Mabe called back feeling rattled and nervous. Then a thought struck him. He didn't need to follow the divine down the cliff. The divine was desperate, but he wasn't. He still had a pouch full of slinger stones. Mabe looked along the crags and saw a section of fissured rock that hung over the cliff. It looked as if it could collapse at any moment.

"What's going on?" Inan called.

"Wait, I'm going to try something." Mabe edged his way towards the overhang and jammed his fingers into one of the fissures. The rock was more solid than it had looked at first. He had been thinking of detonating slinger stones in a fissure and sending the rock crashing down on the divine. Now he had a better idea. With his hand jammed in the fissure, he leant over the edge.

Below, the escaping Mustanian had started moving again, using a vertical cleft to provide holds. Mabe dug his free hand into his pouch. He took aim and threw his first stone. It struck the cliff face just above the divine and bounced harmlessly passed and exploded as it hit the ground.

"What are you doing?" Inan hissed urgently.

Mabe tried again, with more force, but this time his aim was wide. The stone exploded, sending shattered rock flying. The divine clung frantically to the rock face as Mabe sent another stone flying. This one struck the vertical cleft and sent a shower of splintered, rocky shards over the divine. Another stone, then another followed, and finally, as Mabe was about to launch another, he saw the divine slip.

Mustanian warrior looked up towards Mabe with panic written on his face. Mabe let his last stone fly. Another shower of shards engulfed the divine, and his feet slipped from the cleft. His sudden downward motion jerked loose his remaining hold on the rock and the divine plummeted down the cliff.

The attack runs of the fliers had less effect with the defending aneksa spread out, but equally the aneksa had difficulty targeting the fliers. The fighting was intense with the air crackling with energy discharges. A small number of aneksa lost their lives to the flier attacks and several others had severe wounds. Anbooakil and Cal had set up a small group near the tunnel entrance to Toiler's Woe.

"Which one next?" Cal yelled at Anbooakil.

"That one at point." Anbooakil pointed to the lead flier of a group of three.

Five short staff fired upon the craft without causing any apparent damage.

"Next?" Cal yelled again and Anbooakil pointed.

The routine went on with neither side gaining the upper hand. The battle had become one of attrition and one that the aneksa could not win with their smaller numbers.

"That one!" Anbooakil directed.

Energy blasts from the short staff raked the flier. This time the aneksa struck lucky. The flier sped away with a thin trail of vapour behind it.

Cal grinned. It was a small success.

Another trio of fliers lined up for an attack run. They flew directly at Cal and Anbooakil's group. As Cal fired, the energy blasts from his short staff cut flickered briefly and then stopped. Cal looked up in alarm at the approaching fliers as energy discharges razed the ground, sending stones caroming in all directions. Even as Anbooakil pulled him down, several stones struck Cal on the head.

Chapter Thirty One

The three aneksa with them fired at the retreating flier, which suddenly veered off course. It made a small correction as it tried to gain altitude. Its flight path twisted and the craft nosed dived into the ground. A single bright flash of light ripped through the flier, tearing it apart. As if this was a signal, the attacks abruptly stopped.

Chapter Thirty Two

"We can defend! Those narid who managed to land were quickly dispatched." Isla was insistent, even belligerent in her attitude.

"You nearly got beaten up there today. A lot of people got hurt. The only reason we're able to discuss this now is because they decided to leave." Dook spoke earnestly. He trusted Isla, but he felt that overconfidence clouded her judgement.

"Ach! Dook, we hadn't anticipated that level of aerial assault. They still need to get through that narrow passageway." Isla was surprised at Dook's attitude. She thought that he was being very negative for someone who had pushed so very hard to defend against the divines and their machine masters.

"Convince me" was all Dook said.

"Look, Dook, we can't afford to have them on our roof. Who knows what they could do up there?"

"How many people did we lose up there today?"

"Four dead and six injured. They lost many more than we did."

"Aye, but they can afford to, can't they? We can't sustain losses like that."

"Dook, I don't like to see them die or get hurt any more than anybody else. We know the risks."

"Aye, I know that."

"Why did they leave if they were winning?"

"I don't know. They would have overwhelmed us eventually. If they had pressed the attack."

"So what do we do?"

"We leave. We have a place to go."

"What? Abandon Rustick More?" Isla was shocked and unwilling to believe that Dook would simply walk away from the fight.

"Aye. We need to think about what we can achieve by staying here."

There was a disturbance near the corridor as a large man thrust his way through a cluster of people with his long grey-streaked red hair fluttering in the air as he strode. The man wore his dirty morcote open, revealing a substantial and powerful girth. A gaggle of equally unkempt and dirty muckers followed the big man.

Dook produced a broad smile. "Hamadern, what are you doing here?"

"We had to leave Dunirayn in a bit of a hurry. We've been trying to get here since, hiding from the divines. You know that the country is swarming with them?"

"Aye, and most of them on our doorstep. You can't stay here."

"Dook, you know what they are doing. They're killing everyone, not just those who can fight, but the old, our women and even little babes. It is sickening." There was a look of horror on Hamadern's face as he recounted their journey and the death pits where the divines had buried the dead in shallow mass graves.

"I know, but we can't stop them."

"Have we lost then?" A look of intense worry creased the lines of Hamadern's face.

"Nay, not by a long way. We just can't stay here."

"But Dook, where will you go? The forests?"

"Some of us, but we have another place. I think you can be of help though."

Clar15 and Gilmur49 waited. They waited in silence on the bridge of the Command Ship for the arrival of the battle hiu that had summoned them. Clar15 wore an elegant white dress that clearly marked her as non-combatant. Gilmur49 was dusty and unkempt by comparison having come directly from the army at Rustick More. He was about to speak to Clar15 when the battle hiu arrived.

Chapter Thirty Two

There was no ceremony or announcement. The battle machine HIUcom01 simply addressed them without preamble. "It is not known why, but communication from the Interface has ceased. You will now be getting your instructions directly."

"How has this happened?" Gilmur49 demanded to know.

"That information is not available yet." The hius voice ground out the words with no indication of noticing Gilmur49's lack of etiquette. "The Frame requires that the process of establishing proper control in this district must be accelerated. Two attacks have now failed. You must use resources more efficiently." The hiu addressed Gilmur49 directly.

"The last attack failed because the battle aimu failed to respond to signals." Gilmur49 was indignant and spluttered over the riposte.

"No signal was received."

"The signal was sent."

The hiu appeared to ignore Gilmur49's claim. "The Frame has sent a new set of battle plans. Over-General Clar15 has these. You will study them and follow them exactly. There will be no mistakes."

"HIUcom01, I have looked briefly at the data you have supplied regarding the battle plans and I am unable to interpret them." Clar15 interrupted the discourse between the machine and Gilmur49.

There was a pause whilst the hiu cogitated and analysed Clar15's comment. "The data is in the correct format."

"For you, it is in the correct format. For us, it is unreadable. We are warriors not technicians. We need the plans in plain text." Clar15 kept her statements as simple as possible. It was always wise to do this with machines as they translated speech very literally.

"Are you not able to translate simple code?"

"No. Our instructions are always translated into plain text."

"I will perform the translation for you. I have requested the correct cypher to do this. There will be a delay as a result."

Clar15 cleared her throat and addressed the hiu. "Are we to understand, then, that we are not going to be able to understand our instructions until that time?"

"Until the Interface is either repaired or replaced, I will have to operate in its place. This is not a part of my designed function and will be less efficient. You must still perform within acceptable parameters." The hiu turned its headless form toward Gilmur49, raising its plazmetal arm and pointing at the divine General in emphasis. "I will accompany you to the Forward Command where I will ensure your efficiency."

Feelings of anguish and despair flooded Cullin's mind, paralysing him, preventing him from action. Ardcleric Allamued, his tutor from the kirk in Glen Ereged, had always drilled into him that the taking of another person's life was the greatest crime that a person could commit. It was a lesson he had taken to heart.

How could he ever reconcile taking the life of a helpless person, whatever harm they might have caused, with his own conscience? He felt a dull knot of pain in his bowels and his head throbbed. His body, especially his hands, shook uncontrollably. It was as if his own body rebelled against the act of killing.

He let the grief take him in his wretchedness until he was numb from the pain. At last, he lifted his head and opened his eyes. He felt as a dead man. He had given up a precious part of his humanity, but he knew his friends, the people of his homeland suffered. Many had lost their lives. Many more might still lose their lives at the hands of the divine army. He could live for them, not for himself for he had given up that right.

Cullin pushed himself to his feet. He had accomplished what he had set out to do, but had now stayed too long. He had to focus on helping the crew of the Banree. He pushed himself back to his feet, determined to help the others.

As he stepped back into level eighty-four, his heart skipped a beat. There was a hiu standing before the tube and the only exit from the level.

Chapter Thirty Three

There had been a disturbance on the perimeter. A mucker had approached the perimeter guards and hailed them. The guards had almost blasted the man with stols as soon as he had made his presence known to them. Fearing a ruse by the muckers defending Rustick More, they thoroughly searched the individual. They only found a simple rune disc on his person. The mucker called himself Robert the Red and claimed to be working for the divines. He had the rune disc to confirm his identity.

It had taken another wair before a couple of burley Mustanians brought the mucker to the command tent. He looked nervous as he stood before Clar15 and Gilmur49. The man's eyes kept flicking toward the brooding menace of the battle hiu also present. Clar15 had the rune disc in the palm of her hand and gazed at it curiously, reading the data contained within. At last, she addressed the hiu.

"The mucker is who he claims to be. The rune disc belongs to a certain List36 of Port Main who is the Ardmaster in charge of the town's security."

The hiu turned toward Red briefly, its headless form standing over three paces. It grated a response to Clar15's information. "This then, is a divine matter. Why has it been brought before me?"

Clar15 turned toward one of the Mustanians guarding Red. "Well? Has it been interviewed? What does it know?"

The hiu turned toward the guard. A small red light on the rim of the neck-ring winked steadily in the direction of the guard. Another red light flickered on and moved along the circumference of the rim until it faced Red. "Explain."

The guard cleared his throat before answering. "It, it claims to know of a way into the rebel base. We couldn't determine if this is true or not, but it was felt to be too important to ignore. It also claims to be known to the rebels and to have been within the base."

"If this claim is correct, why have you not reported this information to your Master sooner?"

Red had guessed that the question would be asked and had his answer ready. "A report is only sent once a month. The information wasn't previously available."

"It is an inefficient system, typical of inferior muckers." The hiu moved before Red and held out its left arm. This caused a moment of nervous confusion for Red, thinking this might be some form of greeting. It wasn't. A light emanated from the palm of the hius palm and grew swiftly into an image that floated in the air before Red. "The mucker will indicate the way into the rebel base."

Red was suddenly very nervous, his mouth had gone dry and he found himself shaking imperceptibly. "It, it starts somewhere here." Red indicated an approximate position with a finger. "There is a long tunnel that leads directly into Rustick More."

The hiu grated out an immediate response. "The position is not accurate. The precise location is required."

Red moved his finger, searching. His hands felt clammy with apprehension. He traced a small stream that had its source high on the flanks of Rustick More in rocky gullies. Eventually he let his finger settle on a more precise location. "It starts here." It was all he could manage to say; his chest felt tight and a knot a churning discomfort in his stomach indicated imminent sickness.

The hiu turned toward Clar15. "A drone has been dispatched to investigate this possible tunnel. I will formulate a battle plan and instruct you later." At this, the hiu left the command tent.

The morning following the aborted assault on Rustick More started with a light rainfall. Dook and Isla watched the activity of the divine army from the open hanger doors of Toiler's Woe. Isla had posted more lookouts on the summit plateau of Rustick More as she distrusted the divines. She was convinced they were up to something, but was at a loss to think of what they could be planning.

"Dook, I'm going to see if Jon has anything to break our fast with." Isla had suddenly realised that she had not eaten since before the airborne attack. Now she realised that she was very hungry.

Chapter Thirty Three

"Why is that man still here? I'm grateful that he is, but he should have gone with the rest before now."

"He says that the food needs to be managed properly. He thinks, if he stays on, we will have one less thing to worry about. He's probably right." Isla was about to head to the canteen when movement below caught her eye. "Dook, what's that down there? I think I saw something."

"Where? It's difficult to see."

"Hush, there's a noise too." Isla could just discern a deep reverberating noise that the early morning activity of Toiler's Woe almost completely masked.

"Down there, on the right. In that dark gully." Isla indicated vaguely with her hand after a moments pause to listen. "Without the oykaverk it's difficult to see what's going on down there."

Dook peered into the murky grey light of the early morning and cast his eyes about until he picked up a brief, subtle movement. "Ah, I see it. We have guests coming, Isla."

"Divines?" Isla had continued looking, but had failed to see any further movement. "I knew they wouldn't leave us alone for long."

"Ah, no, not the divines. Machines and something else."

"I'll alert everyone." Isla was about to head towards a group of aneksa who had been lounging about in Toiler's Woe. Isla had kept a small squad on alert through the night. She turned back to Dook. "What is something else?"

Dook frowned. "Anbooakil."

"What?"

"Where is Anbooakil?"

"With the lookouts, I think."

"Well, find ey. I need to talk to eym."

"Eym?"

"Him, it, that is eym. Go. Alert everyone."

"Aye." Isla headed quickly towards her troops.

Neither Clar15 nor Gilmur49 were happy about the attack plan provided to them by HIUcom01. It had no subtlety or finesse. Yes, it would work, but it was like smashing whelks or limpets off their rocks with a boulder.

They both watched live, streamed images of six machine grubmoles as they moved slowly forward flanked by enhanced divine warriors. Two thousand divine Mustanian warriors followed in broad files. The machines were slow with a gaping maw and large grinding teeth at their front end. Excavation was their usual function, but here they would chew an entrance into Rustick More.

The head end was flexible and the body short, squat and heavily armoured. The grubs advanced on broad rollers and extruded ground up material from two apertures at the rear. Their appearance was highly suggestive of maggots. They made a deep rumbling noise as they made their inexorable way toward the mountain.

Clar15 and Gilmur49 turned their attention to the other holoscreens. HIUcom01 had planned the coming battle with strict timings. They had argued against this with HIUcom01, but the machines instructions took precedence over theirs. Those timings could not be changed due to the problem with communication between the machines and the Mustanians.

Transport and drone fliers would make their runs as the grubmoles began to force an entrance into the rebel base. A further assault force would penetrate the base via the tunnel guided by the mucker informant. They would crush and pulverise the rebel base. The muckers would have no means of escape.

"Is the Folly charged?" Dook yelled.

"Aye" came the immediate response.

"Then fire at the nearest of those things."

A gimbal system hastily added to the Folly design allowed better movement and aiming. The muzzle of the Folly swung round, aiming steeply down the mountainside at the machines heading the vast Mustanian army.

Chapter Thirty Three

There was an abrupt whine as the Folly charged. Then a huge report seemed to tear the air apart. A twisting mass of green energy spewed from the muzzle and crackled as it roared through the air toward the nearest grubmole.

Several more blasts shook the air even as the first struck the leading grubmole. Plumes of rock and earth enveloped the advancing machine and the ground shook from the force of the impact. The grubmole stopped as successive discharges struck.

"Deetah, Anbooakil!" Dook stared at the giant with shock. "What have you done to that thing."

"I have improved its efficiency threefold. It might be sufficient." The enigmatic giant appeared unmoved.

"Well, let's do it again."

However, as the air cleared it became clear that the grubmole was undamaged and resumed its advance on Rustick More. Slowly, inexorably the burrowing machines progressed.

"What in Irin are those things?" Dook demanded of Anbooakil.

"They are mining machines. They are designed to take enormous punishment without damage. They have no weakness."

Discharge after discharge from the Folly struck the machines, but still they came, each concussion dissipating harmlessly. The very air about the machines seemed to be alive with energy. The divines held back their advance, not willing to chance their lives with the unexpected weapon of the muckers.

"Dook, those things will set off the first line of anti-personnel plazboma at any moment. Those machines are creating a road for that army. This is hopeless, Dook." Dona was staring down at the grubmoles as they started up the lower slopes of Rustick More.

"I don't think that's the intention, Dona, they don't know about your anti-personnel defences. They can only anticipate them." Dook frowned as he replied.

"Then, I don't understand what they are trying to do. Those things can't climb the side of the mountain."

Anbooakil answered in his high-pitched voice dispassionate, emotionless and unreal. "They are going to burrow a tunnel."

Dona looked aghast at Anbooakil, her mouth open wide with astounded distaste at the giant's placid and undemonstrative nature. She looked down at the machines and the trail of devastation. "What happens to all the rubbish; to all that smashed up rock?"

Anbooakil shrugged. "It has to be cleared."

"By what?"

"I expect they will bring machines for that. It will have been planned for."

Dook laughed unexpectedly. It was a cold humourless laugh. "There is another problem. The rubble takes up more space than solid rock."

Anbooakil nodded. "It will have to be cleared. They will do that. It will take time, but then they have time to spare. We are not going anywhere."

"Not yet. There is still too much valuable equipment here. I don't want the divines to know what we have here."

"So you're just playing for time?"

"Aye, and hurt them as much as we can whilst we are still here." As they watched the grubmoles creep onto the lower slopes of Rustick More blasts of energy continued to strike ineffectually at the armoured body. The heavy armour could withstand the pounding of rock whilst excavating beneath the ground without damage. A thought struck Dook. "Anbooakil, can the Folly create a continuous discharge?"

"It can, but I would strenuously advise against it. The constant flow of energy could damage the Folly."

"Why?"

"It would cause a lot of heat. The heat would damage the components."

"Machine components. Aye, heat. Those machines are not designed to withstand extreme heat. Train the Folly's discharge on the mouth of the lead machine. Let's see how tough they really are!"

"I do not know about such limitations. It might work."

Chapter Thirty Three

As the crew of the Folly took aim on the mouth of the lead grubmole Isla caught Dook's attention. "We have another problem."

"What problem?"

"The lookouts have spotted fliers coming our way. They appear different to the ones that attacked before."

"They will be drones." Anbooakil announced as he gazed down at the advancing machines.

"Aye" Dook agreed. Cullin shot down a couple at Dundoon."

"They were fast. Cullin was lucky to survive. We can use short staffs."

"Aye. Oh, and Isla –" Dook stopped the young aneksa just as she started to leave. "Use the energy shields. See if you can't knock out a few of them."

Even as Isla turned to leave there was an ear-splitting high-pitched whine from the Folly. A continuous discharge spewed from the muzzle. Anbooakil was now at its controls and aiming the weapon directly into the gaping maw of the lead grubmole. The heat built up gradually as the machine continued to advance. The grinding teeth glowed a deep red and then orange from the intensifying heat.

The design of the grubmoles did not allow for extremes of heat. A vital component cut out, over-heated and damaged. The advance of the grubmole stopped and Anbooakil turned his attention to the next one.

Isla had wasted no time in setting up the defences on the plateau. Since the previous attack, a small squad had guarded the tunnel entrance. Isla quickly added more energy shields. Twenty aneksa waited for the incoming drones behind those energy shields. They didn't wait for long.

They came in, two abreast, spitting gouts of searing force towards the shield wall.

"Dook, we have a problem!" Neev tugged urgently at his morcote.

"Only one?"

"There are divines in the tunnels below us."

"What? How did they find the way in?" Dook's mind raced, this was not something he had anticipated.

"I don't know, but they're in, and coming this way."

"Dona!" Dook bawled even though she was not far away, talking to Isla. "Go with Neev and some of the aneksa. Neev show them where they are. They must be slowed down." Dook rushed over to the Folly to where a grim faced Anbooakil wearing a cape made from sleeping furs sat at the controls. "Leave the others to do this. They have the idea now. I need you elsewhere."

"Isla, get a squad to the top of the tunnel. We have uninvited guests."

"Aye."

Dook and Anbooakil soon caught up with Dona, Neev and a handful of aneksa. Dona had a lantern lit and a pale yellow glow illuminated the group. Hoarse whispers came from the group as Neev guided them through the narrow tunnel.

"Hush, they'll hear you." Dook whispered urgently as he joined them. Then to Neev he added "how far down are they?"

"Oh a fair way yet. They hadn't got to Eskoramor. With any luck they'll get lost up Blind Alley."

"What were you doing down here?"

"Looking for somewhere quieter to listen for signals."

"The seismocom should work, even with the extra noise."

"Aye, it's working fine, but the noise was disturbing my concentration."

"Ah, look, Anbooakil and myself will go ahead to the falls. We can wait in ambush there." As Dook and the giant moved ahead, Dook added. "Dim that light. It will give us away." Dook paused for a moment, then whispered "and keep quiet, the sound will travel a long way down these passages".

Slowly, Dook and Anbooakil descended, with the only sound being the slight scuffing of their boots on the stone floor. Using augmented vision, they needed the barest minimum of light, which Dook provided with the utility knife he had later developed into the aneksa short staff. Set at a minimum level, the knife glowed diffusely with a soft blue light. Dook moved ahead as the passage narrowed and steepened. Then, with the sound of Eskoramor, dull and muted ahead, Dook stopped. There was movement and light ahead.

Chapter Thirty Three

Anbooakil stopped in his tracks as Dook gripped his hand urgently. They interfaced.

"We are too late. They have found the way."

"There are many. Some are like myself and they are well armed."

A sudden chill of fear shook Dook. He knew that the quiet, polite and enigmatic Anbooakil was bred for one purpose; battle. "So much for an ambush. We should get back to the others."

"We can slow them down. The others will know what is coming. I am prepared."

"We fight, then."

"We fight" agreed Anbooakil.

Anbooakil didn't wait for any further response or agreement from Dook, but charged down the narrow passage. Dook closed his eyes, gripped his force knife and held it above his head. He discharged its energy with a bright flash of light and caught a glimpse of several giant warriors advancing up the passageway. He raced after Anbooakil.

Anbooakil had engaged the leading enhanced warrior, but Dook could see more behind. He charged past the struggling forms of the two brawling giants and discharged his force knife into the next. There was a crimson spray of blood and the headless form slumped to the ground.

Dook continued his charge and found himself outmatched by the next enhanced warrior. A huge hand gripped his wrist and began to twist the knife out of his hand. In near panic, Dook discharged it randomly, catching brief images of more warriors approaching. He heard shouting.

Dook was big strong man, but his opponent was far stronger. He could feel the warrior's breath on his face as they grappled. He searched frantically for the giant's free hand and head butted the space where he thought his head might be. He could hear more divines approaching up the passageway as he felt himself, inexorably forced to the ground.

As he fumbled in the dim light, he caught hold of his opponent's wrist and tried to push it away from him, but the warrior was too strong. There was a brief, bright flash from behind him as his knees buckled beneath him. Dook recognised the flash as coming from a stol. His mind raced as panic built within him. As he sank to the ground, he flicked his legs out and pushed backward. He rolled pulling the giant divine with him.

The sudden movement caused the warrior to loosen Dook's wrist. Dook discharged his force knife into the body of the warrior. Simultaneously another body caromed into the sprawling combatants. There were a couple of bright stol blasts and Dook's opponent suddenly went limp.

As Dook blinked, he recognised the form of Anbooakil standing above him. Dook gathered his wits. Not far away now, more divines were almost upon them. Anbooakil turned to face the threat, but Dook pulled him away.

"There are too many! We cannot beat them all!"

Anbooakil started firing a stol down the passageway with random blasts.

Dook yanked at the giant's fur cape urgently. "Come on! We need to get back to the others."

The drones came in waves of two abreast, pinning Isla's troops down with overwhelming fire power. Despite the wall of force shields, the aneksa were in a poor position to defend themselves against the intensity of the stol fire directed towards them. Isla's troops could barely return fire. Isla was trying to get what shelter she could from behind her heavy, cumbersome force shield, but knew it was inadequate against the bombardment. She pulled her troops back to the tunnel.

Despite the withdrawal, the drones continued their strafing runs. Several of Isla's troops were hit and had to be dragged under cover. Then came the incendiaries. Isla was quick to realise that they could not defend against fire. Wave after wave of firebombs pummelled the summit of Rustick More until the area around the tunnel entrance was ablaze. The brief encounter between the drones and the aneksa on the summit had caused several injuries amongst her troops.

"Cal." Isla yelled. "Get everyone back to Toiler's Woe. We can do no good here."

"Aye" came the shouted response from the heavyset aneksa.

"You and you!" Isla pointed to the two nearest troops. "Use your short staffs against the roof like this." Isla fired away at the ceiling of the tunnel,

Chapter Thirty Three

slowly retreating. She could feel an intense heat from the blazing chemicals of the incendiaries just beyond.

Suddenly, explosions started to rip apart the rock ceiling. "Get back!" Isla screamed at her comrades. "Back, back, get back!"

As the roof of the tunnel collapsed, they were plunged into darkness. They had to feel their way, step by step, until there was a dim light ahead. It was Cal holding a small lantern.

"What, in Irin, happened up there?" Cal's voice was shocked, but demanding.

"I don't know, but I think I know who to ask."

Dook and Anbooakil had raced up the tunnel with the divine troops hot on their tail. As soon as they reached Dona, Neev and the other aneksa a barrage of short staff fire lit up the tunnel.

Dona hunched up behind a force shield hollered "Don't stop! Keep going."

The divines had almost caught up, but an intense barrage from short staffs forced to take shelter behind a shallow bend in the tunnel. The air began to sizzle with a crossfire of charged particles.

Dook crouched behind Dona's force shield, taking it from her. "Dona, what are you doing? We can't stay here. We'll be cut to pieces."

"It's rigged!"

"What?"

"The tunnel, it's rigged with explosives."

"Then do it and let's go."

Dona was about to ignite a fuse line when Dook stayed her hand. "Wait! I see something."

The divines, no more than a hundred paces away. They had stopped firing at the defenders of Rustick More.

"What? Dook, I need to set this off now!" Dona gaped at Dook with incredulity. The dust from the fighting and dim light of the tunnel meant that she could only see a dark shadow of Dook's bulk.

Dook was calm. "You go, Dona. Give me the short staff. I can set the fuse." Dona hesitated, but Dook ignored her. He gazed through the gloom to the bend where the divines sheltered. The stolfire had ceased, but he could make out two of the giant warriors creeping forward. Dook wasn't interested in them. It was a familiar figure behind them that that had tweaked his curiosity. "Go now, Dona."

The recognition angered Dook intensely, but his anger, his rage was as cold as ice. "Robert the Red? Is that you?"

There was some stirring amongst the divines, who had halted their progress at this unlikely turn of events.

"Red, you're a maggot ridden, stinking piece of rotten cac! Come forward where I can see you. Let me see your face before I kill you."

"Kill me? You demented drunken retard! Can't you see you've lost this little game! Your mucker revolt is over!" Robert the Red laughed. It was a short, sarcastic, sneering laugh.

"Not over Red. Not by a long way."

Red had stepped forward and now stood in front of the giant enhanced warriors. Red fired a stol, and Dook's shield flared in response as the energy from the blast was dispersed. He sneered again and spoke with a hate-filled snarl. "Have you seen the size of the army out there Dook?" He sneered again as he took another step forward and fired again. "That army out there is huge Dook! You cannot win!"

Dook retorted "You're a deluded goat shagger Red. That pitiful army out there can't win!" He wanted to irritate Red, to stop him thinking clearly.

Red stepped forward again taking pot shots at Dook with every step. "You're going to die very soon Dook. Not soon enough for my liking."

"You're a gutless slug Red. You won't kill me Red. You've always been a coward and you're going to die a coward."

For a moment Red stopped, incredulous, this was an insult too far. Suddenly, his self-restraint snapped. He charged forward, blazing away with his stol. The divines also charged.

Chapter Thirty Three

"Too slow Red" Dook whispered to himself and lit the fuse with his force knife. There was a wry grin on his face as he suddenly realised that he didn't know how long the fuse was. It was too late to worry about that. "Too late Red" Dook bellowed down the tunnel.

Dook started to back down the tunnel, away from the divines. Professional Mustanian warriors that they were, had paused their attack. After a few shouts and urgent hand signals, they began to back off back down the tunnel. Red was alone and heedless in his charge.

The fuse was taking too long, so Dook aimed at Red with the short staff and, with a single blast, blew the legs from beneath Red. The law of momentum took over and the legless body tumble and slid forward, coming to a halt at Dook's feet.

Astonishingly, Red was still alive and stared up at Dook in Shock. Dook shot him again and muttered to himself "you always were an idiot Red".

At that moment, the first of Dona's explosives detonated with a massive report. The air shook with the force. Dook ran as the roof of the tunnel collapsed. He was almost fast enough. Rocks pummelled him as he used the heavy wooden force shield in a forlorn defence.

Chapter Thirty Four

Dona was in shock. Dook was gone, crushed under morkudram of rock. Anbooakil and Neev re-joined her, shouting at her to move. "Come on, come on. We have to go". She couldn't hear the words or focus on her two colleagues.

Neev grabbed her by the shoulders and shouted directly into her face "Dona, come on".

Slowly Dona began to focus with tears streaming down her grubby face. "He's gone" she muttered almost inaudibly.

"I know." Neev spoke gently now. "Dona, we can't stay here now. We have to go."

"Go? Go where?"

"There is a place. The place Ecta found. Ecta's Ledge"

Dona nodded, a slow almost imperceptible nod and a gentle, resigned sigh. "Aye, Ecta's Ledge."

Anbooakil spoke "We need to gather everybody and leave this place."

Glossary of terms

Amadan – idiots.

Atha – Inalsol's first moon

Aneksa – free people.

Aimu – Artificial intelligent mechanoid units.

Alben – Scots Pine

Atacote – a waxed, heavy duty coat used by sailors

Atalok – Lake to the south west of Mark Ossin.

Ar- east or eastern

Ardclaf – ceremonial sword and energy weapon.

Ardcleric – a clans head priest.

Ardyvinland – main island in the group called Garvamore.

Aylinron – small rocky island, northeast Marlok.

Balcleric – a local priest.

Bancaol – the narrow sea strait north Bandrokit.

Banree Na Mur – Pul's boat.

Barsick – die.

Beetick – the cloth made from Beet fibres.

Begarn – hill north of Dundoon.

Bivvy - bivouac

Brayvik Straits – a narrow sea passage that separates the Island of Brayvik from Anklayv Island.

Breergara – a liar.

Cac – faeces, shit

Calman – pigeon or dove.

Calp – kelp.

Cammic - A device that both records sound and visual data.

Compad – a small computer about the size of a modern credit card.

Com-posts – communication device of the Frame for use by aimu.

Comsat – communication satellite.

Canut Strait – small sea between Willemsbree and Dundoon.

Creet – hard artificial stone used by the Frame to construct buildings.

Darna – second month of the year

Deetah – damn.

Des – south or southern

Desarick – south-east.

Diavals - devils

Divines – the ruling elite in human culture who are overseen by aimu and ultimately the Frame.

Divine's staff – communication and energy transfer device.

Drimneev (poison ridge) – mountain that Cullin and Ecta survey

Dun – an extensive stone dwelling, frequently fortified.

Duvick Namarv – the realm of the dead.

Ey – non-gender form of he or she.

Eyers – non-gender form of his or hers.

Eym – non-gender form of him or her.

Eyself – myself.

Feeaklack – teeth.

Flier – a small flying machine, originally designed by the Frame, but adapted for manual flight by the resistance.

Furlok – Long sea inlet east of Mark Ossin.

Garvamore – a group of mountainous islands lying north of the main continent.

Gelkarn – hill south of Dundoon.

Gunna – gun.

Grubmoles – heavily armoured mining machines.

Hameed – the Latter Prophet

Hesoos – One of the four faces of God, the child prophet in whose name all children are blessed.

Hiu – human interface unit.

Holoscreen – display unit for computers.

Inalsol – the world in which lies Garvamore.

Irin – hell.

Kaylick – witch.

Kerev – fourth month of the year

Kilree – head of the church – archbishop.

Locater disc – device registered to a specific person that signals its position to a specific receiver.

Lok Kruay – sea inlet east of Rustick More.

Mane – a fur or woollen wrap used to keep out bad weather.

Mark – an administrative unit of Garvamore.

Mark Brus – located near Drimneev.

Mark Glaskarn – Mark in Dunban Mountains

Mark Kissom – Mark that includes Dundoon.

Mark Konzie – Mark in Dunban Mountains

Mark Lowd – neighbouring Mark to Mark Ossin.

Mark Ossin – Cullin's home Mark.

Marlok – stretch of seawater separating Ardbanacker from Anklayv.

Matha – Inalsol's second moon.

Morcote – heavy densely woven knee length woollen coat that keeps out most bad weather and cold.

Morven Rebellion – rebellion against the Divines and Frame.

Mozog – the first prophet.

Morkudram – 20 000 oonsa (129 kilograms)

Morven Rebellion – rebellion against the divines and Frame.

Muga – 20 fluid ounces, or oonsa.

Nano - Nanos improve mitochondrial efficiency. Different nanos improve muscular output increasing speed and strength. Further implants improve memory and can process data accurately as fast as computer speeds. The brain shortcuts by making comparisons allowing ultrafast human computation.

Narid – enemy –used in reference as a general term for Divines and aimu offensive units.

Natua – north or northern

Neev – halls of rest (heaven)

Neuro-chips – miniature computers inserted into divines brains.

Nuygev – ninth month of the year.

Oosgrim – The midpoint of the year. Before Oosgrim, there is growth, but after, all things diminish and decay.

Oykaverk – Night glasses

Oyki na Spirad – Night of the Spirits

Oil Beet – a root vegetable that produces a heavy oily sap.

Plaz – A durable light material made from refined oil beet sap.

Plazgunna – plazboma gun, fires plazboma shells.

Plazboma – plastic explosive.

Rayanam – season of souls, runs from the winter equinox for three months (tuseek, Darna and tres).

Rossein – God of thought and enlightenment.

Rune disc – indentification device that is programmed to recognise specific genes.

Salak – dirt

Scaping – digital connection between different minds.

Seismocom – communication device that uses seismic P waves.

Sents – one hundredth of a wair.

Sheedoo – black spirits.

Skits – childs game played with stones.

Skaden – herring.

Slancha – good health.

Slootar – villains, person of low honour.

Stol – hand held energy weapon.

Surwane – spruce

Swithering – indecisive, hesitant, dithering.

Tendays – ten days, equates to a metric week.

Tres – third month of the year

Truarly – expletive - nasty, evil

Truargan – evil ones, a wretch.

Tuaport – divine town on Ardbanacker Island.

Tuseek – first month of the year

Tyber – possible location of the Interface in Desert Zone A.

Varamor Sea – lies east of the Islands of Garvamore.

Venuasal – Lady or Ladyship.

Wagon Master – Leader of a group of wagoners.

Wagoner/s – traders in heavy goods requiring transport.

Wair – 1/16 th of a day. 90 minutes.

Wicks – sheep.

Wifman – woman.

Yayl – a six stringed fiddle.

Yer – west or western.

Zenumerator – aimu central processing unit.

www.ingramcontent.com/pod-product-compliance
Lightning Source LLC
LaVergne TN
LVHW061034070526
838201LV00073B/5028